THE RED SERGE

STORIES OF
THE ROYAL CANADIAN MOUNTED POLICE

HARWOOD STEELE

Author of *To Effect An Arrest*
Ghosts Returning
The Marching Call
Policing the Arctic
The Ninth Circle
Spirit-of-Iron

THE RYERSON PRESS ~ TORONTO

COPYRIGHT

To E. G. C. — W.

PRINTED AND BOUND IN CANADA   THE RYERSON PRESS—TORONTO

FOREWORD

With one or two obvious exceptions, the chief incidents dealing directly with Force work in these stories are based on fact. Some follow the originals very closely, while others are adaptations or composites. The themes and the technical and background details are authentic.

Specifically, "The Red Serge of Courage" is founded on similar recent dangerous affairs. "Sir Galahad and The 'Bad Man'" closely follows the facts of typical single-handed arrests by Corporal Hogg and a constable nicknamed "Smoky Angus." "The Race For Molly Scott" adapts two actual Yukon Gold-Rush episodes, the rescue of a damsel in distress and the first Force run from Dawson to Skagway with mail. "Ordeal By Fire" faithfully adheres to a typical exploit (by Constable Conradi), "Lunatic Patrol" almost as faithfully to the harrowing adventure of Constable Pedley. "A Dog Won't Lie" is based very largely on actual brilliant detective work and the behaviour of dogs in two cases. "A Working Partnership" originated in an actual pursuit by hand-car.

"Pal" is a composite of Force police service dogs, one of them actually so called, the incidents before the man-hunt are authentic, the hunt is factual, but composite, with minor changes and its climax almost exactly describes the end of the real-life association between Constable Rhodeniser and his dog "Tell." "Mighty Mean Indian" is a factual composite. The fight and its ending in "Beaned With Bottle" are authentic.

The theme and detail in "The Missing Link", "A Little and Certain Compass", "A Couple Of Caribou" and "The Little Red Devil and The Deep Blue Sea", like the legal decision at the end of the last-named story, are factual, the plots fictitious. "The Monster and The 'Mountie'" merely exploits public interest in Ogo-Pogo. "Have Done My Best" deals with a Force legend that could fit several real-life incidents, and its background closely follows the experiences of a recruit of the period who was also a friend of mine in his later years.

I must stress however, that the characters, other than famous historical figures such as Jerry Potts, "Buckskin" Charlie and Sitting Bull, are fictitious. Their personal traits and private lives must not be identified with those of the people whose factual exploits provided my inspiration.

The stories, other than "The Red Serge of Courage" and "Have Done My Best", are arranged in roughly chronological order.

—HARWOOD STEELE

CONTENTS

CONTENTS

THE RED SERGE

the red serge of courage

"Cross your stirrups! . . . Walk — *march!* . . . *Tr-r-o-t!* . . .
Can-t-e-r-r! . . . "

The too-familiar, hated orders turned Ernie Thompson
("Get-em" Junior) cold—with fear not of getting hurt but
of disgracing himself and Dad. He'd rather face mechanized
gunmen, liable to bounce up at any time, than hear this
routine summons from "Staff" Richards, instructing the
recruit ride. Eighteen years old, five foot eight, passed
Grade 8 at school, he met the minimum standards laid
down for modern Force recruits. So that wasn't the trouble,
though most of the other 3rd class constables on probation
were older, bigger, better educated. The trouble was that,
being chunky and town-bred (in Regina, right next to the
barracks), he hadn't the build or background for a first-
rate horseman like that old Force hero, Dad.

Yet those orders meant another round of jumping with
arms folded and feet out of stirrups crossed in front of the
saddle, so that you stuck on only by grip and balance. Over
the weeks the jumps had been gradually raised, till now
they looked as big as barns. So, ten to one, he'd fall off,
as he had on Monday.

All sixteen men (except himself) broadly grinning, all
sixteen beautiful black horses dancing and prancing, the ride
rushed down the jumping-lane in single file. Thank the
Lord, he was last. Here, though, was the first jump, simply
charging at him as his Crowfoot put on speed. *Whups!*
Cleared fairly well. *Whups!* Next fence, a bit better—and
Mac, just in front, lost his cap, some consolation—*Whups!*

1

Off balance—Crowfoot was going too damned fast. *Whups!*
"Steady, there!" from Staff, "*Lollipy-pop, lollipy-pop. . . .*"
Too bad, that guy Thompson almost unfolding his arms to
grab the reins. *Whups!* O.K.!

Then suddenly WHUPS! Crowfoot shied sideways as he
took off and his rider bit the tanbark and the deepest depths
of humiliation.

Staff usually dealt with riding-school faults in kind yet
terribly effective "Who'd have thought it?" style. The pupils
too were good at comment. But, seeing this casualty safe,
sound and trying to grin, riding instructor and ride merely
waited in silence while he caught and remounted old Crowfoot—a cinch, as the horse just stood and looked at him. This
hush hit much harder than the fall, as it showed—must show
—that they were thinking:

"Quietest horse in the stable, yet he still comes off! The
kid won't pass recruit class if he doesn't do better soon.
That'll be tough on his Dad, old "Get-em" Senior, too, so
we can't kick poor Junior round too hard—"

A small aircraft waggled its wings in the victory sign as
it roared over the ride, now headed for Noon "Stables."
Three mechanized gunmen, as the recruits well knew, sat
handcuffed and escorted in that newly landing plane, easily
recognized by its smart blue and gold, the Force colours.
The bandits had ambushed the staff of the Traders' Bank,
at Wolseley, fifty miles east of barracks, just before business
hours yesterday. Making it open the strong-room at pistol-
point, they'd grabbed $100,000 held there for harvest-time
transactions, then dashed north in a stolen car—to be caught
by "F" Division's wireless, radio, dogs, road-blocks and the
aircraft two hundred miles from Wolseley at 7 a.m. today.
Quick, good work—so much so that the whole ride, marching at ease, returned the plane's signal with thumbs up.

Cheered a bit, Ernie enjoyed the breeze sweeping over
miles of golden stubble on flat grain-fields till it beautifully
displayed the flag on the tall staff in the square against
Saskatchewan's clear sky. The ride, he thought, looked

grand passing the flag, which the Force, through Dad and others, had served so well. And its yellow-banded caps changed, in his mind's eye, to stetson hats, its khaki shirts to scarlet tunics, its horses glowed like patent leather, pennoned lances flashed above it and, multiplied by two, it became the Musical Ride. That "brilliant equestrian ballet," as some reporter called it, regularly thrilled big cities. And its members, always including men recently freed from recruit training, were given the time of their young lives.

But naturally their horsemanship must be absolutely perfect. As this naked truth fell into line with the sour memory of his riding-school tumbles, the scarlet coats and lances faded away and their men turned back into 3rd class constables. Then, after Stables, his heart sank into his Strathcona boots as Staff deliberately chose to walk beside him towards the square and dinner.

The instructor wrapped his bad news nicely up in talk about this and that, just throwing in, off-hand:

"Without good grip and balance, it's hard to make the Musical Ride."

"Hard" was a friendly way of saying "impossible" and also of hinting that a guy who bit the tanbark all the time would be found unfit for service at the end of the recruit course.

This explained why the buffalo-bull's head, the Force crest carved life-size in stone above headquarters entrance, looked down at Get-em Thompson Junior with an even bigger sneer than usual as he passed under it.

Showered and changed, he joined the rest of the ride and dozens of other men surging into the sunny cafeteria at the first note of the trumpet sounding "Dinners Up!" They filled the big room with a roar of laughter, small talk and plans for this duty-free Saturday afternoon. He found himself with some of his squad at tables near Corporal "Tiny" Shields, who had helped bring in the mechanized gunmen by plane an hour ago. The recruits pounded the tall, lean N.C.O. with questions, but all he would tell them concerned

Constable Holt, who had cornered the only bandit making a stand.

"Ran through his fire and shot the pistol out of his hand—like Get-em Thompson taking Spotted Horses in the old days—"

Everybody looked at Ernie, who, feeling as he did just then, thought the remark well meant, yet a two-pronged pitchfork reminding him of his faults. One prong brought back the time when an officer, lecturing his squad on Force history near the beginning of the course, had mentioned ex-Sergeant Thompson as a model for recruits.

The speaker had made sure that not one shiny button was missing from that model. The squad saw the big, burly, straight-shooting, hard-riding, hard-driving figure take shape before them, heard his war-cry, "Get 'em! Get 'em!" lead patrols into action against "bad" Indians and white "bad men." They followed his entire career in outline, learnt that on going to pension he had settled in Regina just to keep close touch with the Force. His capture of Spotted Horses had been described in full. And, winding up, the officer, looking straight at the old man's son, had told the squad:

"Don't forget that things like that may jump out at you—and when you least expect it."

Sure, sure, he was dead right. His talk certainly impressed the class. And of course he'd have dealt with some other Force hero if he'd known (as every one else did) that the ex-Sergeant's boy was present, suffering hells of embarrassment. Anyhow, from then on, that same boy was christened "Get-em" Junior. Dad was kingpin, with him, and the fellows were just kidding, but the name was much too big for him.

The other prong of the fork—unknown to Tiny Shields but, again, well known to the recruits around him—was this: Get-em Junior couldn't shoot the pistol out of anybody's hand, either with pistol or rifle, for the simple reason that he never hit the bull's eye! Nervousness made him pull the trigger too soon or too late. The whole squad had seen Sergeant-Major Collins, at last revolver-practice, trying hard to cure him, probably for Dad's sake, without doing much good. And all that added up to likely failure in another key subject of the course.

Luckily, the cafeteria crowd soon swung back to questioning Tiny, or to plans or jokes. And Mac, returning dirty dishes, asked, "Care to go gunning for prairie chicken with some of us this aft?"

A great guy, Mac—at least twenty-five, six foot tall, shaving twice a day, worldly wise, super-efficient and anxious to help without making a song and dance about it. Right now, for instance, he issued this bid not only for company's sake but to give a poor shot a chance to improve the easy way.

Yet "some of us" meant other eyes watching the poor shot's blunders. So black depression produced the answer:

"Sorry, I've got a date."

"Shirley, I'll bet!" Mac grinned, then suggested, "Phone her and put her off till after dark. She'll like that better."

She would too. But:

"Not today, Mac—sorry—"

Mac laughed, "O.K.! Well, I sure want some one to share a private workout with me and my pistol tomorrow morning. How about it?"

"You bet! Thanks a lot—"

That cheered him up a bit. Then he felt better still on leaving his barrack-room a little later to get his car. Besides being off to meet Shirley, he was smart as be-damned in cap, dark brown jacket blazing with brass buttons and badges, brown slacks, brown leather belt and etceteras, including, so help me, a riding crop and brown leather gloves. Sure thing, the uniform would make a god out of a gorilla, but at least he did know how to wear it and Shirley loved it.

Fine—till the Force Roll of Honour in the square threw a

shadow across his way to the main gate. He knew every name on its long list of members who had died on duty, had known them, in fact, by heart, ever since reading them as a kid, years and years ago. They inspired him, as they did everybody. But today they seemed to accuse him silently of letting them down. And for a moment he thought grimly that if his own name ever joined them it would be just for going astray like "Dreamy" King, the boy recruit who had frozen to death in a blizzard long ago, though he had left behind a message: "Lost. Horse dead. Am trying to push on. Have done my best." Worse, Get-em Junior wouldn't even wear this smart uniform much longer, at the rate he was going now.

But firearms and gunmen chased gloom from his mind as he drove on towards Shirley's, past hunters with rifles hurrying their cars northward after deer and beside fields over which the bangs of shotguns potting game-birds reached him from all directions. Murder or robbery, he remembered, could be done at this season under cover of hunting or of shooting "accidents."

Soon his intensive training had him automatically noting descriptions of the hunters and their vehicles, while reviewing instructions on how to cope with the type of emergency they brought with them. At least he'd catch any fugitive on wheels, for, if he couldn't ride, he could drive—no fooling! Weaving through the traffic in a way that made the Musical Ride serpentine look like a slow-worm, he passed everything in sight, to throw the dozen miles to Shirley's behind him in as many minutes. With the modern Force, that kind of driving counted—and it made him feel better.

Then Shirley herself, all ready and waiting on the veranda of her Dad's big, if old-fashioned, farmhouse, boosted his morale still more. Couldn't help it! Pretty as a peach in her bright, soft dress, this pint-size, peppy brunette could push the cover-girl off any magazine. She'd been *his* girl ever since they started climbing together through Regina's schools. And now she said:

"You look just *marvellous!*"

Her family backed her too, when they came out to greet him. Mr. Waterton, a big shot in Saskatchewan, as a blind man could see, said, "Boy, you'll soon be Corporal!" Mrs. Waterton (Shirley grown older) cried, "Hullo, handsome!" Jean, the kid sister, murmured, "MY!" Olga, the hired girl, would have joined in as well, only she was busy in the kitchen.

But the rest of the household, seemingly, weren't so pleased. Bill Levine, the hired man—husky, up-and-coming, thirty years old, a black-browed Casanova with one of those close-clipped, movie-type moustaches, just glanced up from the hammock, jeered "Pride of the Mounties!" and went on cleaning his rifle and shotgun, while that glance, quick though it was, suggested that he'd gladly pump a round or two into the visitor or knock his block off. Well, that would be O.K. any time, so long as it went no farther than a strictly unofficial scrap. Anyhow, what the hell—the poor sap was chasing Shirley, getting nowhere and plain jealous. As for Grandpa Waterton, in the rocker and the shadows, he simply went on muttering over the old Bible on his knees, which didn't count, as he was slightly nuts. He'd been brought in from his lonely farm near Prince Albert last year because he couldn't run it any more.

"Where to?" asked Shirley, now beside him in the car. "Paramount," he said, "the Saskatchewan Room for supper —and maybe drive out to the lakes later on!" "Terrific!" she said. "The best picture, restaurant and climax! You know how to spend your pay—and get your gal—"

In fact, the picture was good, the meal worthy of Regina's chief hotel. With Shirley surpassing even herself, they took away his troubles. Unfortunately a tourist brought them back as they headed for the streetdoor afterwards. She was fair, fat and far past forty, a frustrated romantic of the kind Force lecturers on public relations urged the men to treat gently. And she broke in on him with the usual:

"Excuse me, sir, I'm just dying to tell the folks back home I shook hands with a Mountie—er—Canada's finest!"

Then, of course, he'd have taken the hand she put out in a scared sort of way if she hadn't suddenly pulled it back and asked:

"If you're a Mountie, where's your beautiful red coat?"

She'd hit it—where? Her bald, pink, executive-husband grabbed her arm and whispered much too loudly:

"Mabel, you're embarrassing the young man!"

The young man, more than embarrassed, plunged truthfully through with:

"I haven't got my red coat yet—I'm only on probation—"

"Oh, dear!" cried Mabel and was dutifully hurried away.

Back in the car, he cruised with Shirley through flashing city streets to join the endless chain of headlights moving gently through cool darkness towards Qu'Appelle Lakes. She sat close to him but never said a word till they were miles from town, when she quietly remarked:

"You'll get it soon."

"Your beautiful red coat," she meant, the Force's "red serge," which recruits got when they passed their course, as a university graduate gets his cap and gown. Just like Shirley, to know what he was thinking about and pick the thread of it out of silence in exactly the right way—

He tightened his grip on the wheel. This was going to be tough. She knew how he felt. His older half-brothers by Dad's first marriage were born civilians, George a successful mining engineer, Joe doing well at law. But he'd wanted to be in the Force all his life and would never be more or less than a Force member at heart. How, then, could he now find words to tell her that he feared discharge as unlikely to make an efficient constable and therefore sure to be Dad's biggest disappointment?

But trust Shirley again—woman's intuition or whatever it was, sizing things up from the little bits and pieces of news about his progress—or the lack of it—he'd given her from time to time. Squeezing his arm, she said, with hardly a quiver in her voice:

"Even if you did fail—which I'm sure you won't—you can do some other job. Then we won't have to wait till you've saved a lot of pay and got the Commissioner's permission to get married. We can do it the moment they say 'Out!'"

"Well," he commented, "the course is nearly over. But I'll try to push on, like Dreamy King, and do my best."

"That's the stuff!" she said and kissed him in a way terribly violating traffic regulations, yet likely to put new hope into any man able to keep his car on the road while she did it. "Come to supper tomorrow," she added, "Come early! The family's going to see Aunt Nell, Olga's going to see her folks, and Bill's going to town after he's milked the cows, so we'll be alone except for Grandpa and we can really talk."

"It's a date," he said.

Then, much later, when he dropped her at home, she kissed him again, so heartily that Bill, the hired man, and Grandpa, both sitting up late and hearing the car, glared from open bedroom windows and Grandpa yelled, "Quit that!"

Assistant-Commissioner Bennett, commanding "F", felt that something big and bloody was about to happen when he awoke in his Regina-barracks home next morning.

Perhaps the pop of shotguns still after game-birds gave him the hunch by reminding him of the rifle fire of both World Wars and of those murders and shooting accidents liable to concern his division, covering all Saskatchewan, this bright fall Sunday. Or perhaps it sprang simply from the fact that Get-em Senior was paying a social call on him this afternoon. For the ex-Sergeant, having tactfully avoided barracks since his son started training there, might now sandwich questions about the boy's work between yarns about old times. And then he'd have to be told that the work had serious weak points, so that, if Ernie failed the course, his Dad's heart would not be broken.

A job nearly—though not quite—enough to account for that feeling of grim stuff ahead. Normally O.C. Depot, in charge of recruits, would tackle it. But ex-Sergeant Thompson was a Force institution *and* aged seventy-five! Besides, big, grey-haired Art Bennett had trained as a recruit under Get-em Senior thirty years ago. So he'd agreed, at O.C. Depot's request, to deal with that awkward subject when the veteran raised it, even studying reports on Ernie beforehand, to avoid mistakes.

Get-em Senior arrived at precisely the appointed time and place—4 P.M. in the Bennett living-room. To his host he looked as broad as an old Force wagon, straight as the path of duty, almost as ruddy as the old red serge and therefore—thank God—still fit to hear home truths. Soon the two comrades of many a tough trail were sitting over scotch and sodas, well away on a long ride into the Land of Memory. But soon too that led to the awkward subject, as, more's the pity, it was bound to do.

"Of course," said Get-em, "that's all just history now—Force history. And, talking of Force history, how my boy Ernie loves it! George and Jim, my two eldest, never seemed to care for it much. But Ernie! Ever since he was knee-high to a grasshopper, he couldn't have enough of it. Why, often when I'd be holding forth with some old-timer about what I'd seen and done or what the Originals had told me about Macleod or Walsh or Jerry Potts, our pioneers, I'd find that little shaver out of bed and sitting in the dark outside the door, to take in every word. So now he knows Force history backwards, doesn't he? Eh? Doesn't he?"

"He certainly does," Bennett agreed, glad to find the old man opening up with one of Ernie's good points. "Then," he plunged on, "he's first-rate on discipline, naturally, public relations, rules and regulations, criminal law, typing—oh, yes, and comparison microscope, forensic medicine, toxicology — excellent in observation tests, ditto plan-drawing—"

"Glad you think it," said Get-em Senior, beaming like the sun through the smoke of a prairie-fire. "Mind you, I'm not surprised, not one bit. God knows, I've told him often enough about the MacGregor case, for instance: how our experts picked that damned child-murderer's gun out of hundreds by using the comparison microscope to identify its bullets! As for observation tests, from the time he joined his boy scout troop he was a wizard at Kim's Game—one glance and he'd remember twenty objects. Plan-drawing comes natural to him—takes after his mother—a real artist. Fact is, in all those things he's a regular Pennycuick. Remember the O'Brien case?"

"Before my time," said Art Bennett. It was, too, though naturally he was well informed on the details of that Force classic. But as the old man loved to describe it, he let him ramble on:

"Up in the Yukon, it happened, during the Gold Rush, a few years after I joined the Force. O'Brien made himself a hideout, murdered and robbed Ole Olson and two others there, threw away their odds and ends, shoved the bodies under the river ice and beat it. Corporal Ryan found the hideout, sent for Constable Pennycuick. Right off, Penny-cuick recognized the stove in the hideout, though he'd last seen it over two weeks before in the camp of men calling themselves Miller and Ross. He sent out their descriptions. One was O'Brien's. That led to his arrest. Then Pennycuick swept away the snow around the hideout, found the odds and ends. I helped him. Later, we found the bodies and built up a case covering dozens of witnesses and thousands of miles, all starting from that stove. Pennycuick's sketches for the court were perfect. Yes, Ernie's like him—

"Now, what about other good points—Ernie's?"

Bennett quietly refilled their glasses, to fortify Get-em Senior for shocks.

"Let's see— He's good at interviews, interrogations, most

forms of criminal investigation, fair with police service dogs, average in gym, boxing, police holds, excellent in everything to do with motor transport—" A pause— "Oh yes, and in all kinds of drill."

"I expected that." Yet now the prairie-fire smoke seemed, somehow, to veil the sun. "Poor, though, at swimming, life-saving, handling a canoe?" Before Bennett, surprised, could frame a suitable reply, the old man went on, "He nearly drowned in the lakes once. Scared his mother into keeping him away from the water too much. I should have helped him more or got George and Jim to do it. 'Cause those things are mighty important. All those drowned men on the Roll of Honour show that — Mahoney, Hooley, Wahl, Morphy, de Beaujeu, Kern, Campbell, Heathcote and the rest. Remember how we'd have joined 'em in the Hanbury rapids if we'd not been good canoemen—and swum well?"

"Times have changed!"

"Not on the water—"

Hell, thought Bennett, this talk is getting cock-eyed. Here I'm defending Ernie from his Dad.

Get-em Senior glanced at his watch.

"The boys are at evening 'Stables'," he said. "I should have taught Ernie to ride from the first. You know what the Commissioner says: 'There's nothing like a horse to find out the weakness in a man' — yes, and for rough country and crowds."

"Staff Richards tells me Ernie's got the heart of a lion, even if he does fall off. And he's improved—"

Ernie's Dad did not answer and for an awful moment Bennett dreaded tears. Then a breeze wafted many shotgun reports through the open windows and—

"That reminds me," the old man remarked, "I should have taught him to shoot really well." Suddenly he added, looking his friend in the eyes and speaking firmly as could be, "Art, you must 'Maintain the Right', though I'd hate to see the boy thrown out!"

For once, the Assistant-Commissioner was completely at a loss. Trying to sound casual, he said:

"We get six thousand would-be recruits a year, take only ten per cent and even fail some of *them*. Our standard's still very, very high. Perhaps we try to teach too much, with sixty subjects—"

Here he should have quoted the gist of O.C. Depot's notes on Ernie:

"Lacks full confidence. Immature. Very good at some things, seriously weak in others. May fail to overcome these weaknesses before the end of the course."

But he could only consider saying, "We could find him a clerical job and let him try again in a few years' time."

He never said it. For the shotgun reports became filled with menace and the phone in the hall, ringing sharply, recalled his hunch. Answering the phone, he heard:

"Switchboard here, sir. Constable Thompson has just telephoned this message from Mr. Waterton's farm off Highway 1, twelve miles east of here: 'Mr. Waterton's father violently insane, armed and threatening to shoot the hired man, take his car and kill all the young men in the country. Am unarmed myself but moving in to subdue him'."

Ernie heard two shots from the yard behind the Waterton house as he drove up the side-road to the farm. His mind being happily on supper with Shirley and his good morning of revolver-practice with Mac, he thought they meant nothing more than Bill's having a little target-practice too.

Then he heard Grandpa howling like a mad wolf, the most bloodcurdling noise he'd ever come across, half guessed what it meant, sent the car hurtling to a halt beside the veranda and saw Grandpa in the yard, covering Bill with a rifle. The hired man, hands up, had obviously been paralyzed by the shots, fired at or near him. Frozen with fear, Ernie thought, "Shirley!" and charged into the house. White as her own dress but cool as Saskatchewan in

winter, she was feverishly struggling to get the barracks on
the phone.

"Tell me the set-up, quickly!" he ordered — no lack of
confidence here— "Give me the phone, too!"

"After the others left," she gabbled, "Bill spent the
afternoon in his room, like me in mine. Grandpa's been
getting fussy about protecting me from men." She laughed
hysterically. "Seeing the coast clear, he hid every firearm
and all the ammunition in the house except that rifle he's
got now. When Bill had milked the cows and changed into
city clothes, he went to get his car. Grandpa came out of
the garage, yelling that Bill was a seducer and must be killed
but first he must give up his car-keys, so Grandpa can drive
around killing every other skunk like him. Bill won't give
them up, so Grandpa's fired at him. That's all."

The barracks switchboard now answered Ernie's call. He
gave his message like a veteran (didn't even have to think
out the form), then told Shirley:

"Stay on the phone! Give and take reports! I'm going
to disarm Grandpa—"

"He'll kill you!"

"I must go, you know that!"

"For God's sake, don't hurt him!" she wailed after him,
as he ran to the kitchen window.

"I won't," he shouted back.

Of course he hadn't a gun, and there was no time to find
one. Besides, he must rely on judo, in any case, as hurting
a madman wasn't in the Force book.

Grandpa had his back to the window and was raving
enough to scare the living daylights out of a guy, while still
covering Bill, who hadn't moved an inch. Both men seemed
terribly far off *and* stood beyond a high wire fence and a
closed gate which a rescuer must cross before Grandpa
could shoot again.

"Don't forget that things . . . may jump out at *you* . . .
when you least expect it!" The lecturer's words flashed into
Ernie's mind, with two of his own: "And now!" He didn't

consciously recall that Dad, rushing Spotted Horses, or even
Holt, rushing that mechanized bandit yesterday, had at
least a pistol. But he was glad he wasn't cluttered up with
a horse, as it was much simpler to push on dismounted and
do his best, in the mopping, mowing face of death.

His plan came automatically . . . to slip out the back door,
tiptoe to the gate, vault it and rush. With luck, he'd reach
Grandpa in time to—well, in time—

The screen-door twanged like a harp as he opened it.
And Bill, seeing him, stared with dropped jaw. But Grandpa
was raving too much to notice anything.

The words foaming and yammering from his mouth were
all Bible words but almost as bad to listen to as the fearful,
meaningless shrieks and snarls mixed with them:

"Son of the Whore of Babylon—spawn of Satan—
libertine—"

Then he threw in a lot of modern stuff Grandpa normally
wouldn't use in a thousand years, plus things like: "Keep
to your harlots and leave Shirley alone or I'll kill you. Guess
I'll kill you anyhow!"

Step by step, Ernie closed in. Apart from Grandpa's
ravings, a clank, now and then, from the farm windmill and
that ugly, yet unconcerned popping of distant shotguns, the
evening was all peace, just right to die in, and silent as the
grave, so silent that every pebble displaced by creeping feet
seemed to make a noise loud enough to wake the dead.

But still Grandpa showed no sign of suspicion, though
hope had slipped into Bill's ashen face, with something like
thanks (none of your "Pride of the Mounties" now!).

Ernie's hand was on the gate when Grandpa howled:
"For the last time, give me those keys or I'll shoot!"

Ernie vaulted the gate but so clumsily that he fell and
as he fell Grandpa shot Bill through the heart.

Ernie charged on, while Grandpa, quicker than greased
lightning, rummaged in Bill's pockets, found and took out
the car-keys, then wheeled on Ernie, pointing the rifle and
yelling:

"Mountie, stop right there!"

Ernie stopped—naturally and because there was no sense in getting killed at this stage. Grandpa grinned and glared at him, yet held the rifle steady as a rock. But really this horror wasn't Grandpa. Those rolling eyes, that tousled white hair, that sweat-drenched face, that gibbering, drooling mouth and that claw itching on the trigger of that deadly rifle had a ghastly look of an old man Ernie liked but belonged to a fiend out of childhood's blackest nightmare, a fiend holding Grandpa back in some dark room behind the eyes. Somehow Ernie had to slip past the fiend to poor old Grandpa and, so doing, gently collect the rifle and the keys.

The sound of the phone bell and of Shirley's voice answering the call drifted down from the house, but very faintly, as Ernie began his great attempt to carry out Plan No. 2. Still out of the Force book, though he didn't consciously consult it—

"Hullo, Mr. Waterton," he said, "I'm Ernie Thompson."

The fiend laughed, in a terrible voice not a bit like Grandpa's:

"Ernie Thompson? Not you! I know Ernie, known him for years! A little tad, still at school. *Don't come a step nearer!*"

"Sure, sure, but I've left school now, Mr. Waterton. I'm up at the barracks, taking the recruit course. Shirley's having me to supper, remember?"

The fiend snarled:

"Keep your dirty tongue off my grand-daughter! Keep away from her or I'll have to kill you, with all the others out to ruin her. Keep away!"

The muzzle of the rifle, five yards from Ernie's chest, with that claw moving restlessly on the trigger, looked bigger than the muzzle of the obsolete seven-pounder gun near the Roll of Honour in the barracks square. Ernie went on:

"Just as you say, Mr. Waterton. My, that's a fine rifle! Can I have a look at it?"

The fiend yammered and grimaced, while poor Grandpa

fought to push past it in answer to that friendly voice. Would the old man make it? Ernie held his breath. The shotguns popped, the windmill clanked, but the wide world had shrunk to a coffin holding only two people, apart from the fiend—Grandpa and himself. Poor dead Bill didn't count—and Shirley was much too far away.

Grandpa got his head out of prison.

"Sure it's a fine rifle, Ernie, you're right! Can't miss!" he declared, in something like his normal voice. "But then we've a lot of fine guns—all nicely put away. Better'n any you've got in the Force, I'll bet."

"You've said it, Mr. Waterton!" Don't excite them by arguing, that was another rule. But turn the talk off guns! Otherwise, with that muzzle still pointing— "You're looking well, sir, never better!"

"Not bad for an old one," said Grandpa, now right past the fiend (Keep it up, you Get-em Junior!). The claw, now a hand, left the trigger and passed wearily over a puckered forehead. "Mind you, I get awful headaches and dizzy spells—have 'em now. Still, I'm pretty good, considering. How's your own folks? How's your Dad?"

"Fine too, Mr. Waterton—" strolling two steps nearer a slightly wobbling muzzle— If only Dad was here! Instead of just two people in a coffin with a fiend— "Cigarette, sir? How about sitting on those hay-bales for a good old talk?"

"I'd like to, Ernie!"

The rifle-muzzle was pointing to the ground now, the hand stretched out in friendly style. For Pete's sake, Plan No. 2 was going to work! Ernie unbuttoned a side-pocket, fished in it for the cigarettes.

There and then, the fiend sprang back, throwing poor old Grandpa clean out of sight, pointing the rifle, clawing at the trigger.

"No, you don't!" it snarled. "You've a gun in there! Can't fool me. Anyhow, this is wasting time. I've got to take that car and kill a few seducers before sundown. Keep back, I tell you, Mountie, or I'll shoot!"

As it spoke, the fiend began backing slowly towards the open door of the garage where stone-dead Bill's car stood ready.

Ernie stepped over Bill and followed quietly. Plan No. 3! If he couldn't do anything else, he'd grab the rifle when the fiend tried to start the car. Plan No. 3—

"Let's have that rifle, Grandpa!" said Ernie, reaching for it.

The fiend threw back its head with a whoop of laughter straight from Hell itself.

"I'm out to kill, Mountie!" it chuckled. "And *no one's* going to stop me. Now, listen, if you don't stop following me, you're a dead duck!"

Ernie followed. No, not Ernie! He wasn't Ernie Thompson or even Get-em Junior, one lone 3rd class constable, an undersized kid on probation. He wasn't a failure, moving in to a grandstand finish. He was Dad and Dreamy King and Tiny Shields. He was the whole Force, past and present, doing its duty "without fear, favour or affection," as the oath required, and thinking of nothing more than getting that rifle away from the fiend, come what may.

They were right in the garage now. And the fiend was backed up against Bill's car, the rifle-muzzle almost touching Ernie's chest.

"Keep off!" it snarled.

"Come along, Mr. Waterton, I'll hold the rifle while you start the car—"

The world burst apart in flame and thunder as the fiend fired, flash and report multiplied a hundred times in the confined space and darkness of the garage. Ernie fell through space into oblivion and fell and fell and fell—

Till he landed, quite softly it seemed, on something. He heard, far, far away, somebody sobbing, then, even farther off but coming nearer and nearer very fast, the wail of the fiend (or maybe of the siren on a police car), the blare of many horns, the murmur of many voices and a funeral bell (or the gong on an ambulance).

He opened his eyes, not fully taking in or believing what he saw: Grandpa, free again, the rifle at his feet, his hands to his face, tears streaming through thin fingers (which naturally explained the sobbing, poor old guy)—police cars, civilian cars, the ambulance, white-coated men, Shirley, Dad, Tiny Shields and—gosh!—the Assistant-Commissioner himself. A white-coat said:

"Make way, so I can give him this plasma and rush him to hospital for a blood transfusion! Then he'll live!"

That made him glance at his own coat, not brown but red with blood, red as—well, Bennett was aptly misquoting Stephen Crane:

"The Red Serge of Courage! By the living God, you've won it, boy! You've passed the course!"

sir galahad and the "bad man"

"Blue-streak Joe", the "bad man", rode into Mustang at full gallop.

Mustang (pop. 300) lay dozing on a hot midsummer afternoon and on a branch of the C.P.R. a few miles north of the State of Montana. Up till now, nothing could have been quieter. But now Joe proved that this peace had been no more than the calm before the cyclone.

As he dashed past Ping Ling's Laundry, the first place he came to on Main (the only) Street, he raised his hands and began to utter war-whoops, while from his guns blazed a deafening fusillade.

Mustang snoozed on. It had heard the shots and the yells, but waking up Mustang took time. Arriving at the far end of the street, Joe halted. Disappointment, born of the town's seeming indifference, sat heavily on his face, while his lanky, powerful figure, in the conventional panoply of the cowboy, drooped sadly. But, not to be beaten, he reloaded and, putting spurs to his horse, rode back along Main full blast, as if less than one jump ahead of the entire Blackfoot Nation.

So now Mustang yawned, sat up and took notice. Men, women and, inevitably, swarms of children ran out to gape at this strange being, and curious heads appeared at many windows. They did not stay there long. As soon, in fact, as their owners realized that the being was a bad man, firing real bullets from real revolvers, they ducked back into cover. Joe, delighted with results, hastened the disappearance of the staring faces at the windows by firing at them.

20

Opposite the Lone Wolf saloon, he dismounted. Terrified outposts spread the news: "Sacred rattlesnakes, boys, he's comin' in here!" Followed a wild dash for safety. Chick, the bartender, deliberately ignoring the common emergency, protested strenuously against an invasion of the bar, vowing, when the invaders howled down his assertion that they had no business there, that there was only room for himself. As he was a large, fat man, who took up a great deal of space, this was very nearly true.

The announcement of Joe's approach had barely been made when all hands except the gentlemen under the tables had disappeared. These were not cowards. None of them had a weapon. Canadian cowboys did not carry guns on social occasions.

Joe came in. His first procedure was to root everybody out of cover. The bartender, stuck almost immovably in a sort of cupboard, refused to emerge. Joe fired a bullet into the bar above his head and, with quite exceptional agility, Chick, yelping pitifully, bounced out of his hiding-place like a rubber ball from a box.

"Drinks for the house!" commanded Joe, revolvers pointed.

"Ah, say, d'you want to land me in the breadline?" asked Chick, who was also the proprietor.

"Make it slippy," Joe insisted.

The drinks were produced. The house sheepishly, yet not ungratefully, drank "Blue-streak's" health. But the kick in the liquor evaporated somewhat when the visitor made a team of Mustang's leading citizens, long past such capers, dance a Highland reel to "Turkey in the Straw", shakily strummed out by Mozart Schmidt on the Lone Wolf piano while Joe's revolver shots kept time. Worse followed. "Forty-Rod" Milligan, perpetual mayor, who chanced to be present, was ordered to stand against the wall, holding out his hat, which the bad man riddled, poor Chick punctuating the silences between with wails of anguish as ricochets smashed mirrors and went through pictures.

Some murmured a word about sending for a Mounted Policeman.

"Mounted Policeman, huh?" Joe sneered. "One of them red-coated luridly adjectival very improper nouns? Why, there's no such guy in Mustang! But you shorthorns can tell the Mounted Police, from me, that this galoot will fight 'em all at once, free-for-all or go-as-you-please, any time they dare—yep, dare—to poke their snoots into my hog-wash. So long! I'll call agin. An' Mr. Blue-streak Joe, from Antelope, is my name."

With that he left, wisely headed, in spite of all his big talk, for the boundary line.

He was almost clear of Mustang when he saw Betsy, draped over her home fence and watching him coolly. His spectacular arrival Betsy had greeted with delight, as something to break the town's utter monotony. And her scorn for the timidity of its people—"a hundred able-bodied men bulldogged by one lone cowboy"—had held her at the fence for the past ten minutes, in the hope of just a squint at him. After all, wasn't he like one of Tennyson's Knights of the Round Table? Wasn't he? No, he wasn't. But at least he bore a mighty close resemblance to his false knaves, churls and caitiffs, which was something.

At sight of her, Joe halted—Betsy, a strapping, handsome girl, could halt a locomotive. Clumsily he took off his hat, grinned from ear to cauliflower ear, and said, "Lady, How do!" Her reply surprised him, "Put an egg in your boot and beat it!" Then she flounced back into the house. Joe's grin widened. He liked 'em lively. "I'll be back!" he yelled, as he pressed on southward, leaving yet another heart tied to Betsy's saddle-horn.

Superintendent Praed, hero of the White Eagle manhunt and the Case of Pete the Doukhobor,* now commanded the district concerned with these nice goings on but, at the time, knew nothing about them. The catch was that the Mounted Police, totalling only a few hundred men to safeguard an

*See "The Martinet" in *To Effect An Arrest*.

area bigger than most European countries, let alone Texas, could not afford to post a constable permanently in Mustang. And before Forty-Rod Milligan could lay a complaint against Joe in the lap of the nearest detachment, the bad man was safely in Montana.

Praed rasped, "They want me to send out a man whenever a duck quacks!" Still, he promised to post a single constable, temporarily and as a special case, in Mustang, with orders to gather Joe very quietly in, should he reappear. He did not believe that Joe would reappear. But even a single constable would stop Mustang shying at its own shadow. And, if the bad man actually did come back, that constable could deal with him.

Better send "Flaming Andy" (Constable Andrew Clint). Andy's hair was the colour of vermilion war-paint, clashing horribly with the scarlet of his serge jacket and, being big, broad-shouldered, fearless and impulsive, he was the spittin' image of a buffalo bull. His day-to-day record suggested an ambition to raise as much merry hell as he could within the limits of the North-West Mounted Police Act (36 Victoria, Chap. 35). This made him what his sergeant-major called "the thorn in my tortured flesh." But he did everything important well and could and would bring in Old Man Coyote and every other devil known to priest or medicine man if the Commissioner so ordered it. Besides, Andy was getting restless.

So Praed told him, with a grizzly growl: "Go to Mustang! Stay there till Blue-streak Joe shows up again! Arrest him! If he resists, you know the drill—"

"Yes, sir," said Andy, looking as if saddle-soap wouldn't melt in his mouth, "I can use just enough force to overpower him but no more—see *The Constable's Manual*, Sec. 6, Para. 4, footnote!"

"Exactly!" snapped Praed, while Andy made himself scarce with his best salute.

Meanwhile, Betsy made Mustang feel small. Blue-streak Joe, she said, had branded the townsmen for what they

really were; and what *that* was she detailed through a
vocabulary astounding in a nice young girl who had never
even been to Saskatoon.

Now Andy rode into Mustang, not war-whooping on the
dead jump but slowly, with dignity and in full dress, to
restore confidence. Sitting as straight in the saddle as the
lance he bore through the Musical Ride, he looked as if his
entry should be heralded by a great flourish of trumpets.
Mustang shouted its welcome. And even Betsy, back at the
home fence, said "My!" But that was under her breath.
What she added, right out loud, perhaps because His
Magnificence did not so much as peek sideways at the
prettiest girl in the border country, was: "Hail, Sir Galahad!"

Andy scorned to reply. But the sarcasm struck deep, as
no Force member worth his salt ration would boast, "My
strength is as the strength of ten, because my heart is pure,"
much less, "I never felt the kiss of love or maiden's hand in
mine." If it had been Lancelot, now, "the great knight, the
darling of the court, loved by the loveliest" and "bruised
and bronzed" or even Modred, "like a vermin in its hole."
But Galahad! That sissy! So, though keeping mum, Andy
flushed till his neck was ruddier than his vermilion hair.

Getting his own back did not take long. His first duty
being to meet every one in town and establish himself on a
friendly basis, he began a round of social calls that very
evening. Not unnaturally, he started with the home of
Jimmy Cavanagh (Flour and Feed, Insurance, Mortgages,
Money to Loan), who just happened to be Betsy's dad.
And not unnaturally, Betsy just happened to open the door.

Said Andy, very politely, "Are the grown-ups in, Betsy?"

Haughty as be-damned and Queen Guinevere (being
three years out of high school) Betsy retorted, "Miss
Cavanagh to you, sir—" then spoilt the whole thing by
adding "Galahad!" and rushing upstairs. There, locked in
her bedroom—the Lady of Shalot in her tower—she spent
the next half hour making mental notes, for future guidance,
on how Lynette brought Sir Gareth to heel by calling

him names, while Andy discussed crop reports with *Mr.* Cavanagh and a Stonewall Jackson cigar.

Over Mustang hung tension, as at the approach of hail or summer frost.

Till, sure enough, remembering sauce-box Betsy, Joe came back.

He had a keen sense of the dramatic. Betsy, he felt, would be more impressed if he staged his next exhibition of gun-play without notice. Her absence—she was driving around with Dad in the buggy to look at those crops— marred the big moment. But still it had its points — the town again hushed in a summer afternoon, Flaming Andy and the flies dozing together in his temporary detachment and the Lone Wolf peacefully drinking and talking cattle-prices as Joe burst into the saloon in a breeze of bullets.

"It's the bad man!" yelled the crowd, stampeding into cover.

Joe did not make them come out this time. Instead, to improve, as he thought, on his first performance, he began shooting at anything that took his fancy. He put a bullet through the portrait of the reigning Sovereign, another through the matching lithograph of the current President, for Joe was quite impartial. He shattered bottles on the tables. He blew taps off. And he regularly bawled, "Bring on your Mounted Police!"

The answer to his bawling proved worthy of Tennyson at his best. Joe was taking leisurely pot-shots at a match-box trembling on the shiny pate of Baldy Jones and, except for the crash of his revolvers and the chattering of Chick's dentures, the Lone Wolf was absolutely silent when Andy suddenly appeared through the swinging doors. Forty-Rod Milligan had slipped out to get him, unbeknownst. And he now came on the double, buckling on his .45 as he burned the trail. Looking like a big red barn, he coolly sized things up, then, speaking to Joe, through a lull in the firing, gently uttered two tremendous words:

"You're pinched!"

Joe, who had not seen him, spun round, quick as a

cow-pony. He gaped, amazed to find a Mounted Policeman actually in Mustang. But, soon recovering, he grinned and shouted:

"Come an' git me!"

True to the old tradition of never drawing a gun until he had to, Andy marched slowly towards him in silent acceptance of Joe's invitation. Shaken into panic, Joe lost his ugly head, opening up with the full weight of his artillery. In no time, the big red barn turned back into the buffalo bull—charged, head down, through a fury of fire— miraculously survived it—closed—

The bad man, now, had only four shots left and all in one revolver. As Andy reached him, he dropped the empty gun. Andy grabbed the hand holding the other and kicked the useless weapon out of reach. In a blizzard of curses from Joe—Andy never let out a peep—the warriors whirled three times around the room. Three times Joe fired but Andy's crushing grip spoilt his aim. Tables and chairs went flying, Mustangers scattered like steers before the rush of wolves.

Joe managed to beat the policeman to his knees. In half a jiffy, the bad man would get his gun free and his last shot would make Andy the centre of attraction at the next coroner's inquest. But somehow Andy recovered himself and the watchers roared as they saw that this second revolver was now in his hand, then pitched into a far corner, like the first. It was man to man now, unless the constable drew his gun. This Andy scorned to do. He wanted a straightforward trial of strength, nothing less. Appreciating his sportsmanship and on fire to see Canada's Glory pound the Pest of the Prairie into paste, his supporters gave another thunderous cheer.

Round and round again, arms spinning, like two threshing machines in fits. Andy staggered the bad man with a terrific drive. Joe regained control and charged. They clinched. Joe forced the policeman down on to a table. His long fingers were at Andy's throat. The table disintegrated. Andy got somehow to his feet and Joe to his. The bad man seized a chair. The crowd howled a warning. Andy dodged nimbly and the chair was shattered to bits.

Andy might now resort to similar weapons, under the laws of chivalry and of bar-room scraps. But he was more determined than ever to get this gorilla with his bare hands. Wild blood thoroughly up, he closed once more. Locked in a deadly embrace, the two men spun towards the door. To the left stood a tasteful Japanese screen, a veritable collector's piece. A sudden twist threw Andy off course and brought screen and wrestlers down together. Joe rose with his shirt in shreds. As for the screen, no collector—veritable or otherwise, except, perhaps, a junk man—would have looked at it.

They clinched again. But Andy evaded the issue with a wiggle worthy of Minnehaha in her favourite war-dance. Joe rushed him to the bar, pinning him against it with an intense bombardment. Though ruffled, Andy got Joe by the hair—in its mind's eye, the crowd heard the rasp of his scalping-knife. Joe screeched a high C quite as good as a coloratura soprano's and yelled red, white and blue murder as Andy swung him on to the bar for a brisk massage. Bottles and glasses cascaded, crashing, to the floor, then Joe and Andy cascaded into them.

Finding their feet, the punch-drunk pair exchanged haymakers with awful deliberation, till Andy flung Joe into the wall with a slam that shook the building. This was too much for the reigning Sovereign. His picture leaped from its nail to the bad man's head, half stunning him and showering him with glass. Andy, glorious in raw manhood, waited for Joe to recover. But Joe, the caitiff, suddenly stooped and hurled a spittoon straight at him. Andy ducked and the thing rocketed through the Lone Wolf's last unbroken window.

That spittoon really riled Andy. Bottles, yes! Pickaxes, yes! Guns, undoubtedly! But spittoons weren't fair. So now he went for Joe in earnest. Rushing him to the piano, he banged out all the chords in Liszt's "Hungarian Rhapsodies" with the bad man's rump, though normally neither Joe nor Andy could play a note. Then, tossing him into the shrinking laps of Chick and Mozart Schmidt, Andy stood back.

"Had enough?" panted the pillar of law and order, rocking on its base but pulling out handcuffs.

No reply—the bad man tried to speak but could not. And the onlookers were similarly stricken dumb, so that a tomblike hush held the wrecked and smoke-filled room.

"Had enough?" Andy gasped again.

But, no two ways about it, Joe was game. His clouding gaze roved here and there till it came to rest on the Milwaukee brewery's outsize colour print of "Custer's Last Stand." That turned the scale. Suddenly he tottered forward and, taking Andy off balance, collided with him so violently that the handcuffs sailed into the chandelier and the Redcoat Rider, and Joe in his own "last stand," burst through the swing-doors into Main Street.

Here 202 people—all Mustang's 300, less infants, invalids, the aged and those already packed into the Lone Wolf saloon — waited fearfully to find out who was murdering whom. They'd been waiting since Joe's first shot woke Granny Grimes, who'd come west in a Red River cart and bounced her back through many years to the time of the North-West Rebellion, yelling, "Git yer guns, boys! It's Big Bear!" Among them, now, as Andy hazily saw through nearly bunged-up eyes, was Betsy. Newly returned from crop inspection, she was standing on the seat of the buggy. And, in the uproar following the totally unexpected appearance of the gladiators, he realized not only that his own honour and the honour of the whole Force were just about lost but that she was hollering, as no lady ever should—though this was certainly no place for a lady:

"Go to it, Galahad; Rope 'im, ride 'im—" and much, much more.

In fact, she was changing her mind, just as Lynette, when

Sir Gareth fought his last great conflict for her sake, stopped calling him names and shrieked:

Well done, knave-knight, well stricken, O good knight-knave—
O knave, as noble as any of all the knights—
Shame me not, shame me not. I have prophesied—
Strike, thou art worthy of the Table Round—
His arms are old, he trusts the harden'd skin—
Strike, strike—the wind will never change again!

Of course, Betsy, in the excitement, had got a bit muddled between Sir Galahad and Sir Gareth and was shouting with western variations. But the effect, also with western variations, was the same.

Lifted to supreme heights by her support and that detested name, now publicly jammed around his vermilion crown, Andy in turn lifted Joe, with one terrific uppercut, into oblivion.

So it was over—the clash that made the battles of Waterloo and Gettysburg look like the balcony scene in "Romeo and Juliet." Compare the "Moonlight Sonata" with those "Hungarian Rhapsodies"! Or Boadicea in her chariot with Betsy in her buggy! Said Mustang, "Don't be goofy! No comparison—"

Anyhow, the last word lay with Andy. Having delivered Joe to the divisional guardroom and changed his uniform, he marched into Praed's office to follow up his written report on Joe's defeat.

The superintendent looked him over without speaking for almost a minute, eyes like big guns glaring from a turret to take in every detail—the bruises, the swollen lips, the left arm in a sling—and loosed a heartrending groan. Yet his anguish was eased a little by the cocky air, the gleaming buttons and boots. Then he read from the written report in a voice which echoed the snarl of a grindstone sharpening the headman's axe:

Appendix A: Damage to government and private property:

1 jacket, regulation serge, destroyed
1 shirt, regulation (collar size 16), destroyed

1 cowboy outfit complete, ditto
1 antique Japanese screen, greatly prized, ditto
2 lithographs, ditto, ditto
27 glasses, ditto . . .

And, breaking off, he roared;

"Ditto, ditto! I'll ditto you, by Judas! Roast and toast your utterly lost soul, I told you 'Take him very quietly!' "

"That's just what I did, sir. Forty-Rod—er—Mr. Milligan, the mayor, says I used admirable restraint!"

"Speak when you're spoken to! Then how about behaving 'without fear, favour or affection,' as your oath requires? 'Without affection'! Pah! You were egged on by that confounded girl, that Betsy—I know, I know, the poor simp now wants to marry you—but if the Commissioner says O.K., I'll eat my saddle, girths and all! Oh, well, never mind"—and Praed's face broke into a marvellous grin—"you did a first-class job! And I wish I'd seen that arrest!"

"Sir, your own deeds were my inspiration!" said Andy, meekly.

the race for molly scott

"THE HANGMAN'S RACE: *Montreal Comet* (One-eyed Mike), 7 to 1—*Seattle Packet* (Chilcoot Jim), 10 to 1—*Chicago Post* (Tump-line Tony), 16 to 1—*New York Star* (Swift-water Jake), 20 to 1—*London Sun* (Bonanza Pete), 25 to 1—"

Dirty, bearded, buckskinned Tom McGuire studied the betting odds on the big blackboard while the fortune-hunters, fortune-squanderers, touts and hussies packing the Monte Carlo dance-hall roared and shrieked, "Five-hundred on Tump-line!", "My boots on Chilcoot!", "My (this, that or the other) on One-eyed Mike and the Little Nugget, Molly Scott, Molly Scott, Molly Scott!"

Through this tumult, Tom bawled into the most convenient ear:

"Put me wise, kid! What's up?"

Souse Bassett, the ear's half-pickled owner, tossed off his hooch, stared with amazed, crimsoned eyes at Tom and bellowed:

"Where you bin that you don't know?"

"Prospectin'," howled Tom, "Only back in town tonight (Fill 'em up agin, bar-tender!) Now, tell—"

"O.K.! Tomorrow, at what passes for dawn in this Yukon midwinter Pan-Out Jenkins is set to be hung right here in Dawson City, Territorial capital! You savvy, while you was chasin' rainbows for your crock o' gold, Pan-Out clubbed his pardner, Siwash Hinds, then burned him to ashes in the campfire to get rid of the corpse. Only our hawk-eyed Yallah-legs (Mounted Police to you) found out. So 'the

31

trial rockin' two continents' and tomorrow's necktie social's the result."

"But what about the Hangman's Race, the *Comet*, Molly Scott?"

"Hold your huskies, bo, I'm gettin' hoarse. Same agin? Don't mind if I do! Now, this trial's been covered by all the big-time rags named on that there blackboard. And every special correspondent wants his paper to be first with the news that Pan-Out's paid his debt to Sassiety, yes, sir. So each has hired a crack musher and his dawg-train, see also that there board—Tump-line for the *Post*, Swift-water for the *Star*, etcetera. And jest as soon as Pan-Out dances his cake-walk in mid-air, each'll dash off his tale of them last sad moments and rush it by that train six hundred miles to Skagway, then on by boat to Civilization before the rest, if possible!"

"Keep talking. More hooch!"

Souse went on gratefully, "Now every pleasure-haunt in Dawson's bookin' bets and every mother's son and daughter's layin' his or her last cent on who'll lead this Hangman's Race into Skagway post office. 'Cause they'll bet on anything—date of the Yukon's spring breakup, colour of Diamond-tooth Gertie's garters—"

"So! Well, who in thunder's Molly Scott?"

"Correspondent for the *Comet*, slogan 'We cover the universe! Ride our tail!' She's got more word-power and plain grit than any man here on the same job. She always writes the truth. She's prettier 'n Klondike Kate, sweeter 'n San Francisco Belle. An' she's the Little Nugget, good as gold! So One-eyed Mike, her driver, and his dawgs are favourites in this race. And, bust me braces, there she stands!"

Yes, there she stood, on the dance-hall stage, among the other correspondents, the drivers and the gamblers taking the bets. No two ways about it, she did look like a Yukon poppy in a bunch of poison ivy. And her dainty, little up-turned nose for news was sniffing in "atmosphere" for that last despatch, while the rough, tough miners and their fancy skirts yelled her name.

Then, suddenly, it happened. Her heart skipped a couple of beats. For Sergeant Jack Winslow, tall, weather-worn, straight as a spruce, brave as a grizzly, star of the Butcher Man-Hunt and one of the North's best dog-drivers was struggling through the mob and the dense cigar-smoke towards her, his scarlet coat, as always, a red light for danger —danger to her staying single, danger to some breaker of the Queen's Peace. And this time, surely, he brought real trouble.

Why, otherwise, would he mount the stage without a glance at her to give a document to Grease-Paint Potts, boss of the Monte Carlo, and Uncle Joe Gibbons, dean of correspondents? Besides, on reading it, Uncle Joe tore his white locks and Grease-Paint silenced band and crowd with pudgy, gem-ringed hands and a great roar to make this shattering announcement:

"Ladies an' Gennulmen: Judge Dugas has de-cided it's illegal to execute Pan-Out Jenkins on the date fixed by the Govern-ment of Canada, to wit, tomorrow, 'cause it's a re-ligious holiday. Therefore, the Judge is pointin' this out to Otty-wa. And till he gets a noo date from Otty-wa, the execution is *postponed!*"

Then Uncle Joe explained, after pandemonium:

"My newspaper colleagues may feel that they must now postpone this so-called race as well. But, seeing what it means to you and that despatches describing your reactions might be sent by it instead of accounts of the execution, they might rather it should stand. We'll tell you in ten minutes."

Actually, the question was settled in five.

"La-dies an' Gennulmen!" from Grease-Paint. "De-spatches on how you took the Judge's rulin' will go out as soon as maybe but with all com-pet-itors startin' south from in front o' this hall at the same time—9 a.m. tomorrow."

As the band crashed into "There'll Be a Hot Time in the

old Town Tonight!", Sergeant Winslow overtook Molly, battling to reach the main door and, peering down at her, asked:

"What's wrong? You're white as a sheet—"

"Jack," she gulped, "I must see the Colonel right away. Where is he?"

"A step off, inspecting Town Station. Hi, hold on—"

But she was gone.

And in no time the gigantic, veteran Colonel, more accurately the Superintendent commanding in the Yukon, saw her pushing towards him through brawlers still fighting, though under arrest, red-coats dragging in drunks to save them from thieving "rollers" and all the nightly turmoil of Town Station, guardian of Dawson's heart. Like a stern-wheeler breasting White Horse rapids, he broke a path to her, towed her into the backwater of an empty office, put her in a chair, took another and said:

"Now, young lady, shoot!"

Furs framing a lovely face wet with tears or snowflakes, this damsel in obvious distress was as appealing as a scared squirrel as she sketched the changes just made in the Hangman's Race and added:

"So, unless you help me, sir, I'm ruined!"

"Frankly," he growled, "I can't see why."

"I'll explain," she faltered, "You know Corporal Elliott and I are good friends?"

"That's been plain enough ever since you fell off the steamer coming up here on the *Trail of Ninety-Eight* and he pulled you out, then lent you his spare uniform, so you arrived in Dawson in his red serge and yellow-striped pantaloons—"

Flushing so crimson that she looked more like a Yukon poppy than before, she protested, "Making allowances, that outfit was a darned good fit! But let me get on. I wanted to make a scoop with my story of Pan-Out's execution—"

"A scoop—'first with the news'—"

"Exactly. So I—well, I wrote the yarn beforehand, from

my imagination. And, as Don—er—Corporal Elliott was leaving at noon today with a sled-load of official papers and some mail—"

"You asked him to take your story and post it in Skagway, which would get it to your editor before any one else's in the Hangman's Race."

"That's it. Of course, I had and still have to send out something in the race itself. But nothing important. Do you think I'm *awful*?"

"Terrible! Never mind, you merely played one of the tricks of your trade. And now—"

"Now some one *must* catch him before he makes Skagway and stop him handing in that horrible despatch. Otherwise, my paper headlines it and, when it proves all moonshine, I'll be a laughing-stock—and, as I told you, ruined!"

He asked thoughtfully, "Why not send your driver to overtake the Corporal? Or hire another musher and send him?"

"I can't!" she wailed. "One-eyed must carry my follow-up yarn in the race, to—avert suspicion. Besides, Don—er—Corporal Elliott is travelling so fast—"

"You bet he is! First, because the official papers he's carrying must reach Ottawa in time to appear in the Commissioner's Annual Report and I told him to do his best. Second, because you probably asked him to break all records for your sake!"

"You're right," she blushed again, "And I've no time to find a civilian driver good enough to overtake him. But if you could see your way—"

"So *that's* it! Well, the one man with a chance of catching Elliott starts for Skagway with the Judge's letter to Ottawa in an hour." He shook her with the frown normally reserved for hardened criminals and defaulters. "I couldn't possibly tell him to run himself and his dog-train ragged just to stop your story. But—"(here the frown was chased away by a smile which made her think of the sun's ending the long Polar night) "as it happens, I've ordered him to get to

Skagway as fast as possible. And also, luckily for you, he's Sergeant Winslow—"

"Oh, Jack!" she cried, "Another very good friend—"

"So I've no doubt that if you give him a note to Corporal Elliott to stop your scoop, with bits of your 'poor, weak woman' act, he'll catch—er—Don if anybody can. Write the note now and give it to the Sergeant when I finish with him in this room. Oh, don't thank *me*! Thank the good stuff you've turned out for your paper. Ah, that's his knock. . . ."

Still whooping it up at midnight, downtown Dawson, brimful of hooch and admiration, saw Sergeant Winslow off with his tearing five-dog tandem and Skookum Jim Beaver, his solid, stolid Indian special. The crowd knew that he carried the Judge's letter. They'd have gone mad, he thought, if they'd also known that he carried Molly's note and meant to catch Don Elliott or bust. For the Hangman's Race would look like nothing at all to men like these in comparison with this contest between crack Force mushers to make—or save —the Little Nugget's professional reputation!

Plungers aware of all the facts might have backed Jack Winslow, considering these points:

A full moon like a pan of gold-dust, rising in clear skies as lusty Dawson disappeared behind him, shed light so strengthened by the white reflecting snows that it would serve him well while the subarctic sun remained off duty. The trail was in fine shape, the thermometer merely at zero. Of wind, the curse of dog-drivers, there wasn't a breath. Standing high among those drivers, he felt head and shoulders above them now—Molly's appeal would put life into a Tinglit totem-pole! Skookum Jim was the best Indian on the Force pay-roll, Winslow's team the best available in Dawson barracks. And the outfit travelled light, as it could pick up almost all it needed at the small Force detachments dotted along its track, the frozen Yukon, Queen's Highway of the Territory. So its malamutes and mongrels could gallop on and on almost indefinitely, with the men taking turns to ride the sled and with only occasional halts for food and rest.

But the Sergeant grimly noted handicaps: Little Peewee Elliott, game as a wolverine, fast as a wolf, would do his damnedst to reach Skagway far ahead of the Hangman's Race. Chunky, spunky Tagish Charlie Pike, his Indian, was a grand trail-runner, his team of huge Labrador huskies the finest in the Force. Being ahead, he would get the pick of detachment resources, leaving Winslow only the second best. His two hundred pounds of mail would not affect his speed much. And twelve hours was a terribly long start. It would probably give him a lead of seventy miles. So, to overtake him this side of Skagway, the Sergeant must out-march him by something like eight miles for every day of actual travel on the run of six hundred-odd miles to the seaport.

Still, with good luck *and* good management, Jack Winslow had just a chance. And in some ways he relished the odds against him, since, if he overcame them, he would teach the Midget Marvel what was what, once and for all.

At Indian River, thirty miles out of Dawson, red-haired, raw-boned Constable Sandy Macpherson left his bunk to help the patrol. He gave its men a very early breakfast, its dogs a small feed, talked a lot about the Hangman's Race and banging bawbees on Molly. Then, more important, he mentioned, without being asked, that "wee Don went through jist twal' hoors past as if Auld Horny himsel' was after him." So at least the Sergeant had not lost ground.

He pushed on. His spirits rose with the sun above the distant evergreens, naked birch and poplar, soared straight into the air with the chimney-smoke from Ogilvie, twenty-one miles farther on and reached in very fast time. Yet Kid Smart, the Ogilvie constable, shot him down with "Corporal Elliott left here round about half past nine last night, sure burnin' the trail"—and keeping his lead. So Winslow merely inspected dogs and outfit and gulped a cupful of scalding hot tea before he cracked his long whip, yelled "Mush!" and pressed on for Stewart River.

At that point (sixty miles ex-Dawson) he nooned over moose-steak, spuds, fresh homemade bread and still more tea, with canned apricots to follow and Corporal Dude de Courcy as his host. Once of Her Majesty's Guards but now in charge here, Dude pumped him about the Hangman's Race, bet the detachment constable, Pat Hogan, a month's pay on Molly, then remarked casually that Don Elliott "means to sleep tonight at Selwyn," nearly a hundred miles away. "Fine!" said Jack Winslow, adding to himself "God *bless* him!" As his patrol galloped out of sight, Pat mused, "Breakin' records—and crazy as a loon, like Don!"

The sun sank redly behind cold grey trees, ending the short winter day, yet still the Sergeant's train pressed on, though cautiously, to avoid blundering into open water. Never mind, the moon, taking over, made possible more galloping, to go on till some rare riverside spot where the wood had not been cut out or burnt out by Klondikers or steamers offered a campsite. In fact, just before moonset, lights appeared at one such spot, then black pyramids— the wigwams of Stick Indians who redoubled their usual welcome for a red-coat friend as Skookum Jim of their own band was with him.

That naturally decided the Sergeant to call a halt right here. Gripping the sled, he, like Jim, had run forty-five miles since leaving Dawson, while the team had covered ninety, always with one man as passenger. And that was more than enough for one day of a long haul, even for deep-chested hunks of steel and rawhide like the men, greased lightning like the dogs. He declined to share the Stick supper and dog-feed— "You need all you have and we've got plenty!"—But he gladly accepted help in unloading the sled, unhitching the dogs, tying each to a tree well away from the rest, hanging the harness in branches, so that it could not be eaten by animals unsatisfied with a big feed of dried fish. And he thankfully took a place at the Indians' fire for cooking bacon and beans, a space in a wigwam for sleeping.

Later, the patrol topped this routine by smoking and talking for a bit with the Sticks. They knew nothing of Elliott (he must have passed them at a distance). Still, Winslow's guarded questions suddenly struck Skookum Jim with a great light—as the two men crawled wearily into their sleeping-bags, he announced, "You chase Don!" Jack said nothing.

He got Jim up again at half-past-three, with the full moon up before him and, after a bite of biscuit and a drink of tea to fill the gap till breakfast, had said "So long!" to the puzzled Sticks and pushed on by four. This start was certainly early. Yet a supreme effort to shorten Elliott's lead must be made while the patrol remained as fresh, the trail as good, the thermometer as high, the weather as fine, clear and windless as they still were today.

Besides, they had to allow for the dangerously unexpected, soon pouncing at Half-Way detachment, twenty-odd miles from the Stick camp.

Roars and crashes in Half-Way's police cabin told the Sergeant, as he approached it, that its garrison, Corporal Laliberté and Constable Coote, were probably much too busy to help him and needed help themselves. Sure enough, he threw open the door on a riot of whirling arms and legs, of blows and curses representing a civilian giant at war with the law and wrecking the place. Always quick off the mark, Jack Winslow joined that party. Diving in, he brought the giant down with a crash that stunned him. Through the sudden, perfect hush sounded the click of handcuffs suitably applied, then Jack's:

"Holy mackerel, it's Gorilla Gus!"

"*Oui*, mackerel, dat's for sure!" agreed the sturdy French-Canadian two-striper, between gasps, while the extra-long and lanky Coote revived the prisoner. "Found Gorilla up de creek, robbin' caches, "went on Laliberté, "Just now we tak' de 'andcuffs off for 'is break-fast. An', *sapré batème,* 'e give *us* break-fast! Tries to beat it—*Dieu!"*

Clearing things up, the Force men managed a scratch meal and Coote fed the Sergeant's dogs while preparing his own to take Gorilla Gus into Dawson. But the only news of Peewee Elliott was "Guess he dropped in yesterday when the Corporal and I were away. We found some grub and fish gone when we got back."

And Winslow found himself nursing a new handicap. He had hurt his left hand—maybe even broken a bone in it— during the scrap with Gorilla Gus. It didn't matter much, just now. In time, though, it might make all the difference between defeat and victory.

He had it roughly bandaged, then dashed on again, after sunrise, through glare beginning to hurt the eyes, silence and solitude, nooning for a bite by the trail, then plugging into Selwyn just at sundown. Constable Vickers, that one-man detachment, volunteered, with his schoolboy grin, "Corporal Elliott got here round midnight, dog-tired, but left half-past-seven this morning, going like smoke for Lord-knows-where." "The little so-and-so!" thought the Sergeant, with a grin. "Never mind, I'm gaining." Vickers added, "Supper's ready. I'll feed your dogs. And you'll take a shakedown?" "Supper's fine, thanks," the Sergeant said, "But never mind the dogs. I'm mushing on tonight and if we feed 'em they won't keep going." Vickers smelt a musk-rat—to no purpose. Winslow gave him no explanation, merely hit the trail when washing-up was over.

Moonset left total darkness. "Camp now?" Skookum Jim asked hopefully. "No! Light the lantern! Lead the way!" answered Winslow, his face wearing its sternest look, partly because his injured hand was now really bothering him. He hoped for more news of Elliott from Yank Taylor, living nineteen-odd miles past Selwyn, as that grand old veteran of the American Civil War felt himself a brother to the red-coats, kept open house for them and was the Yukon's biggest gossip. So the patrol plodded on by lantern-light, sometimes bypassing weak ice or missing the trail, till the great moon allowed a two-hour gallop and at last revealed Yank's cabin under the pines.

Lifeless windows said, "He's away!" but friendly chimney-smoke contradicted them with, "He's in bed!" Correct, his well-known roar answered the first knock, "I'll blast your guts out, deadbeat, if you don't vamoose!"

"Guts be damned, it's Jack Winslow!"

"Wall, walk in, nitwit! I'll light the lamp. Bring in yer stuff while Skookum feeds yer dogs and I toss ye a mess of flapjacks." But a casual question, later, brought only, "Pee-wee Elliott? Passed me by! Now, the Battle of Gettysburg . . ." which was bad, even though the patrol, bedding down in Yank's cabin, had covered one hundred and seventy-five miles since leaving Dawson just forty-eight hours ago.

Yet Jack slept well, from sheer fatigue, in spite of his sore hand, then mushed away lightheartedly early next morning, as conditions remained good, to reach Selkirk in time for a late breakfast. Only, Selkirk gave him a shock—Elliott, regaining ground, had passed through it roughly eighteen hours ahead of him. And feeding the dogs, getting replenishments and overhauling the outfit (between answering questions on the Hangman's Race) cost two precious hours. That sent him back into the trail and the now torturous sun-glare with a grimmer look than ever. Urging the team relentlessly, his long legs covering as much in one stride as Peewee's could do in two, he did the forty-five miles to Hootchiku detachment in eight and a half hours, nooning included, the last fifteen miles by moonlight. Over supper, Hootchiku's tall, keen-eyed Corporal Barnstable said, "Elliott left here about five A.M." "So I'm catching up again," thought Winslow, then announced:

"Guess I'll make Five Fingers tonight!"

Barney protested, "Moon'll be down. You'll get into the rapids." "Not a chance—but thanks—" As the patrol drove on, Constable Neyland ("Big-mouth" because he talked too much) said, "Sergeant's after Elliott for breaking arrest!" "Bunk!" snapped Barney, though he wondered.

And Jack Winslow wondered, "Should I go on?" when the moon deserted him just as he dimly sighted the faroff water-smoke of Five Finger rapids, a fiend's hand groping for travellers. But he took the lighted lantern in his own un-injured hand, and the post of danger in front. Skookum Jim, driving the team, followed slowly. As they drew nearer the growling rapids, the ice began to tremble and those reaching fingers showed themselves faintly in streaks of foam. Like a lion-tamer sidling watchfully around his animals, the Sergeant found a way past them. And he kept the outfit clear of flooded ice—only to learn when, very late, he made Five Fingers detachment, that from now on his pursuit of Peewee Elliott was to be one of the hardest of his life.

For by that time he had more to endure than a throb-bing, stiffening hand. His wet moccasins were then stone-hard and his feet frost-bitten.

Worse still, the detachment flag fluttered in a rising north wind when hoisted after sunrise next morning, the sky was overcast, the cold increasing. Blizzard soon! "You'd maybe get to Tantalus but no farther," Corporal Bill Kennedy, the sturdy, grey-haired old-timer in charge, told him, over late breakfast, "Better wait!"

But "Can't!" said Winslow. Hadn't Kennedy informed him, last night, "Elliott went through, pretty tired, 'bout twelve hours ago" and therefore with no more than the original lead? Besides, Constable Sharp, ex-medical student, had rebandaged his hand ("no bones broken") then dressed his feet. And now Skookum Jim came in from tending and harnessing the team. So "Thanks, boys, we're off!"

Tantalus detachment gave them lunch but no news of Peewee. Winslow reasoned, "If he's halted for the storm and I push on, I'll cut his lead still more,"—worth doing, with the Hangman's Race only nine hours, at most, behind. Skookum Jim looked doubtful. Yet they pushed on. The stern wind puffed them helpfully along, though it whirled the snow around them and veiled the waning moon in such black clouds that at last they could see nothing and had to find shelter.

Luckily the *Earl of Minto — Earl* for short — offered this forty miles above Tantalus, where she had been beached high and dry when a rock disembowelled her last summer. Covered in snow and largely stripped for her timber and other valuables, the little passenger steamer looked like a shrouded, ravaged corpse in the moonlight. And the litter left in her 'tween-decks by mushers staging there added to her air of desecration. All the same, her fairly intact wheel-house, with its improvised fireplace, could hole up the men, her ruined saloon protect the dogs, planks from her deck serve as fuel. So both Jack Winslow and Skookum were mighty glad to be bedded down inside her when the storm broke at midnight.

They had nothing to do, though, but shiver in their sleeping-bags, nurse their small fire, doze uneasily, munch a biscuit, drink vile tea brewed from snow-water, and feed the dogs. They saw nothing through the short, pale spells of daylight but a birch madly conducting a rag-time band of furiously performing spruce near the wheelhouse, heard nothing but the wind producing the wild music or shrieking like the ghosts of passengers who once raised merry hell here, while it shook the dead *Earl* almost to pieces. The blizzard seemed to rage for an eternity. In fact it lasted fifty hours exactly, by the Sergeant's watch, then suddenly stopped roaring over the clean sweep of the Yukon and left fine sub-zero weather and an uncanny hush behind it.

The patrol moved off at 10 A.M. next morning. Winslow's damaged hand still throbbed, his feet still smarted, his eyes ached in the sunglare. Friction, increased by cold, slowed down the sled. Yet men and dogs had tails up, being tired of inaction. Besides, they had now entered the second half of the long run to Skagway. As sounds travelled a great distance through that weird silence, they soon heard an axe chopping wood miles away—Elliott's axe, Winslow hoped, or at any rate the axe of a traveller possibly able to report Peewee's position. Rounding a river-bend at noon, he sighted not Peewee's modest outfit but quite a crowd of Klondikers, with half a dozen tents, big fires and other essentials to mushing in style. "Grub's up! Join us!" shouted the obvious boss, a hearty red-face in enough furs to stock a trading-post. "You're Sergeant Winslow? I'm Bill Collins. Shake!"

Bonanza Bill had made his enormous pile on the creeks in the first days of the Rush and, he explained, was now escorting these New York financiers to Dawson with a view to making more. He treated the patrol to lunch, with champagne, and volunteered, "Had a word with one of your fellows, Don Elliott, passing by while we made camp here, day the storm started." That was really something—so Winslow pushed on at once for Big Salmon. Pausing only for replenishments there, he kept going till long after sun-set, first by the glow of the Northern Lights high-kicking like armies of brilliant show-girls, then by moonlight re-inforced from billions of blazing stars.

This effort was rewarded. Tracks branching off the trail led the patrol to a rough shelter on the bank. And among its signs of recent occupation were sacks marked "N.W.M.P." and labelled "Corporal Elliott." Peewee, obviously, had been storm-bound all through the blizzard at this point, only sixty-five miles from the *Earl*. So, at least he had not run out of reach. Winslow decided to camp here.

Howling, the dogs and the distant wolves talked all night about the weather, especially the bitter cold—and kept the cursing men awake for an early start. But when Skookum Jim fed them their first snack, King, the leader, would not eat and Winslow found him bleeding from the lungs. Now almost faint with pain himself, also from frostbite and his injured hand, the Sergeant groaned, "King's got to ride the sled to Lower Laberge—and we'll have to change to a fresh team there. That's wrecked us—"

In spite of this setback they reached Lower Laberge in

time for lunch—only to learn that Elliott had passed the
detachment nearly twenty-four hours before and that the
fresh team available was second-rate. Still, Winslow took it,
with replenishments, then toiled on up Lake Laberge. While
the mercury was rising, the Coast Mountains, about one
hundred and fifty miles ahead, promised tough pulling soon.
And a red-rimmed rainbow around the misty moon foretold
"Snow coming!" as the patrol ended a day's run of only
fifty-eight miles at Upper Laberge, roughly four hundred
and forty miles from Dawson.

All this added the beginnings of desperation to pain
and growing weariness, made grimmer by Upper Laberge's
Corporal in charge, bustling Damme Field of the fierce
moustaches: "Peewee Elliott? Not come near us, damme!
Gave us the go-by, damme!" Then his heart sank into his
moccasins, where frost-bite now played "The Maple Leaf
For Ever" on his toes, as a dawn survey found the whole
world buried in the night's snowfall, with flurries still falling.
For trail must be broken through those drifts, at least till
they struck Peewee's trail. Of course, it helped to know that
Peewee must also endure the same slow, tiring job. But
help of that kind did not amount to much.

An extra big breakfast fortified both Winslow and
Skookum Jim for this ordeal. Out came the long trail-
breaking snowshoes, and for two exhausting hours they
floundered southward, often clearing masks of snow from
their faces, cakes of it from the feet and eyes of the dogs
and sometimes taking the long whip to the team as a last
resort.

Suddenly they heard desperate, terrible groaning and
through pelting snowflakes dimly made out a halted dog-
train and a musher doubled up in agony beside it. Blood
streaming over mittens clapped to one eye gave Winslow
some idea of the trouble, a gasping "Slipped on that ice—
fell on that stick—drove it right in!" told more. "Let's have
a look, I won't hurt you." But it took all his strength to
force those clutching hands away. His blood ran cold at

what the look showed him. The stick was not in the eye but the socket was a ghastly mess, hiding the full extent of the damage, though confirming that it must be serious.

"Sit on this log, boy," he told the musher, guiding him to the place. "First aid now—then White Horse hospital, quick as we can make it!" But even while Skookum Jim quickly built a roaring fire to boil a kettle and Winslow whipped out towels for hot applications, the significance of the situation made blood run colder still.

White Horse was twelve miles off, not to be reached through this snow and on this bad trail, with halts to renew the applications, in under five hours. Meanwhile Elliott, with no patient to burden him, must so increase his lead that all hope of overtaking him in time to save Molly's professional reputation would disappear forever. And the musher demanding this sacrifice was a "macque", the lowest of the low, living on the immoral earnings of women. The Sergeant knew him well as Red-light Looie. Ordered out of the Territory, he had been heading for the outside when tragedy struck him. That Molly's interests must now give way to his seemed as cruelly unfair as anything Winslow had met in an unspeakably tough service.

Yet errands of mercy, even for no-goods like Looie, took priority with the Force—which settled it.

Having clapped a towel soaked in the freshly boiled water onto that injured eye, the Sergeant and Skookum Jim put their patient into a sleeping-bag on their sled, tied his dogs to trees with a feed to keep them quiet till some one could be sent from White Horse to collect them and started that errand, the Indian breaking trail ahead.

Almost at once it stopped snowing, but the change made little difference. Struggling over rough ice that had ruined the trail before this snowfall, and wading through drifts barely breached by Skookum Jim's snowshoes, the dogs tired rapidly. Their pace grew slower and slower as their feet, all cut and bleeding, demanded more and more attention. Tongues dangling, they puffed out frozen breath at such a rate that they looked like little hard-driven locomotives. And the sled, as it plunged over ruts and ridges, bucketed so violently, in spite of what the Sergeant could do, that Looie shrieked as if the Windigo, the cannibal spirit, were eating him alive. Also the compresses cooled so fast and he suffered so much without them that the halts to boil more water and renew them became far too frequent.

"He sure is in bad shape!" said Skookum Jim.

Yet the Great White Gods played fair. In early afternoon the patrol struck a fresh trail well beaten by horse-drawn sleighs. Then a herd of prehistoric Yukon mammoths huddled together under snow, their trunks held up, turned into steamers wintering with lifeless funnels at the wharves of Whitehorse. A ring expanding round the sun promised fine weather before ring and sun sank behind the mountains sheltering the town. And as lights sprang up in shacks and cabins, Red-light Looie was delivered into hospital.

"You've saved his eye," said kind old Doc Melbourne. "First time I've thanked a Yallah-leg," groaned Looie. "Shur-r-r up!" said Winslow, then to the doctor, "Mind looking at this hand—and my feet?" For the strain of saving the macque had been so terrific that not only "The Maple Leaf" but "God Save The Queen" were being played on his extremities at the same time—and with variations. "Far to go?" asked the Doc, studying the problem. "Skagway!" "Urgent?" "Yes—very." "I'd give the job to some one else if I were you."

But anyhow he'd not been marked unfit for duty. So he drove into barracks with fresh dressings and in reasonably good heart. There big, soft-spoken Staff-Sergeant Cunningham ("Holy Joe", as he meant, some day, to be a preacher) told him: "Elliott went through this time last night. But look there!" What a sight — Peewee's famous Labrador huskies, strewn all over the dog-corral, played out. "Gave him our best team," went on Holy Joe, while Winslow and Skookum Jim glanced at each other in triumph. Holy

Joe added, "You *and* your outfit don't look any too good, either. What's your hurry?"

"New date's wanted for Pan-Out's execution," Winslow explained, "and I'm rushing the Judge's note on it to Skagway."

"That kills the Hangman's Race!" said freckly young Constable Desmond, who was listening, all big ears. "It doesn't? Fine! Staff, bet some more on Molly Scott."

"Against my principles," smiled Holy Joe. "Well, say a dollar. Now, go get Looie's team. Sergeant, take mine. Supper?"

"No chance!" The sight of Peewee's worn-out huskies had thrown aside an inclination to "give the job to some one else," revived a determination to press on at once and to the end. "I'll just stock up on feed and grub, then take your team, with thanks, and git!"

Only the dogs really enjoyed supper that night and Winslow's rest was bad. A three-sled bunch of mushers breaking trail ahead had allowed the patrol to cover thirty miles by moonlight after leaving White Horse and it had comfortable sleeping quarters in the Eldorado Packers' camp (temporarily closed to business but open, by arrangement, to Force members, who knew where to find the bunkhouse key). But Hell-hounds — the best team from White Horse, serving Peewee—savaged his throbbing feet and aching hand in nightmares, while Molly's terrified face and Elliott's mocking grin swirled around him in mists of worry and pain. Being in front of the three-sled mushers, Peewee must still be breaking trail himself. Yet by now he might well be within a hundred miles of Skagway.

So he had as good as won. Or he would certainly win if his pursuer were seriously slowed down by physical disabilities on the next, critical stage, to Tagish. Jack Winslow saw that clearly. More, he realized that if he did crack up, his plain duty would be to turn over the chase to some one else able to get the Judge's letter to Skagway and Molly's note to Elliott at top speed. A hard fact to face, this was enough to guarantee an almost sleepless night to a man already worn by pain and weariness.

Still, he was no quitter and didn't intend to become one if he could help it. In any case the ghost of a chance soon rode the sled beside him. Having dozed off at last, he overslept, like Skookum Jim. So the sun had been blazing down on the white, still world for an hour before the patrol finished its light breakfast and mushed on into that eye-torturing glare. Luckily the trail remained well-beaten. Braced by the clean, cold air, the dogs devoured its miles at a gallop, to make Tagish post in time for the men to share the garrison's noonday meal. And lean, trim Sergeant Glynn, in charge there during the Inspector's absence, produced magnificently astounding news over the first pot of coffee:

"Corporal Elliott left here just after breakfast. Barely covered thirty miles yesterday with so much breaking trail. Damaged his sled too. Had to mend it on the spot—*and* give his dogs a good long rest last night. Trail's O.K. from here on. And you look as if you'd do with a good long rest yourself. But I shouldn't be surprised if you caught him up at Caribou Crossing."

"Won't matter if I don't!" lied Winslow, cheerfully. "All the same, I'd love to try it—if I'd a fresh team from you."

"Too bad—the Inspector's got a record-breaker but he's gone to Bennett with it for a few days and we haven't another to spare."

That almost decided Winslow to throw in his hand, letting Glynn take it up—almost but not quite. For, after all, he ought to be able to tough it out and overhaul the Midget Marvel this side of Skagway, now that he was so close behind. He dressed his flaming feet, had his crippled hand rebandaged, gave the dogs a small feed, replenished feed and grub, mushed on.

Word of Peewee could surely be had at Caribou Crossing, where Jack had stared in wonder at vast, migrating herds last summer. Sure enough, he got it at Captain Hunter's Road-house over supper.

The jovial, beefy Captain (a courtesy title only) told him by way of gossip, "Elliott and Tagish Charlie looked in this afternoon. Said he wouldn't sleep here, nothing more—but my guess is he'll spend tonight with your boys at Bennett."

This all but took the taste out of the rich Irish stew. Bennett was only thirty-five miles from Skagway, though these miles included the tough climb to the Summit crowning the Coastal Range.

"Can I feed your dogs?" went on the Captain.

"O.K., O.K.," said Winslow, absently. "They're tired, anyhow."

An idea had burst through his dejection. It was based on a feeble possibility, yet might just come off.

Adopting it, he refused cozy beds and waited for clouds to unveil the half-moon enough to allow cautious travel. Though the clouds persisted after the moon hid behind the mountains, they soon gave place to magnificent Northern Lights revealing the trail and the patrol pressed on. It drove up Lake Bennett, between white peaks and miles of cabins abandoned by the Rush, like a mite crawling up a sword on a white cushion littered with bones. Later the Lights danced away to make room for the stars of The Greatest Show On Earth, marshalled in dazzling galaxies. Lights, peaks and stars scorned the mite and the cabins so briefly daring their eternal vigilance. But Winslow in turn ignored them, having eyes and ears only for certain signs of victory.

After hours of riding the sled in a daze of pain and weariness, he thought he saw and heard those signs — a distant campfire and the howl of huskies around it, detecting the patrol's approach.

"There they are!" he yelled, jumping off the sled for a dash at top speed.

His dogs stopped to answer the howl—till Skookum Jim laid into them with whip and voice and they rushed on madly.

Winslow's idea had worked. Tired and over-confident, Peewee Elliott had thought himself so far ahead of the Hangman's Race that he could safely camp for the night this side of Bennett. And his pursuer, cunningly marching while he rested, was now on the point of overtaking him.

Or was he? The fire vanished as suddenly as it had been sighted and a gust of wind carried shouts of "Mush!" and a whip's cracking to Jack and Skookum Jim over perhaps a mile of silent snowfields. Obviously the patrol had closed in just as Peewee—if it *was* Peewee—got ready to quench his fire and move on. And now, of course, he would drive like fury, in case the approaching outfit led the Hangman's Race, after all—naturally, he could have no notion that it was a police train, trying with good reason to catch him.

Cursing his luck, his feet and sore hand, Winslow ran after Skookum Jim and the sled as he had never run before. Skookum Jim, hurled out of his Indian calm, urged on the dogs more fiercely than ever. And the dogs, inflamed with the excitement of the chase, flew, like Jack's imaginary Hell-hounds, along the trail.

No use! Heard through Skookum Jim's uproar, the swish of the sled on the snow, the wind's whistle and the pounding of blood in over-strained ears, the shouts and whip-crackings from the outfit ahead grew steadily fainter. It had the faster team. Gradually that bitter truth came home. With it came this heartbreaking revelation: All the sacrifice, suffering and desperate effort endured since leaving Dawson were wasted and Molly's professional reputation doomed by the very strength, speed and skill with which Peewee was trying to serve her.

A crash like the noon gun's daily firing at Dawson barracks shattered these musings and darted across the trail in front, to echo and re-echo through the mountains. Winslow knew it at once for the crash of thin ice splitting in a long, straight line when suddenly overloaded. Having heard that fearful sound before, he knew why he now heard it. Peewee—or whoever it was—had risked disaster by leaving the trail to cut across a bend. And disaster had struck him.

Pain, weariness, Molly Scott, rivalry with the Midget Marvel and everything else but the thought that men and dogs ahead were drowning vanished from Jack Winslow's mind. His patrol seemed to take an age to reach the victims. In fact it took only a few minutes, yet long enough to allow that bitterly cold water to bring death. So what he found on reaching them was certainly grim.

The lead-dog and the two just behind it were still swimming feebly—no two ways about it, huskies took a lot of killing. The rest of the tandem, pulled under by the sled, must have drowned. The sled itself, its precious mail and despatches lashed in it, was all but submerged. Possibly a foot of its bow projected from the water, as if its stern, by the grace of the Great White Gods, had come to rest on a rock rising almost to the surface from the deeps around it. Clinging to the sled, with only part of his hooded head showing, was a man. Clinging to jagged edges of ice that had newly given way when he tried to rescue that man was another. Men and dogs immersed in that black horror were utterly, ominously silent, as if the doom waiting there struck them dumb.

Fighting a sense of helplessness made worse by those cruelly indifferent peaks and glittering stars, Winslow went into action. A yell, "Don't go too near!", halted Skookum Jim and his outfit well clear of the open water. His brain working at its best under the lash of this emergency, he pulled a long rope out of his sled, tied it to the stern, looped it in the middle, slipped the loop under his armpits and, holding the remaining slack, crept, then wriggled, lying flat, to the man at the ice-edge.

At every move the ice rose, fell and creaked as if to fling him into a void beyond escape. But the starlight was strong enough to show him that the man was Tagish Charlie. Looping the end of the rope around the Indian at surprising speed, he turned to Skookum Jim and shouted "Mush!"

The dogs sprang forward like pouncing cougars, sled and rope took the strain, the ice-edge broke under it again and again, drenching him in water so cold that it almost stopped his heart and breath, but in a few seconds rescued and rescuer were safe.

Now for Peewee! Slipping the loop from Tagish Charlie, who stumbled to the nearest bank, he took up this second task—a very, very tough one, as Peewee could only be reached by swimming. He threw off the rope and his fur outer clothing, replaced the rope under his armpits, told Skookum Jim, "Drive closer!" and slid into the water. Getting the rope around Peewee proved a corker, as Elliott could give him no help. And he hardly knew what happened afterwards till he found the Midget Marvel sprawling with him on the sled driven full speed by Skookum Jim to join Tagish Charlie ashore.

Finding matches and leaving Tagish Charlie to light and build up an enormous fire from the ruins of a nearby cabin, he managed, in underwear frozen into armour-plate and with Jim's help, to drag out Elliott's dogs (two certainly dead) and their sled, by methods similar to those used in saving the men. Retrieving his furs, he joined all survivors in getting dry at the huge fire. Miraculously, the others were little the worse. But he knew that his damaged hand, as well as his frost-bitten feet, recklessly forgotten during the rescue, would soon make it impossible for him to finish the run to Skagway with the Judge's letter. Of course, he'd be fit again in time.

Over piping hot tea Peewee said thickly, "By gum, Sergeant, you lived up to your reputation just now. I can't thank you properly. But what are you doing here? I thought you were the Hangman's Race."

"I guessed that!" Jack told him, adding a word about the postponed execution, with, "The race doesn't matter now. I've something for you which tells why."

Rummaging in his sled, he found and handed over Molly's note.

He could not help smiling down on the Midget Marvel reading the note by the firelight with his face a battlefield for many expressions. Suddenly Peewee's impudent grin won the day. Rocking with laughter, he passed the note over.

It said:

Darling Don:

I promised to consider marrying you seriously (that sounds a bit odd) if you got my wretched scoop into Skagway in time for it to reach my editor before anybody else's yarn got through. But the situation's changed, as Jack will tell you. So the least I can do is to give him his chance as well, if he catches you. Please arrange between you—peacefully—who's to ask me first. I'm a numskull!

Molly Scott.

Jack joined Peewee in such laughter that the Indians thought them driven mad by the recent strain. At last he managed, between struggles for breath:

"Never mind! Now, here's our play. We'll get properly dried out, dress, have a darned good breakfast, then push right on to Bennett. There we'll privately burn Molly's scoop—being in a waterproof bag and a tarpaulin with your mail and the Colonel's report, it's survived its ducking. With it we'll burn all knowledge that it ever existed. I'll ask the Inspector to get a Bennett man to rush the mail and reports and the Judge's letter to Skagway — he surely will. After that, seeing I'd never have caught you if the ice hadn't broken—your bad luck—we'll privately toss for first chance with the lady. Is it a deal?"

"You bet your life! And generous—" grinned little Peewee, "Shake!"

Dirty, bearded, buckskinned Tom McGuire shouldered his way through the crowd jostling around the red-coat guard of honour at the door of a Dawson church and under high summer's Midnight Sun, then bellowed into the first convenient ear:

"Put me wise, kid. What's up?"

"Where you bin that you don't know?" bawled Souse Bassett.

"Prospectin'," howled Tom. "Only back in town today. Now, tell—"

"Biggest thing in Dawson since the first strike on Bonanza! Molly Scott, the Little Nugget, gittin' hitched. . . Colonel himself to give her away, best man Peewee Elliott, groom Jack Winslow. . . Cheer, bo! Here they come!"

ordeal by fire

The east was aflame, as at sunrise, yet all the west was equally aglow with sunset when Corporal Harry Conger and Tom Dixon, his supper host, came out to part at the corral.

"Prairie fire! A real big one!" gasped Dixon, pointing eastward. "And boy, she's travellin'!"

Conger, a Force veteran knowing almost as much about the subject as Tom himself, hardly needed the old-timer's explanation, much less a reminder that the Fire Ordinance authorized him to meet such emergencies by turning out all able-bodied men in the Queen's name. Rapidly saddling his horse, he asked:

"Anybody living out that way?"

Dixon's answer filled him with concern:

"Yes, Jim Grier, a new hand, more or less. Been there a year. Wife and six kids. Their place is right in the track o' that fire. Doomed, I guess. Best thing they can do is clear out an' lick for the Saskatchewan."

Conger mounted his horse. Before him had risen a fearful vision—of a lone man, inexperienced and dreadfully handicapped by a wife and six children, fighting desperately against overwhelming odds to save that wife, those children, his home, his little all.

"You saddle up too!" Conger commanded. "Bring over every man you can—on the dead jump! You'll find me with Jim Grier!"

And he turned his mount to face that easterly glare.

Dixon paled, said doubtfully:

"I'll do it. But it'll take hours. You ain't goin' out there alone, are you?"

"I am," said Conger.

"Why, it's no use. That fire'll corner you and Grier, sure as a gun. It's certain death. Don't *try* to save the place. The thing's impossible."

Said Conger: "Bring over every man, I tell you. Impossible or not, I'm going to try!"

Waving his hand, he lifted his horse into a gallop.

A gallant silhouette, man and mount bulked for a moment against the crimson sky, dwindled rapidly and vanished.

To cross the prairie between Dixon's and the fire took no more than a few minutes. Conger, riding low, all at once smelt smoke and felt a hot breath in his face. The wind brought him a murmur like chanting and drumming from a distant war-camp. The flames rose to incredible heights. He began to find it hard to breathe. A stronger gust of wind carried heat that actually seared his face.

With it came an increase in the clamour of the fire. It shouted a million war cries, cracked a million "Many-shots" rifles, as it leapt, at a pace well able to beat the fastest horse, along the bone-dry grass. Clearly now, except when the rolling smoke occasionally plunged him in deepest night, he saw every object, almost as if by daylight, and his own shadow racing grotesquely beside him. The heat increased until it was almost unbearable. The fire, as he neared it, swept up and up and up. Gathering all its voices into one as he drew nearer still, it ceased to shout. It roared—

He topped a rise and saw before him, on one side, in the ghastly light, Grier's little homestead, a mile or so away. On the other side, his left, bearing down still at unbelievable speed to cross his path, the fire advanced on an apparently limitless front. Its main body was now less than four miles from him. Urged on by the sight of those pitiful buildings, he thought that with a supreme effort, galloping along the line of the fire's advance, he might just reach the place in time.

The fire, a horde of red devils riding as all the Indians of the Plains might ride out of the past on their fastest horses to destroy him, now howled with laughter, flung long torrents of sparks over his head, licked at him furiously and, suddenly guessing his plan, moved as suddenly to defeat it. From one wing, without a second's warning, it threw out a column, a thin and yelling tentacle, to cut off this lone white scout. Stark in his course, the tentacle became a charging band one hundred yards deep between him and the homestead.

"Now," it seemed to shout triumphantly, "get there if you can!"

Conger set his teeth and pushed his mount straight on.

As they neared the obstacle, the wretched horse wavered, not daring to run the gauntlet of that infernal opposition. Conger's heart sank as the poor beast wheeled, plunged, ran blindly round, went mad. He steadied it, stroked it, drew back a little and then, with a shout and a lashing blow, forced it into the raving heart of the flames.

Complete blackness; deafening uproar; smoke that suffocated; fire that burnt to the bone; one unconscious moment; and he was through.

He had reached the homestead now. Out of the blood-red murk loomed a half-crazed man frenziedly struggling to drive two terrified horses hitched to a plunging plough, and behind him little children running frantically about. The man looked up, amazement on his drawn white face, as the enormous blaze suddenly moulded smoke and flame into a Mounted Policeman on a galloping horse and belched them out to his rescue. Conger, dimly aware that his clothes were half burnt off his back and that the animal under him was a smouldering, trembling mass of sweat and foam, leapt to the ground and woke the man to sanity with a shout almost lost in the tumult:

"Get hold of their heads and lead 'em round! I'll take the plough!"

Sobbing hysterical thanks, Grier obeyed, to begin a mad

race, the team against the approaching fire. Three times they circled the main buildings, the horses at a canter, until the fire-guard that appeared in their tracks seemed as effective as in the time remaining they could make it.

Through the smoke and semi-darkness, Conger could make out his companion only as a shadowy figure. But he gasped further orders at him as they unhitched the horses.

"Get your kids busy! Get out every sack and blanket you can find! Get buckets of water — as many as possible! Where's your wife?"

"Sick," the unfortunate settler choked. He swayed. Conger could see that he was almost done. "Sick in bed. Been laid up for weeks."

"Well, let her be! She'll do where she is just now! Get those blankets!"

He led the horses, his own with them, into the yard and tied them up. Removing his belt, revolver and brown field service jacket, he stripped himself to fight. A hasty glance showed him the fire, drawing rapidly nearer, almost upon them. Desperately he assisted Grier and his youngsters, demanded and was given matches.

"We must start a backfire," he exclaimed hoarsely. "You start over there and I'll start here. Beat it out every little while before it gets too big. Make the kids help. Come, grip yourself, man, for God's sake, or we'll all be burnt alive!"

They ran out together and began the backfire. It was painfully slow work, and the menace seemed to be moving down on them with increased speed. Grier, as Conger glimpsed him now and then, was staggering, so played out as to be all but useless. Conger wondered vaguely why reinforcements did not come. The truth was that Dixon, his supper host, had found every available man committed to action against the fire at other points when he rode out to rally them. Conger felt himself alone, battling against impossible odds, and decided then, as death seemed certain, to die fighting.

The fire tricked Conger. With fiendish cunning it crept unnoticed up a gully and, more dreadful than a thousand of those bygone Indian war-parties, pounced out on him from the long grass. Over his backfire it sprang, clamouring. When at last he reeled out of its deadly grip, he looked like a horribly scorched and mutilated insect scuttling out of a burning log into temporary safety.

Now surrounded by dense, rolling clouds and storming, blistering flames, the homestead, cowering inside the frail defences of the fire-guard, became a scene of terror. Dazzling light revealed its every detail and turned the wide eyes of plunging horses and bawling cattle into gigantic rubies, while the younger children screamed in panic and Grier clung to a wagon for support. Yet unconquerable courage, so often bringing the Force victory from defeat, remained with Conger; through all the sound and fury his brain worked almost as clearly and steadily as ever. He dared not depend for his last stand on the fire-guard alone. But a few yards off, in an area not yet touched by the attack, lay a slough. They must carry Grier's wife and youngsters and drive the stock into it, to stand with them in its water and wait for whatever Fate might send them.

Gesturing and shouting as best he could above the uproar, Conger launched this bid for survival, though he was tiring fast and intensely suffering. Grier was not much good but he was able to carry one toddler and handle some of the stock with aid from the bigger boys. Meanwhile Conger dealt with the other children and animals, then went into the house and on into the room where the sick woman lay in bed, praying feverishly.

The sight of her wasted and terrified face, clearly seen in the light of a coal-oil lamp and the fierce glare shining through the window, gave him such a shock that for some moments he lost what was left of his voice. Then:

"O.K.!" he croaked. "We're going to carry you out and put you in the slough with the rest of us, just to take no chances. But the fire will have passed in half an hour."

She stared wildly back at him and burst into hysterical sobs. Muttering more reassurances, the first he could think of, he wrapped her up and lifted her in his arms. Under the very wings of the fire he brought her to the others, all by this time up to their necks in the slough. Fortunately the woman was so small that he could hold her, and a shrieking child as well, for that next half-hour.

In those vital thirty minutes, the danger, as Conger had foretold, rushed away. The fire-guard had not been breached and none of the buildings inside it had suffered seriously. Dazed with wonder, the limping men brought the woman and children back into the house, the animals back into the yard. Here, for the first time, Conger was able to spare some attention for his horse. Blinded, and with feet hopelessly burnt, it was rocking to and fro in agony. So he found his revolver and put it out of its misery with one shot. As it fell, reaction struck its master and tears flowed down Conger's twinging, soot-blackened face.

Rejoining the Griers, he applied first aid to their hurts and to his own. No one spoke one surplus word. And soon the homesteaders were sleeping the sleep of exhaustion in their rooms. Conger took to an old sofa on the little veranda, but was so overwrought and in such pain that he could not sleep at all.

At dawn he got up, still smarting, to walk into a smoking but fireless world. Taking the saddlery from his dead horse, he transferred it to a substitute from Grier's string. A note promising to send the animal back that afternoon was soon written. The people owing their lives to him slept on. He left them sleeping. The last thing he wanted from any of them was thanks.

Back in his detachment, with his wounds well dressed by the local doctor and a square meal under his belt, he sat down towards evening to put last night's doings on record for his commanding officer. Slowly and stiffly his heavily bandaged hand wrote this:

Sir:

I have the honour to report that at 8 P.M. on the 7th instant
while on patrol I observed a large prairie fire bearing down from
the east on the homestead of Mr. J. G. Grier, located about six
miles north of here. I proceeded to the scene and assisted Mr.
Grier in saving his wife and his six children, main buildings and
stock. I regret that, owing to injuries it received on the way to
the homestead, my horse, No. 826, had to be destroyed. The
fire, on reaching the Saskatchewan, burnt itself out.

There he stuck—not merely because, as a typical Mounted
Policeman, he was better at deeds than words, especially
when those words concerned deeds of his own, but also
because he had to muster all his sense of duty to go on.
Saving the Griers was one thing but adding what he now
must add to his report was most hellishly another.

As he lifted his pen to add it, hoof-beats and the roll of
wheels drew his glance to the window, and he saw Inspector
Hinton, his commanding officer, drive up to the detachment
in a Force buckboard. Though he had not been through
anything like so much as Conger, his tired, unshaven face
and smoke-dirtied uniform showed that he too had been out
all night against the fire.

Conger stood painfully to attention but the inspector
waved him back into his chair, sat down on the bed, fished
a letter addressed "Mr. H. V. Conger" from a pocket of his
patrol jacket and handed it over without a word. Taking
it clumsily from its cheap envelope, Conger read:

Inspector Hinton has just dropped in. Jim and I have told
him what you did for us. And, to spare you the heartbreak of
passing on our secret (as a man as fine as you would have to
do officially, no matter what it cost you, after our reunion last
night) we've also told him all about Jim's doing time for forgery
and now trying to make a fresh start under the name of Grier.
Thank God, the inspector says this information will not go
beyond the Force. But we didn't feel it necessary to tell him
that in saving us you'd saved those who wronged you before
Jim took to crime—your false friend and *Johanna*.

So, after all, Conger need add nothing but his signature to his report. And his ordeal by fire, both spiritual and physical, ended with his reading of that letter from "the woman taken in adultery"—and divorced before he joined the Force—the woman once his much beloved wife.

the little red devil
and the deep blue sea

"'Medicine Line' and 'Good Neighbour'," said Sin, "remind me of my most preposterous adventure.

"You savvy, 'Medicine Line' doesn't mean a line of medicine like *Quit!* (for alcoholics) or *Shush!* ("It Stops That Wind"). It's traditional Indian English for the international boundary guarded by sheriffs, marshals and Long Knives, U.S. Cavalry, on that side, and by Red-coats, our Force, on this. But it's also the Copper's Curse, 'cause once the traditional Indian or his white brother on the run from the scene of his crime crosses that line, he's safe, it may be for years and it may be for ever or at least a good long time, unless a so-called 'hot pursuit' is right on his tail. 'Cause why? 'Cause there are great big gaps between the teeth of the treaties 'respecting the apprehension and extradition of fugitives from justice' and queer fish slip through. Then 'Good Neighbour' means more than Jack Canuck saying 'Nice day' to Uncle Sam.

"Of course, this preamble's stealthily approaching yet another random recollection of that Grand Old Man of the Mounties, Regtl. No. 100,906, Constable Sinister, H., more briefly, me. Sure, sure, my yarns exaggerate, yet, like the Modern Miss, are built on firm foundations. So will you kindly keep your trap shut while I talk?"

Recalling former confidences from this long, lank, gallant, if sardonic Guardian of the Last Great West, I let our horses graze, settled snugly into the grass of the Cypress Hills and said, "Talk!"

So he did, as follows:

Your Sin apart, this drama has two heroes, Sergeant Shard on our side, and Sleepy Dent on theirs, and one villain, Shave-tail Lew, on both. Remember "Iron" Shard, so christened by a redcoat lover of poesy who recalled that line about "reeking tube and iron shard" in Kipling's "Recessional"?* A little man but a real bull-pup, combining Jack the Giant-Killer with Hawk-eye, tough as shaganappi (rawhide), sharp as a lance-head, eating raw recruits as appetizers and sacrificing defaulters to his twin gods, Duty and Discipline. Still and all, you were O.K. by him if you stood up to him, as thus:

It was at Maple Creek, to which I'd just been posted for a refresher—drill on the square, you dolt, not a good, stiff drink. First parade, Shard looked my squad over—Doctor Guillotine selecting his first patient. He picked me. And:

"Blood and Blackfoot!" he thundered, "Look at your buttons!"

I looked—and my heart sank right into Australia. Some fool horse had slobbered over me in the stables before we fell in and my lovely brass buttons were foul. Now Iron Shard unmasked his batteries. When at last the guns stopped firing to cool off, he added:

"Look at mine!"

I looked again, at a chest like a pouter pigeon's, its buttons simply dazzling.

"Well," keened its owner, "have you anything to say?"

Granted, ours is The Silent Force. But, back in Fort Macleod, my buttons had been the pride of "D" Division. And the Last of the Sinisters was annoyed—no, raging. So I announced:

"Yes, Sergeant, I have."

"Then speak up, man, speak up! What is it?"

"Your buttons, Sergeant—I can see the sweetest teeny-weeny face in every one of them!"

*See "The Boundary Line" in *To Effect An Arrest.*

Shard didn't say one word. No, sir! He said so many, with such gusto, that folks in town thought the magazine had just blown up with all the barracks ammunition.

Yet that night, would you believe it, he gave me his presentation ticket, for bearer and lady, to the Oddfellows' Ball. And from then on, if he'd a dangerous mission, he took me too. . . A mighty big compliment or—maybe you're right.

One such mission was to put salt on Shave-tail, wagging far too long. Here's why:

Our western pioneers suffered perfect martyrdom from thirst. Not the trifling inconvenience readily quenched from the Old Oaken Bucket, but the horror bringing foam to the lips, steam to the ear-holes, mirages to the eyes and driving strong men nuts. Cold too—freezing the marrow, burning up the cordwood, forcing the toughest to pass the weary days indoors playing poker. And heat—boiling the sweat in the pores, making honest work impossible. But the universal remedy for restoring vigour to the frame, warming up and cooling off was nonsensically restricted by a primitive form of prohibition. The only alcoholic beverage legally available was strictly for medicinal or family use, by government permit, at five gallons a perm. And while the incidence of disease requiring stimulants and the number of very strict family gatherings were remarkable, legal liquor was always in short supply.

That was where Shave-tail Lew came in. For Shave-tail was more than the ideal western bad man, six foot four in his undarned socks and two-hundred-odd pounds in his birthday breeches, outriding Kit Carson and outshooting Wild Bill Hickok. He was Public Benefactor No. 1, the biggest, smartest runner of rot-gut and Montana red-eye, supplementing those government permits, to be found between the Great Lakes and the Pacific.

Trouble was, we law-men *couldn't* find him. We knew he must have caches, pack-trains, wagons and gangs, but apart from trifles here and there we couldn't put our paws on them. The Invisible Man had nothing on Shave-tail.

Besides, his wolves would fight at the drop of a stetson hat.
And no mean proportion of the Prairie provinces and
adjoining states were hand in gauntlet with him. After all,
the rude forefathers of those freedom-loving citizens had
wrenched the sacred right to take a snort from King John
himself, through Magna Carta.

But back to our mission. Picture your pardner Sin, half
a dozen stalwart comrades and Iron Shard, in charge of the
patrol, ambushed down there in that timber north of the
Line, on a little-known Indian trail, expecting a pack-train
of crazy water to be run in that night by Shave-tail for
"Boozer" Bains of Maple Creek. Conditions were absolutely
perfect—raining cats, dogs, pigs and poultry and dark as
Uncle Harry's coal-hole. So there we all were, lying in wait
and water, rifles loaded and cocked, horses parked behind
us and not a sound to be heard but the low mutter of seven
zeal-mad constables cussing their heads off.

Commissioners came and went, boy recruits decayed into
gruff old pensioners crippled with rheumatiz, yet still we
waited and still it rained. Then, suddenly, Shard rasped:

"Here they are!"

And here they undoubtedly were—plain as your snoot,
we heard approaching the squelch of hoofs, the enticing
gurgle of liquor in kegs and the clatter of armed hosts.

"Get mounted, some of you, just in case," Shard ordered,
in a whisper so soft you could normally hear it only about
ten miles away. "Remember, stand fast till I challenge—
and don't fire first!"

"I sprang to the stirrup and Joris and he." Then, just as
the portcullis was about to trap the pack-train, my fool
horse—yes, the one that spoilt my buttons—spotted a Lost
Love, some pretty little palfrey, among the enemy, and let
out a warning neigh like a peal of thunder. In a mass of
gun-shots and shockingly bad language, the invaders broke
back south, the way they'd come, full speed. And "I
galloped, Dirck galloped, we galloped all three," after them,
before them and among them, determined to win a glowing

line in the Commissioner's Annual Report or break our ruddy necks.

The breakneck part was easy. Ever charge on a horse "over hill, over dale, through bush, through briar, over park, over pale, through flood, through fire," like Buck—or was it Puck?—on A Midsummer Nightmare, in a running fight and a pitch-black rainstorm, to "put a girdle round about the earth in forty minutes"? Pistol in this hand, rifle in that, reins in the other, heart in your mouth, fiends in human form trying to murder you and your gee-gee slipping, sliding, zooming, gliding, utterly out of control? It's fun—ought to try it!

For once, words fail me. Unfortunately the rest of the patrol failed me too. The Headless Horseman (me again) was maintaining a "hot pursuit" so piping hot that whenever he hit the saddle it burst into flames. But even with that beacon-light to guide them, Joris, Dirck and the others were left way, way behind and the deep bay of the Hound of the Baskervilles — my Sergeant, urging them on — grew steadily fainter in the distance. Which usually happens when Sinister rides again. Besides, in this case, anyhow, Sinister wouldn't halt. 'Cause why? He couldn't. And Old Moore himself, with his famous Almanac, foretelling world disasters, might have found it impossible to predict the end of that ghastly night if something you'd never guess in a thousand years hadn't happened. I fell off.

Yes, sir, though my bronco-busting trophies fill quite a small suitcase, I fell off. But not alone, by Crikey! At the same time, I fell on—yup, fell right on a whisky-man, fell in every sense, laying aholt of that there critter and landing like a Rocky Mountain snowslide bang in the middle of his bread-basket. So, as the rain stopped and came the dawn, the Infant Prodigy woke with Shard applying eminently suitable restoratives and cooing:

"Great work, Sinister! The rest of the gang's vanished. But you, at least, have made a capture, though it's only Roddy the Runt. Let's see, now, if he'll talk."

He wouldn't. Scared of Shave-tail, I guess. And at last Shard sent him back with the rest of our patrol and said:

"Boot and saddle! We're crossing the Medicine Line, just we two, in search of the nearest Yankee sheriff and more co-operation re Shave-tail."

Which neatly introduces that sheriff, Sleepy Dent. Big and hearty as a buffalo bull, with eyes like arrow-heads, moustaches like the horns of a Texas steer and a face like a prairie sunset, he had forty notches on his guns in memory of men he'd disposed of for resisting arrest. And he was known as Sleepy, in our cryptic western style, 'cause no one ever caught him napping. As for "Good Neighbour", our Force never had a better, you can take it from Sin.

But to hear him exchanging compliments with his side-kick, Shard, you'd have thought they were still fighting the War of Independence.

Said the Sergeant, snarling sideways, "What I want is 'hands across the border' in a real man's grip. But all I get is 'Beat it, I'm busy!' Shave-tail's liquor comes from Montana. His base is here—it must be. His trains and wagons move across a Great American Desert bald as your screaming Eagle and therefore in full view. Yet you know less about him and his set-up than Goldilocks knew about grizzlies!"

Sleepy Dent roared back, with a laugh like C.P.R. No. 1 doing seventy over a bridge, "Little man, how'd you make so sure he's not got all you say up there on your own range, in Canada? You didn't, 'cause you're nothing but a Red-coat. Started running under General Braddock, before 1776. And you've been running ever since."

Sneered the Sergeant, "Take off that tin-can badge of office and I'll knock those words so far down your throat, they'll come out in Washington!"

Tut-tut, I thought, that's not the approved way of fostering better international relations. Only Sleepy then said, grinning like a wild-cat:

"If you'll close that gaping gob, I'll put every marshal, vigilante, posse and Long Knife in this county onto finding

Shave-tail. And I'll escort you tenderfeet back across the
Medicine Line, 'cause the guy might get you and that would
never, never do."

"Star-spangle your Banner," said Shard. "It's a deal."

Who was to guess that the immediate results would lead
us into enough fire and fury to last a timid soul like me for
life? We were totally off guard, though in sight of the Line,
when a bullet pinged out of a pile of American rocks.
Judging by how close it came, I've an uneasy hunch it was
meant for the Riders in Red, Iron Shard or me. But it cut
Sleepy Dent out of the saddle like a thrown rope cutting
the hoofs from under a maverick at branding-time. Then
came more bullets, by the magazine-full, cracking like stock-
whips, buzzing like hornets. Quick as a rifle-flash, some sort
of sixth sense told me, "Shave-tail's gang!"

In the same breath or maybe two gasps behind, Shard
yelled at me, "Get the horses under cover! I'll take care of
this!"

Now, instant willing obedience to orders is a great Force
tradition. "Look after your horse" is another. And who was
Constable Sinister, H., to flout those glorious precepts?
Never, in fact, was he more delighted to follow them. Shard,
rifle in hand, was still springing out of the saddle to Sleepy's
defence when good old Sin scooped up the reins of both
riderless steeds and rode with them for the shelter of the
nearest coulee like a panicking puss.

Once there, I swiftly tethered the brutes to this and that,
whipped out my firearms and looked back to see what I
could do. No two ways about it, Shard needed me now.
With Sleepy slung over his back, he looked like a coyote
trying to carry a cow as he staggered after me in search
of a refuge. And bullets! Two knocked off his hat, one shot
away a shoulder-strap, others punctured what Sleepy used
to call his "cute dude pants." That was enough for Ivanhoe.
Recalling redskin ruses and stratagems, my one-man band
set out to impress the gang with the idea that they were
totally surrounded.

Bounding from rock to rock and tree to tree with the amazing velocity of St. Vitus in a skirt-dance, I made the welkin ring with appropriate war-whoops: "Scotland for Ever!", "Lincoln for President!", "Vive la France!" and blazed away at the dastards like the Fourth of July gone mad. And boy, did I get results? Bear in mind that I'd won a consolation prize for marksmanship in recruit class and the shooting-trophies I'd since collected were of such a character that my comrades laughingly called me Dead-Shot Dick. So, in no time at all, I drove the gang into full retreat—and my pals into the deepest holes available.

Shard expressed his gratitude.

"Sinister," he asked, "what in the name of Sitting Bull and Custer did you think you were doing?"

"Hemming them in, Sergeant," I said.

"Some hem!" he said. "Next time, my lad, be a little bit more careful. You nearly shot *me!*"

No matter, the war was over and we got to work on Sleepy. As we worked, the Sergeant prayed with that pious eloquence for which he was so famous: "Rupture the House of Representatives, Old Glory and all sheriffs!" and so on and so forth. But meanwhile, he padded that shoulder-wound, damned a Colorado River of blood. And Sleepy, opening his peepers, grinned and whispered: "Cuss you, Shard, I'll pay you back."

Leaving them happily insulting each other, I commandeered a Bar-U wagon to rush Sleepy to his hometown hospital. And, after that, the international man-hunt for Shave-tail and his cohorts got really going. Booze or no booze, the citizens didn't want Sleepy Dent, that Monarch of Montana, following the buffalo to extinction. Sin did his humble part when he could be spared from more important duties, like peeling spuds and painting the barracks flagstaff. But even with the master-mind to show them how, the hunters got nowhere fast.

Half the law-men on each side of the Line were standing with ears to the ground, like giraffes, or crawling around with magnifying glasses, like sleuth-hounds hunting sleuth. Others were combing the entire Plains country and leaving no stone unturned in it. Soon the region was littered with combs and well-turned stones. Yet every track petered out in a morass of mystery. At last Dame Rumour whispered that the Commissioner, in sheer desperation, had cabled Sherlock, "For Heaven's sake, come!" In vain — Holmes (went on the Dame) had cabled back: "All tied up with the Veiled Vamp of Piccadilly Circus. Shall I send you Doctor Watson?" To which our Chief had tersely replied, "For Hell's sake, don't!"

You see, his desperation was quite sheer enough without the Baker Street Booby adding London fog to ours and making it worse.

Then one fine day Iron Shard came to me with eyes full of that glint which meant that he was on and up to something.

"Turn out!" said he. "We're hitting the trail in twenty minutes."

"We" meant not only Shard and Sinister, Partners, but a dozen buck policemen as well. First, the Sergeant rushed us at full gallop to the scene of my spectacular capture of Roddy the Runt. Then he led us, Indian file, into the timber on a trail worth hitting—with a club, as it was so poor that no Indian, except maybe a Snake, would have been able to follow it. Branches scalping you, pine-needles blinding you, tree-trunks tripping your horse. . . . Through green depths made blue by some of the choicest words in the Force vocabulary, we struggled for a couple of years, every constable sharing this sad thought: "It was bound to come, of course, but poor old Shard's gone bughouse!" Till, all at once, we saw method in this madness, yes, sir! We saw ourselves in a slash or passage cut like a fairly wide road through the timber and running dead straight, east and west, for ever and ever, amen.

It was that slash you can just make out down there—the slash cut by surveyors to mark the Medicine Line, the 49th

parallel constituting the boundary between those two "Good
Neighbours", Jack Canuck and Uncle Sam.

And in that slash, so help me Hannah, right in front of us,
were a lot of log buildings, with Shave-tail himself grinning
like a wolf from out the nearest window!

At that amazing sight the immortal maxim of good old
Sherlock, so obviously digested by our glorious Sergeant,
flashed through Sin's reeling brain, in words to this effect:

"When you've exhausted all the possibilities, what remains,
however improbable, must be the truth."

Well, Iron Shard had exhausted not only the searchers
but all the possibilities in his hunt for a Shave-tail base on
this side of the Line or that—and so arrived, the clever little
chap, at what remained, i.e. and viz., this truth: that base
must be somewhere on the fence, the Line itself!

More than that, he'd nosed out its location and here we
were!

Meanwhile Shave-tail, still grinning, swept us a bow with
his ten-gallon hat. And now he sneered:

"Howdy, Sergeant Shard! Welcome to my seat — yup,
Castle Shave-tail, where even you can't touch me!"

"I'll touch your seat, all right, in my own good time!"
replied our Sergeant, through those tiger-teeth. "Pending
that pleasure, however, take notice, Lewis Sarcophagus
Montacute Smith alias Shave-tail Lew, I've a warrant for
your arrest!"

"Say, ain't that nice?" Shave-tail said, stepping briskly
southward to another window, "But you can't execute that
warrant, Smarty, 'cause *you* ain't in hot pursuit and *I* am
now in U.S. territory."

Followed a holy hush, while twelve grim Red-coats
caught that very fast ball and swallowed it.

"Still an' all," went on the mocking-bird, "Seein' as you're
here, I'd love to have you step inside an' look things over,
so you can gather what you're up against when you tangle
with Shave-tail Lew. Yup and you can bring along one slave
to keep you company. But leave your rifles in their buckets.

And the rest of the delegation best stay put. 'Cause my braves have got your whole ding outfit covered from the U.S. side!"

Shard signalled me off my high horse to go with him. But he simply answered with a meekness which, I knew from sad experience, boded ill—Christmas, how it did bode! —for some one:

"Thanks, Shave-tail, I *will* have a look, for future reference."

In we went. To our left was just some rustic furniture . . . but to our right enough kegs, cases and bottles to irrigate the Prairie provinces, all guarded by about a battalion of armed brigands, who were also drawing beads from suitable loopholes on our boys outside.

There and then, I knew exactly what ailed the early Christians when they joined the Lions for a Roman holiday. And I wondered why on earth I hadn't taken Mother's advice and a good safe job like clerking in a store or thawing dynamite instead of wasting my undoubted talents in the Mounted Police.

Shave-tail broke into this meditation. Pointing to a thin black line running, I'd say, precisely east and west, down the middle of the floor, he expounded:

"That side of this here building's Canada, this side, where me and my fellers and my booze is standin' at this interestin' moment, is the United States. And since, I repeat, you ain't hotly pursued us, you and yours can't do nothin' to us and our goods and chattels aforesaid so long as we stay where we are. Contrariwise, if that corrugated, dessicated Sleepy Dent pays us a visit like yours when you've shamefully departed, all we've got to do is move, bag and baggage, to the Canada side and we're safe once more!"

Stricken dumber, even, than usual for a while, your Sin eventually broke the silence with this subtle observation:

"Fry my saddle for a mess of flapjacks, but the guy's dead right!"

"Quiet!" snarled my Sergeant, then, still polite as the
minister at a church social, he enquired:

"Would you kindly quote your legal authority for all this
balderdash?"

"De-lighted!" said Shave-tail. *"Milligan versus Regina,
Mulligan versus The People and verb sap."*

"Sap I may be," Shard replied, "but not withstanding
Milligan versus Regina, Moose Jaw, Saskatoon or any other
burg in Western Canada, that doesn't prove you're safe!"

"Damn right it don't!" now roared a Thunderbird, appearing at a window in the U.S.A., like the bird from a cuckoo
clock. And there was Sleepy, new-risen from the dead—or
bed, in hospital, by prearrangement—with his Minute Men
at his back. "Shave-tail," he pealed, "I've got a warrant for
your arrest! Charge, attempted murder of one Sleepy Dent.
So where are you, wise guy? Between the Little Red Devil
and the Deep Blue Sea! Just drop your guns and come
quiet!"

Don't ask me for details of the next five minutes. Sir
Sinister was much too busy to absorb them. Through a
kindly veil of crashes, smashes, dashes and Hell let loose,
with all our patrol in action from the north, Sleepy's posse
attacking from the south, fond memory retains a general
impression of complete confusion. There was little or no
shooting, as we law-enforcement officers from two great
nations wanted no violence and Shave-tail's army dropped
their guns, as ordered. But as for coming quiet, that was
another kettle of jackfish altogether. Suffice it to say that
our fight along that frontier made Grant's Battle of the
Wilderness look like a toddlers' tiff and to recall one episode
which was mighty serious, yet somewhat laughable, to wit:

Constable Lancaster-Lancaster (said by Dame Rumour,
that incorrigible old chatterbox, to be an English Lord in
disguise) had a tug-of-war across the Line with Shave-tail's
second-in-command as rope and Sleepy's chief deputy in
opposition at the other end. And, at the height of the

struggle, my Lord was heard repeatedly bawling, in the accents favoured by Britain's nobility and gentry:

"Release 'is 'eels h'instanter h'or 'e'll 'ave 'is 'orrid 'ead h'off!"

The outcome? Well, of course, Justice won, happily without actually killing anybody. But then the lawyers got busy, discovering more legal complications than even the Queen's Bench and the Supreme Court had thought possible. You savvy, no arrest had ever been made actually *on* the Medicine Line before. And the case brought the position of that Line in the law-enforcement picture to a 'ead, as Constable Lancaster-Lancaster would have so happily expressed it. Allow me to give you a faint idea of those complications by very roughly quoting fragments of a document setting them out—a document emanating from the Secretary of State and covered with Great Seals.

The Commissioner showed it to my dearly loved and revered commanding officer at Maple Creek. He showed it, by permission, to Iron Shard. And the Sergeant, requiring a copy for official purposes, showed it to me, so that I could pass an idle week-end writing it out in a fair round hand instead of wasting my hard-earned pay in the canteen. 'Twasn't his fault. The job was "rush."

The relevant clauses ran more or less like this:

"Whereas *ab initio* (from the beginning) the aforesaid Lewis Sarcophagus Montacute Smith, hereinafter referred to as Shave-tail, *et al* demonstrated a determination to resist arrest, matters rapidly passed *a verbis ad verbera* (from words to blows). Subsequent events are difficult to follow. Howsoever, it appears that a general fracas, melée or free-for-all rapidly developed and that *flagrante bello* (during the war) a great many severe, even very severe, blows were struck with fists, feet and several blunt instruments by either, both or all contestants, at Shave-tail *et al* and *vice versa* as the case may be, Al in particular being roughly handled.

"*Exempli gratia* (by way of example), Sergeant Shard hit

Shave-tail in the *proboscis delicti* (delicate nose) and Canadian territory, while Sheriff Dent kicked the same man in the *posterior* and the State of Montana.

"In consequence, attorneys representing the accused are claiming that the arrests were effected on the boundary line and are therefore *ultra vires* and contrary to the recognized law of nations. Furthermore, they are preparing counter-charges against the aforesaid Sergeant and Sheriff for assault and battery committed against the persons of their clients in the Dominion of Canada, the United States of America or both.

"And *ad interim* (in the meantime) the venue for the trial of their clients is fiercely in dispute and citizens on both sides of the Line threaten to lynch Shave-tail *et al* unless they are suitably dealt with soon."

Most of these contentions will no doubt impress you as *petitio principii* (a begging of the question) or, as Iron Shard more tersely put it, bunk. Still, eventually all came right. Shave-tail *et al* were tried in Canada and got what was coming to them in no uncertain terms. More important, it was agreed, by international arrangement taking a dog's age to put through, that thenceforth and thereafter no building should ever again be erected astride the actual boundary. So Shave-tail's successors can no longer claim immunity by sitting on the fence. Sure, sure, the Medicine Line remains the Copper's Curse, thanks mainly to all that insistence on "hot pursuit." Never mind, Sleepy "paid back" Shard. And between them they proved once and for all that "Good Neighbour" means more than Jack Canuck saying "Nice day" to Uncle Sam.

a dog won't lie

Murder— an accident— or nothing at all— but probably murder—

Constable Tom Baring, tall, young, studious-looking and the best Force investigator in the Yukon, formed those first impressions of his new case from these few facts on file:

George Hind had left Dawson, territorial capital and heart of the gold-fields, on November 25th — nearly eight weeks ago — to visit points up the Yukon River, the region's natural highway. Thirteen days later Dougald Macpherson had followed him, to take a train at Whitehorse, northern terminus of the White Pass and Yukon Railway, for Skagway, the Alaskan seaport one hundred miles farther south, there to board a steamer for Seattle. With Macpherson went Harry Gross, also visiting points along the river. Each of the three men was travelling on business and driving his own dog-team. But only Macpherson and Gross had patronized roadhouses and been seen by other civilians, Force detachments or patrols on the route.

Reaching Big Salmon, 340 miles from Dawson and 260 from Skagway, on Christmas Eve, Macpherson and Gross had put up at the Colossal, Ed Hill's roadhouse. Hind was there and had been there since the 11th, using the place as his base for local trips. Next day, Hind and Macpherson had driven off together towards White Horse, while Gross had left alone for Dawson.

Though Gross had reached Dawson safely, George Hind and Dougald Macpherson had not been seen since.

This information had come from the detachments dotted

thirty miles apart along the Yukon River. It was the outcome of routine under which travellers in this wild, dangerous land told the Force their movement plans, so that failure to follow these could bring about instant Force action on their behalf. In this case White Horse detachment had telegraphed Dawson on January 5th that Dougald Macpherson had not checked in or caught his train there, as he should have, that day. And Dawson, since then, had been exchanging telegrams with detachments on or near the river, trying to trace both Macpherson and Hind.

Tom Baring now looked even more thoughtful than usual as he frowned over the file at Dawson headquarters, for the problem might well prove to be gigantic. The feverish Rush along the Trail of Ninety-Eight had subsided some years ago. The Yukon's population, chiefly of thirty thousand cheechakos (tenderfeet) interested only in making their fortunes, had decreased a little, learnt sense and settled down.

Yet, in spite of Force vigilance as keen as ever, a few men still vanished overnight. They joined new stampedes, moved from one old camp to another, went hunting or prospecting or left for civilization in riches or in rags, with little or no word to any one. They died from sickness, injury or starvation in lonely cabins or on lonely trails, no one the wiser. They were murdered or accidentally killed by partners, strangers or Indians who afterwards kept guilty silence. And a few overworked red-coats like Tom had still to find them and bring their enemies, if any, to justice in a wilderness as big as France.

But thinking about the possible vastness of the problem could not solve it. So Tom put away the file and began a round of calls.

The clean cold air of Dawson's short midwinter day braced him as he swung down busy Front Street among other parka-clad, moccasined men, past panting dog-trains, jingling horse-sleighs, saloons, dance-halls, offices and stores, to knock at a side-street door.

The pretty dark-haired girl who opened that door said, "Why, hullo, Tom, come in!" and admitted him to her well-kept log-cabin home. She added, "Join me, I was just stopping my work for coffee," and soon fell into a casual and friendly yet not intimate chat over the steaming cups. He thought himself lucky to know Ellen Macpherson, Dougald's sister, even as slightly as he did, seeing that she could probably give him a firm starting point for his inquiry and was good company.

From small talk he slid into the indirect questioning of the trained investigator, taking care not to frighten her.

"How's Dougald?"

Her face clouded slightly.

"Fine, when I heard from him last. He's gone 'outside' on business, some big deal—he never tells me what. Selling claims, I guess." She truthfully filled in details of his departure from Dawson, adding, "He wrote me just a line from Selkirk (this side of Big Salmon) saying he and Harry Gross were O.K. But I've not seen Harry since he left Dougald at Big Salmon and Dougald's not written me again. Mind you, he's a terrible letter-writer, the 'No news is good news' kind. But I wish the run to Seattle wasn't so dangerous, this time of year, even by the Inside Passage, and that Skagway and Seattle weren't so tough."

"I'd not worry about the Seattle run, if I were you," said Tom. "I suppose you know what boat he sailed on?"

"The *Alaskan*."

"We'd have heard if she'd come to grief. But we haven't. As for Skagway, it's dead as 'Soapy' Smith — king of its gangsters in Rush days, remember? Then, I don't see Dougald running foul of Seattle wharf-rats. Too much sense. . ."

"You're a help. Anyhow, I guess I'll hear soon."

More small talk, while Tom's keen eyes roved around the tidy little room. They unobtrusively surveyed Dougald's desk stuffed with mining papers, his shelves of technical books and his poker-worked buckskin wall-hanging, a souvenir of Ninety-Eight. They glanced at framed photographs of Dougald, Ellen and their friends, lingered over the names of professional photographers stamped on the mountings and passed to a cabinet photo Tom had not seen before.

Nodding towards it, he said, "Familiar face. Do I know him?"

She blushed—not good at hiding things—or was she?

"That's George Hind, a great friend of ours—Dougald's mining partner till last year—"

"Of course! Should have recognized him. Handsome!"

He had already noted her sparkling engagement ring.

"We're marrying in the summer, when Dougald gets back."

"Well, well! Not only handsome but lucky—"

"I'm lucky too. I love him very much," she said, almost defiantly.

Tom said, "I'd like to drink with him to your future happiness sometime. I think I know his office—"

"Please do. But he's away till next week." Again she sketched in details already known to Tom. "No news from him, either—though, in his case, I don't worry. He's not going 'outside.' And he's a worse letter-writer than Dougald, even."

Tom picked up the photo, studied it closely, without appearing to do so and remarked, "That's a fine collie with him."

"Yes, that's Bruce. I gave him to George when we became engaged. They go everywhere together."

"Pity about his torn ear."

"A husky attacked him," said Ellen. "He's very gentle himself."

Tom was thinking, "Find the dog and we probably find the master. He may well be the key to the case."

As good-byes started, Ellen suddenly asked,

"Why have you really called? Anything wrong?"

He smiled. "You know our Force keeps touch with everybody, particularly girls living alone!"

She laughed and they parted.

Yet, looking over his catch as he strode back to Front Street, he thought, "This mess of fish seems—well, fishy!"

Now, casting his net in other pools, Tom first sought out the photographer who had taken the photo of George Hind with Bruce, the collie, and one of Dougald also noted in Ellen's home. The man promised to rush any required number of copies to headquarters if called upon and gave Tom prints of both photos for his immediate use. Next Tom went to the telegraph office, coded and wired Skagway's city marshal descriptions of the men and the dog, based partly on those photos, and asked him to report whether either man had embarked in the *Alaskan* or some other vessel or if men or dog had been seen anywhere in Skagway. Another coded wire to upriver detachments described Bruce and requested a search for him.

Then Tom visited the Mining Recorder's office and got two specimens of the signatures of the missing men. Keeping one of each specimen for reference, he left the others with the postmaster, who undertook to advise the Force if letters addressed in either handwriting reached Dawson and at the same time to report the names, addresses and postmarks concerned.

His next call was at the nearest bank. Tom Cassidy, its manager, knew him well. It was a case of "first time lucky." Cassidy said that Dougald Macpherson banked there and that his account was flourishing, so much so that after drawing out $15,000 in cash and $10,000 by draft on the day he left Dawson he still had about $10,000 to his credit. The manager was also able to give Tom the serial numbers of the notes making up the $15,000. More than that, he said:

"I felt that a man carrying so much cash might get into trouble. So I memorized key numbers of the series and kept my eyes open for them. And—let's see, I've a memo about it in this drawer—yes, on January 11th Harry Gross paid $300 in those notes into his rather rickety account here. Could mean something—"

"It certainly could," Tom agreed, recalling that Gross had returned from Big Salmon on the day before making that deposit.

George Hind kept his account at another bank, where Tom found it through Homer Falls, the manager, whom he also knew well. This account, he learned, had suffered ups and downs ever since Hind had severed his mining partnership with Dougald and at present stood roughly at $500.

Tom now decided to see Harry Gross. The man was part-owner of "The Road To Ruin", a minor Dawson dancehall. He had made his pile during the Rush and thrown most of it away but had never clashed with the law. That said a lot, even for a mere eddy in the furious rapids that must have flooded Dawson with crime in Rush days if the Force had not dammed them. Yet Harry's clean record might simply mean that he was smart.

Now was a good time to see him, for his ragtime band, fancy skirts turned "respectable" and bar dispensing drinks at moderate post-Rush prices would not need his attention till customers rolled in, much later in the day. So Tom went at once to The Road To Ruin. Serious doubts concerning Harry returned to him there. The shadows purposely maintained in the main hall for those who liked semi-privacy in dissipation were sinister. The office seemed haunted by the ghost and stained by the blood of Flossie Levine, a dancehall girl shot in it by Taku Bill Wilson, her jealous lover, in Ninety-Nine. And jolly, overfed Harry Gross, heartily greeting his tall, quiet visitor from behind its roll-top desk, always sounded like a call played by a trumpeter-recruit— just a bit off key.

"Drink?" he chuckled. " 'No—not on duty!' Ho, ho! Well, I don't mind if I do and here's the bottle. Ah-h-h, real good whisky—Saloo! Now, Yallah-leg—er, excuse me, I should

have said 'policeman'—how can I help you? And what do
I get for it?"

Tom laughed that one aside and again cast his net through
an informal chat. With the minnows thrown out, it confirmed
that Harry had accompanied Dougald upriver, reaching the
Colossal on Christmas Eve. Harry went on:

"I needed a change. And I had to see a boy at Selkirk
I grub-staked on a claim last fall, then talk to Ed Hill of
the Colossal—he wants to put money in this place. On the
way, I took 'bout $500 off Dougald, playin' cards—just takin'
the pants off Junior, to a man like me. Swell time at the
Colossal, too.

"Soon after we ran into George Hind there he said he
and Dougald would join up for the rest of Dougald's run
to Skagway. Suited me fine, as I had to start back for
Dawson next day, when Dougald had decided he'd push on.
You see, I'd promised to see the New Year in at Selkirk.
Nice trip back, using my usual roadhouses, meetin' mushers
and seein' your detachments and patrols. Settled my
Colossal and other roadhouse bills with part of what I'd
won from Dougald, banked some of it when I got back
here and spent the rest on the trip or since. That's my story,
Yallah-leg, an' you can check it if you like, blast you to
hell."—this last remark being hurled at Tom half in jest,
half in earnest, like a snowball with a stone in it.

Returning to the telegraph office, Tom coded and wired
the highlights of Harry's statement, with the serial numbers
of Dougald Macpherson's notes, to all detachments engaged
in the search, asking them to get local comments, trace what
notes they could and wire back a report on the results. At
headquarters he arranged for circulars requesting Yukon
stores and other likely places to look out for the notes and
inform the Force of full details if any came into their hands.
After supper the Skagway city marshal's wired reply to
Tom's queries arrived—quick work! No one answering to
the description of Hind and Macpherson or using their

names had embarked at that seaport, nor could any trace
of them or of Bruce the collie be found there. Tom now
felt convinced that some mishap had struck them.

Seated in front of the big map in the main office, he
worked out the area in which this could have happened,
basing his calculations on the average daily distance dog-
trains covered on the trails linked with Big Salmon and
bearing in mind that reports ruled out many of those trails
completely. The result pointed to the blow having hit its
victims on the main Yukon-Lake Bennett-White Pass trail,
between Big Salmon and Skagway. It also suggested that
he ought to search that trail himself, beginning at Ed Hill's
Colossal as soon as possible.

Inspector Lawlay, his big, brawny C.O., grown grey in
years of successfully fighting crime, came into the office
as Tom reached this conclusion. He listened stolidly to
Tom's report, agreed with his ideas for future action and
said "I'll keep you posted as you go along. Take an extra-
good man with you. Start first thing tomorrow."

So dawn saw Tom whirl out of Dawson with young
Constable Mike Greenwood, Skookum Jim Beaver (the
first-class Indian special once concerned with Sergeant
Winslow in The Race for Molly Scott) and two fast dog-
teams.

Every detachment passed along the river gave him news
from Inspector Lawlay or more information of its own. But
all these contributions supported Harry Gross's story—
perhaps a deep lad, that one—or merely confirmed old
data. Ed Hill brought out new clues, however, naturally,
as a man with the wit to name his small roadhouse the
"Colossal" might be expected to keep his sharp eyes open.

Over cigars enjoyed in his private parlour the little
wizened baldhead described events occurring in his place
at that vitally important Christmas season. He told of
Hind's stay and of rejecting Harry Gross's offer of a share
in "The Road To Ruin"—and disappointing him, as Harry

needed the money. Then, going back to Harry's arrival with Dougald, Ed stated:

"Macpherson was surprised to meet George Hind here. Surprised but very friendly. Hind put up a show on the same lines but it didn't ring true, in a way—my guess is that he may have known Macpherson was coming and possibly doesn't like him. But anyhow, with Macpherson and Harry Gross, I'd all ten rooms taken that night, double beds in some, a shakedown in two—seventeen guests altogether. Yes, here's my register, with names and everything. Then twenty-odd people dropped in for the evening, the Colossal being popular—and at Christmas, why, I like to do 'em proud. Guess Mrs. Hill and I can name all twenty for you.

"High jinks that night, with Christmas crackers at dinner, drinks pretty well on the house all through and Dougald Macpherson, in particular, fairly whooping it up, old Rush style—throwing money round, flashing nuggets and even dropping 'em down the necks of a bunch of show-girls working their way up to Dawson by degrees. One nugget was quite special. Dougald called it a souvenir and said he'd not part with it at any price. Pretty near as big as any ever panned up here, it was, but easy to remember 'cause it's shaped like a star. 'The Christmas Star', we all said, and I'd know it anywhere. Boy, that nugget set 'em staring, George Hind and Harry Gross as much as any. And, if you ask me, Dougald was mighty reckless the way he showed his wealth to that mixed bunch."

Tom said, "Your statement's worth that nugget, perhaps more. So go on."

The little man brooded awhile, then added:

"Gross told me when he arrived he was only staying the night, so I wasn't surprised when he left next morning. But when Hind and Macpherson said they too were going off after breakfast *and* going together, it took me aback, as Hind's room was booked for another week, Macpherson said originally that he wanted to be in on our extra-special dinner Christmas Day and Hind seemed to have got over his dislike for Dougald much too quickly. My guess is those two boys must have had urgent reasons for changing their minds and missing that party! However, they all three settled their accounts with Mrs. Hill, then some of the guests and I saw 'em off."

Tom showed Ed the photo of Hind and his collie.

"Know that dog?" he asked.

Ed's face lighted up in a crinkled smile.

"Sure, that's Bruce," he said. "Lovely dog! Arrived here with Hind and stayed here while his master made little business trips round about, then went off with Hind and Macpherson Christmas Day. But I've not heard or seen hide or hair of him since."

"Anything else?"

"Well, if it's any use to you, Harry Gross had a 40.28 rifle, Dougald a 30.30 and George Hind another 40.28 and a .41 Winchester revolver I saw in his room one day."

"You should be in our Force!" said Tom. "Now, Ed, I want you to keep everything Hind and Macpherson may have had anything to do with while here—even what's left of the Christmas crackers! List every guest and visitor who was here during their stay. Have another try to find the notes used by the three men to pay their bills. Also, let me have copies of those bills. So long!"

And, heaving his lean 6 feet 2 out of his arm-chair, Tom set about preparing a report on Ed's statement and wiring the coded gist of it to Inspector Lawlay in Dawson.

Just twenty-four hours later, burly Constable Greenwood stopped decoding a telegram from the inspector and, looking at Tom across the table at Big Salmon detachment read, with as much excitement in his broad red face as he ever allowed himself:

"'White Horse stopped and questioned George Hind on way to Skagway 11 A.M. yesterday. Account of recent movements unconvincing, so arrested and searched him and sled. Found star nugget and $13,200 of Macpherson's notes. Bruce not with him.'"

"Bruce not with him . . . to say nothing of Macpherson!" Tom exclaimed. "That's bad."

Seven weeks afterwards, Tom, Mike Greenwood and Skookum Jim Beaver drove to Muskrat Yarrow's cabin up a creek on Teslin River.

By this time, Tom thought, the case looked all but hopeless. The Force had sent photos of Macpherson and Bruce, with masses of data, to every part of Canada, Alaska and the States, talked to most Yukoners, closely watched the mails, shadowed Gross and others. And Tom's weary patrol had searched the main trail all the way from Big Salmon to White Horse, then back to the Teslin and up that river, as well as side-trails, creeks, river-banks and the Yukon telegraph-trail, all detachments helping. Yet no trace of man or dog had appeared, so far.

Nor had Hind's story been disproved. He maintained that when he was at the Colossal, before Dougald and Gross arrived, Bill Ireland, from up Big Salmon River, had told him that he'd struck it rich but needed money to finance development, while Henry Butler, up the Teslin, visited by Hind about the same time, had offered him a good claim for a quick sale. When Dougald reached the Colossal, Hind had suggested to him that they join forces with Ireland and buy Butler's claim, Dougald finding most of the cash. Dougald had agreed to run up the Big Salmon to see Ireland and had let Hind have the notes found at White Horse to go up the Teslin and buy Butler's claim. Later Hind and Dougald would meet in Skagway to tidy things up before Dougald took the *Alaskan* for the outside.

In an excess of alcoholic Christmas spirit, and as a wedding gift to an old chum engaged to his sister, Dougald had given Hind the star nugget. Hind, in return, had given Dougald the collie. Then, on Christmas Day, Dougald had driven off to see Ireland, taking Bruce with him, and Hind had gone to see Butler.

Hind denied any knowledge of what had happened to Dougald and the dog. He suggested that they had gone through the ice of the Big Salmon and drowned without leaving a sign. Or some one, perhaps Harry Gross, who had seen Dougald chucking gold and money around at the Colossal, had followed and killed them both.

After leaving Big Salmon, Hind had spent days with Butler, trying to buy that claim, without success, then back-trailed to the Yukon and headed for Skagway, only to be arrested by White Horse detachment.

Neither Hind nor Dougald had told any one about exchanging gifts, as this concerned only themselves. Similarly, they had kept their visits to Ireland and Butler secret for business reasons, allowing everybody to think they had set out from Big Salmon together for Skagway. Ireland confirmed that he *had* talked to Hind about financing his rich strike, though Dougald had not been mentioned and Ireland had not seen him. Also, Butler supported Hind's account of his unsuccessful effort to buy that good claim.

No one except Butler had seen Hind between Big Salmon and White Horse because everybody was indoors, celebrating, on Christmas Day, he could not afford to stay at roadhouses, after paying his Colossal account, and he had no friends, other than Butler, to stay with on the trails concerned. Besides, he had hidden from strangers approaching him on those trails lest they rob him of the $13,200 and the nugget. He could not know that they included Force patrols. As for avoiding detachments, he didn't like Yallah-legs! In any case, he had given his questioners a list of his night-halts between Dawson and White Horse. Force visits had verified that those halts had been used fairly recently. Tom's patrol, covering those from Big Salmon onwards, had made plans and taken photographs of them and had found evidence—an old envelope, grub-sack tags and so on—confirming that some, at least, really had been used by Hind.

Ellen Macpherson was standing by him, though the Force knew that he was wild and not too honest. Then, Gross was still under suspicion.

And meanwhile where, where, *where* was Dougald Macpherson—or his body? Where was Bruce—or his carcass?

Tom, now driving up to Muskrat Yarrow's, had a hunch that if the old man or a second search of the thirty-odd miles between the Teslin mouth and Big Salmon failed to indicate the answer to those questions, they would remain unsolved for ever.

The clamour of Muskrat's huskies and a frenzied counter-blast from the police teams brought the trapper to the door. His leathery, bearded face fell as his sleepy eyes saw the yellow-striped breeches and he growled:

"Botheration! You damn' nosies don't give a man no rest! I've already told your Big Salmon boys I don't know nothin' 'bout that feller an' his dog!" Then, slipping back into his normal kindly self, he added, "Sorry, shouldn't talk like that, when you people do so much for us an' all. But I just got back from my trap-lines an' I'm tuckered out. Come in, come in and I'll boil ye some cawfee!"

Tom's own eyes lighted up as he said:

"If you know nothing, Muskrat, *what are you doing with collie hairs on your shirt?*"

The old man looked as if threatened by a stick of dyna-mite. He glanced down at his shirt-front, stammered, stuttered and at last brought out:

"Them ain't collie hairs, them's husky's!"

"Come off it," said Tom, good-naturedly, "No husky's that colour. I'll bet my boots you've got Bruce here, Muskrat! So trot him out—and remember withholding information's a serious offence."

"I tell you I ain't got him!"

"O.K.! Then we'll have to look around."

"Jumping Japers!" said Mike. "Japers, sure!" said Skookum Jim.

And, Japers sure, they did find Bruce; Old Muskrat had

made him a cozy kennel, cunningly concealed in the nearby bush and shut him up there. Alert and well cared for, he betrayed his hideout by barking a reply when Tom called his name.

Returning to Muskrat, they found the poor old chap near to tears.

"I picked him up runnin' loose and scared o' his own shadow, near Lower Laberge round about New Year's. So now he's my dog—that's the law. An' I've always wanted a nice dog like him, a pet, you see, huskies ain't enough."

"But he'd a collar with a tag on it, Muskrat," Tom reminded him, on information lately given by Ed Hill, "And that tag read 'Bruce. Hind. Dawson City.' Where is it?"

"Well, I threw the collar into the bush, dunno where. But if you want a witness that he had one, I'm it."

"O.K.! Now, Muskrat, will you lend us Bruce for a while? You will? That's fine."

Back at the Teslin mouth, Mike asked, "What's your plan?"

Tom said, "To put the key of the case into the lock—and turn it. Good night!"

First light next morning saw them slowly following the west bank of the Yukon towards Big Salmon, with Bruce trotting beside Tom's sled. The dog looked anxious—as well he might, with his torn ear a token of what the nearby huskies could do. And he looked puzzled, also with good reason, for Tom kept telling him, "Go home, sir! Go home!"

In time his scanning of the bank showed that he apparently understood Tom's orders. And suddenly he proved it. He sat down at a creek mouth, threw back his head and howled a dirge to chill the blood even of two policemen.

Then he started up the creek.

"Wait here with the teams, Jim!" said Tom. "Now, Mike, come on!"

Bruce went back for a quarter of a mile, Tom and Mike following and making him move with harsh orders whenever he sadly checked himself. At every step the creek narrowed, till eventually the trees almost met above it, forming a gloomy tunnel which, Tom felt, might well lead through the cold silence to something terrible.

Still driven on by verbal lashing, Bruce now left the creek by a little trail almost invisible in the brush. Then he lay down, trembling, and would go no farther.

"Stay here with him," Tom said, looking rather like a dog —a hunting dog—himself.

While Mike comforted the scared collie, he went on alone into a small natural clearing. Dark, dismal and deep in snow, it suggested that it would bear investigation.

But, rejoining Mike and Bruce, Tom said:

"We can comb this area thoroughly later on. Just now I've a hunch to follow up at once. Let's go back to the river."

"Couldn't stop me!" said Mike, his face redder than ever from barely suppressed emotion. "This ghastly place gives me the creeps."

They went down to the creek mouth, handed Bruce over to Skookum Jim and walked out onto the Yukon ice. There they dug away the drifts with snowshoes till they uncovered a deep depression, site of a hole existing not so very long ago.

From this depression the face of Dougald Macpherson looked up at them with a frozen welcoming smile, as if to say, "I knew you'd come."

Now it was mid-July and Tom felt the tension, in what the journalists were calling The Trial of the Century, approach its climax as his turn came to give evidence.

Though not allowed to sit in court till now or to read what those star reporters had written about the proceedings, he could well imagine how, for days on end, they had justifiably dramatized everything.

The court-house, next the Force's Dawson barracks, "beside the Yukon, rolling through the Long Day"—Judge Poitras on his high seat, the Royal Arms blazing behind him, "an eagle on a crag backed by the Midnight Sun"—the lawyers and officials, "busy black bears"—the jury, civilian witnesses and public, all rugged frontier types, "the Rush restored"—the red-coated Force orderlies and witnesses, "bright flames of justice"— George Hind, "the swarthy, brooding prisoner" and Ellen Macpherson, "the lovely tragedy queen" in deep mourning and a special chair, their associations providing material almost as colourful as the "copy" lost when counsel wisely decided not to use their statements or put them in the witness-box—

Above all, Tom knew, drama must have shone through the brilliant opening address by Vincent Trent, prosecuting counsel, and through the examination and cross-examination of the witnesses he had called so far: Force members from detachments and patrols, the doctor and dentist who had conducted the autopsy, analysts, postmasters, Skagway's city marshal, bankers, arms dealers and experts, photographers, an engraver, a sled-maker, representatives of Seattle's Midas Mining Company and the *Alaskan*, railwaymen, roadhouse-keepers, merchants, travellers, Muskrat Yarrow, people who knew Macpherson, Hind and Bruce.

Even the hundreds of exhibits filed to back the testimony of so many witnesses must have been given dramatic treatment.

This was the gist of what the prosecution witnesses and exhibits had contended, so far:

Hind was financially hard-pressed and jealous of Dougald Macpherson. He knew that Dougald, carrying a large sum, intended to go with Harry Gross as far as Big Salmon, then on alone from Skagway in the *Alaskan* to make a big deal with the Midas people in Seattle. So he decided to waylay, kill and rob Dougald, destroy all traces of the crime and escape secretly to Skagway and, probably, the "outside." If caught, he would blame Gross. He preceded Dougald and Gross to Big Salmon with Bruce, his collie, reporting to Dawson Town Station at the start but otherwise avoiding human contacts.

While based on Big Salmon's Colossal he heard from Ireland and Butler of attractive business opportunities and bribed Butler to say, if questioned, that Hind had spent days at his place *after Christmas* vainly trying to buy a claim. He also prepared a hideout and stocked it with goods for his secret flight. When Dougald and Gross reached Big Salmon on Christmas Eve, Hind induced Dougald to leave with him next day, probably in hope of seeing Ireland. That night the Colossal had a lively dinner, Dougald showed his money and star nugget, and the show-girls played with the men.

Next morning Gross left for Dawson, Dougald, Hind and Bruce "for Skagway." Gross travelled openly and arrived safely, the others vanished. Later Bruce was found by Yarrow, then recovered from him by the Force. Dougald failed to report at White Horse or take his train, an extensive search began, and Hind was soon "caught with the goods." He failed to implicate Gross, and Butler repudiated his abili.

Young Stanley Richfield, defence counsel, fought this formidable testimony magnificently. Though too shrewd to attack the respected Force witnesses really hard, he almost prevented the production of an axe found in Hind's outfit by White Horse detachment, calling the thing "insignificant." And he tore many civilian witnesses to bits.

Harry Gross was so shaken by reference to his "large part in Dawson's underworld" and his "dire need to sell a share in his aptly named 'Road To Ruin' dance-hall" that his account of how he obtained $500 in Dougald's notes became confused and he was left looking at best uncertain, at worst the murderer. Men living along the main trail who testified that Hind usually stayed with them when he passed that way but had not done so on his last crucial trip were forced to admit that he might have "given them the go-by" to save them expense. Gordon Vernon, the sled-maker, who had sold a sled stamped with his mark to Dougald, agreed that charred fragments so stamped could have come from any similar sled. Big Salmon storekeepers surprised by

Hind's purchase of so many goods conceded that he might not have wanted them all for his run to Skagway.

Poor old Muskrat Yarrow was gently yet firmly driven into saying that throwing away Bruce's collar was "dishonest," always provided that the collar ever existed, and that hiding the dog was "not the thing at all."

Then Gertie Delacroix, a show-girl who had helped pull Christmas crackers at the Colossal, given Hind her garter set with a 'G' in brilliants and allowed Dougald to drop nuggets down her neck, was tenderly roasted alive. She was "working" her way to Dawson by doing "odd jobs"? Surely "working" was hardly the word, while the jobs were "very odd indeed"! Champagne "flowed like water" on Christmas Eve! So she might be wrong in thinking that Dougald pocketed such trifles as a toy whistle, a pencil and a black-cat lucky charm from the crackers and that the dirty object now exhibited was that garter. Again, she must naturally be prejudiced against the man accused of murdering "a *friend* who *gave* her nuggets in Gold Rush style"!

But even Stanley Richfield could not break Butler's contention that Hind had bribed him to provide an alibi, gainsay the engraver who had inscribed a collar-tag with the words "Bruce. Hind. Dawson City" or set aside the expert testimony that bullets found in the body or at the hideout came from a rifle and revolver like Hind's. He so distressed old Yarrow that the jury itself came near to booing him. And Gertie gave him as good as she got, with "*You'd* never understand what 'odd jobs' mean or that snatching garters and dropping nuggets is just *gentlemanly* fun," "A *lady* in liquor remembers everything—and, damn your eyes, that *is* my garter!" In fact, Judge Poitras had almost to break his gavel in silencing the public's cheers for her spirited counter-attack.

That gavel banged again as Tom's name was called and an excited hum saluted this tall, calm red-coat, known to be a vitally important witness. Ellen looked at him striding towards the box, their eyes met, and though he must keep his service oath and do his duty "without fear, favour or affection," her expression touched him. It told him clearly that she was not yet convinced of Hind's guilt and that what she must now hear would hurt her sorely.

Preliminaries over, Vincent Trent asked him confidently:

"Will you now tell the court what you did and what evidence you found from the moment you took up this case?"

In a level, passionless voice, Tom complied, identifying the exhibits he referred to as he went along. After leading his excited audience to the finding of the body, he continued:

"I recognized the dead man as Dougald Macpherson. I at once informed Inspector Lawlay of this discovery, sending him a coded telegram through Lower Laberge. I thought that the body had been placed under the ice through a hole, then had drifted to the surface in the hole, which later froze over, became covered with snow and so was perfectly preserved. Constable Greenwood and I photographed and made a plan of the body in the ice and its surroundings. We then removed the body from the ice and examined it. It had been shot once in the chest from behind and once in the head, both shots at close range. The clothing was much bloodstained.

"We next took photographs at five points between the hole and the clearing, all on the river or creek ice. We removed the surface snow at these points. This uncovered sled tracks. Measuring the tracks, we found that they were made by sleds of a width corresponding to the prisoner's sled and to the fragments of a sled resembling Macpherson's. The tracks indicated that two sleds had been driven up the creek to the vicinity of the clearing, then one had been driven back to the hole in the ice and returned and finally one had been driven down the creek to the river and towards Skagway. We photographed the tracks, then photographed and made a plan of the clearing.

"We then removed and sifted the upper layers of snow

in the clearing. This took us till dark and all next day. We found many articles, marked the spots where we found them on our plan and later photographed the articles.

"First we found ashes of a fire at Point A. In those we found poles and boughs cut with an axe, used to construct a shelter and later broken up with the axe and partly burnt. At points B to H we found the stumps and trunks from which the poles and boughs were cut. Tests showed me that all these exhibits had been cut with the axe found in the prisoner's outfit at White Horse, as the marks made by the axe on the poles and boughs and in my tests are exactly alike."

Uproar! When it had subsided, the judge said:

"The jury will have an opportunity to test the axe. Witness, pray proceed."

Tom proceeded:

"We next found charred pieces of a sled in the ashes, then charred, bloodstained fragments of the following: a letter; a road-house bill made out to George Hind for $61.75; a receipt from Keen's General Store, Big Salmon, for canned goods; a document on bank paper; and six bank notes with serial numbers corresponding to some drawn by Macpherson on the day he left Dawson."

A low growl swept the court and produced more furious gavel-banging as the listeners heard the witness identify the sled fragments with those shown in court to Gordon Vernon, the sled-maker, the letter as one already proved to be from Ellen to Hind, the amount of the road-house bill as that already shown to have been paid to the Colossal by Hind, the document as one sworn to be similar to the draft for $10,000 obtained by Macpherson from his bank, and the notes as previously produced exhibits valued at $850.

Tom went on:

"Scattered around the fire at Points J to M we found a bunch of keys, a toy whistle, a pencil, a black-cat lucky charm and a woman's fancy garter. . . ."

Judge Poitras banged down a roar of laughter, and the listeners soberly recalled that the keys had already been shown to fit Macpherson's desk, the whistle, pencil and charm to be similar to others taken from Christmas crackers stocked by the Colossal, and the garter to be the one identified by Gertie as her own.

When able to continue, Tom said:

"We next found pools of frozen blood, five at Points N to R and one at Point S. We also found the prints of a collie, quite distinct from those of huskies, at many points in the clearing. We photographed all the blood-pools, then cut them out bodily for future analysis. We also photographed and made a plan of some of the prints. Later I took impressions on a card of the feet of Bruce, the collie, and compared them with the photographs of the prints, which I found to correspond exactly."

Checking a buzz of comment roused by the fact that five bottles of the blood Tom referred to had already been shown by experts to be animal, one bottle to be human, the judge set aside Stanley Richfield's protests and intoned:

"The jury may compare the feet of the dog Bruce with the appropriate exhibits later on. Witness, pray proceed."

Tom said:

"At point T we found a 40.28 rifle bullet similar to those fitting the prisoner's rifle and to the one used to shoot Macpherson in the back. It was embedded in a tree-trunk. We photographed the bullet in the tree-trunk, then cut out the piece of trunk with the bullet still in it. In the bushes at Point U we found thirteen empty tins, nine bearing labels as used on cans of food bought by the prisoner from Keen. Hidden in the woods at Point V we found the bodies of five huskies. They had been shot in the head and frozen stiff. We found harness near them. Finally, much deeper in the woods, at Point W, we found a bloodstained sleeping-bag in which was an unloaded 30.30 rifle. All these exhibits were photographed by us where found and later."

The listeners recalled that the pelts of the dogs had

already been produced and identified by their markings as those of Macpherson's team, the bag and the rifle as his.

Vincent Trent now blandly asked, in deathly silence:

"Will you tell the court your conclusions?"

"The prisoner prepared and stocked the hideout. He drove to it with Macpherson on Christmas Day, knowing that no one would be around to see them. While they were making camp that night or packing up next day, Hind fired two rifle-shots at Macpherson from behind. Macpherson was near his sleeping-bag and totally unsuspecting, as his rifle was unloaded. One shot took effect, the other lodged in a tree-trunk. Hind then shot Macpherson in the head with the revolver to make sure of his death. Searching him, he found and took the Christmas Star nugget and $13,200, with at least $850 more, in notes. He also found and threw away the keys and the Christmas favours, with his own trophy, Miss Delacroix's garter. He then broke down and burnt or tried to burn the shelter and Macpherson's sled and put some bloodstained notes and the draft, which he could not use, into the fire, with Miss Macpherson's letter and the bills, all similarly stained. No doubt, some of the notes were consumed altogether but others, to the value of $850, and the articles named were only charred.

"Bruce had escaped. Macpherson's huskies, tied to trees, could not. The prisoner shot the huskies in the clearing, then hid the carcasses, the harness, the sleeping-bag and the 30.30 rifle in the brush. Next, he took Macpherson's body on his own sled to the hole in the ice and put it under. Nature, he thought, would finish his work of concealment there and in the clearing and the woods. Lastly he returned to the clearing, loaded his sled, hiding some of Macpherson's notes in it, concealed the rest of the $13,200 and the nugget on his person, and started secretly for Skagway."

Through an uncontrollable roar of applause Vincent Trent said, "Thank you," and signalled to Stanley Richfield to start his cross-examination.

But Richfield asked only a few trival questions before Tom stood down.

Ellen, Tom saw, looked stunned, yet still unconvinced.

Vincent Trent now reminded the jury of Bruce's appearance by showing them previously produced photos in which the collie's markings and torn ear could be clearly seen. Then he asked and received permission to bring Bruce into court. Sergeant-Major Nash testified that the dog had been guarded by the Force day and night from any sort of interference. And in a hush so great that men talking in the nearby barracks could be clearly heard, a constable brought in Bruce.

Stepping daintily, yet looking around for a friend in the nervous way of collies, the beautiful dog was led into the well of the court. All eyes were on him or on Hind. And Hind's eyes were on him in a desperate burning stare.

Suddenly Bruce saw the prisoner. Only Vincent Trent, smiling so serenely, seemed to anticipate the result.

The dog gave an indescribable shriek of terror, then broke free and fled madly from the court.

Neither the judge nor his subordinates, not even the red-coated court orderlies, could control the instant pandemonium. But, as the pencils of the star reporters flew over their note-books, some one bellowed:

"There's your final proof! A dog won't lie!"

And final proof Tom thought it. Or at least it crowned a certain prosecution victory, in spite of Stanley Richfield's gallantly handled case for the defence that followed it. Eventually, Tom knew, the judge would give him most of the credit for a combined operation that had covered such vast territory with such effort and against such odds, though he hardly expected the bench to call his Force "the glory of Canada and the envy of the world." In any case, he cared mainly for this fact:

The dog had convinced Ellen, as nothing else could, that Hind was guilty and that justice would be done. For, as she looked at Tom again, her wan, pale face, he saw, was now at peace.

a working partnership

I.

Escorting Dave Wendall, riding Trix and thinking about Jean Matthews, Constable Quentin ("Q") was in quite a situation.

For Wendall, the most dangerous brutal bandit in the Rocky Mountains, needed constant watching, even now, with his hands manacled behind his back and his horse held by Q on a leading-rein. Trix, the best mount in the Force, big, handsome, glossily black as Q's full-dress jack-boots and shrewd-looking as his sergeant-major, perfectly suited the name Jean had given him: could play dead, walk on his hind legs, shake hands, do anything, in fact, but talk, thanks to his own brilliance and Q's patient teaching, which had welded horse and man into a perfect working partner-ship. And Jean, the best girl in the world, sweeter than any peach in British Columbia, prettier than any mountain flower, provided the finest possible excuse for thoughts wavering between Love and Duty.

Besides, Q had been thinking of nothing but Duty for over a week. Through all that time he had been scouring the mountains far and wide, life in hand, with only one thing in mind—the imperative necessity of capturing Wendall. So now that Wendall was captured, it was not surprising that Q allowed his tired brain to busy itself an instant with Jean.

But that instant brought disaster.

The trail on which the men rode wound tortuously through the autumn forest. They came suddenly to a point where a low bough overhung it. Wendall, almost a horse's length ahead of Q, stooped to pass under the bough. As he stooped, he realized that to negotiate the obstacle and follow him Q would have to check Trix. With Q in the middle of these negotiations, Wendall put spurs to his mount and broke into a gallop.

He had reasoned well. The sudden jerk on the leading-rein snapped it cleanly. He was free, and tearing along the trail on the dead run.

There and then, Q came down from heaven to earth as though that leading-rein had been the cord by which he was suspended. In a moment he struggled out of the grip of that confounded bough. In another he was away, full gallop after the bandit.

That started a chase that might well have made the heroic "mounties" of romantic fiction lose their man: now bounding over a fallen tree—now shaving under a drooping branch by the breadth of a finger—pounding at leg-breaking speed down awful descents—plunging up terrifying slopes—taking a hazardous shortcut across a loop in the trail—fighting through the furious torrent of a mountain stream. The trees zipped past them. The fir cones flew like sparks from beneath the speeding hoofs. The wind roared. The white spray flew. The ice-cold water took away the breath.

Q didn't mind—much. He knew that sooner or later, unless the unforeseen happened, the bandit, with his manacled hands, must again become his prisoner. He gently cursed the loss of his lariat in working his way across an over-swift river some days before and his resulting depend-ence on that faithless leading-rein. But that was all.

Wendall, a flying dot ahead, riding in masterly style, was nearing the railway crossed by this trail. Q felt certain that he could catch him there. He might have drawn his gun. But traditions forbade a Mounted Policeman to use a weapon except as a last resort.

The bandit, reaching the railway, suddenly did something that for an instant took Q by surprise. He wheeled his horse dexterously with his legs and galloped off to the right along a little path that followed the track. Q could not account for this unexpected change of course. But a second later he saw it all. About a hundred yards ahead of Wendall was a cutting. Over the cutting was a little wooden foot-bridge. Round a bend to the left a fast freight was approaching the bridge. Wendall had heard it coming while Q was still too far away to do so. His purpose was to dismount at the bridge, drop from it on to the roof of the train as it passed beneath, and so be carried away to comparative safety.

Q might have admired the bandit's quick thinking. Manacled as he was, Wendall could only have boarded the train by dropping on it from above, as he evidently intended to do. There was courage in the idea, too. Unable to use his hands to grasp the roof, the chances of his falling off were very great.

But Q had no time for admiration. Desperately he called on Trix for full speed ahead. The horse answered nobly. It seemed, however, that nothing could bring them to the track in time. Q shouted frantically and, drawing his revolver, fired several shots in the air above the train, but none of the crew could hear any sound through the echoing uproar of the train's progress, and none had eyes for the slopes above them. Q thought of trying a long shot at Wendall. Many trees got in the way. His last hope was that the engineer would realize that the man on the bridge was up to no good and would stop the train; failing that, that Wendall would miss his leap. But Wendall had by this time dismounted, and was standing on the bridge in an uncompromising attitude. The train rushed on. Wendall poised himself for the drop. Q watched breathlessly. A moment later he saw the bandit plunge from the bridge, fall to his knees on the top of a box-car, sway perilously—

Directly assisted by his big boss, Satan, he recovered himself. He was overboard—no—yes—no! The train swept away, Wendall triumphantly upon it.

New thoughts raced through Q's head as he galloped after the train, thoughts which, pieced together, gave him a full and minutely accurate conception of the situation and of what Wendall yet would do. Half a mile ahead a trestle spanned one of the mountains' mightiest rivers. It was impossible to lead Trix over it. Horses have been led over trestle bridges, but it is an infinitely slow and dangerous proceeding, and the time consumed in doing it would kill all chances of overtaking the bandit. It was equally impossible to cross the wide and raging flood beneath by swimming. Wendall had foreseen this clearly. To wait for another train was much too risky—there might not be another for hours. To gallop to the nearest telegraph office and from it warn Force detachments beyond the river was also too slow. To walk alone across the trestle was equally unthinkable, for the same reason. Q foresaw that Wendall would stay undiscovered on the roof of the train until it slowed at the nearest downgrade. Then he would jump to the ground and make his way to the nearest house in quest of a file with which to remove his manacles.

And here a terrible truth flashed into Q's mind. Under its urging, he galloped furiously along the little path, hoping desperately to reach the trestle before the train had crossed it, and from its head, in some way or another, to attract the attention of the men in the caboose. But when he reached it the train had disappeared.

II.

Jean, just then, was bustling and singing at her work in her father's cabin.

She was alone, "Dad" Matthews being away in the middle of a month's business trip. Worse, she had no weapon and no near neighbour. But she was brave as a cougar and fortified by knowing that Q or some other Force member dropped in regularly for the popular job of keeping an eye on her.

The familiar ring of spurs and the shadow of a big man

in a stetson hat reached her from the open doorway behind her and made her heart leap with joy—marred by vexation.

"I'm cleaning the stove," she wailed, "so I look a sight and I can't give you any coffee!"

"Get me a file," growled a voice never heard before, "and the coffee kin wait!"

That drowned both pleasure and vexation in horror; whipping around, she saw not Q nor any of his comrades but a huge and handcuffed lout in the stetson also worn by some civilians. She recognized Dave Wendall—badly wanted by, and now obviously escaped from, the Force.

Remaining undiscovered on the roof of the train till it slowed down, then jumping to the ground, Wendall had made his way to the nearest house — Jean's, about a mile from the track and clearly visible—to get, at all costs, a file to remove his manacles. And realization that he would do just that had been the terrible thought which had sent Q and Trix galloping furiously after the train till it disappeared.

At sight of the bandit, Jean had equally terrible thoughts —that Q might well be hunting him or that he had possibly murdered her lover.

In such circumstances even cougar-hearted women might give way when Wendall shouted, "Get that file, you slut, or I'll break your neck!"

But "Go to hell and grill there!" Jean shouted back.

Whatever other cougar-hearts might do, this one would help no "fugitive from justice" and certainly not a fugitive from Q suspected of murdering him.

The bandit cursed her at the top of his voice for fully half a minute. Still cursing, he passed into the living-room, then the two bedrooms, overturning everything in his desperate hunt for the means of securing freedom. Jean, dead-white under streaks of soot and stove-blacking, watched him dumbly. As she watched, she prayed wildly, incoherently and frantically that help would come—prayed, above all, that Q was safe and on his way with Partner Trix to help her.

Back into the kitchen came Wendall, yelling with fury. In a frenzy he went around the room again, climbing on chairs and twisting himself painfully to open cupboard after cupboard, drawers and boxes, and search them awkwardly with his manacled hands, scuffling and peering, all without success. Swept by crazy panic, he rushed at Jean, towering over her, his face purple.

"I know damn well you've got a file!" he shrieked. "Every place has one! Tell me where it is, tell me, or I'll kick the stuffing out of you!"

Jean shook her head, rallying her courage magnificently.

She knew exactly where the file was, as she had used it only that morning.

But "I won't, I won't, I won't!" she told him, her voice now reduced by excitement to a whisper.

Wendall resumed his mad searching and Jean her wild prayers that it would fail him. Suddenly her heart almost stopped as a howl of joy came from her bedroom. The bandit had discovered the file on a small bracket there. In another moment he was back with it in his hands, spitting and snarling:

"Now, you file these bracelets off'n me or I'll kill you somehow!"

Yet Jean clung to her decision to die rather than help him. She tried to shriek, but no sound rewarded her. A dread of what the man would do next welled up in her. For the first time she felt that with diabolical cunning he would bend her to his will, in spite of herself.

Now he charged at her like a football forward, again and again, knowing that if he could only corner her or knock her down she would be at his mercy. She dare not risk trying to get past him to the door or the windows. But a girl able to dance all night with the best of them could nimbly dodge his charges.

Confidence returned to her . . . till Wendall stopped for breath, an unspeakably evil grin slowly wiped rage from his ugly mug and he howled triumphantly, as he went out into the little porch:

"By God, I know the very thing to master you!"

III.

Held up at the trestle, Q looked up the track, down the track, into the woods and even at the sky, as if to find help there. Otherwise, he would never have seen the handcar.

It stood on a short spur, half-hidden behind a pile of planks dumped near the trestle for some repair work.

Seeing it, Q ran to it like a recruit to the men's mess when the trumpeter sounds "Dinners Up!" It would take him across the trestle in ten minutes. Then it struck him that he could never get to Jean's in time without Trix. Somehow, he must get the horse over too.

How was he to do it? Presently he saw that with a few planks and one or two of the ropes lying with them, he could enlarge the platform of the car sufficiently to take them both! But here was the catch. Would Trix stand still if he put him aboard? Then, remembering what a clever cuss he was, Q decided to chance it.

The contraption was rigged up with remarkable speed. He thought that to get Trix aboard would be a job. But the big horse just hopped up as if he were a canary and the car a branch.

They started. Cold fingers played ragtime up and down Q's spine as he trundled the car on to the trestle, with Trix breathing down the back of his neck. He felt that he now understood the feelings of Blondin, the tightrope walker, when he carried a man across Niagara Falls in a barrow. A hundred feet below, and Heaven alone knew how deep, was the river. There was nothing to grab if anything went wrong. Trix and Q would have been in the water for a certainty. Between the piers the rocks raved like Blackfeet in a war-dance. The thought crossed Q's mind that should

Trix become restless Jean would probably attend a funeral instead of a wedding. It was Trix that worried him.

Pumping that car into the middle of the trestle seemed to take two or three centuries. Occasionally Trix swished his tail and sent Q's heart to the bottom of the river. To stop that nonsense, Q talked to him with a "Steady, boy, steady there!" He thought it would keep him quiet if he sang. So he started the only thing he could think of—"Home, Sweet Home." But Trix didn't seem to care for it. He had a musical ear and could keep perfect time while waltzing to the depot band. And Q's voice was making merely awful noise. Somehow the notes refused to come out right. So he had to stop.

The middle of the trestle passed, prospects brightened. Yet Q found things little easier. His arms were played out. Years before he had rowed in a Varsity boat race. Now he felt that he was back there, pelting down the home stretch, with the other boat gaining hand over hand. Meanwhile terrible visions of what was happening to Jean harried him.

And something worse than a vision, worse even than the worst of nightmares, came roaring down on him around a curve—an eastbound harvesters' special unscheduled in the C.P.R. timetables and so totally unexpected by Q till he actually heard it coming. It charged straight at him, howling blue murder and red ruin. Brakes drummed, sparks flew. Then the rocking locomotive struck the handcar, smashing it into excessively small bits and hurling them into the faroff capital of Kingdom Come.

IV.

The cabin now stood without a sign of life or the slightest sound coming from it. There were no voices, no poundings, no crashings to disturb a total, terribly ominous silence. And around it sounded nothing more than the chatter of squirrels and the sigh of the cool mountain wind in nearby pines.

But on the wind came a growing mutter of swiftly

galloping hoofs as Q and Trix dashed up the trail into the cabin's clearing.

Though the special had shattered the handcar, they were not on it. Trix cool as any horse trained to stand field-gun fire, and Q well matching him, they had jumped off the thing just as it reached solid ground at the end of the trestle, a matter of seconds before the locomotive struck it. Better still, Q was back in the saddle and away on Trix before the harvesters gaping at every window of the long train had more than an inkling of why they had come to a halt with a "Down brakes!" flinging them headlong.

Now Q was out of the saddle again and into the cabin.

No one, living or dead, was to be seen there. But the fearful wreckage and confusion made of the place told him that a desperate struggle had ended in Wendall's killing or kidnapping Jean and making good his escape.

Whipped by this horror, Q rushed from room to room in the fastest search he had ever made with or without a search warrant, till he saw a pair of feet sticking out from under Jean's bed.

Jean's comparatively dainty No. 5s! Blind rage and the dim light made them so. Then somehow they turned into huge, dusty, spurred and easily recognized boots on Dave Wendall, dragged out ruthlessly.

"Heard you comin' too late!" gasped the bandit. "Or, blast your guts, I'd sure have made my getaway!"

Roared Q, "Where is she?"

"Right here, Q!" piped what was left of Jean's voice from somewhere in the kitchen.

And what was left of Jean rose shakily from behind the stove.

"He found a broom and tried to jab me with it till I'd file off his handcuffs!" went on the voice. "But I got in here and he couldn't get at me. You see, old Q, I couldn't go back on you and Trix—the partnership—"

"The threesome, you mean!" gulped Q, as he kissed away fast-flowing tears, stove-blacking, soot and all.

lunatic patrol

"Everything's quiet—except the Rev.'s gone crazy!"

Sergeant Mercer groaned as young Constable Tavistock, in charge of his Fort Chipewyan detachment, greeted his return to the little Athabaska settlement with that short, yet vivid summary.

He was tough as his own huskies, a fact he'd taught most of the North through years of doings like those concerned with the murder of Siwash Pratt.* But Tavistock's words foreshadowed his having to take the Rev. David Wentworth, Protestant missionary, five hundred dog-sled miles to hospital, in the year's worst travel season—though he was tired and strung up after a long, hard trip, sick of "lunatic patrols," longing for the settlement's Christmas party.

So he groaned, yet merely asked, "Violent?"

"Not yet. But thinks he's a saint fasting in the wilderness —won't eat, wash, shave or have a haircut—prays, sings and yells day and night— Scared his Indians away, 'cause they guess he's 'gone Wendigo,' to eat them up. Now the Catholic priests and I take turns in his house, looking after him. . ."

Still in his trail outfit, Mercer said, "Let's go over."

They went, through deep silence, great cold, grey noonday and midwinter snows, to the Rev.'s place, between the Hudson's Bay Company post and the Catholic mission.

He barely knew the Rev., who had been transferred to

*See "The Force Can't Fail" in *To Effect An Arrest*.

Fort Chipewyan from Labrador only last summer and had stayed at the fort while he was away on patrols. But even David Wentworth's best friends would not have recognized the hideous figure crouching over a neglected dinner table with boyish, frightened Father Lecroix. The parson's clothes, dog-collar and other symbols of peace, love and respectability were put on so badly that they horribly caricatured themselves. The eyes glaring from a skeleton face ringed by tousled, grizzled hair and beard were soul-less, like an eagle's, while froth dribbled from the twisted lips.

"Too long down North. It's 'got him'!" Mercer said. "I'll have to start with him for Edmonton tomorrow."

Returning his look with a scowl, the Rev. said, "I, Peter, say to you, Judas, 'Get out'!"

"Hullo, Peter," Mercer said, "I'm not Judas, though, I'm Paul, come to take you to Rome."

He sat down at table, helped himself to stew and remarked, "Boy, that's good. Me right off the trail, too, with no dinner. Come on, Peter, dig in!"

The Rev. obeyed, fairly gobbling.

"A miracle!" cried Father Lecroix.

"No," said Tavistock, "a tribute to your cookery—and a lesson to me in handling mental cases. Am I going with you, Sergeant?"

"Who'd run the detachment, with our only other constable sick?"

The meal finished, Mercer took Tavistock back to their quarters, gave him instructions for preparing the patrol's requirements, had a word with Jack Dean, the sick constable, and went to bed. He thought himself facing the trip of his life, as Fort Chipewyan had used up all its sedatives on the Rev. Also, aching head and limbs spoilt his rest.

Big Pierre Gladu, his Indian special, harnessed two dog-trains after breakfast next day. He too suggested a mighty tough patrol ahead, as he looked tired from the one finished yesterday—and scared to travel with a Wendigo who was also something like the white man's God. All the same, he loaded things cheerfully, was the best runner available. And Mercer must trust to luck.

Luck would surely be needed. For the patient had now decided to spend Christmas with his Fort Chipewyan parishioners. He fought Mercer and Tavistock like a cornered wildcat. Fortunately saintly old Father St. Cyr, who had tamed bloodthirsty plains tribes in his day, was there, with Father Lecroix and Jock Maclean, the Hudson's Bay factor. So the patrol, with their help, at last got the Rev. into furs, extra large moccasins, a sleeping-bag and the toboggan, cozily strapped down under rugs.

Pierre, meanwhile, had loaded the second toboggan with the patient's outfit and with appetizers — chocolate, fancy biscuits and the like—donated by the traders and priests to tempt the Rev. out of self-starvation. So all was ready.

"Save me some scotch from the party!" said Mercer.

"So long!" said Tavistock.

"Pax vobiscum!" said Father St. Cyr.

"Lead me in the right way because of mine enemies!" said the Rev.

"Mush!" said Pierre.

And the patrol started, to the sound of whip-crackings, the wind's cruel piping and the voices of the priests as they knelt in the snow and prayed for this poor afflicted soul.

Prayers were needed even more than luck. The Rev. gave no trouble; exhausted by his struggles, he slept like an uncouth baby. But at 20 below, the gentle breeze blowing over frozen Lake Athabaska worried men and dogs as soon as they cleared the islands near the settlement, and rough ice meant terribly hard hauling through the whole four-mile crossing.

Then the Rev. made up for lost time as soon as the patrol had settled into its night-camp on Fallen Timber Creek. He refused to take his arms from the bag to feed himself, spat out the beans, sent the soup flying — and grabbed

Pierre's rifle, carefully placed (as Pierre thought) out of his reach. He may have downed two gulps of grub but not more.

And then he brought in Rosie—"the Rose of Sharon, the Lily of the Valleys, fair as the moon, clear as the sun" and so on, endlessly. All in the sub-Arctic night's work, of course, to veterans of loony patrols who knew that even clergymen might rave about some woman and give in to her wiles, but tough on trail-weary, aching tent-mates kept awake by it for hours after bedtime. Particularly as this unknown she would probably keep them company all the way to Edmonton—

Besides, a sleepless night was hardly sound preparation for a miserable march next day, its worst stage six miles along Embarras River ice, deep-flooded under snow, to the patrol's first camp on a mightier stream, the Athabaska. For floods spelt soaking clothes for the two keepers, toboggans to be repeatedly cleansed of clinging snow—and terror for the Rev., who took the swirls of water-smoke for an army of damned souls escorting him to the hereafter. "Embarrassed I sure am!" grinned Mercer, through chattering teeth, his pun dear to every traveller using that river. Also he knew too well that bad colds and frost-bites usually followed the cold baths it gave them.

To prevent such troubles, he and Pierre built a huge fire and paraded almost in its flames, warming their naked bodies. Bone-dry, the Rev., still in his bag, stared at the muscular pair and insanely chuckled, "Glad Rosie can't see you! A modest flower, my daughter—" "Your daughter? That's good news, anyhow!" said Mercer, chucking a chest. Another good thing: the Rev. ate a fair supper.

Once started on Rosie, though, there seemed to be no stopping him. At last, long after bedtime, Mercer, goaded nearly to the limit, growled, "I wish your Rose—or wife, if any—was nursing you, instead of coddling some damned fool in civilization." "Wife's dead," the Rev. replied, quite rationally. "As for coddling some fool, Rosie's not married."

The dogs began acting strangely next day, as if to freeze blood already chilled by bitterly cold weather. For the first two miles they steadily followed Pierre as he broke trail through deep snow along the Athabaska. Then both teams suddenly stopped, growling, pricking their ears and staring ahead, hair on end with rage or fear. They howled like the Rev. at his worst and galloped on as fast as the drifts allowed them. Before they could be halted they had passed the neighbouring islands, and the men at last heard the sounds disturbing them: shouts, the barks of other dogs, and the chop, chop, chop of axes, rising, apparently, on the ice just ahead, though not a tent nor a whiff of smoke could be seen in the brilliant sunshine. . .

Surely these sounds came from a camp of ghosts or devils!

The Rev. thought so, anyway. He made desperate efforts to get out of his bag and repeatedly screamed:

"O Lord, make haste to help me! Rosie, help!"

Mingling with those ghostly sounds, his yells made the dogs still more uneasy, frightened big, boyish Pierre and even sent cold prickles along Mercer's spine. But he pulled himself together, ordered, "Mush on!"

They mushed, though the sounds grew more terrifying and louder than ever, coming from all sides as they echoed among more islands and the patrol approached Point Brulé. With them, of course, the poor Rev.'s ravings also became louder and more horrible—so much so that as the dog-trains drew near the true source of his fright—the Indian camp on the point—all the alarming noises stopped, for the campers, dreading madness, ran away into the bush.

Mercer took the situation in his stride, nooning at the camp as he had planned, then pushing on to his night-halt at Poplar Point. But here too the Indians fled from the Rev.'s ravings, so the over-worked patrol got none of the help it hoped for, the Rev. ate little and the keepers were again kept awake for hours. The Rev. and his daughter — the "Cedar of Lebanon," with "doves' eyes" and "breasts like two young roes"—upset things enough. But cold threatening pneumonia was there too.

Then phantom-men and phantom-dogs made next morning's march more terrible than the last. For these were also on the march, moving steadily towards the patrol with whip-crackings and shoutings from an invisible source apparently not far ahead. Later a three-train phantom actually appeared, yet for a long time got no nearer. The effect on the Rev., his guardians and their dogs was naturally just as before.

At last the three-train ghosts turned into Hudson's Bay men and dogs travelling from Edmonton to the Mackenzie trading-posts. Mercer longed to noon with them, for a change, but they scared the Rev. so much that he had to leave with no more than a bundle of newspapers they gave him for campfire reading and assurances that they had saved him trail-breaking till the next heavy snowfall.

Yet the parting did not lay the other ghosts, far from it. They took to firing rifles, all around the patrol, while slyly hiding in the woods along the river. They whispered terrifying messages, laughed mockingly, kept up with the march by rustling scampers through the bush. "It's Satan and his legions," shrieked the Rev. "My adversary the Devil, who walketh about like a roaring lion, seeking whom he may shoot and devour!" Nor did the night-halt bring relief—it had to be made beside those echoing, murmuring woods, which at times half-convinced Mercer himself that the Rev.'s ideas were right.

Especially as the Devil suddenly looked out from bushes only twenty yards off the trail as they plodded on next day. . . . The Rev. howled, Pierre bolted and Mercer whipped his rifle from his back, then out of its buckskin case and shot the apparition right between the eyes. A young caribou with horns only ten inches long, it certainly did resemble Satan . . . and in death relieved the tension. Pierre laughed like a great big kid, getting more fun out of the affair than Mercer himself. "Sure, sure," he agreed, "devil-guns just cold trees cracking, devil-talk just wind in bush, devils running moose or caribou!" "And all those other things just freaks of Nature!" added Mercer.

Also the Rev. really enjoyed their fine caribou-steak supper. And afterwards he talked so sensibly about "My Rosie—how I wish she could see us!" that Mercer even hoped for a peaceful night. No such luck . . . instead he suffered muscular pains, fever, lung-congestion and unaccountable nightmares about demons led by a Rosie with horns and tail, her lovely face distorted in a horrible grin.

Masses of such demons flew past him overhead, wailing, threatening to pounce, reviving Pierre's fear and throwing the Rev. back into convulsions throughout the following march. Tired and jumpy from broken rest and sheer hard work, he could hardly bring himself to realize that those enemies were just black cloud-banks driven by a wailing, strong North wind. Later the Rev. terrified the half-breeds, Chipewyans and Crees camped around the day's objective, Fort McKay. Bob Meredith, the Hudson's Bay trader, calmed this dread, so that the half-breeds, crossing themselves, helped the patrol to feed its teams, though Bob said:

"I wouldn't do your job for all the furs in Canada!", adding, "Why not lie over here for Christmas? It's just three days away—"

"Christmas!" coughed Mercer. "I'd forgotten it. No thanks, I'll try to spend that day at Fort McMurray. But we'll share your roof tonight, if you can stand it. . ."

Stand it Bob did—a severe test, with the Rev. throwing his supper every which way and carrying on for hours about "the Rose of Sharon." Luckily, his keepers, played out, slept through most of this performance and Mercer, though racked with coughing, had no dreams.

Morning showed him his southward trail almost smothered under last night's snowfall. "Sure you won't lie over?" Bob asked. "Well, it's your funeral!" Certainly the pace that day was funereal, thanks to more trail-breaking on snowshoes. So was the scenery, with grim, impressive natural ramparts rising on both sides of the river to rake those never-ending clouds.

"The Gates of Hell!" screamed the Rev., at sight of them. "For God's sake, boys, turn back!"

Instead Mercer went on, being already in that frozen Hell he'd read about somewhere, yet burning (to get out of it). So, naturally, the Rev. went on screaming, the more so as devils in hordes began howling a welcome from the gloomy depths beyond. In spite of them the uneasy patrol kept going till darkness called a halt with only twenty miles covered today but next thing to a certainty—thank God— of reaching McMurray tomorrow.

Now the howling devils—or wolves—closed in on the new night-camp. Long green eyes dimly flaming in shadowy forms prowled constantly around it, dreary yelps and keen-ings offered it a constant, threatening serenade. As the smell of supper grub—or of three defenceless souls—might tempt a rush, Mercer told Pierre, "We'll scare 'em off with a big fire kept up all night." Still, the dogs raised a terrific row, defying the fiendish shapes, Pierre muttered, "I no like it, me!" and the Rev., utterly convinced that he was really lost in Hell, screamed again, through the baying:

"O Lord, make haste to help me! Rosie, help!"

The hairy raving madman in his bag, the shaken Indian and the clamouring dogs, all blood-red in the fire-glow, with the green eyes and the keenings so near them in the lonely, vast, black night, made Mercer think that this was his hardest patrol. Worse, it strengthened his notion that the Rev. could just be right. So, for the first time in years of Northern service, he too tasted sweating, stinking fear.

Suddenly, now, he found himself staring at a metal tower and, flogging his tired brain, recognized it as a sign of civilization, a derrick used in drilling for oil. Clearly he had broken camp and left those yelping fiends or wolves behind him hours ago. How, though, had he so quickly escaped the wilderness? Then he understood: this derrick was only civilization's pioneer, symbolizing man's first effort to tap the Athabaska's mineral riches—and closed down for the winter.

With laughter so strained that Pierre stared anxiously at him from behind the toboggan on which the Rev. now slept, worn out, he yelled:

"I'm Wendigo too! I know this place, just six miles from McMurray! *Mush!*"

In no time, now, they made the friendly trading-post, perched high above the junction of the Athabaska and the Clearwater, a bit of heaven only sixty-odd miles short of the half-way point to Edmonton. And Alex Ramsay, the Hudson's Bay man, Mercer's hearty friend, came roaring: "Welcome, Santa!", then gasped, "Is that loon Dave Wentworth? . . . Why didn't you wait to bring him out by steamer and York boat next summer?" "It was now or never, Alex, boy!" "Well, by the look of you, it'll soon be never, anyway. But see here, we'll feed your dogs, unload your toboggans, you'll lay over here tomorrow, Christmas Day, and we'll put things right or bust!"

The post did its best to keep that promise. After huge slugs of whisky all round, Alex and his assistants, Dick Sloane and Pat Lafferty, joined the patrol in giving the Rev. his first bath, haircut and shave in weeks. He fought them furiously but later ate a good supper and afterwards slept so soundly, without a word to Rosie, that his keepers were also able to clean up and follow his example, with reasonable prospects of improvement in the twenty-four hours of rest ahead.

Alex, next day, served a marvellous Christmas dinner, featuring a huge turkey brought down from Edmonton last August, carefully fattened since, and washed down with plenty of liquor. So Peace on Earth entered even that lonely cabin in the wilderness—till the Rev. broke it.

The coloured-paper decorations rang a Christmas bell in his muddled head and revived a determination to go back to his Fort Chipewyan parishioners and see them through this holy season. More, he was going to hit the trail northward right now if it killed him. His desperate arguments and struggles threatened to do exactly that, though at last he quit, exhausted, and was left to cool off in his bag and Alex's bedroom, with the door shut.

Cool off he did, but near midnight his luckier friends, all smoking, drinking and yarning around the stove, suddenly heard hoarse and unearthly singing:

> While shepherds watch'd their flocks by night,
> All seated on the ground,
> The Angel of the Lord came down,
> And glory shone around. . .

As verse after verse of the old hymn came rolling out of the darkness beyond the stove, Mercer's cheerfulness melted before a horrible realization of the ordeal still before him and more of that sweating, stinking fear, while Alex actually shivered as he said, against the squawling background:

"God save us, not even a policeman can stand that for another month on the trail! Wait here till he's better—or, sure as Fate, he'll finish you."

"Not on your life!" said Mercer, still tough as his own huskies—maybe, "Besides, he must have treatment as soon as possible or he won't get over it."

Tossing off his drink, smiling and squeezing Mercer's broad shoulders, Alex said, "Duty first—that's you and your whole Force. But," he prayed, "sweet Jesus, stop that awful noise! Now, see here, friend, Pat's going back to our new sub-post twenty miles up the Clearwater, so he might as well leave here with you tomorrow and see you off the river."

Mercer said, "I'll certainly appreciate that," and meant it, knowing that the Clearwater stage was the hardest of the trip.

He launched the patrol into it, with Pat, a half-breed and their own dog-train, early next morning. As the exercise would help the Rev., the traders walked him on a lead.

Otherwise progress would have been almost impossible. Cold and deep snow, even on the wide, well-frozen river, forced the men to join the dogs in the hardest hauls and often to rest them. Then fallen timber on four portages so cluttered those essential short cuts that the teams had to be unharnessed, while the gasping, sweating men strained powerful muscles to carry the toboggans bodily over the worst obstacles. Fourteen hours were needed to cover the twenty miles to the sub-post, that day's goal, the last stage plodding through darkness.

The Rev. had a ravenous appetite and slept well, thanks to his walk, but Mercer felt too sick to eat much of Pat's fine supper, his cough troubled him, his pains returned and with them came more awful dreams of a devilish Rosie. Pierre too seemed to gain little from sheltering that night in Pat's cabin.

While more cold and deep snow, with gusty winds heralding a blizzard, troubled all next day, its worst part was the desperate mile-long struggle through huge drifts up a steep bank maddeningly encumbered by large spruce, tamarack, birch and poplar, to get off the river. Like big, quiet Pierre and the half-breed, Mercer pulled with the dogs till sweat poured down his straining body, his heart drummed like a crazy partridge and mists blotted out the world. Slips, falls and toboggans fouled by trees or turning over doubled the work. In the meantime, the Rev. merely strolled along behind under Pat's escort, chanting gladly about this delivery from Hell and his wish that those do⟨...⟩ves could see him, till Mercer cursed and beat the wretc⟨...⟩ m as he never did normally.

The patrol collapsed from exhaustion at the top of the slope. Reviving first, Mercer built a small fire, made tea and rustled a scratch meal, so that Pat's outfit could turn back for the sub-post with something in their bellies and the rest find strength for the day's last effort, to the Swan Lake fish-cache. Though the cache lay only eighteen miles from Pat's cabin, it was not sighted till nearly dark. Mercer, by then, would gladly have sold his soul to the devils chasing them if only they would take the Rev. off his hands or let him hole up like a bear for the rest of the winter. But with the blizzard's white vanguard already swirling around the cache, screaming its war-cries, he dared not quit work till, with Pierre, he had prepared defences against it.

As the tent could not be pitched—the storm would batter it down and tear it to shreds—he used it to roof a burrow hastily dug in the snow under the lee of the cache. In the burrow he laid the sleeping-bags, side by side, with the Rev. snug in the middle, tethering them to trees. At their feet he made a fire, with tea, biscuits, utensils and wood beside it. He placed a lighted hurricane-lantern next his own bag, within easy reach. The dogs he tied in the lee of the toboggans, which he put on edge and banked with snow.

He had barely followed this work with an apology for supper when the blizzard began attacking. It was blowing full blast well before midnight. For sixty hours, off and on, it made charge after shrieking, roaring, wailing charge, drove huge waves across the sea of forest, smashing and crashing among the trees, tearing them limb from limb or hurling them flat, in desperate efforts to reach its prey, then at last faded away over forest, lake and muskeg — till next time (all too soon). At the peak of its assaults, particularly of those raging in utter darkness, with cold, sickness, hunger, thirst and terrible responsibilities supporting them, Mercer felt that not only was he besieged in this vast appalling Hell by demons but that, as Alex had said, the trip really might "finish" him.

Though toughness, skill and luck had served him on many other Northern journeys, this might well be his last patrol.

Yet in the lulls, when he rallied bone-weary, aching body and soul to take turns with Pierre in feeding fire, men and dogs, he somehow felt differently. He neither knew nor cared why a man tough as his own huskies should gradually become softer. The fact remained that as the strangely quiet Rev. took grub from him with babyish confidence, really personal interest in his patient grew up in him. Later, even, as the poor wretch went obediently to sleep, muttering, "Rose, my darling, if only you could see me," true pity, with determination to unite this pair—and see the girl himself—at any cost, became his chief emotion.

The storm passed—leaving new troubles behind it. Two dogs, still worn out by the frightful haul up from the Clearwater and now disabled by frost-bite, required replacement. And Pierre, looking as sick as the dogs, muttered over breakfast:

"Me quit right now, Sergeant, go back Chipewyan. Me finished."

Mercer had seen this rebellion coming for days and knew that Pierre meant it. So, making another effort to rise above utter weariness, he tried to handle it without mistakes that could land him neck-deep in disaster.

"If you quit," he said, "you lose your pay. Then, what'll Chipewyan think if you desert a man as tired as you are— *and* a loony? They'll call you yellow. You could find yourself behind bars too, if we go down through you."

For an hour he drove his tired brain and strained patience to carry on this exercise in Force diplomacy, till Pierre growled:

"O.K., I come to Jackfish Lake. You get nudder Indian there."

While Jackfish Lake was merely tonight's objective, Mercer had no choice but to accept this and march on in suspense.

He marched, the patrol carrying a load of fish from the cache, to be paid for at that objective, the Rev. on a lead tied to the second toboggan. As intense cold still cut to the bone and trail-breaking through the drifts left by the blizzard became harder than ever, the failing men and dogs moved ever more slowly, with glare from the white snow torturing them. So the sun was a burning wigwam among the trees before the tiny half-breed settlement on the lake offered sorely needed rest and shelter.

The Rev.'s behaving well and eating a good supper made the people forget the Wendigo and practically take over all the work there. One man even volunteered:

"Mush with you to Edmonton."

Pierre snapped, "Mush to blazes!"

That ended Mercer's fear of his special's desertion. Prompt, generous payment for the fish from the cache made it easy to get two strong, fresh dogs for his sick ones. It also helped arrangements for picking up supplies here on his return trip to Fort Chipewyan.

So the twelve-mile march to Whitefish Lake next day seemed nothing, in spite of bitter cold and a heavy snowfall.

Snug for that night among kindly Chipewyan, he had a shock. His faithfully-kept diary ran out.

"How not to see the New Year in," he told himself, "Alone with a few bush Indians—and no liquor!"

He lay over next day, when the settlement nobly produced a roast of moose and an amazing gift of home-grown potatoes. Only the Rev. did the feast justice. Never mind, Mercer's cut, frost-bitten, swollen hand ironically entered in his new diary:

"Happy New Year!"

On next day's march a strong wind raged over comparatively open country burnt out by Indians to make a moose range, and his thermometer that night registered 60 below, the worst cold so far. But the Rev. favourably reacted to big fires and glorious Northern Lights.

"O Rose of Sharon and Lily of the Valleys, I'm still in Hell," he said, solemnly bowing to the flames, "No matter," bowing to the Lights, "a great multitude of the Heavenly Host is guarding me, even if you can't see it, so I'm safe!"

Yet the day's sufferings, wakefulness required in taking turns to maintain the fires and this relapse into insanity had Mercer wondering if he could stand much more.

In spite of it the steadily weakening patrol made Little

Jackfish Lake, where God-turned-Wendigo behaved so badly that the Indians would not come near him and Mercer decided that he must ride the toboggan in a bag again, at least through tomorrow.

That march brought in a four-day trudge through largely burnt-out woods and over muskeg to Heart Lake, head of the last leg but one to Edmonton. And through those four days, praise be, Nature proved merciful. Only, the devils were back—scuttling through tamarack and poplar, whispering in breeze-swept bushes and sometimes wheeling across the trail, disguised as crows, yet chilling the blood.

They set the Rev. yelling so much to get out of his bag that at last Mercer, for the sake of that unknown Rosie and his own peace of mind, returned him to the lead. This calmed him enough to eat well and talk sense of a sort at one noon-halt.

Standing straight, tall and very much the parson, he gravely addressed a huge congregation of trees:

"As our choir is not with us today, we will now read the 23rd Psalm."

And read it he did—or recited it, every word:

"The Lord is my shepherd, therefore can I lack nothing . . . Yea, though I walk through the valley of the shadow of death, I will fear no evil, for thou art with me . . . But thy loving-kindness and mercy shall follow me all the days of my life; and I will dwell in the house of the Lord for ever."

Strangely, the trees and even the devils seemed to listen, for the poor Rev.'s voice went strongly on in utter silence, while Mercer felt the ice in his heart melt just a bit more.

This growing softness, with the fearful fatigue and sickness now clouding his mind and draining his body, soon cost him dear. Next morning he was changing the Rev.'s moccasins before marching off when a tremendous crash in the bush made him jump, threw Pierre off-balance over a toboggan, hurled its team into a terrific fight and scared the wits (or what was left of them) out of the Rev., who yelled, "It's Satan!", grabbed an axe and was off down the trail in a flash. Not only that but it was a misty morning and with a dozen strides at top-speed he vanished in the mist completely.

Wasting no time on the cause of the crash—the fall of a tree uprooted by the recent blizzard, a running moose, or, as the Rev. said, Satan—Mercer left Pierre to stop that dog-fight and pounded away in pursuit. His heart, drumming like an even crazier partridge, sank into his moccasins as he realized that if his patient took to the bush in this mist he might well be lost for ever and all the patrol's devotion, agony and effort be thrown away. His frozen breath, steaming down wind, roared out at a rate grimly betraying his weakness. His wobbling legs, moving, as it seemed, so slowly, confirmed his fear that the Rev. was much too fast for him. His eyes, seeing only vague shadows in the mist, his ears, straining to catch a hopeful sound but deafened by the roar of his own blood, brought him no sign of success.

At last, so far from camp that the noise of the dog-fight had faded into the white silence, he dropped onto a rock, exhausted. Once he felt up to it, he started shouting:

"Mr. Wentworth! David! Rev.! Come back!"

No use—the mist deadened his calls and not even an echo answered him. This was terrible! Somehow he must flog some plan of action out of that weary brain. Suddenly, thank God again, he got it—a thing so simple that, at any other time, it must have flashed up immediately. Track the man, you fool, track him! Almost at once, he picked up prints of those swift feet, followed them easily through crushed bushes and heard at last a terrible, triumphant screech:

"Saul has slain his thousands but David Wentworth his ten thousands! Get thee behind me, Satan!"

Then out bounded the Rev., eyes flaming with rage and fear, axe raised to kill him.

Blow after furious blow flashed around him, many so close that he heard them whistle, others so close that they brushed his parka. Dodging for dear life, he tripped over a fallen tree, while Death leaped at him with axe swung high but also tumbled in the last split-second. With a desperate effort he clung to consciousness, now threatened by near-collapse, rolled clear of the fallen Rev. and struggled to regain his feet and grab that terrible axe. No use! Made quick beyond belief by mania, the madman sprang out of his reach. The blade flashed back once more. Floundering, he threw himself for shelter behind a poplar.

At that critical moment God in His mercy entangled the up-raised axe in another young poplar. While the Rev. yanked at it and Mercer tried his best to recover his balance, the watching sun seemed to stand still. Another moment and he struck the Rev. with a terrific flying tackle. Not even Goliath, let alone David Wentworth, could have resisted it. The axe whirled away into this snowdrift, the men into that . . . and into a weaponless fight as primitive as it was deadly.

When trees and snow and sky stopped spinning, Mercer found the Rev. crushing him in a bearlike hug to be broken only by one particular trick of unarmed combat.

He tried with all his fading strength and all his determination to apply it. But furs and the Rev.'s maniacal grip seriously hampered him. Flames blinded him, thunder roared in his ears, sweat drenched him, blood gushed from his nose and mouth and dripped into the snow, where it mingled with blood from the Rev.'s bare feet. Their panting, crashing battle in the bushes broke the intense silence of the wilderness with what he thought was uproar. Feeling that the Rev. would very soon squeeze his soul out and accepting that, as Pierre was busy with the dogs, he must see this crisis through alone, he put all he had left into a final immense effort, got nowhere with it—

Then suddenly felt the Rev. go limp, unconscious.

He too must have fainted, for a minute or so, as his next clear picture was of his fairly-well-recovered self clinging to a tree and staring down at a Rev. now ominously still. Not dead, though— a hurried examination reassured him.

What next? Well, first he must bind the man, to guard against the possible, if unlikely, chance of another outbreak. Having no cords with him, he stripped off his parka and put it on the Rev. with sleeves still empty, as if it were a strait-jacket. Those bare feet were freezing, so he rubbed them with snow till they seemed better, then put them in his own moccasins. By this time he was so bitterly cold himself that he shivered convulsively. Now find the all-essential axe and get back to camp! If only Pierre would bring up a dog-train! Pierre did not come. So his only course was to walk back with the unconscious Rev. in his arms and the axe encumbering him.

Time and again he fell or had to rest, twice he was violently sick. Yet he managed that walk—a full quarter of a mile. Subconsciously making up a reference to it for his diary and report, he produced: "I am a pretty strong man but in the wind and numbing cold it was really a difficult job. . . ." Then, finally staggering to his goal, he saw the terrible reason why Pierre had not joined him. The dog-fight had been so ferocious that two dogs had been killed, another so bady injured that the Indian had stayed with it to staunch its wounds and save its life.

This setback might have been fatal to the patrol if it had not been near Hart River. Even so, coming on top of all his other handicaps, it almost broke Mercer.

He redistributed the fit dogs to make trains of four and three. He reduced the loads by caching everything he could spare, with the idea of recovering the cache on his return trip to Fort Chipewyan. He changed his wet underclothes and socks, noting that his feet, like the Rev.'s, were frost-bitten, dressed for the trail, prepared tea and biscuits, gulped down what he could and struck camp. Then, with the Rev. still asleep in his bag on the first toboggan, the injured dog and the gear on the second, he mushed on with Pierre into the mist.

That night he slept dreamlessly, from exhaustion, though

the Rev. and Rosie talked all night beside him on the thread-bare theme of seeing each other. And Macfarlane, the Hudson's Bay man at Hart River, did all mortal man could do when he trudged into the place next evening—took over the injured dog, lent him three others and replacements for the cached outfit, arranged supplies for his return march, cared for the Rev., put up the entire patrol. Yet he could barely talk sense now, frame plans or take soup without spilling it. His feet burned, his cough racked him, his night-mares returned in full force.

It was as if all his strength was being sucked out of him by the Rev., who again ate heartily and behaved well.

Still, he, Sergeant Mercer, tough as his own huskies, would see the job through, come what may, as with any sort of luck it now involved only two more days of dog-train travel. Shutting his sore eyes to Jimmy Macfarlane's anxious looks he hit the trail again for those two long marches, with the Rev. again exercising on a lead and the devils in the nearby woods steadily keeping pace beside the patrol as it struggled on, first through that persistent mist, then through a last snowfall, to Lac la Biche.

At this—the front-porch to Civilization and quite a little settlement—he hired a horse-drawn sleigh and driver for the closing stage of his journey, arranged for a thankful Pierre to lie over till he came back and could have got men to relieve him of his patient—if he hadn't been too tired and stupid to arrange it and too damned conscientious anyhow. Here too he might have rested a few days but the Rev., learning that Edmonton and Rosie were not far off, suddenly went wild with excitement and made pushing on as urgent as before.

So on he went, with really nothing to do, now, except watch and nurse the Rev., listen to incessant praise of those "doves' eyes" and dimly long to meet them and have done with it. Sergeant Beverly, at Saddle Lake detachment, sheltering his party on the second night out from Lac la Biche, told him bluntly, "You look about a hundred—and all

in! I'll take your man the rest of the way." Brushing aside
the offer—and a similar one from Andrew detachment next
morning—he endured another night of fearful dreams at a
roadhouse and drove into Fort Saskatchewan just as its
trumpeter sounded "First Post" through the twilight of next
day.

Edmonton hospital lay only twenty miles to westward and
he would have delivered the Rev. there right away if
fatherly old Superintendent Finch, commanding at the fort,
hadn't said, "No, Journey's End and bed for you right here,
my boy! We'll carry on your job!" He tried to answer this
with "Then I won't see Rosie!" but the right words refused
to come. And anyhow Finch was calling him something like
"a hero" and ordering him into the care of the sergeant-
major for a full week's rest. So he got shut of the Rev. and
turned in without satisfying his curiosity after all.

The idea of going into Edmonton to make the necessary
contacts unofficially occurred to him—uselessly, as he learnt
at the hospital, when he called there on the following day,
that the Rev., with Rosie in his escort, had already been
packed off to Brandon's insane asylum, nine hundred miles
away by train. O.K., to hell with it! He was Sergeant
Mercer, too tough (and old) for that stuff—and going back
to Fort Chipewyan in no time, besides!

He bluffed Finch, the post surgeon and everybody else
that he was really fit, though he still had many awful dreams
and his feet were still sore. Then he started back. But at
Saddle Lake he met something bad enough to scare the
gizzard out of the toughest guy that ever cracked a dog-
whip.

Tall, broad, friendly Sergeant Beverly in his scarlet coat
turned suddenly into a huge red devil, Satan himself, all
grins and snarls, reached out great claws and seized him. . . .

Satan Beverly dragged him into the very bottom of Hell—
following the Rev., apparently, to Brandon. There Time
ceased to be, yet became an endless jumble of nights and

days ridden by rage and terror, while countless demons in white uniforms, all strange men or Rosies, fought with him, stuck things into him and forcibly fed him, while other poor damned souls like himself shrieked and yelled for mercy. Then, somehow, Hell faded away, giving place to Force headquarters in Regina, and July, and he was back in uniform, standing shakily at attention before the Commissioner himself.

Also, the Commissioner was waving him to a chair and making quite a little speech:

"You've had a very nasty illness, Sergeant, and a long, long day down North—a great day too. So from now on I want you here in comfort, for a change. You could even go to pension, if you like—it comes to all of us, you know, as the years go by. Very well, I understand! We'll leave you in Regina, training—and inspiring—recruits! Now, thanks for that very fine patrol. No, don't get up. I'm going—but you sit right there, because some friends are here to thank you too."

Of course he might have guessed it: the friends who came in as the Commissioner went out were the Rev.—and Rosie—

He barely recognized the Rev., looking stronger, better, yes, and far younger than he did himself, barely heard even snatches of the Rev.'s remarks: "Completely cured—just lost a toe—I've a new church, in Winnipeg—I owe it all to you— And this is Rosie!" For, as the Rev. talked on, he found himself really staring at the girl, because she really was "fair as the moon, clear as the sun," and more.

At sight of them, smiling so happily together, he knew that his last lunatic patrol had been thoroughly worth while. Yet a lump rose in his throat, confirming that he wasn't really as tough as his own huskies, after all. For he also knew, now, why the Rev. had raved so about "doves' eyes" and wishing she could see him. At the same time, he grasped why she'd not been North, looking after her old Dad.

The girl was blind.

the missing link

Riding slowly back to his one-man detachment in the little prairie town of Saddle River, Constable Chick MacLean, a tired, dusty man on a tired, dusty horse, had no thought for the Bad Bill man-hunt, which he had just helped to end successfully, none for similar adventures liable to pounce on him at any time, and none for an Eternal Triangle.

He was thinking of an Infernal Rectangle (much worse) involving himself, Dashing Danny Dale ("*The* General Store"), Miss Nellie Seacombe (Saddle River schoolteacher) and Johnny Crimp, aged ten, alias Johnny Chimp alias the Idaho Kid alias Wandering Spirit alias Robin Hood alias Dick Turpin alias any reckless outlaw in and out of books.

If Dashing Danny upset Chick's relations with Nellie, Johnny Chimp, "that perfect little monkey," was in a fair way to ruining them altogether.

No two ways about it, Chick would rather hunt Bad Bill a second time or join the escort now taking that ruthless murderer to trial than cope with Johnny. For Johnny was the Scourge of Saddle River. He could blunder into more trouble in less time than any youngster between Winnipeg and the Rockies: always trouble with a funny side to it, but always trouble with a great big T, and always with Miss Seacombe intervening in the end to save him from Law and Order, namely Chick.

Take, for instance, the Case of the Burning Barn. One fine day, soon after Chick's posting to Saddle River, a buckboard had come tearing up to the detachment on the dead jump, its driver Old Man Saunders, red as a turkey-cock, mad as a hornet, its passenger skinny, cheeky, sharp-eyed, tousle-headed, barefoot Johnny Chimp. Leaping out to meet this urgent call, Chick asked:

"What's up?"

Beside himself with rage, the turkey-cock just gobbled.

"Cool down, Mr. Saunders," Chick urged, "Is it homicide —suicide—grand larceny—?"

At last Old Man Saunders managed to roar:

"This damned little devil," shaking Johnny till the tousle-head nearly flew off, "This hound of hell—this—this—well, never mind that! Whatever he is, he's just burnt down my barn!"

"Burnt—down—your—barn?"

"Are you deaf?" bellowed Old Man Saunders. "That's what I said—just burnt down my barn!"

"With a candle!" grinned Johnny.

"Not a word!" from Chick. "Better make no statement till you've seen your lawyer. Now, Mr. Saunders, tell me the whole story, slowly, step by step. Then we can decide if you want to lay a charge and if so what. Arson's a serious offence, can send a man up to the pen for years!"

"How many?" asked Johnny, impressed.

Old Man Saunders, ignoring him for the moment, snarled, "I see this kid sneaking into my barn. And the next thing I know the whole place bursts into flames."

"It was the hay," Johnny explained.

"Don't interrupt!" Chick said. "What did you do, Mr. Saunders?"

"Well, as luck would have it," said the complainant, cooling off, "my boy Jake, Ted, the hired man, were there with me, we'd buckets handy and the horse-trough was full. So we put the fire out."

"Then the barn didn't burn down, after all?"

"Not exactly. But, by gum, it could have. And I'd have lost quite a sum if I hadn't been covered by insurance."

"Which company?" asked Johnny. "I hear the Providential is the best—"

Though now quite cool, Old Man Saunders had to be restrained by Chick from giving the inquirer a clout on the ear-hole.

He said grimly, "I want this kid punished!"

"Aw, Mr. Saunders," this kid said, "it was an accident. You see, I was Robin Hood, in Nottingham Castle, unknown to the Sheriff of Nottingham, the wickedest sheriff in the world—that's you. And I had to signal Will Scarlet—that's Jimmy Neal—by showing a light at an arrow-slit. And I only just lit just that one candle—"

Johnny Chimp, of course, was very much a minor. Mrs. Chimp or Crimp was a lone widow woman who had to take in washing and couldn't pay a fine or a red cent in compensation. Miss Seacombe came forward. And Miss Seacombe, a pretty little redhead full of fun, stubborn as a mule, yet brave as a grizzly in defending her pupil-cubs, could hold even big red-coats like Chick under her thumb. So in the end Johnny got away with it—or with a good talking to from Nellie, Chick and Old Man Saunders. Which satisfied everybody, except the insurance company, till the next burst of trouble.

This was the Case of the Indian Scalp Dance. On another fine day, very soon after Robin Hood set fire to Nottingham Castle, another buckboard came thundering up to the detachment. The driver, this time, was Mrs. Knowles, wife of Nosey Knowles, who farmed just outside Saddle River and had nine children, including Frank, aged eight, and Freda and Leda, heavenly twins aged seven. In her fine, large, bossy style, Mrs. Knowles whipped Chick away from a mountain of files and forms by shouting, "Hi, come here!" then reported:

"All the kids in town are going crazy in my pasture. I want it stopped."

Chick jumped into the buckboard and said, "Drive!"

His homely yet "nice" face (as Miss Nellie Seacombe called it) was red with vexation and anxiety.

They drove—like Jehu or Ben Hur or the Devil—and when they reached their goal Chick all but fell out of the buckboard at the sight that met his dust-filled eyes.

In the pasture about thirty Cree warriors and squaws, averaging eight years old, really were "going crazy," or pretty near it. All paint and chicken-feathers, bows, arrows, sling-shots, air-guns, cap-pistols, yes, armed to the teeth—or to such milk teeth as remained among the little ones—they were dancing solemnly around in single file and a big circle, chanting "hi-yah, hi-yah, hi-yah, hi-yah . . ." and sometimes shrieking war-whoops. Nothing much wrong with that, Chick thought, a very creditable imitation of the real thing and damn Mrs. Nosey Knowles! Then he saw that all the squaws had been scalped and all the scalps, golden, carrots, black and mousey, were dangling at the belts of the shuffling warriors.

At the same time the Crees saw Chick and, true to tradition, instantly stopped fooling out of respect for the Mounted Police.

Now really taking things in, Mrs. Nosey let loose a yell fit for Sitting Bull but quite unworthy of her usual calm, stern self, whirled into the circle and gathered her ill-used twins to her ample bosom.

"My babies, my darlings," she cried, "What have they done to you?"

"Scalped the both of us," said Freda happily.

"Yup, the both of us!" Leda confirmed.

Chick, looking again, saw the full truth. It was bad enough but not so bad as what it had seemed originally, an outrage unprovided for even by the Criminal Code.

The assembled squaws had not been actually scalped. Their locks had been merely shorn off—painlessly, as they obviously loved it.

Through the now deathly silence and the motherly noises of Mrs. Nosey, Chick demanded:

"Who's responsible for this?"

No need to ask that silly question! Wandering Spirit Johnny was obviously the chief of the band. Besides, his bristling armament included his mother's largest scissors.

"How! And ugh!" said Wandering Spirit, raising his right hand in the traditional salute. "Red-coat, it's me. I have spoken."

"Stop that!" Chick said, his gorge rising. "What have you to say for yourself, this time?"

The hush, if possible, deepened, though broad grins still shone on most of the streaked and dirty little faces. Through it Wandering Spirit said:

"Well, you see, Mr. MacLean, we wanted to have a Sun Dance—or Thirst Dance, as it's called among the Crees. 'Cause we were short of warriors, had to 'nitiate some more, you know, through the ordeal by torture. Stick skewers into 'em, then tie buffalo skulls to the skewers and make 'em dance till the skewers came out or they fainted dead away from loss of blood! But we couldn't find any buffalo skulls, I guess they've all been cleared away. And the Great Council decided cattle skulls won't do. And anyhow we didn't really want to hurt anybody!"

"Thank God for that!" cried Mrs. Nosey. "Go on!" said Chick.

His tone suggested that Wandering Spirit was to be hanged at dawn.

"Well, then we thought we'd have a Scalp Dance instead. And you can't have a Scalp Dance without scalps. And so— and so—"

Mrs. Nosey broke in passionately, turning on her gawky son, Frank.

"It's all your fault!" she hissed, seizing the warrior, hurling away his "many-shots" rifle and his tomahawk, then spread-eagling him on the buckboard and spanking him till the dust flew out of his breeches in a great grey cloud.

At the same time Chick grabbed Wandering Spirit and

marched him into a corner of the pasture, with "Young man, I want to talk to you!"

Meanwhile, the rest of the band vanished as the Vanishing Race should do.

That, though, wasn't the end of it. The cyclone struck within an hour, when outraged mothers came *en masse* to the detachment. Chick explained, as best he could, that he didn't think the Force was meant to deal with juvenile delinquency that merely "scalped" quite willing little girls. But somehow the school trustees got involved and dragged him deeper into the slough. Then there was a real tussle when it was decided that Miss Seacombe should punish Wandering Spirit and his counsellors with a good, stout strap.

"I'm not responsible for discipline out of school hours!" Nellie told Chick, blue eyes blazing. "Besides, Johnny's a darling—just misunderstood."

Chick controlled himself, remembering the rivalry of Dashing Danny Dale.

"Well, Mrs. Crimp's agreed he needs a licking. And, if you don't give it, some one else will—much harder—"

So, in the end, dear little, misunderstood Johnny got away with it again, apart from a few taps from Miss Seacombe that didn't hurt a bit.

And so, of course, it went on, till Chick realized beyond all doubt that Johnny, with Nellie to protect him, was his Cross. The Case of the Saddle River Circus, when his Cross caught the whole town by surprise with an equestrian show that put three kids into hospital. The Case of the Prairie "Nautilus," when his Cross became Captain Nemo, out of Jules Verne, turned a derelict water tank into a submarine, dived with it into Saddle River and was nearly drowned. The Case of the Big Stampede, when the Idaho Kid and his gang tried to round up the Bar-U cattle, which were never the same afterwards.

And now the Case of the Decorated Detachment.

It came on Chick like a deadly flash of summer lightning

as he left the Bad Bill man-hunt behind him and thankfully
sighted home. For home was no longer a group of neat
white wooden buildings, as he had left it. No, sir, it was a
blaze of glory. Strings of little flags fluttered from the house,
the stable, the storehouse and even the privy at the back.
"The Maple Leaf For Ever" hung on a bright red banner
over the main door. And that door, the gate posts and,
worst of all, the privy were now red, white and blue.

So Chick, there and then, saw not only red but red, white,
blue and every colour of the rainbow. No use to tell him, as
his kinder self did, that yesterday had been Empire Day, a
national holiday forgotten in the whirl of the man-hunt!
Intolerable liberties had been taken with Force property.
His hide would be nailed to the detachment door if his
superiors saw or even heard of the outrage. And, sure as
shooting, that fiend from the Pit, Johnny Chimp, was at
the bottom of it.

He spent over an hour in putting things right—which,
naturally, he did at once, though all he wanted then was a
good square meal and bed. Fortunately the work reduced
his wrath, so that when he set out that evening, in civilian
clothes and a hired buggy, to take Nellie for a nice quiet
drive, it had simmered down and was more or less under
control. A good thing, as he had decided to tell her, once
and for all, that "something had to be done" about Johnny
Chimp.

At sight of her, radiant and smiling in one of those bright,
light summer dresses, all ready and waiting on the veranda
when he drove round to collect her at her boarding-house
after supper, he forgot about Johnny. But once they were
clear of town and bowling along the trail through the cool
of the evening towards a magnificent prairie sunset, she
stumped him for a while by bringing the lad into their chat
of her own accord. He was so cute, she maintained, im-
proving every day and doing so well at school, he was now
quite far from the foot of the class. Take composition! Such
power of language, originality, imagination—and to find all

this in such a little place as Saddle River! Last week, for instance, when she told her pupils to write an essay on anything they liked, he had produced one so good that she had brought it along, so that Chick could hear it for himself. Would he like to?

Swallowing a desire to consign Johnny and his essay to perdition, where they undoubtedly belonged, Chick said, "Sure, I'd love to," and, fishing the document from some mysterious place about her person, Nellie read:

My Gopher Hunt

There is a gopher that lives in our backyard. He lives in a hole. I live in our house. I have a air-gun, so what do I do? I make up my mind to hunt that gopher, so my mother can make him into moccasins or maybe mittens. So what do I do? I hide in our back porch and watch with my air-gun good and ready. After a while, the gopher comes out. So I go out to get a real good shot. The gopher goes in, so I go in. Then the gopher comes out again, so I go out again. The gopher goes in, I go in. The gopher comes out, I come out. The gopher goes in, I go in. The gopher comes out, I come out. The gopher goes in, I go in. The gopher comes out, I come out. The gopher goes in, I go in—and stay in. And that is the end of my gopher hunt.

Silence, broken only by the soft thud of old Whitey's hoofs, the roll of the buggy wheels and, at last, an irrepressible snort from Chick, "Stop giggling! Oh, I think you're mean!" from Nellie, then such a gale of laughter from both of them that Chick found his kinder self saying, "Don't knock the kid! Forgive him!"

Next thing he knew, Johnny had won again, as Nellie tactfully changed the subject to the Bad Bill man-hunt, pouring out gallons of admiration for the bravery and endurance Chick must have shown through all that dangerous high adventure. And the Case of the Decorated Detachment might actually have done good if polite enquiries as to Nellie's doings during Chick's absence hadn't brought up Dashing Danny Dale.

Apparently that snake in the grass had been coiling his

way into a nest right alongside Nellie's heart, if not actually
in it, while Chick was risking his neck in pursuit of Murder.
And Nellie, a true daughter of Eve, had let him do it.
Specifically, he had added a magnificent pair of carriage
horses, "far, far better than old Whitey," to his string and
graciously received permission to call the mare Nellie, "after
the loveliest girl in Canada." He had twice taken her driving
behind them—"they go like the wind." Then, he'd made her
the sensation of last Saturday's church social.

"Oh, Chick," she exulted, "it was gorgeous. Must have
been three hundred people there. And dozens of supper
boxes, done up beautifully, a credit to Saddle River! And
when Reverend Dogood auctioned them off among the
men, you never heard such bidding. Of course, everybody
knew who'd fixed each box! Ada Inkster's went for $50,
imagine—but who wouldn't bid $50 to have supper out of
that box with the prettiest gal in town—all right, then,
second prettiest. And Jean Foley's went for $70, which was
nice, as she's the plainest and a cripple. Then mine came up
and it went for—what do you think? Do guess!"

"$500," said Chick, "and the guy who bought it was
Dashing Danny D.!"

"Don't be jealous. You know quite well it never touched
that figure. But it did rise to the highest price ever—$150,
think of it!"

"I am thinking of it," Chick growled. "After all, it's equal
to my pay for about five months. But do go on, I'm
fascinated."

"Well, every man still without a box—say, thirty altogether
—was out to get mine, maybe wanting to spite Danny. But
would he let them? No, Sir! Gerald and Charlie and Walter
and Martin pushed her to $75 but still Danny hung on.
Then Charlie and Walter and Martin pushed her to $90.
But still Danny hung on. Then Walter and Martin shoved
her up to $100—and *still* Danny hung on. Then Walter
banged her up to $110, threw her up to $115, kicked her up

up to $120. The crowd was yelling, Walter mopping his brow. But Danny dug his toes in, got his teeth in—"

"Shoved his snoot in," said Chick, "and made damned sure that the star prize went to 'The General Store,' the richest guy in town!"

"It did," laughed Nellie, refusing to be squashed, "and, let me tell you, from every point of view, I'm glad!"

"No wonder!" Chick said. "Fine horses and box socials!"

That was a mistake, as Nellie lost her redhead temper.

"You're always knocking Danny. . . ."

Then the world blew up, with Chick, in the end, saying, "I won't chase any girl for ever," Nellie saying, "I've a right to choose my friends—and take time to choose my husband," and a parting exchange of volleys at the boarding-house gate, where the lady snapped, "I never want to see you again!" and the gent retorted, "Well, you won't!"

Which, come to think of it, was a damned stupid remark, as, in a place as small as Saddle River, you were normally bound to see each other again about ten times a day.

"Normally" was the key word . . . Chick patched things up with a big box of chocolates and an invitation to partner him at the next Quadrille Club dance. But before the dance things suddenly ceased to be normal.

Bad Bill escaped from jail and the man-hunt had to be staged all over again.

From then on, Chick had no time or room to think of Nellie, Dashing D. or Johnny Chimp. His entire division turned out to waylay the murderer before he slipped across the boundary line or possibly killed some one else. And, as the Force happened to be short-handed, Saddle River detachment had to take part—and take the risk of leaving the town without police protection for a while. It was not, in fact, a great risk. The strong red arm and the good sense of Saddle River's citizens had established law and order so firmly that offenders other than Johnny were practically unknown in town. Besides, Bad Bill wasn't going to put his neck into even so small a noose as Saddle River. He knew it was wiser to keep to lonely places.

But Saddle River quickly spilled over into something verging on panic. Though it carried on as usual, obedient to the Mayor's advice, it joined the rest of the district in seeing Bad Bill in every shadow, hearing him in every gust of wind and every hoof-beat. And it was against this uneasy background that Superintendent Oliver, his officers and his men rode, probed and scouted day after day, night after night, to retake a man who swore not to be retaken alive and not to die unless a lot of those who hunted him died first.

Chick again found himself in the thick of it: ordered here, ordered there—left, at times without any sort of order except those issued by the voice of his own experience—with five patrols, one patrol, no patrol whatever—hemming in a coulee, combing a neck of the woods, burning out long grass, chasing a rumour, stalking a rustle of leaves—straining bloodshot eyes in shimmering sun-glare or utter darkness, longing for sleep, starving for a bite, thirsting for a drink, aching in every bone and muscle, nursing an exhausted horse along—ready to spring, braced to be shot at point-blank—sure that Bad Bill was here today, told that he was gone tomorrow.

So the first headlong chase slipped into a long grind and Inspector Lesage, Chick's sub-divisional commander, said at last, "You've done enough for now, MacLean. Go back to Saddle River and rest. I'll turn you out again if we still need you later on."

By the best of good luck Chick got rested in plenty of time for the Quadrille Club dance. And as he could bound through a polka without actually crushing his partner's toes, he might have tied up his reconciliation with Nellie in some fancy steps if it had not been for Johnny Chimp.

The Scourge of Saddle River struck him again at sunrise of the day that should have ended in that touching tie-up. Chick was then deliciously wrapped in much-needed slumber. But through dreams and the open window came suddenly the drum and roll of yet another deputation on wheels—a big one, this time: Nellie, Jack Burke (who owned her boarding-house) and Mrs. Crimp in one buggy, Nosey Knowles, Mrs. Knowles and Frank Knowles in the other. And as he opened astonished eyes on this procession, they all yelled, with one voice:

"Johnny's missing! Please wake up!"

Still in bed, with his head poked through the window, Chick heard the ghastly truth from a scared, sobbing Frank urged on by infuriated parents:

"It's this Bad Bill man-hunt, see? Johnny's talked 'bout nothin' else, see? And he's wanted to join the Force for ever so long, Mr. MacLean, 'cause he thinks you're It, see? Well, yesterday, in school, he says to me, 'Frank,' he says, 'lend me your pony, so I can get into the man-hunt—good practice for when I'm in the Mounted Police!' And I thought he was just playin', see? So I lent him the pony, all saddled up an' everything, and he high-tailed away after supper with his air-gun and a haversack and that's all I know, see? *Wow-ow-wow!*"

Mrs. Crimp, thin, pale and overwrought, took up the tale:

"He sneaked out almost behind my back, Mr. MacLean. And when I said, 'Where are you going and what have you got in that bag?' he said, 'Oh, just to play! And nothing!' But he's not come in all night and me out of my mind with worry. And when I had a look, I found he'd taken a towel and a tooth brush, two cans of beans, a can of tomatoes, matches and a loaf of bread. And what if that Bad Bill gets hold of him?"

What, indeed? thought Chick. He might make the kid a hostage for his own safety. So, even if a broken leg, a drowning or simply getting lost didn't lie behind this situation, it was serious—damned serious.

"Oh, Chick," cried Nellie, on the verge of blubbering like Frank, "you really must do something!"

"Think I don't know it?" Chick returned, bitterly, then aptly muttered to himself:

"*Dear* Johnny Chimp—The Missing Link!"

But all he said openly, just then, was a cheerful:

"He won't starve, anyhow, with all that grub. And he's quite a rider and knows his way around! Don't worry, Mrs. Crimp, I'll be out in a minute and we'll have your Johnny back in no time!"

He meant it too. Kids were always going astray on the wide prairie and, like other members of the Force, he was used to finding them.

When he joined the deputation, he was fully dressed, armed and ready for the trail. Nosey Knowles took him aside and said:

"I feel kind of responsible for this, Chick. So I'm at your service."

Then Jack Burke joined them, adding, "Me too!"

So Chick said, "Thanks, I'll accept your offers," adding, "We've got to make this quick and thorough. What we want's at least two more buggies or buckboards and a dozen riders, everybody with a gun, 'cause it wouldn't do to meet Bad Bill empty-handed. I'll get mounted, wire subdivisional headquarters what's happened and rustle up some volunteers. You take your people home and meet me outside the post office with a rifle, ammunition and a day's grub at exactly 5 A.M."

By four-thirty his posse was made up—except for Dashing Danny D., the last man on Chick's list. After all, Danny was a bachelor, active, able-bodied, with plenty of horses and plenty of help in "*The* General Store." And Chick couldn't help thinking with some satisfaction that it would do him a lot of good to take orders on an errand of mercy for a change.

But Danny wouldn't come. Scowling and growling in his nightshirt at the door of his big house, he paraded a whole division of excuses:

"Holy smoke, Chick, I can't—it's plain impossible. You

see, I'm stock-taking, a hell of a job, got to be done now and done by me! My chief assistant's sick, I haven't a saddle horse fit for such rough work, I'm a poor shot, you know that, you've got lots of men already and anyhow the kid's sure to turn up just as soon as you get started, little devil. No, I'm sorry, but I must refuse."

"Even if Nellie wants you out?"

"Now, don't you worry about Nellie. She'll calm down after a while. And oh, by the way, I'll take care of her at the dance tonight. Good luck!"

Remembering Force policy—"courtesy at all times"—Chick turned away without a word. But what he'd have liked to say wouldn't bear repeating.

By five-twenty, his armed men were ready to go—twelve riders and eight others in four vehicles—and he had issued his orders for a search of the main trails, Saddle River, its banks and a wide belt of country on each side of it, with a noon-day meeting at Pinto Bluff to report progress. One minute later they were off, Chick tossing a last "Don't worry!" to Mrs. Crimp and answering Nellie's last query with a simple, "Danny? No, not here—"

She could put that in her medicine-pipe and smoke it!

But by sundown his thoughts about Dashing D. and the possibility that Nellie, to distract her mind, really might go to the dance with him had faded away. So had a desire to spank the tar out of The Missing Link, root-cause of all the trouble. For Johnny had not been found, all but the farthest-flung members of the posse were retiring to Saddle River for replacements and he, Chick, was by chance alone on a very tired horse, twenty miles from home, with no hope of success, if any, till tomorrow morning.

On top of this, of course, he had still, incidentally, to reckon with Bad Bill.

He recast his plans: one more probe of the densely wooded south bank of Saddle River, just below him—camp for the night—then rendezvous again at Pinto Bluff at 8 A.M. to hear the news and maybe launch another day's searching.

In the fringe of the bush he dismounted, tethered his horse to a tree, took his rifle and began his probe.

With twilight waning, the woods were very dark, no place to wander around in with Bad Bill loose. So he had to work fast. A coyote howling in the far distance, the hiss of his own breath and the pounding of his own blood in his ears emphasized silence so deep that the swish of bushes and the crackle of twigs disturbed by his peering movements seemed multiplied by ten. If by the wildest chance Bad Bill were really here, such noise must convert this Chick into a sitting duck!

Suddenly more bushes swished behind him, though he had been standing still and listening for the past half-minute. His scalp tingled, his grip tightened on his rifle, he turned cautiously, stared right and left, listened. No sound! Imagination! He went on searching—and the bushes swished again. More staring and more listening! And, again, no result! Hell, it was just a bird or some scared wild animal.

A bird, eh? A wild animal? What bird or animal ever made that new and slithery sound as it crept to a flank to evade—or get the drop on—him?

He looked around for some avenue by which to checkmate that movement, some natural path in the trees leading to a position covering the present hiding-place of this unseen enemy. There it was, just the ticket! Along it he crept, towards a big rock offering both an observation post and shelter.

The rustling began again, in an obvious counter-move. He got ready to challenge—just as the situation reminded him of Johnny's "Gopher Hunt": "The gopher comes out, I come out. The gopher goes in, I go in"—and he heard giggling.

"Johnny Chimp, you little fool, I might have shot you!" What a relief! And what luck to uncover that dirty, grinning, far too familiar little face, to hear that "Aw, Mr. MacLean, I was just pretending to be Bad Bill."

Then Chick started to laugh himself. Blast and damn the kid for the biggest nuisance in the world but their stalking each other *was* funny!

Somehow Chick managed to hide his mirth and ask, "Well, where have you been this long time, Johnny?"

"All over," Johnny said proudly, "But I've got a night-camp right over here. Come, look. . . ."

And, by gosh, he had—neat and tidy, with an open tin of beans warming up by a small fire, a saddle-blanket for a bed and the pony cropping grass in a little nearby open space close to the river!

"Only," said Johnny, "I'd have to rustle more grub real soon."

Then he added something that stopped Chick dead in his tracks.

"Mr. MacLean, I've seen Bad Bill!"

"You've—*what*?"

"Yes, sir," Johnny went on, "Saw him right over there, maybe an hour ago—big man, green shirt, brown pants, no hat, rifle, pinto pony!" and he pointed to another open space, about three hundred yards away.

He had the description pat.

"Great Slave Lake!" said Chick. "Did he see you?"

"No, sir, I took good care of that."

Chick rallied bewildered thoughts.

"Listen, Johnny," he said, "this just about wipes out all your misdeeds. You'll make a fine Force member some day! Now, here's what we'll do! We can't go on looking for Bad Bill in the dark. Ten to one, he'd get the drop on us and shoot. And we can't keep a good lookout from here, too low. Furthermore, we can't go back to Saddle River tonight. But we can shift camp to that high ground, watch for him when the moon rises, and first thing next morning I'll take after him again and you ride off to Saddle River with a telegram for Superintendent Oliver and get reinforcements. O.K.? Then let's get busy before it's much too dark."

"Gosh!" said Johnny, "But I certainly wish we could look for him now!"

Camp made, with their fire in a little hollow invisible to eyes that might be watching down below, Chick saw to it that the Lone Scout had the big meal he obviously needed, then said:

"We'll mount guard by turns, pardner, and make sure no one creeps up on us or makes a move down there all night. I'll take first turn, so you'd better roll into your blanket right away."

Johnny obviously needed rest. He kept on talking (in a deliberately adopted whisper) twenty to the dozen and this, with constant giggling, showed young nerves strained to snapping-point. Also he accepted Chick's ruling without a murmur, falling asleep the moment his head touched his haversack-pillow.

Chick, as he looked down on the white, tired little face by a mixture of firelight and moonshine, found himself getting sentimental as Nellie herself, with thoughts that this "poor little fatherless chap" really was just high-spirited and misunderstood. But he had little time to waste on such reflections, with Bad Bill probably on the prowl down there and requiring him to stand an all-night watch, protecting Johnny and himself and possibly marking the murderer down for early capture. All-night the watch must be, for of course he had not the slightest intention of burdening the kid with even a small share of such responsibility.

The hours crept by, with nothing to break the tense silence but the keening of those distant coyotes and faint sounds from the hollow—the scrunch made by his horse and Johnny's pony as they grazed in the rich grass, the twisting and muttering of the kid himself as he slept and slept away. The moon set, then the stars, and the vast world wheeled into the darkest hour, traditionally—and rightly—said to precede the dawn and offer the best chance for surprise attack. Through that long, long spell, Chick strained eyes and ears for the slightest sign of Bad Bill.

Once he caught the killer creeping up the slope, twice rustling through the riverside bushes, got ready, every time, for instant action—and found, at the critical moment, that the creeping was due to a cloud-shadow, the rustling to a sudden wind.

Not for years had those solitudes heard a war-whoop in dead earnest. Yet, with the night black and still as the grave itself, Chick felt the tension that had reigned here when hidden braves stared down from this very hill on some unsuspecting camp, strung their bows, cocked their trade-guns and waited, breathless, to swamp their enemies in a howling wave of slaughter. He could almost see the dark crouched forms, hear the quick breathing, smell the blood and war-paint.

In fact, though, that peak hour slipped into dawn's first timid light and its tension went with it before he caught the reward of his unceasing vigilance.

Then he heard the faint but unmistakable hoof-beats of a slowly approaching horse, crossing the very space in which Johnny had seen Bad Bill yesterday. More, he saw a rider, at first a mere uncertain silhouette but soon quite definitely a big man, armed and hatless, looking stealthily all around him and bestriding—yes, undoubtedly—a pinto horse. Bad Bill! Chick, in his chosen nook on the high ground, slid his cocked rifle forward. A moment more and the rider was in his sights and Chick could have shot him out of the saddle, just as Bad Bill would undoubtedly have shot him had their positions been reversed.

That, however, wasn't done—not by the Force. An effort must be made to take men like Bad Bill alive and unharmed, even at the risk of a point-blank duel that might easily end the wrong way.

So, when the rider in the half-light was within easy shouting distance, Chick yelled from his cranny:

"Drop your gun and come here with your hands up! I've got you **covered!**"

And the rider dropped his gun, came there with his hands up—then turned into Dashing Danny Dale.

For the second time in less than twelve hours, Chick roared, "I might have shot you!" adding, "What the hell—?"

"Sorry, Chick," gulped Dashing Danny, "but if you had, it would have been your fault, not mine."

"My fault?" roared Chick, "And you hatless—on a pinto?"

"Lost my hat in the bush," said Danny, "And this horse, I'd have you notice, is a grey—though I admit the saddle-bags and whatnot could deceive you in a light like this."

Turning, he cupped his hands and bawled, "Nellie, here's Chick!", then, as he took in the full situation, added, "Johnny too!"

"What the hell—?" said Chick again, as Nellie rode out of the bush below and loped up the hill, flung herself out of the saddle and swept Johnny Chimp into her arms, sobbing, "Thank God!"

Danny and Chick exchanged glances brimming with masculine superiority. For the first time ever, they grinned at each other cordially. And Danny said:

"We didn't go to the dance—Nellie wouldn't, things being —well, as they were. And she insisted on our coming out here to join you in the search. Nosey Knowles said we'd find you about here."

Chick growled, "A fine thing to do—bring a woman into this, with Bad Bill uncaptured."

Nellie said, over Johnny's shoulder, "But it was perfectly O.K., 'cause Bill *is* recaptured—they got him yesterday afternoon."

"*What?*" Chick shouted, just about at the end of his patience. "Johnny, were you lying to me?"

For once in his life, Johnny had the grace to look a bit ashamed.

"No, I wasn't lying, Mr. MacLean," he protested. "I *did* see him! I was hiding in those woods—when the patrol took him!"

"But why in the name of all that's holy didn't you come in with that patrol?"

"Well, I was having fun out here. And when you came along—I just wanted to go through a big night of adventure here with you!"

Once more Nellie broke in to save her favourite.

"He's a link, all right, Chick, though he's not missing now —a link between us. And, as Frankie said, he thinks you're It!"

a little and certain compass

Alex Fraser, returning after an hour of unsuccessful bear-hunting to the camp on Linton Island, in Dolphin Sound, where Jenny Dean, her brother Tom and their Eskimo servant Toonee waited for him, never guessed that he was on the edge of great danger.

The igloo, as he drew near it, was unusually silent but the glow from the primus stove and the seal-oil lamps shone bravely and reassuringly through its walls into the February night. Furthermore, he was thinking pleasant things: It would be nice to sit down to the hot supper Jenny had prepared. This journey to Banks Island from the Polaris Company's trading-post, some twenty miles due south of the camp across the sea ice, had been very enjoyable, thanks to good companionship. The Mounted Police boys at Bernard Harbour, fifteen miles to the southwest, were a grand bunch. He was more than lucky to know the Deans, as old Dean, in charge of the trading-post, was a prince, and Jenny the most beautiful, charming thing that ever gladdened the heart of an Arctic exile. Things like that—

And he was not thinking for one second of the possibility that before another hour had passed he might have to save Jenny, save her father and face black-hearted Murder, with human blood spattered over its drooling jaws.

So, never catching the note of warning in the cry of "Alex!" with which Jenny greeted the row made by his returning dogs, he shouted "Hullo, sweetheart!", crawled down the passage, heard a tense "Hands up!" and rose from his knees to stare into two rifle-muzzles and two fierce white faces.

Mechanically he obeyed the command, dropping his own rifle to the floor. As he did so, he glanced around the igloo. Jenny, Tom and Toonee, seated on the sleeping-platform opposite, had been tightly bound, hand and foot, with seal-skin lashings. At the sight of Jenny so ill used, fury welled up in him. But he kept his head. Over the prisoners stood a stocky, bearded thug in a pilot coat—poor defence against the bitter Arctic cold. He held one of the rifles now covering Alex. The other glared from the hands of a second thug, skinny and unshaven, who also wore a pilot coat.

Both these men were pale with the pallor of those who work in a close, unhealthy atmosphere. If Alex had met them in civilization, he would have thought them wharf-rats or vermin from the catacombs of some great city. Actually he recognized them both. The whites in the Arctic are so few that though vast distances may separate them they generally know one another by sight or reputation. And sooner or later their trails cross. The *Ptarmigan*, a trading schooner now wintering directly to the east off Banks, had called at Bernard Harbour last autumn on its way "inside" and Alex had seen them there. Their names he had never heard. But he was sure that one was the ship's cook and one a fireman; and he had been strongly convinced, from the time when he first set eyes on them, that both were landsmen who had joined the *Ptarmigan* to escape the aftermath of some crime.

"Alex!" gasped Jenny. "They want our compass!"

That was a grand tactical error. The two fugitives from the *Ptarmigan*, Alex realized, had blundered into the camp a short time before his return, announcing that they wanted a compass and meant to have one. Jenny, Tom and Toonee thought of the compass in Alex's pocket and would say nothing. The cook and fireman searched them, then tied them up and searched the igloo. When Alex came in, Jenny should have kept quiet, instead of saying "They want our compass!" and immediately betraying in those few words that the party had a compass, after all.

Alex, though taken aback by the situation, thought rapidly, saw that a new hunt would quickly discover the compass, had an inspiration, and at the risk of being shot dead grabbed that inspiration on the spot. It was not a thing to do except on impulse. But, done on impulse, it succeeded because, before the enemy could pull a trigger, it was over.

"Here's the compass!" said Alex. With that, he lowered his right hand, fished around in his pocket and flung the flashing object from it clean across the igloo. The cook and fireman followed it with their eyes, then turned back to Alex, finding him with his hands submissively in the air, as before.

"You blanking dash, keep your paws up!" growled the cook. "You're lucky I ain't shot you!"

The fireman was burrowing among the fur rugs—to come up, not with the compass but with a nickel-plated matchbox. He cursed vigorously.

"What's the trouble, Bill?" asked the cook.

"This!" raved the fireman, showing him the box.

"Well, I'm stabbed!" the cook said. "Never mind, Bill, I bet it's on him somewhere! Search him!"

Toonee, in the semi-darkness, grinned happily. He had seen Alex whip the compass out of his pocket while the eyes of the invaders were diverted to the flying matchbox, then drop the compass to the floor and put his foot on it, at marvellous speed, as quickly as a seal could catch fish. Not for nothing, thought Toonee, was this white man a great *angakok* or sorcerer, who could make playing cards vanish in a flash!

The fireman, with no time for that grin, was now searching Alex, to the tune of a string of oaths that were hotter than the blast from his own furnace. He went through Alex with the industry of a puppy looking for bones. But apparently he never thought of pushing his victim to one side just in case he had the compass underfoot.

Though he could not yet see daylight, Alex was pleased. First blood to him! These birds were undoubtedly flying from the *Ptarmigan*. Greenhorns do not fly during the Arctic winter from the security of a ship in a desperate attempt to cross death-strown wilderness to faroff civilization, unless they have done something serious. In this case, they were probably murderers. Well, they would not be aided and abetted in their flight by his compass!

The cook and fireman, still watching Alex closely while keeping him covered, drew back from him a little and went into conference. He decided to find out what he could by questioning and took a deep breath. Now for it!

"Which of you boys actually did the killing?" he enquired engagingly.

"What in hell are you talkin' about?" asked the fireman.

"Don't answer!" said the cook to his partner.

"I'm talking about you!" Alex persisted. "I know you've bumped off some one or you'd never dare to cross the strait alone, in winter. You left in a hurry, or you'd be better equipped. My guess is you've killed the mate. A real driver, that lad! He'd make you know-nothing gangsters toe the line till you just went crazy. And he probably found out you're wanted by the cops back home and told you so. Which was enough—you sent him West!"

"Go to it, mind-reader!" jeered the fireman.

This pretended indifference did not fool Alex. It merely told him that his casually directed flares were lighting up the darkest places.

Tom growled, "Sure, go to it!"

So Alex went on:

"You'd choose the right time for the killing—when every one except the mate and maybe one other man to stand 'watch and watch' was away trapping. You'd find least risk of interruption then—except maybe from the other man— and you'd have a head start of hours—perhaps days—because

no one could come after you till the skipper and crew came
back. Am I right?"

"Of course, you're right!" from an eager Jenny, no reply
from the enemy.

"Yes, I am!" Alex said. "That's fine! Too bad you boys
didn't stay ashore. You'd not have got into this jam then!
Now, tell me, what in thunder do you want a compass for?
You can see the mainland from here in daylight. And all
you have to do is make for it!"

"How are we goin' to find the place we want to go to
without a compass?" snarled the cook. "That there coast
looks all alike from one end to the other!"

"Just go along it till you strike the river you want—it's the
Coppermine, I know. Then keep moving south. With the
devil's own luck, Indian help and so forth, you might just
make Great Slave Lake, Fort Chipewyan and Fort McMurray and come out alive at Edmonton." Then Alex changed
his tone from one like maple syrup to molten lava. "Yes,
you might just make it—so you don't get the compass!"

With the cook still covering him, the fireman strode over
and cracked Alex in the face, almost unbalancing him and
revealing the compass. Toonee burst into Eskimo protests,
Tom roared with rage and Jenny shrieked, partly in fear
that the all-important instrument would be seen, but mainly
in fear for Alex.

Turning pale, Alex said shakily, "By God, you'll pay for
that!"

"Shut your trap!" barked the fireman.

He went into conference with the cook for the second
time. They produced a map and studied it closely. Alex
could see that it was a Canadian Government map of the
Western Arctic, on which the trading-posts and Mounted
Police detachments were marked with fair accuracy. He
knew the map well, having a copy of it himself.

He said, "That's a mighty poor map to get to civilization
on. Not enough detail. Why didn't you swipe a chart? I'll
bet you never even thought of it!"

The fireman shot him a glance full of menace but made no reply.

"So, obviously, they know darn little about the sea or anything connected with it," Alex thought.

He waited tensely for further developments.

They came quickly—bringing death and terror with them.

The fireman spoke.

"See here! We just got to make the Coppermine. And on the way we aim to stop in at that there Polaris Company post and stock up good for the run south. So, if we're without a compass, we got to have a guide. Well, we're goin' to take your girl. An' if she don't put us straight, if she double-crosses us—God help her! Now, then—what's it to be? The gal or the compass?"

Horror began tearing Alex's heart to pieces. Jenny gave a little, gasping cry. At the mercy of those brutes—!

Alex wondered what on earth to do. Give up the compass and have two murderers escape? Let them take Jenny and maybe rape and kill her? Refuse to do either and be shot dead trying to rescue her?

"What's more—" the fireman added, as if by an afterthought, "you so much as bat an eye to stop us and you'll be knockin' for admission at the pearly gates. Then we'll take the girl anyway!"

Whichever way he turned, Alex thought, no escape was possible.

He had almost made up his mind to hand over the compass when Jenny, as if reading his thoughts, cried sharply:

"Alex! Remember Dad!"

That brought another dilemma into the herd surrounding him and impaled him on its horns. He understood. Jenny's Dad had only two feeble Eskimo servants, a married couple, with him at the post. The other natives were away, hunting or trapping. Besides, Dean was an old man. Even with two Eskimos to help him, he could hope to put up only a feeble resistance to these bloodthirsty desperadoes bent on looting the post for supplies. Yet resist the old man would, since it was part of his creed that the company's property was sacred and must be guarded to the death. Death, therefore, he would get—that was certain.

The whole thing amounted to this: If Alex gave up the compass, he delivered old Dean into the hands of the assassins. If he did not give up the compass, he sacrificed Jenny. If he tried to compromise by attacking these thugs, he would surely die—and uselessly, because, as the fireman said, they'd "take the girl anyway."

A straw came floating across that ocean of black fear. Alex clutched at it.

"Look here—I'll go with you!" he volunteered.

Perhaps he could lead the men astray and still escape with his life.

"No you won't!" leered the fireman. "One thing or the other—gal or compass!"

The straw drifted away. Jenny had all the courage to be expected of a woman born and bred north of the Circle. She held her head high, her eyes were fearless, her mouth set. Yet Alex could see what she was suffering—he knew her well enough for that. Desperation seized him. This infernal quandary had two sides—girl or compass (and old Dean's life) and the two sides were slowly closing on him, like two huge bergs drifting together.

"Hurry up! What's it to be?" shouted the fireman.

Still Alex hesitated. The fireman jumped up suddenly and began to untie Jenny's lashings. It was as if a strong wind rapidly decreased the gap between the bergs. Alex frantically asked himself:

"Isn't there a way—some way?"

There was a way. Not a clear way but a thousand-to-one chance, just a chance— It came to Alex out of the awful night, like a line thrown into his hands.

The facts he had learned in talking to the murderers had changed into this line, through some mysterious process in his subconsciousness. Even though the line was thin as pack-thread, he would use it.

While Jenny protested and Tom swore his head off, Alex lifted a foot and said:

"There's the compass! Also you can take my dogs and komatik. Now beat it!"

The fireman pounced on the compass, opened it clumsily and stared at it, while the cook could scarcely keep his eyes and his rifle on Alex, he was so delighted.

Alex went on firmly:

"Follow the compass south till you hit the shore, then keep it on your left. You'll see the lights of the post. Better take the place by surprise, or there'll be bloodshed."

Jenny was amazed. She forgot that Alex was in a terrible position and realized only that he was giving detailed directions to a couple of homicides determined to harm her father.

"Alex, are you crazy?" she screamed.

But Alex made no reply. He was praying, praying with all his strength, that his plan would succeed. The cook and firemen bound him up like the others, replaced Jenny's lashings, helped themselves generously to biscuits, ammunition and fur clothing and went outside. Soon they whipped up Alex's dogs—the deep bay of North, the leader, as he hit the trail was unmistakable — and were swallowed by the night.

As the sound of their going died away, all restraint left in Tom and Jenny went with it and they turned on Alex.

"You ought never to have handed over the compass!" Jenny exclaimed passionately. "Never, never, never! You've helped those men escape—and you've probably killed Dad!"

"That certainly was a fool thing to do!" Here Tom took up the whip and carried on the scourging. "What's more, we're all tied up like salmon in a trap and if we don't get free, we may die of cold or starvation."

Toonee kept quiet. The situation was a bit beyond him.

Alex also said nothing. His face was as white as the fox fur trimmings of his kooletak. He had done his best, risking everything on one wild hunch. If he had judged wisely, then all would come right eventually, and no one be any the worse, while Justice would take its course. If, on the other hand, he had made a mistake — well, freedom for the murderers, death for old Dean and a miserable end for the quartette bound helpless in the igloo on this isolated island would be the result. He could not help that. It had been a case of following that wild idea or throwing Jenny to the wolves. The girl, he thought, had been unfair and hasty in condemning him.

The night crept on. After a long useless effort to get rid of their lashings, the party fell into grim silence. Aside from a chance band of Eskimos or a pursuit party from the *Ptarmigan* that might just possibly arrive in time, no one was in any degree likely to come to their rescue. If the murderers went near the Polaris post, as they had said they intended to do, they would make sure that old Dean never learned what had happened to his party. So no help from that direction was probable. The Mounted Police might take it into their heads to visit the island, but this too was no more than a flimsy possibility.

Everything rested on the success or failure of Alex's gamble.

Slowly the lamps in the igloo burned low. With no one to attend to them, they would not last long. Then cold would creep in on its soft-shod feet and wrap its white arms around the helpless group and — Alex felt the sweat start from his forehead.

Outside there was also silence. It could almost be felt, like stifling velvet. Alex strained his ears but heard no movement. Not even a stray wind whistled, nor was there so much as a moan from the dogs left in camp.

The larger of the two seal-oil lamps was out now and the smaller would soon follow it. Colder every minute! Alex's feet were freezing, and so were the tips of his fingers. God keep the sturdy little primus roaring for a good while longer! Having missed Jenny's nice hot supper, he was ravenous. He could have eaten a can of beans without opening it, as starving polar bears had been known to do. Death by freezing would be more comfortable than death from hunger.

Dawn came—enough sunshine broke through the ice window to announce it. Alex's hunch must work now or never. Just enough time had passed to bring about success or failure.

The wild howling of the dogs crashed through the intense stillness. Jenny seemed too far gone to grasp what it could mean but Tom and Toonee sat up, their haggard faces shining with something brighter even than dawn-light. Alex felt the chilling blood in his heart grow warmer. Could be the dogs merely starting a fight or sighting game and about to chase it. But usually such outbursts meant—strange teams in sight.

Answering approaching howls settled the question. Yet North's familiar bay tragically, unexpectedly dominated them. "Stabbed broad awake" by it, Jenny screamed:

"Those thugs have missed their way. They've come back!"

And, for the first time in her life, she fainted.

When she recovered, with two armed men bending over her, she got ready to scream again—till she recognized a native helper and young, grinning Constable Edwards from Bernard Harbour.

Over breakfast, quickly made ready, he answered questions.

"North gave tongue as they drove up to the detachment. Like you, we knew his voice, but when we saw the driver in the light from the window we didn't know *him*. Suspicious! So we covered those beauties before they reached their guns. You should have seen their faces! Examined separately, they confessed to killing the mate, each blaming the other. We locked 'em up and I tracked the komatik back here. But how in the world did you induce 'em to go to Bernard Harbour?"

Alex explained, "I guessed those landlubbers never heard about the magnetic variation of the compass and there's nothing about it on their map. The variation here is fifty degrees east. The compass points northeast and if you follow it south, as I told them to do, you really march about southwest, to Bernard Harbour, not Dean's post—and both look alike at night. Or, by apt quotation from my student days, 'Truth lies within a little and certain compass but error is immense'."

"Darling," said Jenny, "you're undoubtedly the smartest corporal in the Mounted Police!"

the monster and the "mountie"

" 'Mountie'? A monstrous word! But, speaking of monsters, Ogo-Pogo, the Terror of Okanagan Lake, brought about my most difficult, dangerous arrest, my scrap supreme, as per my scrapbook, with its carefully preserved press accounts of an episode unique in Force history. 'The Monster and The Mountie'—a banner headline! Now listen —Here's Ogo-Pogo's tale—"

And Constable Sinister, H.—aptly known as Sin, for short —that gallant, if sardonic, spinner of "tall" yarns combining fact with fiction, trotted out this narrative:

The thing really began at Coyote, Alberta, shortly after the excitement caused in that little prairie town by my sensational capture of Sadie the Snitch and her gang of bank robbers.* More precisely, it began in my one-man detachment there, with a one-man conversation between Inspector Albert Slaughter, my illustrious commanding officer, and me.

The Inspector was in a kindly, reminiscent mood.

"Sinister," said he, "I've been thinking about your future. Nothing new in that, of course—I guess I've given more damn thought to it, from time to time, than to any other Force problem. Mind you, I've always seen your good points. If any man, I don't care who—the divisional commander, the Commissioner, even the Prime Minister—said the slightest thing against you, some trifle like 'That guy Sinister's the biggest boob in Canada,' I'd take your part, by

*See "Lambkin and the Mounted" in *To Effect An Arrest.*

162

cracky, and come right back with 'Second biggest, sir! Be just!'

"But pshaw, since you got your woman, Sadie the Snitch —I speak, you understand, in police terms—all doubts have vanished. And I've good news. You've also got your reward. No, no, not money—who cares for that? Something much better — promotion. It's just come through. To Corporal! Like Napoleon, 'The Little Corporal'! Like Marlborough, 'Corporal John'! Why, if it comes to that, like me, in my day— The first step on the ladder, lad, with only a hundred rungs and a thousand men between you and the Commissionership! What do you say?"

"Sir," I replied, "you've struck me dumb—for once. The honour's so high, I'm dizzy. Never in my wildest dreams did I think I'd come to this!"

"Fine!" exclaimed my beau ideal, somewhat doubtfully. "But that's not all. Coyote's unworthy of you. Oh, I know it produced the Sadie case and swarms with desperate characters—Ma Patterson, who gyps her boarders, Hop Sing, who loses laundry, Skunk-Child, who scalped his mother-in-law way back in '75. But we need you in really tough spots like the North—just the place for a chap thirsting for distinction, like you. Patrols that freeze the pants off you, murderers that shoot you at sight, loneliness that drives you stark, staring mad! Anyhow, we're transferring you forthwith."

"Sir," I commented, brokenly, "I know we've had our differences—you've caught me calling you Robert the Devil and Jack the Ripper and Ivan the Terrible (strictly in private, of course)—and I haven't had to catch you calling me—well, we won't go into that! But, honest Injun, sir, I'm quite content to remain an exceptionally simple constable in little old Coyote."

"Too late!" declared my leader. "It's settled. You leave here to open another one-man detachment in Penticton tomorrow."

At that, I all but fainted dead away—like the missionary

when the cannibal-cook cast him aside with "White-feller ain't worth eatin'!" 'Cause, you see—well, let me read you this description of Penticton, as clipped from a pamphlet issued by the Canadian Pacific Railway, which serves the local tourist traffic and therefore is unprejudiced and should know:

"Cradled,, as it undoubtedly is, in the magnificent Okanagan Valley and nestling, as it undoubtedly does, at the splendid foot of the sparkling, unfathomed, 70-mile-long Okanagan Lake, Penticton, Queen City of Central Southern British Columbia, stands surrounded by ladies-in-waiting in the shape of towns whose charms are suggested by their sonorous names: Kelowna, Summerland, Peachland, Wilson's Landing, Gert's Neck. . . Its neighbouring bench-lands, which rise from the lake — or fall into it, depending on whether the visitor is going up or down — its occasional bottoms and even its hilly slopes are radiant with orchards growing subtropical peaches, apricots, cherries, apples, plums, walnuts, almonds and grapes. Game and upland birds are hunted, good fishing obtains, yachting, swimming and other aquatic sports prevail and an equable climate makes the entire region an Earthly Paradise. Change here for Kettle Valley Railway."

And, joshing apart, Penticton, its people and its setting are as lovely as all that—and more.

So no wonder I nearly fainted! Though at last I managed to stammer:

"From now on, sir, I call you just Inspector Albert Slaughter—or preferably Albert the Good!"

Well, in due course, Satan—or, at any rate, Sin—ascended into the aforesaid Earthly Paradise. His tall, stalwart figure in brilliant full-dress uniform, with those new badges of high rank a golden glow on his arm, might have been seen riding into Penticton at noon on a splendid horse to occupy that new one-man detachment. As he passed by, peaches (in skirts) might have been heard gasping "Oo!" and rustling down in swoons, small boys calling, "Mister, where's your cart?", prominent citizens growling, "Jumping Jackanapes, what's that?" They might have been — but they weren't, 'cause I came in quietly on the midnight train.

Never mind, Ogo-Pogo also came in, a few days after I did, and in really spectacular style! Eyes big as platters and red as blood, face blue as those famous Okanagan plums, teeth chattering, wide-open, gaping mouth belching, he crashed right into my simple office. My hand flashed to my six-shooter. Then terror passed and I saw that the invader was merely Dizzy Dan, a booze-hound I'd already met officially.

Yet Ogo-Pogo did come in too. In this way:

Dizzy stammered, "Sarg, I've seen him!"

"Seen who—or whom?" I demanded.

"Ogo-Pogo!" he shrieked.

"Now, what in the name of God and the Continental Congress—?" I enquired—then remembered:

The Immortal Founders of Our Force had often held me and other gawking recruits absolutely spellbound in long winter evenings, gabbing about the hideous monster reported to them by awe-struck Indians when they penetrated into British Columbia. Later white and red men sometimes swore to the creature's scampering before their dod-gasted eyes in Okanagan Lake. And accounts of these astonishing experiences even got into the press. But, after all, our Immortals were like my old Aunt Emma—very fond of embroidery. Dod-gasted eyes generally need glasses. Then, of course, you know the press. So I'd always said, "If you believe in Ogo-Pogo, well, you're a bigger fool than I am—if possible!"

And now, practising "public relations" in a way that would have charmed the Commissioner, I merely said, very kindly, "Take a chair, hold your breath, say 'Ninety-nine' and then speak."

"Well," stuttered the Horrible Example, collapsing, as requested, "I was simply reclinin' on the beach, tendin' my own affairs, thinkin' it too windy for fishin' and takin' little

nips, by doctor's orders, me bein' so frail, when *whoosh!* this
Thing swims round the bend like pink elephants gone to sea
—or like a hell-blasted Mountie in hot pursuit, a ring-tailed,
pie-eyed, pot-bellied, red-coated son of—"

"That'll do, Diz!" I said, kinda sharp. "Keep that sort of
talk for the Judge. And pull yourself together!"

"I can't, Capt'in, I can't!" wailed my informant. "Look at
me—a-shiverin' and a-shakin', a-quiverin' and a-quakin', like
a jelly that won't set. Furthermore, Major, I bin like this
ever since I set my perishin' peepers on that Devil from the
Depths, that Ogre from the Oooze, that pie-eyed, pot-
bellied, red-coated son of— O.K., O.K., I was only goin' to
say that son of Bluebeard and the Witch of Endor! What
I need is a snort from your medical comforts, for to set me
up—"

"Best humour him," I thought. "Steady his nerves!" So
I sat down at my desk, pulled out an official form and said:

"Never mind the snort, just give me a full description.
Answer these questions:

"Height?"

"Five foot ten and one-sixteenth!" said Dizzy, right off the
old bat.

"Weight?" said I.

"A hundred and forty, stripped and *after* bathin'," said
Dizzy.

"Galloping goons!" I said — take my word, it was pretty
exasperating— "Describe Ogo-Pogo, not yourself!"

"Why in carnation didn't you say so? Let's see, a couple
o' hundred feet long—eyes like searchlights—humps—looked
like an ocean liner—or maybe an express train—"

Laying down my pen, I took a firm mental grip of the
following passage in my *Hand Book of Ready Reference*:

"A perfect command of temper is absolutely indispensable
in the proper discharge of the duties of a policeman. Harsh
language on his part to the public and persons in custody
is not permitted."

Then I said, gritting my teeth, "Dizzy, this is a case for

the town force or the provincial, not for mine. But, seeing you're round the bend even more than Ogo-Pogo, I'll lock you up till you're sober — and later let you go with a warning."

Now, as you know, I don't normally make mistakes. Oh, I admit to trifling errors, such as accidentally imprisoning the Sergeant-Major in the barracks icehouse till he was nearly frozen stiff. Still and all, as I reminded him when he came out of hospital, "to err is human, to forgive divine," and it wasn't really serious, as he'd only had double pneumonia *without* complications. However, in this Ogo-Pogo matter, I blundered badly. Thinking that Dizzy's fantasies could be safely disregarded, I wrote the whole thing off with "Case concluded." My Uncle Harry, it was just beginning!

Next thing I knew, Chief Always-Resting informed me, when I visited his lakeside reserve in the course of my traditional job of keeping a protective—yet watchful—eye on our red brothers, that he too had recently seen Ogo-Pogo, helpfully described at "heap big snake turned fish and go like hell!"

Then Bob Quint, Prop. of the Paradise Hotel, reported that, one windy night, two lady tourists asettin' in their rockers on the hotel veranda had seen Ogo-Pogo dancing "Swan Lake" beneath a beautiful full moon. And, mind you, the Paradise was bone-dry, the ladies ditto, so it was no good sniggering that more than the moon was full. Besides, Mrs. Tourist had a heart attack and went on the danger list in the local hospital, while Miss Tourist beat it East by the next train, swearing she'd never come back. And in no time, the whole town was talking Ogo-Pogo, except, of course, old Doc Windows, attending Mrs. T.— he never broke the seal of professional secrecy when he could steam open the envelope.

Yet Friend Sin still said "Pish!"—and might have gone on saying it till the whole scare or Ogo-Pogo died a natural death. Only, Colonel Wellington-Wolfe now laid information against the monster. This meant something, as the Colonel had nerves of steel — or malleable wrought iron, anyhow. Also, he was an amateur naturalist of no mean order, being the author of several highly unsuccessful books—*Fish, Flesh and Fowl in the Foothills, Birds and Beasts beyond the Behind, Cougaring with a Camera* and the like. So he'd watched the Terror with technical knowledge and binoculars from his lakeside fruit farm for over half an hour and delivered his report with the military precision and speed of a machine-gun:

"Ogo-Pogo or properly Ogo-Pogolipius measures 75 or possibly 76 metres in length, weighs an estimated 51 tons, has a bovine-cum-equine or cowlike-horselike head, oscillating or revolving—"

"How'd you spell 'osculating'?" I cut in, writing away like mad.

"Not 'osculating', that's 'kissing'!" growled the Col.

"All Greek to me, sir," I quipped.

"Very droll," he reproved. "Now, where was I?"

"Oscillating or revolving, sir," I said.

"Oh, yes—oscillating or revolving optics about 1 metre in diameter, a viperine or snakelike neck, two large, membranous dorsal fins (that is, batlike and on the back), five circumvolutions or coils and a prehensile or grasping posterior or rump. He, she or it — the sex being as yet undetermined—is aquatic though not amphibian, appearing to appear, disappear and reappear in or on the lake without ever actually leaving it. Means of propulsion uncertain. Maximum surface speed, 10 knots. Normally dumb but sometimes utters a jubilant sound resembling 'Whoops!' or possibly 'Whoo!' and reminiscent of the mating call of a particularly passionate moose. Enough?"

"More than enough, sir," I said, hastily pocketing my notebook.

"Clear?" added the Col.

"As the very best family crystal," I assured—for who was

I to contradict Okanagan's most important Justice of the Peace?

"Good!" beamed the Col. "Sorry my account's so vague. But the day was misty, also windy, like myself — ha, ha! Keep watching. And keep touch!"

Then, speaking of wind, the hurricane—or possibly the cyclone—came fast.

The Penticton *Weekly Intelligencer-Examiner-Sun-Globe-Star-Clarion-Echo and Fruit-Farmers' Gazette*, known as "The Rag", or sometimes "The Dirty Rag", for short, began a series of articles under such headings as: "Ogo-Pogo, The Inland-Sea-Serpent— The Prehistoric Pentictonian— The Okanagan Outrage— The B.C. Bogie— The Canadian Cetacean— The North American Newt— Myth or Monster? —Tosh or Turtle?", with sub-heads like "Colonel Convulsed" and even "Corporal Convinced." There they all are, right in the scrap-book.

Not that anybody really minded "News-hound" Smithers, Editor and Sole Owner, spreading himself in this way. Things were so quiet, you could hear a compositor drop, and he was hard-pressed to fill, let alone sell, the paper, while advertising revenue, like a newly-mounted recruit, was steadily falling off. But when it came to "Corporal Convinced", I got emotionally upset, as my superiors detest personal publicity and "News-hound" had reported, "Corporal H. Sinister, brilliant career-man of the Mounties, when asked to express his views on the current crisis, stated that he had none and that if he had had, he'd not consider them worth having," when all I'd said was, "No! And don't quote me." Worse still, the damned articles were syndicated from coast to coast, first in the national, then in the international press. And that brought the Hungerford Ogo-Pogo Expedition to my very door.

Which was so terrible that we'd better have another drink before we examine it in detail. 'Cause the entire weight of that ghastly outfit fell on me.

This crash was admittedly traditional. When the buffalo

vanished, did the Vanishing Race vanish too? No, Hiawatha, Minnehaha and Granny Nokomis simply gathered in their thousands at Force cook-houses and gently grunted, "Grub!" When the cattle strayed, Lazy-W told its cowhands, "Shucks, the red-coats round 'em up!" So by now the cry was "Get the Mountie!" in any hour of need. Furthermore, as I was practically the Indian Act and the Game Laws in a stetson hat, my provincial colleague rightly said, "It's your problem and, boy, are you stuck with it!" So I put aside more urgent business, notably a dance at the yacht club, to expedite the expedition at all costs.

Which was quite a chore, as Professor Hungerford arrived with two assistants, a freight-carload of equipment, Chief Always-Resting and a mighty big proposition, namely, to camp on the chief's nicely isolated reserve and from it photograph, study and possibly trap the monster.

"Sir," elaborated the Prof., oscillating or revolving magnificent eyes behind aggressively glittering specs and waggling a long, keen nose, "I am a Ph.D., M.A. and B.Sc. of the Universities of Harvard, Oxford (England) and Bonn (Germany)—also a zoologist, ichthyologist, atheist and Elk. This is my Deputy, Mongsewer le Docteur Apollinaire Bis, Maitre ès Arts de la Université de Paris, Paris (France)," a young man remarkably like my old Aunt Emma, seen from the side, "and my Deputy Deputy, Doctor Low (pronounced 'Loo')," another young man aptly resembling my Uncle Harry's cow, seen from the back. "And of course you know our hoped-for collaborator, Chief Always-Snoozing."

"How!" said the Chief.

"And how!" I said. "May I add, Professor, I'm certainly glad to know you? I'd ask you to sit down but Always-Resting has already taken the only chair except mine, which is in use, as you see. Pray proceed."

"Well, now," the Prof. duly and warmly proceeded, "We have everything you could think of and much you'd never think of in a dog's age to further this project—cameras, phonographs, collapsible boats, collapsible camp-beds, nets and trawls for netting and trawling, high velocity elephant gun with armour-piercing bullets for self-protection, dessicated coffee, dehydrated potatoes—in short, the works. And we're all set to go, once the Royal North-West Canadian Mounted Rangers say the word."

"*Précisément*," said Mong-sewer.

"*Oui!*" I returned smartly, mighty thankful to belong to a bilingual Force. "But before I say a word of any kind, Professor, let's understand each other. To put it delicately, is this a bare-faced money-making stunt?"

"Sure, sure, making money—ho, ho, ho!" grinned Always-Resting, "Get-rich-damn-quick—"

"Strong *and* silent, Chief!" the Prof. admonished, then to me, "Continually-Dozing's quite a joker. But you do me an injustice. We might clear a few thousand—but the Indians will be paid handsomely and science will benefit to a supreme degree."

"*Exactment!*" agreed Mong-sewer.

"*Bien!*" said I, playing for time. "The Indian Agent administering the Chief's reserve will have to give permission re. camping. And I must take your other proposed activities under consideration—*considération, vous comprenez—*"

"Will this take long?"

"About a thousand years!" I said, with more truth than poetry. "No, no, leave me an address and I'll let you know in due course. Meanwhile, no liquor on Indian reserves, help prevent forest fires, mind the step, *au revoir* and rest assured I'm delighted to see you go."

Once the screen-door had twanged behind them, I started to think—not easy at any time but hell when the biggest baby ever dumped on the Force sat bawling in my lap. To start with, what section of the Game Laws applied to Ogo-Pogo? Was it technically a fish, an animal or a migratory bird? Was there an open season for Ogo-Pogos, if not, why not, if so, when? Maybe it was an Ancient Monument or even an Historic Site. In that case, it concerned the National

Parks Department. On the other hand, it might come under the Department of Fisheries or of Agriculture or even of Militia.

Encore, was Ogo-Pogo subject to the Canada Shipping Act, the Juvenile Delinquents Act or the Department of Transport Act? Or was my provincial colleague wrong and did it concern some provincial statute like the Dangerous and Mischievous Animals Act? I tell you, I had to be careful, as the provinces are more than jealous of their rights and the slightest mistake might precipitate a political crisis forcing all governments concerned to go to the country and old Sin to follow them and stay there.

Fortunately, in this hour of agonizing appraisal, I remembered that a particularly bad Bad Man had once told one of our Immortals, "You Mounted so-and-so's just make up the laws as you go along!" And I decided to make up a law now, as follows:

RE. OGO-POGO:

It is strictly forbidden, without special licence of the competent authority, to trap, catch, seize, net, hook, snare, lasso, decoy, waylay, beguile, delude, inveigle, nick, touch, stroke, beat or otherwise interfere with or molest the myth, fish, bird, animal, vegetable or mineral commonly, if incorrectly, referred to and known as Ogo-Pogo, the Okanagan Lake Monster, under penalty, on summary conviction, of a fine not exceeding $5,000 and not less than $500 or of imprisonment for a term not exceeding sixty years or six months or of both fine and imprisonment. Pleas of self-defence will in no case be accepted.

By Order.
H. Sinister, Corporal.

I delivered one copy of this masterpiece to the Hungerford Ogo-Pogo Expedition, c/o the Bartender, Bide-a-Wee Hotel, Penticton, one to "News-hound" Smithers, for publication in next week's "Rag" and one to Colonel Wellington-Wolfe. The Prof.'s copy bore a note, saying "further instructions will follow," the Col.'s another, saying "for information only," as, for the moment, I wanted no action whatsoever by any Justice of the Peace at any price.

Incidentally, "News-hound" welcomed the notice with tears of joy, as ultimately the Force would meet his exorbitant charges for its publication (no doubt with deductions from my pay). For the plain fact was that the poor sap was financially in deeper water even than Okanagan Lake. "I've had to sell one of my presses," he lamented, indicating the vacant space left behind it. "Any amount of ink, paper etc. is also gone and frankly, if it wasn't for Ogo-Pogo, I'd be sunk."

What next? Well, rightly or wrongly, I thought I'd stopped the chief causes of probable disaster. At the same time, I guessed I'd better get my past, present and future action approved by Inspector Slaughter and place responsibility in this matter fairly and squarely on the proper shoulders, namely, any shoulders whatsoever except mine. I therefore decided to inform my revered commanding officer of all the facts and get his invaluable advice by telegram, reading thus:

Inspector Fort Blackfoot Alberta:

Filthy lustful incompetent pancake greetings repeat greetings delicately breathed . . . stinking illegitimate fraudulent galloping dishpan oysters birthday-cake saddle-soap colic . . . playful angelic diabolical cesspool erupting roundabout Penticton ravishing Summerland revolting Kelowna dashaway hush . . . beautiful bell-bottomed talkative obsolete pie-crust you are another persistently yes persistently nuts . . . muttering mermaids absorbing dynamite kisses tintacks hair-oil Okanagan students hatefully flavoured deliciously fried . . . Peachland cockahoop show-girl passionately. . . .

Sinister.

Then I went to bed and slept well, conscious of duty nobly done.

But next morning, when I got the telegraphed reply, I was horrified to read:

Corporal Penticton:

Utter scoundrel grossly insubordinate and furthermore condemned by Rachel.

Inspector Fort Blackfoot.

For ten terrible seconds I feared that the Inspector, forgetting that nowadays I called him nothing but Albert the Good, had taken "filthy lustful incompetent pancake" and other choice phrases in my wire as new impertinences. I also suspected that this Rachel had complained against me as the outcome of an unfortunate love affair, with the net result that the two of them had tried me by drumhead court martial in my absence and sentenced me to be shot. But who in the world was Rachel? Patricia, Molly, Helen, yes!—but Rachel? The name drew blank. Then I remembered in the nick of time that I'd coded my message to avoid leakages. Young Bill Mulligatawny, the local telegraph operator, could be trusted not to speak. But as to showing his chums my wire without speaking, that was something else again. And so of course the reply was also in code and really meant:

Your excellent report passed to Commissioner carry on as suggested.

Soon afterwards the Hungerford outfit was given official permission to begin its proposed investigations from the desired camp, though the ban on harming Ogo-Pogo, whether myth or monster, remained applicable to the expedition and to every one else.

Things now became so nearly normal that I was able to catch up on my dancing. But Colonel Wellington-Wolfe never left his post, only climbing down from it one day when I visited him to make sure that isolated settlers were still unscalped and enjoy a glass of lemonade. Then he made a very, very serious complaint.

"Corporal," he barked, "the Indians on Always-Resting's reserve are dancing, singing and yelling all night, so a body can get no sleep. Please look into it."

Naturally I looked, popping over in the detachment canoe.

And when I looked, what a sight met my disgusted eyes! Always-Resting and the entire band lying dead to the world —massacred, it seemed, by the treacherous Prof. But when I looked again, very closely, I thought, "Not dead but dead drunk—a very different, though stinking, kettle of fish." "Still and all," I said to myself, then sharply, "Still! That's it! This vile wretch Hungerford is operating an illicit still to placate the natives and make money—"

"Yup, making money! Red-coat, I have spoken!" muttered Always-Resting, opening one eye, then drifting back to Dreamland.

At that moment, the Prof. appeared from his nearby camp, with "News-hound" Smithers, who was obviously snuffling around for another story.

"Mighty pleased to see you, Mr. Minister," said the Prof., heartily glad-handing me. "I've been hoping for just such an opportunity to show you round my camp."

Reverting again to the *Hand Book of Ready Reference*, I recalled:

"Information can be obtained in a quiet way, without exciting comment."

So I politely murmured, "Same to you, I'm sure," and around we went, with Mong-sewer joining us.

Well, I literally looked into everything—living-quarters, mess-tent, photographic dark-room, cookhouse, storehouses piled high with cases of supplies—but all was still in the usual sense of that ambiguous word. Of alcoholic beverages there wasn't a gurgle or whiff.

"*Bon!*" I commented.

"*Trés bon!*" Mong-sewer agreed.

"But," I went on, "You and I, Doctor Hungerford, must now have a word with Always-Resting alone. Yes, 'News-hound', I insist, *alone*."

Eventually the Prof. and I managed to shake and haul the recumbent warrior into a squatting posture and semi-lucidity and I said, sternly:

"Chief, on information received I have reason to believe

that you have committed about forty breaches of the Criminal Code and various Acts, under which you and yours may well be convicted of creating a disturbance, compounding a felony or high treason—You savvy, raising hell and getting pickled, tippled, stewed—"

"Making money!" grinned the Chief.

"That's right," the Prof. confirmed, "All the braves have done is celebrate the new-found wealth provided lavishly by my expedition as rent, etc. And, exhausted by these junketings, they are now merely sleeping them off. But as for liquor, there hasn't been a drop on this reserve, Mr. Minister, while we've been here."

"O.K.," I said, "but understand, Chief, there are limits. No one objects to an occasional Indian croon, a distant muffled drum-beat, a solo dance—a *pas seul sauvage*. Beyond that, quit! You have been warned. Doctor, one more thing before I go—how's Ogo-Pogo?"

"Dandy!" cried the Prof. "Just dandy! Sighted him twice, photographed him once. Naturally, though, I'm keeping details secret till I submit my full report to you folks and to science later on."

I paddled away pretty well satisfied as to Indian rumpus. But as to Ogo-Pogo, I wasn't so sure. And was I right? In a few days I was swamped in further evidence. Local inhabitants, visitors, sportsmen and the captain, crew and passengers of a lake steamer had not only seen but heard it. All missing particulars were filled in. The creature looked and sounded exactly as described by "Booze-hound," "News-hound" and Colonel Wellington-Wolfe, except when it was totally different. At the same time, mark you, it was hard to be specific, as Ogo-Pogo was never seen or heard except on a windy night or day.

This, though, was certain: even courting couples were driven off the lake, the mayors of the Okanagan towns telegraphed the provincial government demanding instant action to end the Reign of Terror, local Chambers of Commerce similarly pestered Ottawa, and I received the following urgent wire from Inspector Slaughter: "Indigestible Arabic molasses"—

Meaning, "Get that beast!"

So now I abandoned even dancing to pursue my sacred quest. And as a first step, recalling that "knowledge is power," I started to acquire really reliable information on my own hook.

To begin with, I cast that hook into the reference room of the Penticton Public Library with truly gratifying results. First I went through about a million cards in the card-index —no laughing matter, as almost every card referred me to another, saying "See Such and Such" and, after seeing Such-and-Such, I had to see So-and-So, This and That, ad infinitum. Next, with this advice to guide me, I went through enough volumes to flatten Ogo-Pogo himself—from Darwin's *Origin of Species* to Buffon (or Buffoon) on vertebrates, Osler on inebriates, all the encyclopedias and dear knows what else besides.

I looked up Ogi, in Japan, Ogod (in the Soudan, not, as you might think, in Heaven), Dago, Ego, Sago, Togo, Pogar, in the Ukraine, Pogge, Pogum, Pogrom and, in short, every possible and impossible clue. After about a week of this intensive research I knew everything worth knowing about sea-serpents, lizards and other repulsive critters and a lot that wasn't. Also I'd boiled Ogo-Pogo down to a figment of mass hysteria or a Plesiosaurus, an extinct marine reptile no longer extinct, as he'd been left behind by the March of Time because he had no feet. How he'd managed to hole up in Okanagan Lake to survive there long after his relations were fossils in museums defeated me. But being an old bachelor or spinster, like poor Og, I was sure he must be terribly lonely without the company of the opposite sex.

Soon after I finished this phase of my investigation, the "Rag" published a social item: "Corporal Sinister, our jovial and popular Mountie, has been summoned to Fort Black-foot for an indefinite period, during which his detachment will regretfully remain closed," and I duly departed as I'd come, by train, with a capacity crowd to see me off at the tiny little station, all kindly shouting, "Have a good long rest, don't hurry back!" Then, some windy nights later, a canoe might have been seen gliding quietly away from the detachment wharf with a tall, stalwart uniformed figure at the paddle—might have been seen but wasn't, as it was dark as the inside of Little Black Sambo, the canoe was already hidden in the reeds off the point and you can't tell how tall a figure is when it's sitting down. Never mind, you're right—the mysterious canoeist was none other than your trail-mate, Sin, slipped back from Blackfoot unbeknownst and lying in wait.

Let me add, with emphasis, that the operative word is "wait." I waited till every light in sight except a street-lamp in town and the sign over the "Never-Close" Cafe had gone out, till I was literally devoured and completely digested by mosquitoes and profanity, till the canoe slowly melted into the primeval slime, with me a primitive ape-man fossil inside it, and hope was a dead thing in my breast. In fact, I waited so long that I was just wondering whether Inspector Slaughter (who'd approved this waiting) was a bigger chump than I was (who suggested it) when, speaking of who, I heard, far off but running fast before the brisk north wind:

"Whoo!" and again "Who! Who!"

Yes, Ogo-Pogo, no less, advancing rapidly upon me, as anticipated, and just as described by Colonel Wellington-Wolfe, always providing that it wasn't the alternative, a particularly passionate moose.

Imagine my feelings, in that moment, a Lone Patrol, a single-handed Corporal, about to come face to face at last with the monster that had defied old Father Time himself and driven the bravest men and women in Okanagan Valley off the lake for keeps! More than that, about to effect the arrest of that habitual criminal or sacrifice his life for his Force, his country and whatever else that occurs to you with nothing but a fully loaded Lee-Enfield rifle, a similarly charged Smith and Wesson revolver, a fishnet, a pitchfork, a flashlight and a bottle of smelling salts. No, don't imagine this—it's too difficult.

"Whoo!" cried the creature, much nearer now, "Who, who!"

And round the point came he, she or it, enormous, crimson eyes ablaze, wide-open, hideous mouth aflame, membranous dorsal fins aspread, prehensile rump aflapping, all at maximum surface speed. I freely admit that even I momentarily quailed before it. Then I remembered the Force motto, *"Maintiens le Droit,"* also *"Noblesse Oblige"* and *"Cherchez la Femme,"* took my courage in both hands, as well as I could for paddles, pistols, nets and so on, commended my soul to Albert the Good, my estates to the Public Administrator and sallied forth.

"Halt, in the name of the Law!" I thundered, "Halt or I fire!"

But my challenge was lost in "Whos"—or maybe my tongue was stuck to the roof of my mouth and refusing to come down without the help of the entire Penticton Fire Brigade.

Followed a terrific crash. And when at last I got the duckweed out of my eyes, the canoe out of my way, my flashlight into action, there was Ogo-Pogo—

Just a couple of expiring gig-lamps, a painted barrel on a pole, two fallen dorsal fins or sails, a kind of kayak, a string of water-wings, a moose-call, Doctor Hungerford and Doctor Low (pronounced 'Loo'), the Deputy Deputy you and I have totally forgotten.

Also, in the kayak—and waterproof cloth to protect them from the damp—were about a million dollars in counterfeit notes, which, but for Sin, would have been into a waiting land-vehicle and over the nearby international boundary before you could say Plesiosaurus.

What lay behind it all? As was amply established at the trial, "News-hound" Smithers, desperate for the needful, had arranged with Always-Resting to fake up this Ogo-Pogo with materials he smuggled out to the reserve, so that he could syndicate sensational articles at sensational prices all over the continent in the resulting scare. Then Doctor Hungerford, alias Andrews the Ape, Ritchie the Rat, Frog-eyes and Nosey, had decided to muscle in on the racket. He came secretly to Penticton, interviewed "News-hound," saw the new golden opportunity offered in the "Rag" having a spare press, etc., suggested setting it up, well hidden by supplies, in a store-house of a camp on the reserve and bought over Always-Resting and his braves. Then he'd brought over the expedition, his counterfeiting gang.

The Indian singing, dancing and yelling was to drown the noise of the press printing the notes, Ogo-Pogo to scare away the curious, then get the "queer" out of the country without using police-haunted trails more than was necessary. Ogo-Pogo had been concealed in yet another storehouse when not in use.

But Always-Resting's talk of "making money," with the Prof.'s magnificent eyes and long keen nose, well known to law-men of two nations, had put a certain brilliant career-man of the Mounties on the scent, with Inspector Slaughter sniffing along behind. The rest you know.

No, you don't! For a terrible thing happened just as Our Hero, covered with mud and glory, was escorting his captives and the "queer" ashore at pistol-point. From the black depths of the lake, with a rush and a roar, rose nothing less than the real Ogo-Pogo, furious to find his reality doubted, his ancient nobility exploited. We fished out the counterfeit notes and rounded up the Prof. and Doctor Low much later on. But for the time being the cry was "Every man for himself!" In far less time than it takes to tell it, the Prof. was over the Rocky Mountains, the Deputy Deputy on the Pacific Coast and young Sin heading for his old homestead in Coyote, *"Maintiens le Droit"* and even *"Noblesse Oblige"* discarded as so much useless impedi-menta.

When the Prof. recovered from his nervous breakdown, he contended that this real Ogo-Pogo was just a school of sturgeon, a floating tree-trunk or wild fowl rising. If you believe that, you too are second biggest boob in Canada. And anyhow, the Okanagan Valley people bear witness that Ogo-Pogo's still there.

a couple of caribou

From now on, for good or bad, Fort Moccasin beside the Barrens would never be the same again.

Its entire population—say forty people—saw that well enough as they stared at the unfamiliar speck in bright mid-summer skies and listened to the approaching drone.

The drone became a roar, the speck a float-plane splashing down on Moccasin River. The Conquest of the Air reached the fort—at last.

Then Sergeant Fane, at least, learnt that bad came with it.

Being, with Constable Nield, Canada's entire government in these parts, he was first to come alongside the plane in his canoe—though naturally the mission priest, the traders and prospectors, the Indians and half-breeds, also gathered around in other craft. The *Mercury's* cabin-door opened and Tom Drew, the pilot, stuck his head out.

The New North—young, bronzed, grinning—he perfectly contrasted with the Old—with thickset, hard-bitten, grizzled Fane.

The Sergeant quietly, yet officially asked:
"Why have you come here?"
And Drew said:
"To lift you moss-backs from the Stone Age!"
That was all—but quite enough. Fane said to himself:
"This cockiness spells trouble!"

In spite of Tom's cockiness, things, at first, went smoothly. Fane listened patiently when, between trips from this new

Fort Moccasin base, the self-employed bush-pilot lectured the detachment with:

"Look at Yellowknife—not even a trading-post three years ago, a big mining town now. Look at Aklavik, Norman Wells, Port Radium—all done by aircraft. We're carrying passengers, freight, mail, taking sick to hospital, fighting forest fires, bringing civilization to your doorstep—and across it—"

Then Fane conceded:

"Sure, young Drew, when it comes to quick, easy travel you're a godsend to us moss-backs. In fact, you should start a flying division for this Force!"

And he said nothing about civilization ruining the lovely, unmapped, primitive Old North where men were Men—and brothers.

But then came bloodshed.

Fane smelt its first red drops as he chugged back from patrol in the detachment motorboat a few days after Tom's arrival. He found Constable Nield in the canoe talking to Tom in the plane. Nield looked grim as a super-cheerful disposition would allow, Tom sheepish as an Indian caught with home-brew, yet fierce as twenty wildcats. And in the *Mercury* were caribou antlers, hides and meat enough to fill the cabin.

Once in the detachment with this loot and the policeman who had confiscated it, Tom snarled:

"All this fuss about a couple of caribou! You'd think I'd murdered somebody."

"You have," Fane said sternly, "just as much as any Indian or Eskimo killing off the herds with high-powered rifles, like kids trying new toys. Because once the caribou go—and they're going fast—the natives freeze or starve to death."

Tom growled, "I've broken no law!"

"You have," Fane said again. "Listen to the Game Ordinance . . ." And he read from a small book, " 'Schedule D: Close seasons: Caribou—from the first day of March to

the fifteenth day of September'—it's now July!—'Section 15
(4): The meat or the skins or pelts of game shall not be
transported in an aircraft except by written permission of
a game officer', which you haven't got. But you've a copy
of this book. I gave you one."

"Too busy to read it," snapped Tom.

"The gist of it," Fane said, "is publicly posted all over
the place."

Good-natured Nield put in, "This is Drew's first season
in the Territories, Sergeant."

"But he's flown two years in Northern Quebec, under laws
like ours."

"O.K., O.K.," snapped Tom, "I'm guilty. What do I get
—hung by the neck or exiled?"

"A warning might meet the case," persisted Nield.

"Speaking out of turn!" Fane reminded him, adding, to
Tom, in a voice like a blizzard's, "You may get 'a fine not
exceeding $500 and not less than $5' or 'imprisonment for a
term not exceeding two months' or 'both fine and imprisonment'—Section 99 (b)."

Tom said, "I couldn't pay $500 for a thousand years."

"In that case, you'd lose your plane, guns, ammunition,
etc., for a thousand years—Section 93 (1)."

No King of Vice or Queen of Beauty could move Fane
from the trail duty blazed for him. Yet he saw that Tom got
off lightly for the first bloodshed. Unfortunately he also
saw that the case left bad blood on Tom's side.

And then came more bloodshed—the worst—wholesale
murder, not of caribou but of men.

Paddling day and night down the Little Moccasin for
nearly two weeks, Moose-boy and Beaver-child brought
Fane word of the killings—word well-chosen, as they had
been to the mission school:

"Squint-eye fell in love with Big Fish's wife, Boil-the-
Kettle. That made real trouble. Then Squint-eye got tired
of Boil-the-Kettle. He told Big Fish, 'Quit bothering me.'
But Big Fish wouldn't. So Squint-eye and Flat-face—his

brother, remember?—shot Big Fish, Boil-the-Kettle and their three kids with one of those new rifles. Our head man's holding both killers. Very sad!"

Fane's stout soul was shaken. Five people dead through another misuse of firearms! The natives got them legally. But too soon—He'd gladly stop the traders providing those rifles and Tom flying them in. As he couldn't, he began instead to return Tom's dislike. And the prospect of patrolling up the Little Moccasin in this heat and fly-time to investigate the crime increased his resentment, as many breakneck portages dictated a trip by canoe, the motorboat being no good in shallow rapids.

"Drew'd take me up for a reasonable fee," Nield remarked, when he got back from a duty call on the mission and heard the news.

Fane mentally thanked him for tactfully failing to add, "But he'd not take you," then said, "No, the Force won't pay. Start loading!"

With Jimmy Bear, his Indian special, he launched the canoe that afternoon, while Moose-boy and Beaver-child, still in their own craft, led the way up the Little Moccasin for a three-week journey. At least they called it the Little Moccasin. It was really the Styx, for it flowed through Hell.

Its clouds of black flies, midges and mosquitoes bit Fane till he streamed with blood from countless bumps. Its raging current fought his paddle or track-line till his heart broke and his muscles quit working. Its cold, when he waded through it for hours waist-deep among clinging weeds or slippery boulders, chilled him to the bone. Its long steep portages crushed him under loads that made his knees give way and his forehead throb against the tumpline. A merciless sun roasted him through most of the Long Day. And silence haunted him—silence so deep that the fall of a faroff spruce sounded like a roll of thunder.

The mere fact that his Indians shared all this did not really make it easier. And even fish fresh-caught in icy water get damned monotonous when a man lives on little else.

But of course these hardships were all in the great name of keeping the peace on the Last Frontier. So they would not have mattered if a nasty surprise had not met him at what he thought of, now, as Murder Camp, "the Spot marked 'X'."

When the canoes of his patrol glided through reeds and pond-lilies to reach the wigwams, the entire band rushed to the riverbank and old Jack Chipmunk, the head man, produced that surprise.

Another graduate of mission school, he said in tolerable English:

"Squint-eye and Flat-face got away ten days ago, I don't know where!"

Such news was enough to make resentment against Tom Drew and the traders glow as fiercely as the eternal fires burning the natural gas Fane had come across on the Athabaska years ago.

Still, he kept that resentment in hand and out of sight, like the gas. For he had a lot to do: learn all about the killings and the escape, open the graves (neatly marked by rustic crosses), view the bodies, take notes and make a plan.

Jack Chipmunk's people would thoroughly search for the murderers and bring them to Fort Moccasin if captured or driven by hardship into rejoining the band. Meanwhile Fane would go back to the detachment with Jimmy Bear, his special, prepare a full typed report and rush it to subdivisional headquarters with recommendations for a widespread search operation, if necessary, after freezeup—an earlier start now being impossible.

This settled, he duly started back, down the Little Moccasin—or the Styx, "like a bat out of Hell," as Jimmy Bear aptly put it. Aptly because the swift current now helped instead of hindering and extra time might be saved by running at least some rapids. Besides, the fewer portages were not so tough, being now, of course, downhill, tracking

in icy water was no longer necessary and the insect pests
had died with the heat. Not that it was really cold, so far,
but winter could be seen approaching from the non-too-
distant Pole as autumn's colours deepened day by day in
the surrounding wilderness.

So he rode his canoe like a race-horse through the white
fury of those chosen rapids, with rocks sometimes drumming
the Devil's Tattoo beneath him and "life on the twist of a
paddle." He rushed his loads down those remaining portages
at top speed. And in little more than a week he swept into
Fort Moccasin—to meet his second surprise.

"I've brought you Squint-eye! He's inside."

That was the second surprise—a glorious one if it hadn't
been offhandedly thrown at him, just then, by Tom Drew—
a Tom lounging outside the detachment after another trip,
looking hideously cocksure, sleek and clean in a new flying
outfit and contrasting more vividly than ever with a tired,
thin, grizzled, empty-handed sergeant in dirty clothes.

Naturally, smouldering resentment could not be loosed
on Tom in the teeth of that news. Still less could Tom be
given the satisfaction of visibly riling Canada's government
by atoning for the caribou business in such a conceited way.

So Fane merely said, "Well, isn't that something?" and
added, pleasantly, as he helped Jimmy unload the canoe,
"Tell me!"

"Nothing to it!" said Tom, grandly. "I got back here soon
after you left. Pete (Nield) let me have the story of the
killings, as all Fort Moccasin was gabbing about them, anyway. I'd a repair job on my hands. Did it, then, to test it,
took the *Mercury* for a little flip, keeping a lookout for this
and that, as usual, while in the air. Spotted a camp-fire by
Jackfish Lake, up Jackfish Creek—you know, off the Little
Moccasin. Flew low. 'Stead of waving, like most men, white
or red, Indian at the fire beat it into the bush. Suspicious!
So I just landed on the lake, took my gun — the one you

might have confiscated—followed him, recognized him from
that squint, brought him in. No reward?"

Fane grinned, "No reward! But thanks — thanks a lot.
Come in and have a drink—to celebrate?"

"Guess not—too busy. See you later."

"Still sore," Fane thought, as Tom strolled off and Nield
came on the double to hear the news and lend a hand.

"It's Squint-eye, all right," the constable reported.

This was final, as both policemen had met the killer before.
Nield went on, "He's a poor fish, that Squint-eye. Made
a full confession to me, giving details of what Flat-face
is doing, so as to save his own skin, if possible, I guess.
Unfortunately, what Flat-face is doing doesn't sound too
good for us. In fact, I'd say that whoever follows him to
settle his hash is in for almost certain death."

"Interesting!" said Fane. "Please explain."

"Well, Squint-eye claims that Flat-face did the actual
killings—which, from what we know of both men, is probably true. Furthermore, Flat-face swears he'll kill every
red-coat in the North rather than be taken alive. Finally,
he means to cross the Barrens right to Hudson Bay."

Fane sat down to rest on the woodpile, got his dirty old
pipe fairly going, then remarked calmly:

"Almost certain death's an understatement."

Perhaps the understatement of the year, as, apart from
Flat-face, a man of his word, any patrol chasing him across
the Barrens must cope with enormous distances, winter cold
or summer heat, the risk of accident and sickness far from
human help, fuel shortages and, above all, possible starvation
from a failure to find caribou.

O.K., of course, if these were found: in spite of regulations
restricting men like Tom Drew, the Game Ordinance
expressly allowed any Force member on a winter patrol to
"hunt . . . such game as may be necessary to supply him
with fresh meat."

But that "if" was big as Great Bear Lake, for the movements of caribou, the mainstay of the Barrens, were utterly unpredictable.

Such natural hazards explained why no one—white, Indian or Eskimo — except the Pelletier patrol, years ago, had crossed the full length of that northern waste or even tried to cross it.

Yet, later, Fane said, "Guess I'll cross it now, if necessary."

This was after interviewing Squint-eye in the detachment lock-up, making a hearty supper and typing out all the documents required in connection with the case to date.

Nield obviously understood, as he placed another sheaf of typed papers on Fane's desk, saying, "That's from Drew."

"That" was a well-drawn-up plan for an airborne pursuit of Flat-face.

Fane galloped through it, his heart warming.

"Perfect!" he said, "Except for the cost—it calls for at least two aircraft and no other pilot's likely to accept Tom's idea of waiving all profits. Still, I'll forward it with my humbler scheme for doing the job with dog-teams and canoes—and strongly recommend it."

"Now you're talking!" Tom said, suddenly appearing at the door. "So finish off your typing, give me the entire dossier and I'll slap it into subdivisional headquarters by noon tomorrow. Then I'll be back with two ski-planes when the ice will bear 'em. Meanwhile, moss-backs, I'll rev up."

Fane sighed, "If only we could cure that cockiness!"

As agreed, he rushed his typing through, then over to the *Mercury*. But next day he began preparing to go after Flat-face by dog-sled.

A long-faced Tom landing one ski-plane on the Moccasin a few days after freezeup endorsed this foresight.

He brought "Long John" Silver with him—Corporal John, as tall, wild, woolly and expert a trail-runner as any in the Force. He also brought orders for Fane to go into the Barrens after Flat-face with John and two or three Indian specials. But as for airborne pursuit — that was ruled out "with regret, because of the prohibitive cost."

"I was right!" Tom raged. "Still in the Stone Age, you red-coats. . ."

"Shut up!" Fane said sharply.

No outsider could talk that way about the Force to any member—but this reopening of Tom's old wounds was a pity, all the same. For the kid's plan had been good, his offer to forgo his profits more than generous.

It looked, now, as if the breach were permanent, as Tom was the only living soul in Fort Moccasin not on hand to see the patrol off in pursuit of Flat-face some days later. This might mean merely that he was too busy with his own forthcoming trip (to fly Jacques Leroux out to his winter trap-lines). Anyhow, what the hell! Fane could give no more thought to a sulky young bush-pilot, when he had Corporal John, Special Constables Jimmy Bear and Freddy Trout, twenty-five dogs and three sleds loaded with grub, dog-feed, outfit and two canoes in his care and must lead them into the Barrens and "almost certain death."

Once, as the North wind, cutting like a knife — no, like countless swords in the hands of ghostly, charging cavalry —drove the patrol off the ice of Great Slave Lake into the shelter of nearby timber, he saw Tom's plane sweeping south before the gale. Safe and comfy way up there, looking down, in every sense, on him and all his troubles! And once, as the pale sun nooned on an ever-shortening daily journey towards midwinter, Freddy Trout, at the campfire, suddenly said "Listen!" and the plane's drone came to the party from infinitely far away. But not another sight or sound of it reached the poor boobs stewing—or freezing—in their own juice far below.

Oh, sure, the thing they saw was probably a falcon, the thing they heard some freak of Nature, who plays strange tricks to break the great subarctic silence at sixty below zero! And, anyhow, the kid undoubtedly had jobs to do, most certainly had been politely given the brush-off in regard to chasing Flat-face. So, once more, what the hell!

Particularly as Artillery Lake, three weeks' march from

Fort Moccasin, claimed a patrol-leader's whole attention—
for water-smoke blanketing vast unfrozen reaches of the
lake made it a death-trap to earthbound travellers. At last
the mist got so bad that he could not see the lead dog of his
own team in action.

"Camp here till it thins!" he ordered.

"By Judas, yes!" said Long John Silver.

So camp they did and waited for the next cold spell to
throw a film of young ice over the open water and cut off
that fog at the source.

They waited a week, Fane consoling himself with the
thought that every trail-runner in these parts must be pinned
down, like them, by similar conditions.

He was wrong. For, as they waited, Freddy Trout, still
the man with the best hearing, again said, suddenly,
"Listen!" And, through the fog, they heard a very strange
something. "Ghost!" whimpered Jimmy Bear, turning pale
under his bronze—no wonder, as the sound really was like
the wail of spirits heard on certain rivers, such as the
Qu'Appelle . . . and as ghosts—or swirls of water-smoke—
had haunted him for days. "Listen!" said Freddy again.
They heard it again. "By cripes, a man shouting!" said
Long John.

Then, all at once, the splinter and crash of downtrodden
brush hurried madly through the fog towards them. Fane
held his men in a state of constant readiness, mainly because
of Flat-face. Besides, you never knew. So his rifle stood
near at hand. He flashed it out of its buckskin case and
cocked it in one swift movement. And, as the breech-bolt
clicked, a shadow burst out of the mist, charging straight
at him.

A moose? A bear? No, undoubtedly a man, armed with a
shotgun and completely crazed with panic, yelling, "Help!"

The entire patrol swamped him. Disarmed and firmly
held, he stood there, simply gasping.

"Well, well," said Fane. "It's Tom!"

He was right. As they sat him down by the campfire and

calmed him with a mug of tea, he stammered out his story.

"Flying back from Cambridge Bay via my caches on Back River and McLeod Bay, I had to come down on Walmsley —engine trouble. Overnight, it got warmer—water-smoke everywhere, like this. Couldn't take off. Not enough grub. Started out to shoot something—" He grinned self-consciously, "I can, you know— Got my licence and the season's open. But first thing I knew, couldn't find the plane. Next thing, lost—abso-bloody-lutely lost! Been lost ever since! How long? God knows! A week, say—maybe more— And only shot three rabbits—"

He started to blubber.

"Stop that!" Fane barked, "You're O.K. now! Also it's getting colder—fog will be gone tomorrow. Better still, we know where we are, if you don't. So I'll send you safe back to your plane with Jimmy Bear—and grub aplenty."

"You've saved my life," Tom choked.

"For the love of Mike," Fane said, "forget it!"

He hadn't the heart to crow over downcast cockiness— or to curse Tom for delaying the patrol still further while it waited for Jimmy Bear to guide the bush-pilot back to the aircraft, then rejoin. He could only think, "That's patched things up." And wonder if the future would prove him right or wrong.

A month later, he found Flat-face.

The Indian had taken over a deserted cabin cowering on the north bank of the Thelon, about one hundred miles down from the Hanbury in the very heart of the Barrens.

Three chance-met Yellowknife hunters told the patrol where he was and that he had holed up there for the winter. They even described the place minutely, to avenge themselves on a man who had driven them away from the spot with threats to kill them.

Fane recalled "this man is dangerous" and no doubt cunning as well, though, in deciding to winter in the cabin, the fugitive had evidently misjudged the length of the Law's red arm. So, to avoid premature detection, the patrol hid in the timber a good way from the river and ten-odd miles from the cabin, while Fane shouldered a pack, some blankets and a rifle and scouted on alone to see what he could see. For two bitterly cold days and nights, he shivered without a fire in the brush, watching the cabin at fairly close range, yet not so close that the sled-dogs tethered around it would notice him and raise an alarm.

Chimney-smoke told him that somebody was there. And at last, on the third morning, a man came out with a rifle, grub and outfit for a short hunting trip. Fane could have shot him dead in his tracks but the Force took its men unharmed and alive, if possible. Besides, this fellow's parka-hood was up, so his identity was uncertain, though in height, slouch and long swift stride he answered to the fugitive's description. Alternatively Fane could have told him to throw up his hands, but if in fact he were Flat-face that would probably mean a murderous duel, with at least one life thrown away. All this considered, it was better to leave him alone and ambush him with the whole patrol when he came back. Or if, by the wildest chance, he did not come back, he could be overtaken in the open.

Dogs harnessed and sled loaded, the hunter drove off, luckily downriver, away from the patrol's hiding place. When he had vanished around a bend, Fane went the other way. The long trail-breaking snowshoes hampered him, and he was tired, but muscles toughened by months of hard travel quickly carried him to his men.

As the sun sank like a burning ship in a lonely, vast white sea, the hunter came swinging into Fane's carefully laid trap. The surest way of taking him by surprise would have been to wait for him in the cabin but the place was so small that only one person could have room enough in it to tackle him effectively and fresh tracks near the place would put him on his guard before he entered it. So Fane, Long John and Jimmy Bear hid some distance from the cabin, beside the trail to be followed by the returning dog-train, while Freddy Trout stayed with the police teams a mile away.

The plan was for one man, unarmed, to challenge the hunter quietly. If he resisted, all hands were to rush him. If he opened fire, they would shoot him down, preferably merely wounding him, but not one would pull trigger except as a last resort. The scheme bristled with hazards, but every one agreed that Force doctrine demanded some such action.

Fane took the post of danger — the role of unarmed challenger—as a matter of course.

He waited till the lead-dog was on the point of discovering him, then stood up from behind his bush with his arms held out as a sign of peace and said:

"Hullo, there—just a minute—"

The hunter, obviously, was taken completely by surprise. But he, in turn and a flash, surprised the patrol. Instead of standing still or rushing, he darted into the trees, whipped his rifle out of its case and fired at Fane pointblank. As the shot broke through the dusk and the utter silence with a blinding flame and stunning roar, Fane went down. At almost the same instant Long John and Jimmy Bear charged home—they could not return the fire, even if they wished to, trees being in the way. Long John's spring was one that a cougar might have envied. Yet another shot flamed and roared at Fane before the corporal sent the hunter flying. Jimmy Bear pounced one split-second later.

That settled it. Pinned down by two big men, their prey sprawled motionless and panting.

Fane also sprawled motionless but panting not at all.

Long John called, "Are you hurt, Sergeant?"

No answer. Again:

"Sergeant, are you hurt?"

And again no answer.

"Keep this guy covered," Long John told Jimmy Bear and rushed over to the shadow that was Fane.

The shadow did not move. Long John let fly with a furious monologue. Many of his words would have taxed the resources of the Oxford Dictionary, complete and unabridged.

"Quiet!" said Fane. He sat up, gasping. "I slipped on that damned rock and stunned myself. Did he start shooting?"

"Bang-bang!" shouted Jimmy Bear, in happy confirmation.

"By Judas, you're the luckiest guy I know," said Long John, wringing Fane's hand. "Two near-misses, the closest I've seen in my life."

But Fane plunged over to throw back the captive's parka-hood and stare at him through the gloom—

"Praise be, it's Flat-face!" he announced.

Jimmy Bear said, still more happily, "Bang-bang!"

Fane formally arrested Flat-face. So far, so good! Unfortunately, "so far" was still very far from complete success. In spite of the murderer's boasts, he had been taken alive. But he had still to be brought alive out of the Barrens, with, incidentally, no loss of life in the patrol.

That night, Fane's aching head could not plan this last phase. Penning Flat-face, with Long John, as guard, in the cabin — which could hold no more — taxed all his powers. Next morning, though, he really got to work. He could push eastward till he reached Chesterfield Inlet detachment, on the west coast of Hudson Bay, or retrace the trail to Fort Moccasin. Naturally, he preferred the second course. In any case, thorough stocktaking showed him that supply questions made it the only wise one. Even with Flat-face's cache of caribou-meat, fish and a moose he had been marvellously lucky to get yesterday, the grub and dog-feed in hand would support the men and dogs, Flat-face and his team back-trailing through the lifeless Barrens only till they reached a cache Fane had left on Artillery Lake and only if the party killed at least a few more caribou and if conditions generally remained average.

If! There, again, was the world's worst word, written here in letters covering miles. So Fane thought, as he weighed the pros and cons, saw absolutely nothing move in a snow-covered "abandonment of desolation" twice as big as France and was reminded of Scott's remark at the South Pole, "This is an awful place!" Not that the situation should upset him, as some one else, somewhere, had rightly called Force members "trail-mates of death." Nor could he let fear of the terrible responsibility of getting his party safely home fill his mind, when the ways and means of saving it must be given top priority.

"If" began fighting him almost as soon as he turned his followers westward two days after he had captured Flat-face. In bitter irony typical of the North's cruelty to many patrols, it threatened the travellers largely through Flat-face, who had forced this journey on the others and could make it useless by dying on their hands. Then, still ironic, it struck through the prisoner's dogs. Almost at once, prisoner and dogs fell sick. Fane thought this surprising in Flat-face, as skilful, tough an Indian as he had ever seen, but later he recalled the hardships of singlehanded flight through summer wilderness with a canoe-load of dogs and of winter life in the Barrens and felt no surprise at all. Next, "if" brought cold and blizzards equal to any in the Barrens' scanty records, with two nearly normal, always dreaded Barren negatives—no helpful Indians and practically no game.

Fane's stiff, swollen fingers faithfully noted the results in his diary with entries short and sharp as coffin-nails:

"Shot two ptarmigan. Nothing else so far. . . Flat-face sick. Too cold to travel (60 below) . . . Wind. Cracked lips. Flat-face dog sick. 11 miles. . . Heavy snowfall, so trail-breaking hard but made 12 miles. . . Very hard trail-breaking, 12 miles. . . Flat-face sick again. His sick dog dies. Trail-breaking so hard, only made 10 miles. . . Trail-breaking still hard. All tired. . . Too cold to travel (50 below). Two Flat-face dogs die. . . Corporal's face frost-bitten. . . Wind. Cracked lips very bad. Flat-face sicker. 12 miles. . . Blizzard. Lie-over. Flat-face dog killed in fight. . . Heavy snow. Only 8 miles. . . All sore feet from trail-breaking. Flat-face barely walking. Still no Indians and no game. 13 miles."

Veiled by his parka-hood yet easily recognized, Death

crept nearer Fane's small campfire: "Conference. Agreed cut rations, but not dog-feed, as our survival depends on teams. . . Jimmy Bear skins hand through picking up axe, which sticks to it in cold too bad for travel (79 below). . . My throat sore. Can hardly swallow. 10 miles. . . Shot three hare. 10 miles. . . Can only speak in whisper. . . All very tired, sore feet, etc. Flat-face's last dog dies. . . Now no wood within reach for 80 miles ahead. Begin breaking up canoe for fuel. Must keep the other for use when ice gone. 10 miles. . . Giving Flat-face best food and carrying him on toboggan. Snow very heavy, so only made 9 miles. . . . Still 60 miles from cache, rations low, no Indians, no game, blizzard coming."

To meet that blizzard, Fane pitched his tent under a cut-bank, buried it in snow, stocked it and tethered the dogs in the lee of the toboggans—which was wise, as the storm was the worst in his long experience. Swinging through the weird grey twilight with nothing in the world to stop it, then prowling awhile around the tent like a gang of robbers, it finally struck that poor shelter like the wrath of God striking a tiny star. With it came five days and nights of roaring near-destruction. And with it Death closed up, squatting just outside the tent, all ready to crawl in and end the business.

As rations disappeared and the men revised their plans, eating the dried fish left for dog-feed and offering the team a bearskin robe, even those half snowblind saw that the end was very near.

But on the morning of the sixth day, Fane's ears, though still ringing with the storm's wild music, somehow detected an unearthly silence. Swaying weakly in the centre of the tent, he thought, "Now we can move on—but first, at any cost, we must find Indians or food!" Long John, Jimmy Bear and Flat-face slept heavily but bright black eyes smiled bravely at him over the rim of Freddy Trout's bag.

"Come on, Freddy," he croaked, "We're going to look for Yellowknives— or caribou."

"Sure, sure!" grinned Freddy, as if to say, "You're crazy! Still, I'm with you."

He too left the tent with rifle and ammunition and trudged manfully on snowshoes over ice-clad Lake Ptarmigan.

Slowly and heavily Fane pushed through the cold hush, Freddy muttering, "Sure, sure!" close behind him. Like the special, he searched the nearby snow at every step, alert for any sort of track from man or beast or bird and from time to time scanned the shores, the vast expanse beyond them and the steel-grey sky. More than once he took the streaks and spots before his eyes for campfire smoke or a worthwhile target, but in fact snow and sky remained pitilessly empty and "if" still whispered through the creaking swish of snowshoes: "No Indians. No game."

Too tired now to feel more than the crushing weight of his responsibilities, he found himself repeating half aloud:

"Give us this day our daily bread . . . our daily bread. . ."

Suddenly Freddy Trout said, "Listen!"

Recalling how effectively this man had used that word in the past, Fane listened obediently. Thanks, perhaps, to the blood-throb in his ears, he heard nothing, not even the wind. But Freddy had gone mad, was literally running around in circles, waving and yelling.

Then, of course, he heard it too — the drone that had startled Fort Moccasin last summer—saw too not just specks before his eyes but *the* speck that, like the drone, was unmistakable! An aircraft surely and proudly covering as many miles a minute as a dog-team travelled in an hour—the New North to the rescue of the Old—

Yes and more than that, Drew to the rescue of Fane—For the pilot, sighting two frantic exclamation-marks on the white page far below him, swooped down and flew so low straight over them that the type of plane was easily identified! It was even possible to see a friendly arm waving from a window by the cockpit.

Still more, Tom was not merely squaring accounts. Instead of just dropping grub or whatever else he carried for the patrol, he obviously intended to land on the lake with a view to giving more active aid if necessary. Probably no trick of Northern flying was more dangerous than coming down on ice with its possible roughness or weakness hidden under snow deceptively smooth, like this, as Fane knew well.

Too dangerous! The aircraft ploughed through the snow, struck an unseen obstacle, pitched on its nose and exploded tremendously into a mass of flames.

Gasping and reeling after perhaps the hardest run he had made in his life, Fane stood with Freddy as close to the blazing plane as he dared to go and watched it burn its way through the ice with everything in it.

Tom and Constable Nield stood beside them, after hopping out in just the very nick of time. Poor Tom was stricken dumb by the disaster but Nield said, very quietly:

"Yes, we got worried so Tom volunteered to fly supplies in and take out your sick, if any, free of charge. Now he's lost everything—he can't get insurance-coverage for flights like this—too risky—"

Fane was also stricken dumb, with pity for the bush-pilot and the awful realization that now he must save not only his own party but these newcomers as well. Roles reversed —the Old North saving the New, after all—

Then Tom spoke at last, with a gallant grin, reading his thoughts:

"Guess we know this now: we need each other! Only *you* can get us out of here. But only airborne eyes could find what you *must* have to do it. Behind that ridge—not just a couple of caribou, old Fane, but hundreds!"

pal

"Pal's missing!" said Dog Trainer Vickers. "Absent without leave."

"Good grief!" said Constable Frank Darwin.

He had just finished preparing Pal for the hard, dangerous life of a police service dog and was to take him to Winnipeg tomorrow. On the course Pal's playfulness and enthusiasm had made him the hardest animal to handle. Yet this magnificently handsome German Shepherd (Alsatian), though barely two years old, had shown, in all eighty-five pounds of him, that he, in his own way, might match that bygone sled-puller Okemow, The Ace of Huskies*. So to have him missing now brought exasperation and anxiety into Dog-master Frank's voice, good-humoured face and twinkling eyes.

"Got to find him right away!" said Frank. "Let's go!"

With six other dog-masters he set off, under Vickers, to search around the training kennels, in an area of woods, fields and rocky paths criss-crossed with roads and trails of varied surfaces, ideal terrain in which to teach canine recruits but difficult for searchers.

Suddenly Frank said, "There he is!"

Yes, there he was, on the training field. All by himself, just for the love and the hell of it, he was hurrying over familiar obstacles put up for developing a dog's ability to follow his quarry anywhere. He ran up and down the eight-foot ladder, then along the narrow plank, sprang through a waist-high window, rushed across the chest-high

*See "The Ace of Huskies" in *To Effect An Arrest*.

tables, scaled the eight-foot wall, and sidled along the narrow rail from end to end like an acrobat on a tight-rope.

"Well, I'm damned!" grinned Vickers. "Can't get enough of it!"

Then, of course, with a laughing, applauding audience, Pal had to show off, going back over the obstacles before throwing Frank flat under excited caresses from a tongue like an oversized sponge.

A born dog-master, patient, firm, understanding, strong, athletic and a lover of animals and the great outdoors, Frank, as he took Pal to Winnipeg next day, thought about the dogs that had shared his life so far: Toots, a cocker spaniel, teaching him, a toddler, to play ball; Jumbo, a black Labrador retriever, keeping him off roads and pulling him out of the creek; Wag, a Newfoundland—Kerry blue—Airedale, strong as a bull, and as unpredictable except with friends; Heinz, with "57 varieties" of ancestor and enough tricks to make him the mascot of Frank's recruit-class, years ago; many others; and now Pal.

Though born and bred in the Force, Pal was out of the puppy stage and ready for training before he met Frank. But at that meeting each had looked at the other and said to himself, "You're mine!" Important, this, for by well-established practice Pal had to be a one-man dog, with Frank the only one to feed, groom, exercise, train, handle and control him throughout his nine years of service, unless Frank ceased to be a dog-master.

It was an exacting partnership, for, in the words of Dog Trainer Vickers, it was "for business, not pleasure"—how exacting Frank realized when, his short dog-master's course over, he started training Pal.

That job lasted a year, double the period spent by Frank himself in preparing for general service, because recruits on four legs naturally must train twice as long as recruits on two — and no wonder, the course being as tough and varied as Force life.

Frank had not only to build up Pal's courage and tenacity

to supreme heights, and make him efficient over obstacles and instantly obedient to many words of command. He had to improve the dog's marvellous power of trailing or finding on just a whiff of scent. Then he had to teach Pal to protect and warn two-legged comrades, overtake, disarm and guard a criminal, guard prisoners and property, make water-rescues and "give tongue" to announce "mission accomplished."

Above all, Pal had to learn to face violent, terrifying resistance, notably gun-fire, and to break that resistance by furious baying and snarling, yet never to hurt any one. He must be taught to take work seriously and curb affection. These were his hardest lessons, for they repressed his natural fear, rage, gaiety and love. The trouble was that whatever the task Pal's tail seldom stopped wagging, while he worshipped Frank so intensely that even a mild reprimand upset him for days.

Ah well, training was over now and all he needed to perfect him was practical experience.

Dog and man together burned to get it, and they began to get it almost before Pal had settled into his Winnipeg kennel.

Sergeant Rance, in charge of the dogs there, said to Frank:

"Corporal Lambert at Portage has just the job to try out you and Pal. Run over and tackle it."

Frank popped Pal into the wired-off back-compartment of the dog-car and covered the sixty-six miles to Portage la Prairie in little more than an hour.

"Sad case," Lambert told him. "Old Jerry Turnbull will put you in the picture."

Frank and an eager Pal listened and watched as Jerry and his Missus outlined that picture on their nearby farm.

"Happened yesterday, somewhere in those fields," said old Jerry, pointing over fifty of his acres. "Missus walked across them from the bus stop on the highway with $500 she drew out of the bank in town—" ("Almost all we have to live on for months," from Missus.) "She left the bus round about eleven. Money was in a dark leather wallet in her bag here. She opened the bag now and then to take out her hankie—" ("Head-cold!" from Missus, mopping her eyes.) "Well, she left the path with a message for me in that field, Lord knows where, then another for my boy Steve in that one, Lord knows where again! Then she chased a prairie chicken every which way, damn it!" ("And when I got to the house," sobbed Missus, "the wallet was gone!")

"You've searched thoroughly?" asked Frank.

"Ever since, till we phoned your Mr. Lambert. Me, the Missus, Steve, the neighbours!" Jerry assured him. "No real idea where to look, understand—so we found no trace."

Missus wept on and even Jerry wiped his eyes over their serious loss. Frank and Pal considered the problem, Pal having obviously taken in every word. Fifty acres, thought Frank, the same area as twenty-five of Winnipeg's big city blocks: mostly plough, with clods of the same colour and often the same size as the wallet, much stubble and some scrub also offering it concealment—and a scent over a day old. Only Pal or a dog like him could find that wallet, and then only by a miracle.

Planning aloud, Frank said, "We'll start from the bus stop, giving Pal a smell of the hand-bag there."

At the stop Pal whined and bounded, mad-keen for action. Let go, nose down, tail up, he rushed along the track for about two hundred yards, then darted this way and that, like a puppy having a good aimless run, yet really hot on the scent. Frank could almost see a ghostly Missus leading Pal over yesterday's course.

Suddenly Pal hesitated, stopped and came galloping in at top speed. The wallet was in his mouth. He dropped it gently at the old lady's feet and look around for approval.

"Dear Pal, God guided you!" sobbed Missus. "Thank you, thank you!"

"Nothing to it!" said Frank, speaking for both.

All the same, he whistled jazz for most of the way back to Winnipeg, with Pal's tail more or less keeping time.

Some failures followed. As Sergeant Rance put it, "A dog can't follow a trail through a city rush hour, wet fields or heavy rain, pick up a scent over three days old or work tired out!" But there were brilliant successes too.

One morning the Sergeant told Frank, "Report with Pal to Inspector Grayson on Highway 59 this side of Morris."

Frank found the tall, rugged young inspector, Constable Wheeler of Morris detachment, the highway patrol and a shifty, protesting civilian beside Force vehicles and the civilian's ditched car. Taking Frank aside, the inspector told him in his usual crisp style:

"Man's Mike Ayalik. Patrol saw him ditched. Offered help. Mike said 'No'. Suspicious! Patrol looked into the car. Full of new kitchenware—fishy! Mike explained, 'Bought at Perfect Wholesale Hardware Co., Winnipeg, yesterday. For my store in Pembina, U.S.A.' Patrol contacted Morris and Emerson detachments and sub-div. H.Q., two-way radio. Morris phoned Pembina. Reply: 'No Mike Ayalik in hardware business here.' Sub-div. phoned Perfect. Reply: 'Don't know Mike.' Smelly! Now, look at this!"

"This" was a string of footprints leading from the ditched car into the bush but soon petering out there.

Frank put Pal on to the trail of the footprints. Off Pal went, with a deep nose and working fast, sure signs that he was on a strong fresh scent. After ten such minutes, Pal swerved into the dense woods. From these burst "a reasonable facsimile" of Mike, yelling "I quit!" Pal pinned him down.

Inspector Grayson overtook Frank, Pal and the prey.

"Name?" he panted.

"John Andrick!" gasped the prey, with an aside to Pal, "Say, Mister, let me up!"

But, after the usual warning, he would add nothing to this. So every one went back to the ditched car and Frank let Pal try again.

Pal now behaved like a kid on a nursery treasure hunt.

He found and carried in, one by one, a frying pan, a kettle, a saucepan and two boxes of kitchen knives.

"Burgled!" commented the inspector. "Rushed south till the car was ditched, then men started hiding the loot in the bush. But patrol interrupted. So John beat it, dropping these things as he went!"

"You win!" growled Mike. "Burgled at Selkirk last night. What in hell can a man do when dogs turn into cops?"

Soon afterwards, Frank was rushed with Pal to a farm near Stonewall, just northwest of Winnipeg. Inspector Grayson, two plain clothes men, the constable from the local detachment, Ken Brown, the farmer, and his badly, justly scared family were waiting there.

"See here!" said the inspector, pointing to a big hole in the foundations of the farmhouse. "No, not mice—gasoline! Fired last night. Now come inside. Burnt beams, rags, kindling. Might have blown everything sky-high. Attempted murder and arson—damned serious. Brown hasn't a clue who did it. Nor have we. How about it?"

Frank thought awhile, then said, "I'll give Pal a whiff of this gas-soaked rag and let him try."

Just that one whiff and Pal shot across the fields like a hunting tiger, dragging Frank after him. The others toiled along behind. At last Pal led them all to a house so shut up that it seemed deserted, rushed to the front door, sat down and gave tongue.

"Jeff Smith's!" Brown exclaimed. "A friend of mine. Impossible!"

After much knocking, a scared woman unlocked the door.

"Talk to your husband?" asked the inspector.

"No," snapped Mrs. Smith, "he's sick in bed."

But Pal wasn't having any of that stuff. Uninvited, he dragged Frank upstairs to a closed door, where he again gave tongue. The woman sullenly opened the door and they all trooped through.

Wild eyes glared from under the bedclothes.

Inspector Grayson solemnly gave Smith the statutory

warning that anything he said might be taken down in writing and used as evidence.

"Hell, what's the use?" Smith said wearily. "Ken Brown did me dirt when he bought my twenty-acre field. Last night I took across the long way with the gas. Explosion wasn't big enough. But you'd never have pinned it on me if it hadn't been for that blamed dog!"

"You're telling us!" said Grayson.

That winter, as he now kept in touch with this dog-man partnership with a view to helping it if it still worked well, he asked specially for Frank and Pal to join him at Plum Coulee. "Breaking and entering case!" he told the senior partner, "Got me puzzled!" Then he led them to a rear window in the office of the Blossom Cartage Company. A pane of glass was missing from the window. Grayson pointed to a mass of footprints in the snow below it and ordered:

"Follow!"

Neither Frank nor Pal needed anything more. Pal snuffled around above the footprints for a few seconds, then meandered along the alley at the side of the office, into the street, along other streets, over vacant lots to an isolated house, then through more streets to the fringes of the town. The men hurrying behind him sometimes saw prints or traces of them, but for the most part even Frank, an expert, could note not a sign of the trail he followed so surely.

Suddenly swinging back into town, he led a mystified Frank and the grinning inspector to the front door of the Blossom office. It silently opened for them. In the office Frank found Constable Osborne, of nearby Morden detachment, Harold Quill and Ike Partridge, senior company officials, and Leo Flitch, their Plum Coulee assistant. Pal charged straight at Flitch, showed him his great white fangs and sat down in front of him, snarling.

The inspector said, "Constable Osborne, repeat the report you made to me just now. Mr. Quill, Mr. Partridge, please check it."

Osborne, at attention, said, "Sir, at 9 A.M. today Mr. Flitch telephoned me at my detachment. He stated that on opening for business he found that a pane of glass had been broken out of that window, then the window had been opened and some one, entering through it, had broken into that desk, taken $150 from that cash-box and gone out the way he came. I examined the premises and vicinity. Mr. Flitch then phoned his story to Mr. Quill and Mr. Partridge and I phoned you. When we were all here, Mr. Flitch repeated his story and I made a private report to you."

Quill and Partridge said, "Correct, as far as we know."

Grayson said, "Now, constable, tell these gentlemen what you told me privately."

"Sir," said Osborne, "I found no evidence of melted snow in this office. The dust on the window-sill was undisturbed. The robbery was an inside job, faked to look like an outside."

Flitch turned deathly white, while Grayson said, "Dog followed a roundabout trail to your house, Flitch, then back here. Straight to you. Comments?"

"Damn the dog!" shrieked Flitch, throwing a roll of money from his pocket to the floor, "I did it!"

Pal solemnly picked up the roll and presented it to Frank.

Matters of life and death also concerned their partnership, as Frank and Pal often had brought firmly home to them. Frank saw one such matter ahead in the midsummer following the Plum Coulee affair, when a desperate appeal called him at top speed with Pal to rough farming country around Gimli, sixty-odd miles north of Winnipeg.

They found the local people, chiefly Icelanders, in a turmoil. Stephan Stephansson, the leader, told Frank:

"Mrs. Sigurdsson — she's eighty-six — went berry-picking this morning. Family got worried when she was overdue— bush very thick, full of deadfalls and bears. We've had a hundred men out since two. Now it's eight, dark any minute, no trace. A night in the bush, tired or hurt, will finish her."

Frank looked at the anxious, silent searchers and vast,

silent woods, then at Pal, confidently ready, tail wagging, and remembered a good omen: the Force had scored its first success around here with a winter patrol against whisky-traders back in 1873.

"Let your fellows carry on," he said, "But we'll start from Mrs. Sigurdsson's with a whiff of something she wore recently."

Though limited to places a person of her age could reach, the hunt proved very difficult, with only flashlights to dispel the utter blackness of clinging bush wet with scent-destroying dew. Time and again Pal went wrong and was put back into the desperate struggle with Frank's order, "Find!" After six hours he was clearly faltering, while, apart from torches like glow-worms, calling voices and the rustle of startled birds or animals, the woods seemed lifeless.

"How could an old woman vanish so completely—or get so far?" Frank asked himself, adding, "I'll have to get a relief tomorrow."

Just then Pal, after forcing his way down a natural trail apparently too narrow even for a child, gave tongue sharply. Going twice astray in fifty yards but guided always by impatient barks, Frank and the men who rushed in behind him came across this tableau:

Old Mrs. Sigurdsson, tousled, dirty, exhausted but safe, with Pal sitting beside her, both blinking in the glare of the flashlights—Pal one ridiculously self-satisfied smile, its chief feature a red tongue apparently a foot long.

"The dog is my saviour!" she sobbed, burying her face in Pal's thick ruff, to be comforted by a warm, wet lick.

Death sometimes threatened the partnership itself. A year and many cases later, Frank, Pal, Constable Phil Ashwood (a plain clothes man working for Excise) and the constable from the Lac du Bonnet detachment east of Winnipeg drove on a search for illicit liquor to a place near the lake farmed by the two tough North brothers. The house was closed, but smoke from its chimney told Frank that the closure was only temporary.

He loosed Pal with one magic word:
"Booze!"

One word—but enough. It sent Pal snuffling around like
an alcoholic madly looking for his misplaced bottle. This
went on for twenty minutes, till a joyful yelp from behind
the garage called, in what was nearly plain English, "Found!"
His grinning comrades joined him. He was digging furiously
to uncover a jar buried four inches underground.

Phil Ashwood uncorked the jar and smelt it. Looking as
happy as a Yukon miner unearthing a record nugget, he
said, "That's the stuff! Now if only we could find the boys
as well—"

"Maybe we can!" said Frank. "Hold on."

Poking around in the garage, he dug out a pair of gloves.
Hardly waiting for a good sniff of them and another command, Pal shot into action once more. He wandered between
the garage and the house several times, into a field and back,
over to the gate and around the front yard, obviously following somebody recently busy with chores. At last he plunged
into the barn and gave tongue. There was a fearful yell, then
ominus silence.

Leading a rush, Frank saw almost nothing in the barn's
dim interior but a familiar object sticking out from behind
many bales of hay. It was Pal's tail. Beyond it, wedged between the bales and the wall and so covered with hay that
only a dog was likely to find him, was Bert, the younger
North brother. Pal was holding him by the leg of his overalls
and was evidently ready to do so indefinitely.

The statutory warning scared Bert into a blunt refusal
to say anything but, "You better get outta here before my
brother Wilf comes back. He's got a huntin' knife and a
shotgun and he'll kill one of you, that's for sure!"

Judging by Wilf's record, this was more than probably
true.

The police party handcuffed Bert to a tractor in the barn
and laid an ambush for Wilf beside the trail leading to the
farm. The wait was long and broken only by an occasional

visit to Bert to give him a rest from the handcuffs, but eventually a truck ground its way up the trail. It was about 100 yards off when it suddenly stopped and out sprang Wilf with the gun and the knife. He had seen the ambush.

Frank loosed Pal at once, with an order to "hag" the enemy. At sight of him, roaring and racing in utterly regardless of danger, Wilf dropped the gun and fled into the bush.

He knew that natural maze perfectly, and somehow the party lost him in it. Frank led a zig-zagging three-mile search. Suddenly Pal fished an empty tobacco package out of the grass. It told him something important, for he spent ten minutes tracking slowly and carefully from it—then rushed on through the brush at full gallop.

Frank and his party raced after him, yet were too late to see him dash across a clearing and through the open door of a cabin.

Terrific bays, yells and poundings from inside suggested the worst.

"Wilf's killing Pal!" gasped Ashwood, "Hurry, hurry!"

Frank in the lead, they burst upon a half-dismantled still for the manufacture of rotgut whisky, the hunting-knife on the floor beside it, Wilf cringing in a corner; and Pal, holding him by the knife-arm, helpless.

As Frank called Pal off, Wilf gabbled:

"You'd never have found me without the dog. And I'd have had the still hidden in another five minutes. But I don't bear him no grudge, 'cause he got the knife away without so much as scratchin' me. Some pal!"

"You're right;" Frank said, "Some Pal!"

So it moved on, step by step, into the desperate, bloody Hampton man-hunt.

Pal was by now a dog-star shining brilliantly, though soon due for retirement. The Commissioner praised him in print. Grayson, now Superintendent commanding in New Brunswick with Frank and Pal under him by special request, said,

"Pal should be a sergeant and get a good fat pension."
Frank, now corporal, added, "Sergeant, at least!" Newspapers wrote him up and published his portrait in all its
regal maturity. Judges, policemen and law-abiding citizens
blessed him, criminals cursed him till they ran out of
breath.

Seven years of success in finding, rescuing, warning and
guarding often at the risk of his life, in cases ranging from
murder to petty larceny had earned him this renown. And
they had bound him to Frank with a love stronger than
pain, weariness or death.

The man-hunt called the partners out from their Moncton
quarters at dawn of a beautiful summer day to as ugly a
sight as they had ever seen, which, as Frank remarked,
meant "really something."

The body of a young man and a girl, dressed for an
evening party, lay on a secondary road some miles east of
Hampton. The man was at the wheel of a car, the girl some
yards off, and man, girl and car were a gory mess riddled
with bullets. Inspector York and a detail from Saint John
city, twenty-odd miles to the southwest, were taking finger-
prints, casts, photographs and measurements.

York himself briefed Frank. Safe-blowers had stolen over
$20,000 from Hampton's Self-Service Store during the night.
Apparently their victims, on the way home from a dance
in the city, had blundered into their getaway and rashly
given chase. The gang, unable to shake off a fast car well
driven, shot it to a standstill, then finished things off at
point-blank range. The man tried to hold them off while
the girl escaped, but without success. Then the flight went
on, destination unknown. Sam Mead, driving early to Saint
John, found the mess and phoned Corporal True of Sussex,
who phoned York. The inspector flung out road-blocks and
extra patrols and discovered the safe-blowing.

He ended, "True's searching down the road. Set Pal to
work here—he'll smell out something."

Pal did: four spent bullets, some of them distorted

ricochets, and two empty cartridge cases buried in or near the ditch or in the road where the pursuing car had passed over them. As these items were scattered along the road, Frank thought them relics of the burst that stopped the car. Two more spent bullets Pal found buried in the ground near the car, a third cartridge case trodden underfoot beside it.

"Nice work, Pal!" said York. "Now True's picked up some interesting things near this road. Better join him right off and see what you can do."

Frank grinned, being used to getting orders more or less addressed to Pal, who seemed to understand them anyway.

Corporal True was waiting beside his car perhaps fifty yards from a sharply westward turn in the road and twice that distance from the Bay of Fundy, sparkling in early morning sunshine.

He pointed out tire tracks swinging left into the long drive of a big, empty summer residence, swinging out again and so west along the road, evidently in continued flight. Then he led the way to a rough shed behind the house. Here the car had stopped, then returned to the road.

Waving to a sock lying on crushed grass with three paper bags for carrying money, True said, "Found in those bushes. Your deductions, my dear Watson?"

Frank picked up the sock and said, "Soapy—used in the safe-blowing (to prepare the explosive charge). The gang sat on this grass while getting rid of incriminating evidence and dividing the loot, then drove on to separate somewhere else."

"Elementary—but good," said True. "Now find more stuff while I make casts of these tracks."

A sniff of the sock sent Pal plunging under the shed through a hole too small for a man. In three such plunges he brought out five socks and a pair of gloves, all soapy and evidently pushed through the hole with a long stick nearby. Then he looked at Frank, clearly saying, "I've fetched you everything from under there. What next?"

The rest of the search was a tough two-hour effort taking

Pal a long way into wet underbrush. But it produced one by one some highly important clues cleverly hidden between rocks, in gullies and even overhead among branches.

Frank said, "Good boy! I'd not have found these by myself in a dog's age."

He collected the finds with care, to preserve finger-prints. They included three assorted revolvers, two auto-loading pistols of different calibres and ninety-nine rounds of ammunition. This last was of three types, one of which corresponded to the relics recovered at the scene of the crime.

"An arsenal!" said True. "I've taken my casts. Let's go back to the cars with this stuff and report."

York commented, over the two-way radio:

"Still dangerous. I doubt if they've ditched all their arms, even now. And cool too, hiding those things and splitting the loot so soon after the murders, and so near them. Stuck to a prearranged spot. This suggests local knowledge and local men concerned. Now come in, quick. I want to rush your finds to the lab."

He had vital news for Frank at the Self-Service Store, now his headquarters.

Early that morning, a tall, dark, grey-eyed man, with a two-day beard, a hunted look and a New Brunswicker's accent, aged about thirty and dressed in a grey shirt and blue overalls, had driven at high speed in a black sedan with Quebec licence plates to a small store near Havelock, forty miles north of Hampton. He had bought Sovereign cigarettes, asked whether the day's first radio newscast had referred to any local crime and driven on northward. Here, it seemed, were one murderer and the getaway car. As the man was alone, the gang apparently *had* separated.

Learning this from the storekeeper, a patrol had driven after the car, picking up a Good-o potted-meat tin and a Sovereign pack, both empty—but not the man. His success-ful avoidance of roadblocks confirmed that he knew the country.

Great Force assets were now being thrown into an intense, grimly determined effort against the murderers. Frank and Pal joined a reinforced hunt south of Hampton, another developed north of Havelock. True's tire casts were rushed to the small store for comparison with tracks found there. "MP Hawk" (Mounted Police aircraft CF-MPH, of Air Division) took off from Saint John to deliver Pal's finds, soap from the blown safe and finger-printed glass from the death car to the Force's eastern laboratory at Rockcliffe, near Ottawa, 450 miles to westward. York cabled a description of the man seen near Havelock to Cuthbert Vine, owner of the empty summer residence, who was holidaying in Europe with his family, asking him to identify the description, if possible. New Brunswick's city police and Maine's law-enforcement officers were put on their guard. Force patrols, supplemented by radio broadcasts, warned farmers and villagers to look out, then sought their co-operation, stressing, "These men are dangerous."

Noon found the province tense, with excitement increased by announcements that the butchered young couple were socially prominent Moncton people who were soon to have married. It was now known for certain that the black sedan was the getaway car: the pattern of tread and the blemishes seen in the tracks left by the sedan outside the store matched those in True's casts. Then a long-distance Force phone call received within a few hours of the arrival of "MP Hawk" at Rockcliffe stated:

"The finger-prints belong to Buster Sims and Dirty Davis, safe-blowers with bad records in Vancouver (a continent's breadth away). The soap on the gloves and socks and the soap from the safe are similar."

But the call added, "The bullets and cartridges used in the killings do not fit any weapon recovered at Mr. Vine's residence. Look for a 9 mm. Spanish Star auto-loading pistol or a .45 Thompson sub-machine gun." This Frank thought discouraging, for the search he had shared with Pal and other comrades all through the afternoon had brought no results and many false alarms had plunged them in fog as dense as any plaguing the Bay of Fundy in wintertime.

Yet he felt less at sea (though at sea, in a good sense) early next morning, when the telephone orderly at Moncton told him:

"*Fort Starnes* has been out all night in hot pursuit of some of your murderers, maybe—and she's still at it. Here's the dope—"

His verbal sketch was so vivid that Frank could almost see hunter and hunted racing through the summer darkness, under blazing stars and over rolling seas, the long fierce beams of the pursuer's searchlight relentlessly pinning the pursued, the wakes boiling, could almost hear whistling winds, crashing waves, sharp orders, throbbing engines.

The chase came about because a resident of Harbourville, Nova Scotia, across the thirty-mile width of the Bay of Fundy and southeast of Hampton, stumbled on a fine cabin-cruiser lying up along the coast. By sheer chance, he recognized her as the *Cheetah*, Cuthbert Vine's boat, and guessed that she had been stolen from the owner's wharf near his empty summer home. The resident instantly informed Kentville's Force detachment. And, as instantly associating the *Cheetah* with the mysterious escape of some of the murderers, Kentville's men drove full speed to her berth, only to find her gone.

But she had just got under way and could be seen streaking westward in a novel, probably long-planned getaway obviously intended to carry the thieves roughly 120 miles to Maine, the portal through which they could vanish into one of the many states beyond. And Kentville detachment also saw one chance of defeating them. A priority phone call to Sackville detachment, in New Brunswick, relayed to the *Fort Starnes* lying off that port, put her on the track of the *Cheetah* at once.

The fastest patrol ship in the world, and one of the most modern, this motor launch of the Force's Marine Division, Canada's Coast Guard, left at eight bells, midnight. Soon her two high-speed engines were driving her down the Bay of Fundy at over seventeen knots. But even with her searchlight sweeping the waters, her wireless asking every vessel within range to report the *Cheetah*, she might miss the fugitive in the wide, dark bay. Besides, the *Cheetah* was worthy of her name, if not so fast as the *Fort Starnes*, and had an eight-mile start. So it really was "touch and go."

At 7 A.M. Frank's suspense was ended by a phone call from York:

"The *Fort Starnes* intercepted the *Cheetah* fifteen miles (just fifteen miles!) from the Maine coast an hour ago. The men aboard *are* Buster Sims and Dirty Davis. They had $10,000 of the stolen money hidden in the engine room. Carry on looking for the murder weapon."

Frank carried on. This gun might well be near the road between the scene of the murders and Vine's summer home, hurled from the getaway car in momentary panic while the men rushed southward. Pal apparently agreed, for he plunged eagerly into the undergrowth. Never had he been more thorough. Yet two hours of rummaging brought no luck.

"Hell!" said Frank. "Twelve o'clock!"

And just then Pal gave tongue, from deep among bushes over a Tommy gun covered with finger-prints.

The vast Force trap was closing. York, whom Frank reached by phone at Havelock where he now had a powerful radio transmission truck and many patrols, said:

"That's the gun. Bring it in. Sims and Davis won't talk. But we've just found the getaway car twenty miles north of here. And Quebec Provincial Police say it was stolen in Montreal two weeks ago, I think by Sims and Davis coming from Vancouver."

Pal went into action again at the car. In three hours of hard trailing through woods he found another empty Good-o potted-meat tin bearing telltale finger-prints, then a slip of paper inscribed "Hampton Self-Service", a death warrant—

if the Force could serve it. But then came darkness, with all trails and roads blocked for many miles around.

At daybreak the hunt launched a supreme effort to capture the fugitive before he broke through to Maine, Quebec or the nearby Game Reserve, in which he could live on moose and deer till the hue and cry died down. Another long-distance phone-call, reporting overnight on the Tommy gun, meat-tin and slip of paper, flown to Rockcliffe as quickly as possible, had stated that the Force could not identify the finger-prints on these items but that all had been made by the same man. And a cable from Vine in London indicated that man as Gordon Jacques, a shiftless character formerly employed at his summer place and probably tempted into the affair by Sims and Davis. Jacques' description was broadcast, and Frank and Pal led the day's work with new confidence.

Gold, a young second-string dog rushed in from Moncton, helped them. Yet Pal, almost saying "I'll show the puppy!", was foremost in exhausting hours that found a trail of meat tins, biscuits and banana skins clearly pointing into the Game Reserve. Patrols with walkie-talkies then took over till nightfall, when the trail was lost.

True to the Force tradition requiring senior officers to be in at the death in hard and dangerous man-hunts if they could manage it, Superintendent Grayson lent his skill and experience to his subordinates next day, sensing that the man who had fired that Tommy gun at the murdered couple was still armed and would stop at nothing if trapped. He also took to the air, guiding the hunt and searching the ground from "MP Hawk." But Jacques, evidently travelling at night and hiding by day, had vanished into the thick woods. And forty-eight hours of rumours and blind groping went by before an Indian reported seeing him two miles away.

He had a .303 rifle and a .45 revolver.

Inspector York threw a wide but steadily tightening noose of patrols around the vital area and thrust into it himself with Frank, Pal and two constables, Grayson being over on a flank in support.

This was to be Pal's great hour, for success in his biggest case—and in these woods—depended mainly on him. He rose to the occasion, like the magnificent lion-hearted veteran he was.

The dense thickets and dark glades smelt of death, utterly unseen but waiting in there somewhere to open a murderous fire. All the hunters could smell it as readily as Pal himself, particularly as night compelled them to resort now and then to flashlights, each light an easy target. But with rifles and revolvers ready all pushed on steadily, facing that hidden death in the old Force way.

Suddenly, on a cow-path, Pal picked up the trail. Growling, he sprang into the trees and brush to the left. Frank at once ordered him to "hag" and followed him with those nearest him. But Pal, true to his long training, would not attack, for as yet the quarry had not made a false move. He simply went on barking and growling.

Grayson, still on the flank, now saw the beam of a flashlight leap through the darkness in the dog's direction. "Good!" he thought, "Pal's got his man." An instant later a shot crashed from the bushes, the flashlight went out, Pal shrieked, and a voice said, "My God, he's killed!"

Clearly one of those terrible mischances bound to occur from time to time in such dangerous Force operations had happened now. Grayson grasped this at once and dashed to the spot where the light had been, reaching it in a few seconds. Yet another light, this time carefully screened, was shining at that spot before he got there. Inspector York, his face grotesquely white in that new beam, was bending over Frank. And crying over him was Pal.

The superintendent did not need York's hurried explanations. He saw all too well that Frank, like himself, had thought the fugitive captured and turned on the first light to complete the work, only to be fired at by a .303 rifle at almost point-blank range.

Grayson, in that black moment, showed the stuff that had made him a typical Force officer. Though Frank and Pal had meant so much to him for so long, he did not give way to sentiment. Instead, sharply reminding Pal that duty must come before love, he ordered his four-footed comrade to attack again.

And Pal, a Force member, again rose to the occasion as Frank had taught him. Regardless of the loss of his best friend and heedless of the next-to-certain death ready to strike at him from the gloom ahead, he charged his enemy. Grayson, York and the men with them rushed after him, found him circling that utterly beaten enemy, and snapped on the handcuffs.

Only then did Pal go back to mourn again, while, trying to comfort him, Grayson stroked the thick ruff and said:

"This settles it. You're going to pension right away. Yes, from now on, boy, you're mine!"

mighty mean indian

"But look out for Joe Moose. A mean Indian — mighty mean. And tonight he'll be fit for murder."

"Thanks, Mr. Wilson," said George, going properly formal for this official occasion with a man he normally called Keith. "I'll be careful."

He meant it, as Joe was the district's biggest Dog Rib, bigger even than George himself, and the toughest hard hitter and high kicker.

"Good boy!" said Keith. "You see, I'd hate to have a new Mountie in charge here at Fort Desolation, just because Corporal George Brodie's been transferred to Heaven through Joe Moose. Well, so long!"

And the trader heaved himself out of his usual seat, the police detachment's only easy chair, flashed George a smile from a face deep-weathered but still handsome, and left the building.

George watched him thoughtfully as he stepped from the little wharf into his boat, started the kicker and roared off across the shining river to his white post on the point. A good citizen, to come over specially to lay information that the Dog Ribs were making home brew, contrary to the North-West Territories Act. A very good citizen—

At two A.M. George switched off the electric light (rigged up for him by the signallers in charge of the local radio-telegraph station) and went down to the wharf himself. Constable Goldie MacGregor and Indian Patsy being away in the motor launch on patrol, he had to shove off alone, in the canoe. But two policemen and an Indian Special

220

Constable would have been two men too many and there was nothing like a canoe for a silent approach. Besides, George had his gun, for use if things got really hot—not otherwise.

The short sub-Arctic summer night hid his movements, and no one was stirring in the little settlement. Yet George hugged the river bank and barely lifted his paddle, for after all you never could tell. Only two miles like that, the Indians being camped close to Fort Desolation for trading and for enjoying the simple pleasures of the place, brought him near enough to see, by the light of a huge fire in the camp, that he was up against an ugly situation, the usually well-behaved Dog Ribs being drunk as Arctic owls.

Beaching his canoe a bit away from the rest, he appeared among the revellers before they knew it.

George quietly took the dipper just as Joe's huge hand lifted it, brimming, from the wash-boiler. He smelt and sniffed the stuff inside it. Rotgut, all right, stinking of yeast and tasting like prehistoric eggs.

"I want this, Joe," said George, moving the boiler out of harm's way. "Now, come over here and we'll talk."

Joe's answering high kick must have smashed in George's face if it had connected. And his head-down charge was like the charge of a wood-buffalo bull over there on Slave River.

George met that rush with a left that used to put recruits to sleep in the old depot days. But Joe still came on, threw enormous arms around him and started to hug him to death.

The other Dog Ribs staggered in the background, baying, while every husky and papoose in camp, including Joe's seven kids, howled with them. Only the head man, doddery, reeling old Mike Larondeaux, tried to stop the fight. But only Mrs. Moose, helping her husband, as a good wife should, actually joined it—with an axe. Through flickering firelight and a mist already hugged into his eyes, George saw her swing her weapon. She, Big Mary, was even bigger than Joe. If that axe got home—

The blow came so near to beheading George that it knocked his cap off and into the fire.

Joe also fell into the fire, as George broke his crushing hold with a judo twist. The Indian sprang out, a mass of wood-ashes, red-hot embers and soot. Mad with rage and pain, he bored in with a rush nothing could stop. George sidestepped but fell, with Joe on top of him.

That huge red hand clutched George's throat, the other, clenched into a cave-man's club, battered his head, while Big Mary made slash afer drunken slash at the Law's pinned feet. Head and feet seemed likely to fly off together. Just in time, George threw Joe aside and managed to scramble up again.

The Indian was slower, so that he plunged into a hay-maker, the fiercest George had delivered in seven years of Service rough-and-tumble. As he sprawled, the axe whizzed past, so close that George felt the wind of it and with such force that it buried itself to the helve in a stump and even Big Mary could not pull it out. Seizing this chance, George tripped her into the bushes, where she passed out from utter weariness and alcohol.

Which was as well, with Joe kicking again, a pack-mule kick apparently cracking three ribs. It doubled George up —and was followed by blows enough to kill a Sergeant-Major, let alone a Corporal. . .

With a whoop and a roar, M. P. Falcon, the Aviation Division's old Norseman, smart as all get out in the Force's blue and gold, dropped onto the river in front of Fort Desolation detachment. Inspector Hardcastle, flown in from Fort Smith to try Joe and the other home-brewers, stepped from her cabin into the waiting canoe.

As Goldie and Patsy swept him up to the wharf, excitement ran through the Dog Ribs, crowding the bank in their bright trade-shirts, like a wind through flowers. They grinned happily. The Inspector would probably give them a stiff jolt. But he was also giving them a real good show.

Even Big Mary Moose and her seven little mice managed a smile, though hers was tempered by some fear of what she and her scowling Joe might get from the Inspector.

George saluted, his well-kicked yet well-bandaged ribs hurting like hell.

"Cut yourself shaving?" asked Hardcastle, twinkling grey eyes on the adhesives plastering George's head. Then, noticing Joe's similar dressings, "Oh, tangled with a grizzly —I see—"

George managed a dutiful grin, disregarding the fact that the end of his fight with Joe had been no grinning matter.

Somehow, using another judo trick, he had whipped the Indian into a remarkably awkward kneeling posture, both arms doubled up behind him, blubbery mouth howling for mercy.

T' 'n steel had flashed as George flicked on the handcuffs, saving himself from death, Joe from murder.

"Put the boiler in the canoe and bring everybody to the detachment in the morning," he had told Head Man Mike, as well as he could through numb and swollen lips.

Lastly, he had marched the high kicker down to the beach, bound for the clink, while the bleary eyes of a camp shocked into sobriety and silence looked on glumly.

Court now opened in the detachment kitchen-living room —much too full, in spite of Big Mary driving the kids out from among the boots and spurs with blows and curses. But the Queen's scarlet, the swarthy, bright-clad Indians and Keith Wilson's contrasting blond glamour made this glimpse of Law and Order at work in the North impressive.

Keith was the first witness.

"I sold Joe Moose, the prisoner, Mike Larondeaux, and one or two others what added up to about a case of yeast last Monday," he began. "Next—let's see, yes, it would be on Wednesday—I happened to hear Moose and his wife in my store sort of planning to make home-brew with that yeast."

Hardcastle asked, "Didn't it strike you as unwise to sell

the band so much in the first place—enough to—er—bake buns for a Mounted Police division?"

"Never gave it a thought!" Keith assured him. "Why should I? But I warned George—Corporal Brodie—soon as I knew."

"Good of you!" remarked the Inspector drily.

So the trials went on, till Joe, Mike and half a dozen more had been found guilty of various charges and awarded sentences rising in Joe's case to a year with hard labour and in Mike's to six months of the same.

"Can't jail 'em at Fort Smith," the Inspector told George. "Our cells are overcrowded now. But when we've room, I'll take Moose off your hands. An ugly customer—"

As he returned to the Norseman, Hardcastle added, "Keep an eye on Keith Wilson, Corporal. Looks as if he's trying to discredit the Indians for reasons of his own. We'll see."

George thought he began to see later that month as he sat on the detachment steps with Keith for a minute or two of a drowsy afternoon while keeping an eye not only on the trader but on Joe at work and Keith suddenly exploded, "Call *that* hard labour! You treat him much too soft. Look at those huskies over there!" He nodded at the fine, big fellows of George's team, all wagging friendly tails as they stood each on a long chain before a separate kennel. "Got to handle dogs and mean Indians just the same, to my mind —and that's rough."

George smiled, thinking of the reaction of the Indian prisoners to the white man's idea of punishment. Young Goldie MacGregor, acting jailer, held them down to strict routine, confinement and actually strenuous work. Very early every morning his iron-throated gong hurled them out of their blankets to tidy their cell and endure an unaccustomed wash. Early every evening, unless some job delayed them, he locked them up. And in between they chopped cord after cord of wood, sorted and re-sorted heavy cases in the storehouse, shifted big rocks to deepen the water off the wharf. But, for the first time in their lives, they were sleeping in a nice, dry house and nice, clean beds and eating three square meals a day.

They were getting sleek and plump, Mike slowly expanding, like one of the sunflowers in the detachment garden, though Joe still looked sullen.

So George smiled.

"Our way seems O.K.," he pointed out, "both with dogs and men. Cigarette?"

"Huh," said Keith, then, unconsciously quoting the Inspector, "We'll see."

He left George to a detested job — filling up forms for Indians claiming Family Allowance.

Soon afterwards, as fall set the North aflame with fire-weed, turned the cottonwoods from green to gold, and frosted windows, they did see, through still more serious trouble.

Two of the seven little mice paddled madly over from Keith's store to announce its beginnings to Goldie, who was supervising Patsy, Joe and Mike in beaching the motor launch for the winter. And Goldie hurriedly passed their report on to George in the storehouse, overhauling dog-harness.

"Damn that Wilson!" said Goldie. "He's giving the Dog Ribs short weight. They're over at his store, cashing their Family Allowance credits for grub. And he's palmed off bags of flour that aren't quite full, boxes of tea with a few packets missing—and sparked off something like a riot. Seems if we don't step in, there'll be bloodshed!"

"Come on!" said George. Without wasting time in getting his rifle or revolver, he sprang like a deer from the storehouse into the stern of the detachment canoe, Goldie taking the bow paddle, while Special Constable Patsy and Joe grabbed the paddles in the Moose canoe and followed with Mike and the mice as passengers. Swishing through reeds, dead water-lilies and young ice melting in the noonday sun, the two craft fairly rushed across the open river beyond towards the trader's post.

As they got nearer, George noted murderous roars from inside it and many Dog Ribs running around it.

"Stay here and keep these people quiet!" he yelled to Goldie, grounding the canoe on the sandy beach. And, elbowing the angry crowd aside, he plunged singlehanded into the racketing store.

It was full of scowling Indians, surrounding Big Mary, who faced Keith Wilson across his counter. Both were howling like huskies over a last whitefish, Mrs. Moose hurling threats and protests at Keith in a babel of Indian English and her native tongue, Keith answering with threats and orders.

The trader had his finger on both triggers of a twelve-gauge, double-barreled shotgun, pointed at the crowd in general and Big Mary in particular.

"Out of my store!" he was bawling. "Out of it! Out! Or, by Judas, I'll shoot!"

His face, now, would have cracked any Hollywood camera.

"Too long down here!" thought George. "The North has 'got' him!" But all he said was, "Take it easy, Keith! Put your gun down, very quietly, and tell me what it's all about."

Keith lowered the gun but still kept a finger on the triggers as he muddlingly repeated the Dog Rib charges against him.

George patiently heard him out, then the complaints of Big Mary and the rest. Backed by vouchers Keith had given them and by many bags and boxes undoubtedly holding less than the vouchers called for, their statements seemed gospel truth.

"How about it, Keith?" asked George.

Keith snapped, "Those bags and boxes came up to Waterways from Edmonton by rail, then on here by barge. Train and barge crews are only human. They're probably responsible."

"Somehow, Keith," said George, trying to keep the talk on a friendly basis, "I don't see an old trader like you accepting anything short weight from Edmonton. Furthermore, let me remind you—of that!"

He pointed at a poster reading, "Any one selling or giving directly or indirectly to Indians any intoxicant or intoxicating fluid in the form of patent or proprietary medicines, cordials or perfumes will be liable on conviction to a fine of $300 or to six months' imprisonment."

Keith let go the gun and chuckled, "Imagine working up a jag on perfume! But just where does that concern me?"

"You almost broke that law when Joe Moose got into the jam he's in today," George explained. "It should warn you to be careful now."

"Get out of my store!" yelled Keith, snatching up the gun.

It went off, sounding like the Crack of Doom in that confined space and shattering two windows. The Dog Ribs all but panicked, on general principles and because killing a Mounted Policeman was second only to killing the missionary's God Himself. Fortunately, George had whipped the gun upwards and out of Keith's hands almost before the trader had touched it.

Through the stunned hush he said, "Don't ever do that again."

"An accident!" stammered Keith, now white as the short-weight flour.

"Sure, sure!" George replied smoothly. "And I'll let you off with a warning if you make up that short weight here and now."

"O.K.!" grumbled Keith. "Little mistake, that's all."

But there were dog-whips in the smile he gave the Indians, as big Mary grabbed George's hand, with tears fat as herself rolling down her cheeks. And the hatred his eyes exchanged with Joe, who had crashed into the store when the gun went off, told George that this case was not yet closed, maybe not more than started.

So George felt almost unqualified relief as he sat in a Mackenzie River Oil Company's six-passenger ski plane blaring steadily over monotonous winter landscape between Fort Desolation and Fort Smith and reminded himself that in an hour or so Joe Moose would be occupying room now available in Inspector Hardcastle's jail, well out of Keith Wilson's way.

Word that Joe would at last be welcome at Fort Smith had come in by radio-telegraph soon after freeze-up. And then the oil plane, unexpectedly dropping into Fort Desolation for some minor adjustment, had offered to take the Indian and an escort to the jail when its repairs were completed. George had gladly accepted this chance. Now complete with side-arms, his Smith and Wesson .38, he filled a back seat, carefully watching Joe in the seat ahead of him.

Too bad that Keith Wilson, also accepting a lift to Fort Smith on business, should be in a seat across the aisle, particularly as Joe was as sore as Joe could be! Bitterly homesick for Big Mary and her papooses, recently returned with the other Dog Ribs to their trap-lines on Moccasin River, and bitterly jealous of Mike, who, having served his time, had gone too, the Indian, obviously, was finding Keith's presence in the plane just that little extra bit too much.

Glancing out of his window, George had a shock.

He saw fog, the terror of the bush pilot.

More than that, the co-pilot came out of the cockpit, swayed over to Gordon Murray and two other company engineers in the remaining seats and shouted something. Murray passed the bad news to George.

"Radio's hay-wire!" he shouted. "Can't pick up any one to talk us in. So we're landing first chance, before it gets too thick."

The lights flicked on, "No smoking. Fasten safety-belts."

George got puzzled, clumsy Joe fixed up, fastened his own belt and waited, while, across the way, Keith sat tense. . .

The coldest wind George ever felt in his life licked back his senses, the hottest pain throbbed in his left knee. He was in a white bed—no, a snowdrift. Shadowy, motionless forms looked down on him—his "G" Division on parade—no, trees in fog. Inklings of the truth came as he struggled up in agony and stared down the swath of shattered spruce to a hint of frozen river. For now he could see a nearby misplaced motor bus become a cabin plane with its back broken and its wings gone God-knew-where.

All was now terribly clear. Trying for an emergency landing on the ice down there, the pilot of that plane had overshot it, to crash among the trees. And, of course, it was the oil company plane—George's. He suddenly remembered the spruce trunks rattling and swishing like the pickets of a huge fence along which a boy-giant ran an outsize stick, as the aircraft ploughed through the tree-tops, and the screeching, metallic roar of wings incredibly crumbling just before the black-out. . . In some unaccountable way he had got off—and out—with that injured knee. But what about his fellow-travellers?

Gritting his teeth, he floundered through deep snow to the plane, put his head in at a door burst open. Keith, pinned under wreckage, burst out crying:

"For God's sake, George, get me out of here! We're the only ones left. Look at that shambles ahead! That damned Joe Moose of yours has skipped—I knew he would. Not a scratch on him— Grabbed a gun and a grub-pack and beat it to his people on the Moccasin, leaving us to die!"

George staggered along outside the plane, peering in here and there. Keith was right. Joe was gone. And the rest were dead.

Keith shrieked when George managed at last to lift him clear. His leg was broken. But George, thank God, thanks very much, God, was able to find the first aid kit, an axe and a case of canned soup.

"Soon bandage you up, Keith," he said, thickly. "Give you some chicken gumbo. Fog'll lift soon, bound to—"

In no time, considering, he had a fire going, put on splints, improvised for Keith's leg. He might even have started walking for help along the river, if it had been possible to leave Keith alone or if he'd an idea of where he was or if survival training didn't lay down that it was best to stick to the plane—and if his knee hadn't been a pretty well unworkable source of constant agony.

"For God's sake, don't you beat it too!" sobbed Keith.

George hacked off his retort and the tops from two cans, with self-control and his knife. Quickly heated, that gumbo was marvellous—put new life into both of them—

Bed-rolls dragged from the plane assured more comfort. And George tried to get maps from the cockpit, to pinpoint his position. But debris and dead men were in the way.

A look-round led him painfully through the drifts to the river and a familiar-seeming mound. Clearing part of it from snow, he uncovered a painted board reading:

"Royal Canadian Air Force. Cache 17."

Anguish and a splitting headache were ruining his powers of concentration. But memory told him that Cache 17 was on Moccasin River, two days' march from the Dog Rib trapping area but a long, long way from any place frequented by white men and far off the plane's proper course. Joe knew this country thoroughly, though George did not, and, therefore, should reach home soon. Once there, even if he intended to abandon them, he would not be able to hide the facts from Mike. And good old Mike would come. They were practically saved already.

Yet "Hell, George!" Keith groaned, hearing the glad news, "That's finished it! The Dog Ribs won't come here for me —or for you, while I'm with you!"

"Bunk!" said George, sharply, "I'll make some more soup!"

Night came, another very short day, another terribly long night, another day, so many nights and days that a George starving to keep Keith alive on most of the soup turned too muddle-headed to count them. Yet the fog persisted, thickening in the tree-tops and cutting visibility at ground-level to about fifty yards.

Suddenly, the humming in George's ears seemed to change in key and volume for a few seconds at a time, getting

louder every time, then fading into what it had been before.
Mosquitoes, of course, the enormous kind specially created
to torture Northern patrols— No, it couldn't be, in winter.
Then, also suddenly, George realized that the changed
humming came from an Air Force Search and Rescue plane,
sweeping back and forth, back and forth, along the river.
Greatly daring and with next to no chance of spotting them
but an aircraft, just the same—Keith croaked, "Here we are!
You boneheads, can't you see?" and George hopped madly
to the cache with some idea of making it a signal by setting
it on fire. But the plane flew away long before he got there.

After that the White Silence closed right in, allowing
nothing much to break it except the ghostly howl of far-off
wolves, Keith's disappointed weeping and, eventually, his
senseless talk. He counted countless muskrat pelts and
solemnly assessed their worth in trade for stone-stiff, snow-
white Gordon Murray and the pilot, who stared at him
from shadowy wreckage but offered no reply.

Clearly the man was dying, in spite of George's efforts.
And, by the time he went, George himself would be so weak
that he too would die in his turn. But meanwhile he must
look after Keith as long as wheezing breath rose mistily
from the trader's lips and served his shrinking body.

The hell of it was that the Dog Ribs weren't coming.
Keith had been right, Joe was mean all through, not to be
changed by kindness. But other things were coming. George
drew his .38 to deal with them as the occasional howls got
nearer and at last the animals producing them broke
through the fog in a final rush.

At Fort Smith, later, the Inspector said:
"You nearly shot up my teams, Corporal, after I'd run
them ragged to reach you in time. Sure, huskies sound and
look like wolves—but wolves won't attack a man on guard.
However, you'd gone nuts. And memory'd failed you too,
earlier on. Cache 17, where you crashed, isn't near the Dog
Rib trap-lines, it's just a week from here by trail. So Moose

came here to tell us your location—not scratched but almost
crawling, from injuries inside—came back to prison, because,
he said, you used him right. That saved you, boy — *and*
Wilson!"

Still weak and with a big lump in his throat, George
asked, "But is he—dead?"

"This is the hospital, not the morgue. He's going back to
Big Mary and the mice when he's well."

Then George saw Keith and Joe, in nearby beds, both
smiling.

"beaned with bottle"

They were going to charge. . .

Reality replaced Romance, the death and danger often found in Force life pushing its lighter aspects out of the mind's eye, as the stetson-hatted, scarlet-coated young men with pennoned, flashing lances swung their magnificent black horses into one long straight line. Silence fell and tension rose, silence so deep that the few sounds breaking it—the jingle of curb-chains, the clang of a stirrup-iron—seemed merely to deepen it, tension so great that it became intolerable.

A trumpet sounded. The line instantly changed into a wave of surging, tossing light and colour in furious motion to the roar of a cheer, the thunder of hoofs at full gallop. This for some utterly breathless seconds, till the rush halted and froze on the verge of overwhelming the dense mass of people in its path, applause shattered the tension, fairly lifting the roof of the vast arena, and yet another Musical Ride reached its dramatic end.

Corporal Jim Harington, right-flank man and a realist, wondered if the girl who had watched it, night after night, from a centre box, at last sensed the death and danger. When the riders wheeled to salute the guest of honour and then make their exit march to lilting music and that sustained applause, he got his answer. For a side-glance showed her smiling straight at him, as usual, and briskly clapping, as usual, in romantic fervour. Ah, well, women were built that way! Besides, the Ride regularly toured the chief cities of Canada and the States, performing at fairs

233

and horse shows like this one, to maintain the goodwill represented by her attitude. So he had "no complaints."

As the men off-saddled and bedded down the horses after filing into the stables, Inspector Bellhouse, Jim's commanding officer, brought in the usual very important visitors. And there she was, beside him.

Halting, she said, "Hullo!"; Jim said, "Hullo!"; the inspector said, "So you've met Miss Kemp?"; she said, "Well, he has—now!" and Jim called himself a chump, for this very good reason: the girl was Susie Kemp, socialite daughter of Andrew Kemp, a big industrialist standing behind her; their pictures were often in the papers and he should have recognized them both from the moment he saw them on the first night of the show.

Next thing he knew, he was seeing her in boxes and at parties at other shows on the circuit, at Andrew Kemp's country-house during a few days' leave when the Ride tour was over, at the wheel of her fine fast car, and lastly at a big hotel in what was supposed to be a final meeting before he went back west to a remote detachment. And he was telling her:

"A Force wife has no easy time—never has had, since the days when she tried to make both ends meet in a log cabin while the Old Man chased horse-thieves and cattle-rustlers. Sure, things have improved. She may live in a big city now, in modern barracks or a house with all mod. cons. She's on the phone, has radio, sometimes TV, usually a car, always more money. But on detachment she still fills in when the Old Man's away. She takes messages, passes 'em on by radio-telephone, does the housework, puts in a long day. She still doesn't know when they won't bring the Old Man in with his head shot off by gunmen. As for glamour, she'll hardly ever see a horse. O.K. for a Little Prairie Flower but not for a hothouse orchid like you!"

To which Susie dreamily replied, "I'll have a diamond and platinum engagement ring—"

So they were married, with the blessing of Andrew Kemp,

who told his son-in-law that like many big businessmen
he thought the Force a fine preparatory school for later
graduation into the top executive circles of civil life. The
press justly raved over "the lovely bride." Seven hundred
guests consumed one hundred pounds of wedding cake, 288
bottles of champagne. And the honeymoon was spent on a
Caribbean cruise, Daddy Kemp's chief wedding gift.

Jim's first misgivings vanished in six months spent with
"F" Division at Regina barracks, to which he was posted to
give his bride a chance to settle in and down. Veteran Force
wives, often little older than Susie herself, taught her the
fundamental facts of Force life, how to cook, what subjects
not to talk about and what questions not to ask even her
husband. Detail she picked up quickly for herself. She
became popular, winning or helping to win swimming,
badminton and other trophies for the Force.

As for Romance, "Why, Jim," she said, "the place is full
of it!"

He knew that she found it among the horses concentrated
here for recruit training, the scarlet-clad parades, the
coming and going of planes and cars on mysterious business
eventually reported in the papers as another Force victory
against crime. But she also found it in the chapel, the
museum, the old guns and the memorial to Force heroes
in the square, the old cemetery.

"O.K.!" he said, warmly, "Let's hope you feel the same
when we go out on detachment."

Go out they did—to a place that would really test her, as
Jim saw quite well. Tadpole Lake had a brand-new set of
modern buildings specially designed for a married N.C.O.
and a single constable, each with entirely self-contained
quarters. But it was haunted by memories of bitter fighting
in the neighbourhood during the North-West Rebellion or,
if you preferred it, "troubles" of 1885. The presently peaceful
yet disturbingly silent descendants of the Indians concerned
were still there, in hundreds. So too was a small Roman
Catholic mission. But the rest of the slice of Saskatchewan

policed by the detachment was wild woodland interspersed with isolated farms, ranches and only two villages served by just a few rough trails and one main highway.

Then, although there was not much crime, Jim and big soft-spoken young Constable Ned Paley were always terribly busy and too often away, unavoidably, at the same time.

So Jim feared that a gay big-city orchid would find Tadpole Lake no hothouse. He also wondered if occasional breaks, when Susie drove to Saskatoon or Prince Albert, and occasional visits from a girl-friend made up for a lot of housework and "filling in."

Yet she took it all in a way that made him very proud of her.

Only a hint of horror sounded in her voice as she called him while he was out patrolling in the detachment's radio-equipped car to report "an Indian badly hurt by farm machinery and just brought in here . . . multiple injuries . . . better come quickly." He drove back to her at the highest speed allowed by a dangerously winding, skiddy trail and expected something grim on sighting many Indians, trucks and cars at the house door. But big red splashes in the dust and over the front steps hardly prepared him for the full ghastly truth:

Her living-room swam with blood, an enormous, slippery pool, covering the floor, her nice, new scatter-rugs, her embroidered cushions. In the pool and on the cushions, arms crushed and mangled, lay the young victim of that terrible farm-machine. Beside him stood and knelt three other Indians, stupefied, helpless. Beside him too knelt Susie, white face, hands, dress and apron all bloody, trying to apply first aid, Mounted Police style, to one beyond any sort of aid for ever.

Jim quickly made an inspection, told the Indians all was over, then said, "Susie, you can leave the rest to me." But she said, "No, we'll finish things together," and tried to make herself useful till there was nothing left to do except to wash the room out thoroughly, a job he insisted on tackling

himself. Later, over a picnic meal in the kitchen, he told
her, "You were . . . magnificent!" and wisely made no
comment when she ate nothing.

Again, she happened to be with him when he drove down
to the Saskatchewan ferry and saw that this swift-flowing
river had added yet another to its long list of victims. Pushing through a silent little cluster of people on the bank,
they found that the inert, dripping object of their interest
was Skinny Webster. Twelve-year-old son of the farmer
living nearest the detachment, Skinny was Susie's favourite,
always trying to help her, always hungry for pies and
cookies. Jim went to work on him with swift, tireless
efficiency—and with Susie as a worthy second-in-command.

She made sure that his instructions were instantly obeyed,
sending this man off for blankets, that one for a doctor, took
turns at artificial respiration for three long hours, till the
doctor came to call it useless, coaxed the boy's weeping
mother to tell Jim what he had to know of how Skinny fell
off the ferry in midstream. Then she calmed the woman
down, took over her battered old car and drove her home.

"I'm not going to cry," Susie told Jim afterwards. "It's
all in the game—you said so yourself."

This was true—though her words set him wondering.
More exploits on her part lulled that wonder for a while.
But soon it woke again.

Coming home when Ned Paley was away, he found that
Susie had locked herself in, with all the windows bolted—
on a stifling hot afternoon. A haunted look on her face
betrayed that she sensed his disapproval, but she said
nothing till he quietly asked her, over coffee, with the
windows open:

"Remember, Susie, when we first met, I said I was a
realist and we agreed we'd always tell each other the truth?"

She nodded, so he went on:

"Well, do you always lock yourself in when you're alone?"

"Yes, always," she said.

"But why?"

"I'm scared of the Indians. Ever since they brought that dying man in here, I feel I can't tell what they'll do—and I can't forget what happened here in the Rebellion. Some of the tough characters coming here for you get fresh—I wouldn't have told you if you hadn't asked, as any girl with any looks at all gets used to that. The trouble is, the nearest white man's old Father Savoie at the mission. If I phoned our next white neighbour, he'd take half an hour to get here. Calling you or Ned by radiophone mightn't get help any quicker. And I'd hate to use my gun. Rather play safe!"

"I see," he said, slowly, "I see."

He thought the situation over for two days and, while relaxing under a tree and so well fixed for a good talk after supper, put his conclusions to her with:

"Susie, I guess I'll leave the Force."

"*What*?" she asked, sitting bolt upright.

"You heard," he laughed. "After all, I've done nearly two terms of service and I'm not so young as I was—or so enthusiastic. Your Dad has a good place waiting for me the moment I say the word, you know that. It's time I made real money and had city comforts. How about it?"

But the flash of joy he expected did not rush into her face. Instead, she looked him straight in the eye and said:

"Jim Harington, a fine chap you are, saying we must always tell each other the truth and then coming up with lies! Yes, lies, at least when you talk about not being so young and enthusiastic and wanting big money and the rest of it! Think I don't know that you're heart and soul in the Force, that you'll probably be sergeant if you take on again and that your chance of a commission's extra-good? The Commissioner himself told me you're one of his best men. So don't give me that stuff. All you're thinking about, my boy, is—me! And I won't have it. I'll stick it out!"

In the end, as she admitted that she might never be a real Force wife at heart, they agreed on a compromise, which she summed up:

"I'll drive home for six months' change and see how I

feel after that. If another round of social life doesn't sicken me of Tadpole Lake, nothing will."

So off she went and in no time he was batching it again. Ned Paley was cut off from him in the single man's quarters, the lowest part of the house, and was often away in connection with a long complicated case soon to come to trial. That meant loneliness and missing her all the more. Soon he marvelled over the fact that he had ever been able to put up with unmarried life on detachment and queried whether he could remain a grass widower for long. But at least he could console himself with this: Susie was apparently having a grand time and really submitting herself to a thorough test.

As if to prove it, she mailed him cuttings from the social pages of the papers in cities in which she stayed a while with relations and friends on her leisurely homeward drive. Headlines and columns of flowery trash, occasionally reinforced by pictures, reminded him of the spreads devoted to their wedding by the press. "SUSAN KEMP HARINGTON LOCAL GUEST" solemnly proclaimed the Saskatoon *Star-Phoenix*, the Winnipeg *Free Press* featured "DINNER FOR FORMER SUSIE KEMP," the Chicago *Tribune* insisted "CANADIAN MOUNTIE'S WIFE THRILLS EXCLUSIVE BARBECUE." Fortunately she knew enough to keep the Force out of all this as much as possible, to scribble on the *Tribune* and similar offerings "*Not* my work" and supplement it all with long letters.

Yet the sum total of her cuttings and letters depressed him. They seemed to say that he would have to choose between Susie and the service, which plainly meant that his days in the Force were numbered.

Murderous hands darted into his life without the slightest warning while he was reading this Chicago news. A woman left alone for only an hour or two on a farm near Yorkton, about 250 miles away, had been found manually strangled by a man who broke down two heavy doors and faced two revolver-shots to reach his strong, active victim, crushed her desperate resistance and got away by car. The radiophone

call reporting this to all "F" detachments warned them to
keep a sharp lookout and made arrangements to catch the
killer with special patrols, roadblocks and police service
dogs. Jim set Susie's news aside, put local people on their
guard and spent more time than usual running around in the
car as a direct result.

He felt confident that he would soon be told that the
murderer had been captured. But a week passed with no
concrete success, though Force aircraft joined a greatly
extended hunt and dozens of false clues were followed till
they faded into thin air.

Then the Prince Albert *Herald* came out with "THE
STRANGLER STRIKES AGAIN" over details of an attack on
another woman, this time on a secondary road thirty-odd
miles from the city. The victim was having a picnic lunch
in her car by the roadside when she was seized from behind
by some one moving so quietly that she had no idea he was
there until too late. Luckily for her a noisy truck came along
and frightened her enemy away at the critical moment or
she would have died then and there. But, unluckily for the
Force, the truck-driver, naturally, revived the girl before
he reported the assault to the first roadblock he passed
while rushing her to hospital. And this reviving took so
long that by the time the first police car reached the near-
fatal picnic-place it could find no more than blurred tracks
of the getaway car in a minor trail leading to fields where
all trace was lost.

That second crime started the western press and many
westerners screaming about "The Strangler," who became a
household word in next to no time. Also it swung the main
hunt into an area barely a hundred miles from Tadpole Lake
and put Jim very much on the alert, as the map showed him
that The Strangler was moving northwestward and so might
suddenly wrap those deadly fingers around some throat
under Corporal Harington's protection.

Such protection, Jim saw, was clearly needed, for the
calls now frequently blaring through the radio-telephone

outdid the press in giving him a constantly clearer and more terrible picture of the quarry. Probably a local man, he knew the country intimately enough to choose isolated points for his assaults and to evade patrols and roadblocks, no doubt by night travel. Evidently well-spoken and inconspicuous, he had not permanently impressed people who must have seen him. Resourceful, he had apparently laid in a good supply of food before making his first attack, as no word of his buying or stealing any reached the Force, and he might be disguising himself and his car, as no suspected driver or car even remotely glimpsed near Yorkton could be linked with any in the Prince Albert district.

Worse still, Jim thought, The Strangler was probably mad, yet sane outwardly. For no motive underlying his crimes had been discovered so far. No violent lunatic was known to be at large. No man thought likely to have gone suddenly insane was absent from his usual haunts anywhere within striking distance of the points where this killer had found his victims. Nor had any one reported to the Force as acting oddly turned out to be worthy of suspicion.

So with isolated Saskatchewan women liable to be murdered by a probably local, well-spoken, inconspicuous, resourceful madman also shown to be fearless, ruthless, determined and immensely powerful, Jim thanked God that Susie was safely far away. More, he told himself that, as inescapable service in remote detachments like Tadpole Lake must expose her to such dangers sooner or later, he really would have to leave the Force.

Then The Strangler made another pounce, radically altering the picture. The Moose Jaw *Times-Herald* suddenly trumpeted, "CREEPING DEATH INVADES THIS DISTRICT —LEADING FARMER SEIZED IN DARK." And more official messages almost swamped Jim in further details.

Suffering pangs of "night-starvation," Leading Farmer had left his bed and gone downstairs to raid the ice-box. The electric-light bulb serving the stairs concerned failed to respond when he tried to switch it on. He remembered recently discovering that it needed replacement and deciding to let it be till morning—a plan that now exposed him to disaster. For he could get along without it and without troubling to cross the living-room and kitchen to switches off his well-beaten track to the pantry. So get along he did, in the dark—

Till, suddenly, an unseen something hurled him flat on his back, then leapt on him, seeking his throat. The split second between the hurling and the leaping gave him just time to let out a yell of terror, the leap crashed over four crates of eggs and the uproar roused the house. By the grace of an exceedingly kind God, the house included Tom, his gigantic son, and Bob the husky hired man, both sleeping with loaded rifles beside them, no matter how he pooh-poohed them. These rushed to the rescue like midwestern tornadoes. That saved Leading Farmer, for by the time his boys pounded in the assailant was out of the window and of range, by car, leaving a sack of food behind.

Jim joined the entire province in rendering grateful thanks. But whereas most people were thinking only of a providential escape, to Jim the move meant much more. It relieved him of an enormous burden, as the location of this new attack suggested that The Strangler had run far south of Tadpole Lake, probably in full flight for the United States, with the main hunt springing to cut him off. Again, it apparently proved The Strangler less dangerous and more vulnerable than he had seemed so far, his readiness to rush on men as well as on women partly disposing of the idea that he was a sex maniac, while his obvious need of meeting his new food shortage would expose him much more frequently to capture.

The phone rang soon after subdivisional headquarters had told Jim about these developments. It was Ned Paley, calling from Regina.

"I'll be finished with this trial tomorrow," he reported, "so expect me back at lunch time the day after. The

Inspector's driving up with me and we'll make an early start."

"Good boy!" said Jim. "Then I can get some rest."

As he swung the car into the approach to the detachment just forty-eight hours later, after another routine patrol, he felt better than he had for some time. He had just heard by radiophone that The Strangler was surrounded near Leading Farmer's home, the Inspector and Ned would be waiting to give him companionship, with the latest Force gossip, and he should hear from Susie at home in the East this afternoon.

Sure enough, Ned's tall, broad form could be partly seen between the curtains of the single man's kitchen, probably fixing a meal for all three of them—a good cook—good old Ned! Jim tootled a cheery greeting as he pulled up in front of the garage, slipped from behind the wheel, entered the kitchen.

And The Strangler—not Ned but The Strangler—turned and pounced on him.

Dashed against the wall with such terrific violence that it left him breathless, he was too stunned to grasp the full facts:

That the man concerned with Leading Farmer and now cornered down there was one of those cranks always ready to imitate some criminal "in the news" or a tramp whose attack on Leading Farmer at this time was pure coincidence; that The Strangler had been hiding near Tadpole Lake ever since he had tried to kill the girl near Prince Albert; that being now, in fact, short of food, he had watched Jim leave the detachment, then broken into Ned's kitchen to get it; and that this act, in broad daylight, confirmed his supreme daring and cunning, as no ordinary man would burgle even an empty Force building or foresee that chance passersby would think him there on lawful business, simply because such a burglary was bold beyond belief.

This, though, Jim could tell at once: not only was he up

against The Strangler but the Inspector and Ned had not arrived, which left him facing the fight of his life.

As his huge enemy dashed at him again with those deadly hands outstretched, he punched the snarling face with the hardest right he had ever driven home, side-stepping as he did so, in the dire knowledge that if once The Strangler clamped him in that famous grip he was a dead man. He felt the great head snap back, saw the powerful body reel back against the kitchen table and upset it. For one joyful instant he also felt that one blow had given him swift, decisive victory with a knockout. But in the same moment, yet another feeling—a white-hot flame shooting through his fist and up his arm—crushed his hopes. It told him he had broken his right hand—and with it his best chance of drawing his pistol and shooting his man into surrender. For the pistol hung in its holster over his right hip and to draw it with his left hand at the speed now required was practically impossible.

He tried to do it, only to find that before he got the holster open The Strangler, recovering from that tremendous near-knockout as if it had been little more than a tap from a baby, was charging at him again. He kept his chin down, still grimly aware that he must guard his throat at all costs. He had neither time nor room to make another attempt to draw the pistol. But he beat the rush back with a straight left and followed it up with a grip on the open shirt-collar while The Strangler was still stumbling among overturned furniture, the table and two chairs.

A useless grip—with one mighty twist The Strangler tore himself out of the shirt, revealing a torso Hercules might have envied. Plunging in once more for Jim's throat, he fell into a judo trap, Jim dropping the ruined shirt to seize a wrist and twist the arm in a way which should have brought The Strangler to his knees, yelling for mercy. Again no use—The Strangler evidently also knew something of iudo, was perhaps an ex-commando. At any rate he broke the hold before Jim could make it effective.

Now they were locked together in a grizzly-bear hug, easier for Jim to maintain with one hand almost paralyzed than any other form of defence and better to endure than choking under the pressure of hands like steam-shovels. Reeling around the room in a hideous, burlesqued waltz, they banged into shelves and cupboards, from which boxes and tins and bottles cascaded over them, all smashing and crashing like high-explosive shells. Then, tripped up by the litter of obstacles, they fell into the mess, rolling over and over and back and forth like two fighting dogs, each mad to get on top of the other and stay there.

Jim kneed The Strangler off, so that he flew backwards into the bedroom and, springing after him, got in another judo grip—only to have it broken once more. Regardless of that white-hot hand, Jim battered away at face, chest and ribs, driving his target this way and that with blows that should have killed a mule. The Strangler counter-attacked, tearing Jim's face with great scratches, gouging at his eyes, pummeling lips and nose as he went on struggling with that ruthless, terrible determination to get that throat-hold. Poor Ned's books, pictures, bedside lamp and radio were knocked, kicked and trampled into utter ruin. A few moments more and the place would have been as devastated as the kitchen if The Strangler had not driven Jim back into that first battlefield.

Thrown from his feet by the rush, Jim hit the stove with a force appalling enough to crack two ribs and all but wind him utterly. But, rallying somehow, he repulsed his gleefully yelling foe with a judo chop that had a staggering, if not decisive, effect. As The Strangler reeled and gasped, Jim made one last attempt to draw his pistol. Again no use—a new charge made him fall back once more on a bear-hug. And once more they rolled and struggled on the floor among the wreckage.

Wreckage it surely was—nothing short of a blitz could have done more damage. The men too seemed almost beaten to pieces, were less like human beings than like sweat- and blood-drenched beasts thrown into an Ancient Roman arena to fight to the death. And death was surely not far off for one of them. Though barely able to see, Jim could see that, as they stumbled to their feet for one last effort. More, he saw that victory might well lie with The Strangler. For he knew now that The Strangler was stronger and in better shape than he, besides being a real killer at heart.

Somewhere at the back of his mind he thought vaguely that this was the Reality, as apart from the Romance, of Force life. And through the thunder of his heart, the roar of two almost exhausted men panting for breath, he heard birds twittering and leaves rustling outside as peacefully as if the fiercest fight Tadpole Lake had known since the Rebellion meant nothing.

So much while the kitchen clock, still gamely ticking among the debris, marked the passing of one half-minute . . . Then the Strangler charged again, driving Jim back into the bedroom, this time on to the bed underneath him, into a position that must prove fatal.

With the last shred of his strength, Jim struggled to get free. It was no good. He could not throw aside that crushing weight. And inch by inch The Strangler's iron fingers were closing on his throat. He was done for. . . .

Yet through the blackness and the thunder of this prologue to violent death he suddenly heard what at any other time he would have recognized as a tremendous thud and the sharp breaking of glass. The crushing weight rolled off him to hit the floor with an even louder thud, the pressure on his throat went with it, and Ned Paley in his red serge with its buffalo-head badge swam through clearing mists to solidify at the foot of the bed and stand there staring.

Slowly Jim, recovering, grasped a situation which the Regina *Leader-Post* soon turned into this lead for the year's most sensational story:

BEANED WITH BOTTLE

Corporal Jim Harington of the Royal Canadian Mounted Police detachment at Tadpole Lake owes not merely his capture of The

Strangler but his very life to miraculous timing, quick thinking
and splendid courage not all his own, a spokesman for "F"
Division, with headquarters in this city, revealed today.

It appears that Corporal Harington, being alone when he
surprised The Strangler in the act of searching the detachment
for food, had to bear the full brunt of the attack. But at the
critical moment, when The Strangler was choking him to death,
help arrived in the shape of a handy beer-bottle, with which a
gallant supporter beaned the criminal so effectively as to knock
him cold. . . .

Then, still recovering, Jim also grasped who that supporter
really was.

"Susie!" he gasped—yes, Susie, white as a Saskatchewan
midwinter snowdrift, yet fierce as one of its timber-wolves
at bay, her red dress remarkably like Ned's serge, her Force
brooch like his badges.

"Don't waste time talking!" she snapped. "Give me your
handcuffs—"

"But where's the Inspector?" Jim croaked. "Where's Ned?
What are *you* doing here? Why didn't you let me know
you were coming?"

"Simple!" said Susie, expertly handcuffing the unconscious
Strangler. "The Inspector and Ned can't come till tomorrow
—held up on duty—asked me to tell you. As for me, when I
heard about The Strangler in Chicago and thought of other
women on detachment facing him with their husbands, I
knew I couldn't go on home. I had to turn back and join
you. But I didn't tell you for I knew that with that brute
still loose you'd try to stop me!"

"Sure would!" said Jim, visualizing his gallant little comrade driving alone, day and night, through murder-haunted
country just to be with him. Then he added, with a lump
in his throat not entirely of The Strangler's making. "From
now on, you're a real Force wife!"

"have done my best"

Seventh place on the long, long roll is held by "Dreamy," officially designated as Constable Daniel King.

On the Force's sixth birthday and his eighteenth—a good, omen, he thought—the recruiting team summoned him to the Windsor Hotel, Montreal, for an interview and medical examination. Joy and anxiety fought for first place in his heart: he had now a chance of filling one of this year's seventy-six vacancies, sought by seventeen hundred would-be constables like himself. Yet he was not quite up to standard and he knew it.

Though the interview went well—his character references and education were satisfactory and an awkward defect in his background was disregarded—the medical examination was another matter. Its requirements in height ("not less than 5 feet 7 inches"), weight ("not more than 160 pounds") and constitution ("sound") did not worry him. But, after fiddling around with a tape-measure, the doctor said "H-m-m!", paused terribly and declared:

"You're an inch under the minimum chest measurement for your height of 6 feet 1, not fully developed and far too skinny. Come back next year and you'll probably pass."

"Hard luck, kid!" said Pete Cowan and five other fellows also trying for enrollment. He said nothing but, "Please, sir, I'd like to see the Commissioner."

This to the Adjutant, not to the doctor.

"Great snakes!" said the Adjutant.

He evidently felt that the request was sheer blasphemy.

How dare a newly-arrived soul ask to step over St. Peter's head to appeal to Heaven's highest authority?

He stared and stared, then remarked, with a smile:

"I like your spirit! Wait—"

So Daniel King found himself standing at his civilian version of attention in front of a Commissioner very busy at a desk in the next room.

Eyes much sharper than issue razors bored into his own. A hand like the hand of Providence twisted a magnificent moustache over a full beard. The Adjutant looked anxious, as the twists were many and an unfavourable verdict was usually foreshadowed by too many twists.

A deep voice booming through the twists soon produced this kindly lecture:

"One inch under the minimum chest measurement may seem of no account to you, my boy, but the doctor's right. And great strength is needed in our Force. We patrol through some of the toughest winters and summers on earth. Often we're on short rations and water for days. We usually ride broncos and that's killing work. Then, the Indians out there are still in the thousands—and often as hard to handle as the broncs."

A long pause—with a particularly fancy twist, the Commissioner, who seemed to expect some comment, broke the silence by asking, rather sharply:

"Well, my boy, have you nothing to say?"

His boy gulped, found a voice and said:

"Only this, sir. How many men in the Force have died of all those things since it was formed six years ago?"

The Adjutant muttered, "Great guns!", while the Commissioner twisted his moustache till it almost came out by the roots, then said:

"Your point's well taken. But remember we've had wonderful luck, just wonderful. The number we've lost is roughly six."

"Only one a year? Well, sir, I guess I can trust that luck and count on setting-up exercises to build me up in no time."

The keen eyes suddenly beamed, the Adjutant grinned openly and the Commissioner said:

"Very well, young man, I'll see that you get on."

And get on the young man did, at least in one sense of the term. He first got on a train to Toronto, his father, mother, kid brothers and Gwen, his sweetheart, all very proud, the females tearful, seeing him off on this opening stage of the long journey to what he called, privately, the Land of Great Adventure and the Last Great West. But he made a mistake on the train when he settled down to getting acquainted with Pete Cowan, the only other survivor of the recruiting team's attentions. He said that he liked poetry. Of course, he had sense enough only to praise the rugged kind—this sort of thing:

> Then up spake brave Horatius, the Captain of the Gate:
> To every man upon this earth Death cometh, soon or late,
> And how can man die better than facing fearful odds
> For the ashes of his fathers and the temples of his gods . . .

And of course Pete liked that kind too. But he began to get out of his depth when told that the men and the work of the Force should remind him of these passages from Scott:

> Nine and twenty knights of fame
>   Hung their shields in Branksome Hall;
> Nine and twenty squires of name
>   Brought them their steeds to bower from stall . . .
> They quitted not their harness bright
>   Neither by day nor yet by night . . .
> They watch to hear the bloodhound baying.
> They watch to hear the war-horn braying. . . .

After all, said Pete, only the Force's team-horses wore harness and the men didn't use shields or bloodhounds. But, though a great joker, inclined to make fun of every one and everything, he kept his new friend's poetic inclinations to himself, for the time being anyhow.

Then, that awkward background-defect led to near-disaster during the three weeks spent by the recruits in assembling and preliminary drilling at the Old Fort in Toronto. A careless recruit said, one morning, "King, you're to collect the Adjutant's horse from Smith's livery stable and bring it into barracks." Even brave Horatius might have turned tail at this, as the Adjutant's horse was nasty, with only its magnificent appearance to recommend it. And, though regulations laid down that all recruits must be "able to ride" on joining—this particular King had never ridden, in a peaceful field, let alone Toronto's downtown traffic.

But "The Charge of the Light Brigade"—"theirs not to reason why, theirs but to do and die"—braced him and he went out to get that horse. Smith's livery stable put the saddle and bridle on for him, hoisted him aboard, asked, "Have you made your will?" and drove him forth. For ten solid minutes, the horse did its level best to go back into the stable. For five minutes, it created a traffic-jam by balking at one of the busiest road-junctions, till at last two blue-coated policemen, two dray drivers, two newsboys, a militia colonel and the worst language its rider had ever heard got it under way again. Then it bolted, weaving in and out among street-cars, cabs, buggies, wagons, bicycles and pedestrians like a bat at dusk and feeding-time. Then it bucked and bucked and bucked. . . .

When he had time, he thanked God that he wasn't a Force member yet, so was not in uniform, disgracing it. Meanwhile, "King Bruce and the Spider" and "if at first you don't succeed, try and try again", kept this particular King in the saddle till at last his foam-splashed, baffled steed walked quietly past morning parade to trail-end.

Sergeant-Major Weatherby, supervising the parade, never blinked an eye. But his brain reeled, as he had not intended this particular King to get that horse. No, he'd meant Corporal Nathaniel King, one of his assistants, who had four years' service and rode well, to do it.

Still, the affair had its good points. The recruits remarked, "Gee, the kid sure can handle a horse!"; the S.M. said, "A queer fish but he sure has guts!"; and Pete thought, "What the hell if he does love poetry?"

This was forgotten on the party's next stage westward, the train-run to Sarnia. They were feted at every eating-place, more females kissing them good-bye, crowds cheering them and everybody helping them to sing "The Girl I Left Behind Me." But Pete gave way to temptation when the time came for organizing a concert aboard the steamer carrying them across Lake Superior from Sarnia to Duluth. He suggested to the Sergeant-Major, in charge of Force contributions, "Do get Dan King to spout. He'll be marvellous."

The S.M. hadn't been born today, much less yesterday. Also he knew his Pete. He followed up the idea, though, only vetoing the artist's proposal to render "The Wreck of the *Hesperus*" because it might scare nervous civilian passengers. Even Pete was astounded by the results. "*Recitation*: 'How They Brought the Good News from Ghent to Aix'—Daniel King" brought down the house, appealing particularly to the recruits because of the Adventure of the Adjutant's Horse. An encore was inescapable. And because the civilians looked on the party as heroes, Indian fighters like Kit Carson and Buffalo Bill—though, as yet, they were not even Force members and still had no uniforms, no weapons and precious little equipment—the encore had to be "The Riders of the Plains." The performer again showed sense. He declaimed only six of the thirty-odd stanzas and got an ovation.

So his comrades now said, "Sure, he's a queer fish but he can put over poetry," and marked him down for all future Force concerts.

From Duluth they got on another train, to Bismarck, Dakota, where they had a chance to see the sights after transferring the eastern remounts with them and the baggage to the flat-bottomed steamer *Red Cloud* for their trip up the Missouri. So they saw the sights and much more than they bargained for.

It was a Sunday but every one of the saloons, gambling

hells and dance-halls lining the muddy streets of this wild
and woolly town was open for the entertainment of roughly
five thousand other travellers heavily armed with rifles
and six-shooters. Suddenly a tremendous row broke out
in the heart of the crowd as Daniel King, Pete Cowan and
three other recruits were passing the "Mud and Blood"
saloon. Shoving their way forward, the boys found two
miners about to draw on each other.

Pete rightly said, "This has nothing to do with us!" and
began retreating, all his comrades—except Daniel—falling
back too. But Daniel stayed right there in the lions' den.
"The Sergeant-Major says to keep our eyes open and learn
all we can," he said, "and I'm doing just that!" Then the
guns roared and one man lay dead, the other dying, on the
rickety sidewalk, in blood enough for a butcher's shop. "Get
a doctor, you fellows," Daniel told the lions, adding, "And I
guess we'd better all wait here for the city marshal."

After that the recruits said, "Dan King's the queerest fish
in the Force—but *cool*!"

The long trip up the Missouri was a delight to him, as
they passed buffalo and a lot of huge, ferocious Sioux,
"never likely to settle down on a reservation," the steamer-
captain told him, "while they can find one of them there
animals to keep 'em going." And Fort Benton, end of the
river-line, gave him and his comrades another ghastly thrill.
Having gone into camp near the town, they were again
allowed to see the sights. So they saw three men hanged by
the vigilantes.

All but two of the Force sightseers hurriedly went the
other way. But Pete Cowan was curious and the queer fish
would not leave him. Then a man on the scaffold begged
for mercy and next thing Pete knew he was coming out of a
dead faint with his comrade holding him up and calmly
murmuring, "Drink this!"

Now the recruits said, "Guess that fish is about the coolest
guy in the Force!"

Next, coolness and drinking—or the lack of them—led to

another exploit. On the last stage of their 2,000-mile westward journey, a week-long march from Benton to Fort
Walsh, the heat was terrific, the water-supply scanty. And
at the noon-day halt, word went around, "Dan King's
missing!" Sergeant-Major Weatherby, in charge of the
column, now that the Commissioner and the Adjutant had
ridden on ahead, detailed the other King to lead a search-
party if the wanderer did not return before the time came
to march on. He returned, all right, but with his horse in a
lather, his face red as a buffalo steak, his parched lips caked
with dust.

Sorely tried by the fearful job of shepherding a lot of
greenhorns, the S.M. barked at him, in the hearing of the
entire column:

"Where in the name of Beelzebub, Mephistopheles and
Lucifer—in short, the Devil—have you been?"

"Looking for water, sir," he croaked. "Saw a lake just
off the trail a little way back. But gee, Sergeant-Major,
aren't distances deceptive out here? Took me half an hour
to reach it. And when I did it was nothing but mud. Very
sorry, sir, but that's me—the hazy, dreamy type."

That night, Pete Cowan and others arranged what they
called "a campfire christening" for recruits particularly
deserving it. "Last Post" Barker, who had spent two hours
in Toronto trying to obey some rascal's order to find and
paint that post, only to learn at last that it was a trumpet-
call—"Redskin" Jenkins, who had roused the entire camp by
reporting "hostile redskins out to steal our horses," though
the Indians were just bushes in the moonlight—"Star-boy"
Smith, who had fiercely argued that a distant lantern was
the planet Venus—these were among the victims.

But the best man in the show was dealt with when Pete,
sprinkling dish-water, declaimed, "I christen thee 'Dreamy'
King!"

Those nicknames would stick to most of the men as long
as they stayed in the service. "Dreamy" King, however,

Pete realized in a strange vague way, would last as long as the Force—maybe longer.

A welcoming troop of trained men and trained horses met the column ten miles out of Fort Walsh. And the recruits were sworn in and issued with uniforms, arms and equipment next day.

Staring entranced at the veterans, their white helmets, bright scarlet, pennoned lances and prancing mounts all sparkling or gleaming in the prairie sunshine, Dreamy was reminded of the Knights of the Round Table, "a glorious company, the flower of men, to serve as model for a mighty world." And when he swore to do his duty "without fear, favour or affection," the oath King Arthur imposed, "to ride abroad redressing human wrongs," sprang to his mind. Again he kept these thoughts to himself, perhaps because, when he staggered out of the quartermaster stores with his newly issued outfit, the storeman said, "Sure, the red serge is a bit too big but you'll fill it out, don't worry."

Better still, Fort Walsh proved to be a bastioned, stockaded stronghold straight out of a painting by Paul Kane. It held the border, just like Branksome Hall. It held many thousands of fiery, restless Indians, among them Sitting Bull and other Sioux refugees from the United States who had crossed the border after wiping out the 7th U.S. Cavalry in the "Custer Massacre." And it held all this with only headquarters and two weak divisions, including detachments—a hundred riders, not more.

His work was full of drudgery—cookhouse fatigues, putting up and repairing buildings, mucking out stables. But there were also riding instruction, drill, target practice, police procedure, scouting. Even a twelve-hour day passed quickly when filled with things like that. Besides, look at the men they worked with . . . For instance, "Buckskin" Charlie, a kid of only sixteen, so help me, yet a star bronco-buster, and Jerry Potts, the best scout and guide in Canada, let alone the states to the south.

Look too at their off-duty friends, such as old Scotty MacIan, the saddler. Scotty had ridden in the charge of the Heavy Brigade at Balaclava with the Scots Greys— "the *successful* charge, ye ken," not the Light Brigade's heroic failure. You sat in his shop and listened to inspiring yarns about his army life, about the Force's great March of '74, the longest march in history of a mounted column carrying its own supplies, and about Force exploits without number. Here too you could talk about Scott, Tennyson and even Shakespeare without being laughed at, provided you could get the hang of Robbie Burns.

On top of that, you could have a verbal bracer here when you felt you weren't doing well:

"Laddie, tak' a guid look at thon leather. Grand, is't no'? Aye, the verra best. Noo, tak' a look at this saddle I'm jist gi'in' its last wee stitch. It tak's 'oors an' 'oors an' 'oors to mak' this saddle oot o' thon grand leather. Forebye, gi'en patience, aye, an' guid work, it *can* be made, provided the leather's lak' thon. So never heed, ma mannie, if ye dinna' hit the bull's ee every shot! The leather's a' it should be an' we'll mak' a grand saddle o' ye yet!"

Above all, look at the Indians, whose gaily painted teepees covered all the hills overlooking the fort. Almost every Plains tribe was represented there. As the Commissioner had said in Montreal, they were "almost as hard to handle as the broncs." They raised merry hell day and night, beating their tom-toms, firing their guns, yelling and dancing till they seemed to shake the earth. Often they came charging down in huge multi-coloured waves, war-whooping, shooting, circling around on their cayuses and roaring for grub till the sentry peeked through the main gate and said, "Keegally!", meaning "Get out!" Often too small patrols sallied from that same gate and into those enormous camps to stop a pitched battle between war-parties or to chase horse-thieves and came back with prisoners, recovered horses and badly wounded braves for the fort cells, corrals or hospital.

All of which he summed up in frequent letters scribbled

to the family or to Gwen from his bunk in a long log-barrack-room with the fellows singing, skylarking or playing cards around him.

"I love it here," he wrote, "Fort Walsh is It" and "Am having a wonderful time."

He filled up that red serge, just as the storeman had said he would—with all that fresh air and exercise, he could eat a horse, let alone his full share of first-rate rations. He also filled up some good reports, though he never saw or heard them. "Got the makings of a darned good rider," said Buckskin Charlie. "Good scout soon," said Jerry Potts. "Soon be fit to go on detachment," said Sergeant-Major Weatherby. And soon he went.

Fall was just beginning to touch the poplars up with yellow as vivid as the braid on his uniform when he rode away from Fort Walsh with the other King, now a sergeant, Pete Cowan and a third constable to reinforce East End detachment. "Tak' guid care o' yersel', laddie, an' come back before too lang" old Scotty called to him, from the saddlers' shop. "You bet I will!" he shouted, little guessing how and when he would fulfil that promise. His carbine was loaded—for East End, total strength eight men, guarded many thousands of desperate Sioux—his heart beat high and he would not have changed places in that moment with Prime Minister Macdonald or the Vanderbilts. After all, why should he?

Settling down at East End was easy, a matter of routine into which a man slid as easily and smoothly as his pistol slid into its holster. Sergeant King drilled Dreamy King and his comrades, mounted and dismounted, every day, and every day solemnly put them through rigid inspections. Antelope, a friendly Sioux, often came to teach them his language, by special arrangement. They hunted venison, prairie chicken, rabbits and even grizzly bears for the pot. They caught whitefish with nets in a convenient lake. They took turns as cook, sometimes baking their own bread. Then they frequently patrolled to the Sioux camps or along the trails but never alone—too dangerous.

Yet he was alone, by chance, when the two strange white men came to the detachment demanding instant action to recover two horses, stolen, they said, by the Sioux. Strictly speaking, Pete was with him but Pete had a badly sprained ankle and was of no use, while Sergeant King and the rest were away for several days on patrol to Wood Mountain.

He patiently, politely heard the complaint, then said, "O.K., I'll saddle up and come with you."

"Where to?" asked the strangers, adding, "Just *you* with *us*—to *Sitting Bull's camp*?"

He nodded, saying, "There's no one else to come—and it's now or never, if you ever want to see your horses again."

One stranger, white as the foam flecking his pony, said to his mate, "No need for the both of us to go, George. And I'm ailin' a mite today. Guess I'll wait here and rest awhile. You go!"

"Guess I'll wait here too," said George. "Feelin' kind o' poorly myself."

Pete, from the background, said:

"How's he to identify your horses if you don't go with him?"

"Easy," George said. "One's a sorrel, 'bout 15 hands, t'other a black with white points, 16 hands, both branded with a broken W." Then he threw in, "Say, why don't *you* go? Your pard's just a kid. Maybe you could even go along with him. . ."

This behind the back of Dreamy, who had gone into the stable to saddle up.

"No chance!" said Pete. "I couldn't put a foot in a stirrup. Anyhow, my pard's one of the best. But look here, mister, guess you're asking a lot too much for him to ride alone into Sitting Bull's camp and get your horses without you along to say beyond all doubt, 'That's mine'!"

"He's right, Tom," said George. "I've got a nasty tingle in my scalp, like as if I'd soon lose it for good. All the same,

we must go with that kid red-coat, though we're scared to
death."

So the three of them started, Dreamy wondering if the
sergeant would give him Hail Columbia for tackling such a
mad proposition the very first time he tackled anything
important single-handed, yet fortified by the feeling that no
policeman worth his six bits a day could do anything else,
in the circs.

They rode, at last, over a ridge and saw below them a
scene the like of which had shaken many of the boldest
white frontiersmen with stark fear: a vast circle of teepees
surrounded by thousands of grazing horses and ponies and
in its turn surrounding a vast crowd of drumming, chanting
Indians who, again, surrounded a horde of buffalo-headed
devils in a fantastic dance. This was Sitting Bull's camp
seeking luck in a forthcoming hunt through the buffalo
dance and in no mood whatever for dealing with white men.

Dreamy, looking down into that camp, might have compared himself with Dante looking down into the Inferno,
if he hadn't been thinking, a bit ironically, that he was in
the same fix as brave Horatius and his two comrades—the
Dauntless Three in the poem—when they found themselves
about to hold the bridge against Lars Porsena's huge army.

Ironically, because, however he might feel, George and
Tom obviously felt anything but dauntless. Tom, now, was
even whiter, if possible, than the foam lathering his pony,
and George looked as if he wanted to be sick.

"Come on!" said Dreamy, adding sharply, as George made
to draw his Winchester, "None of that! If you pull a gun,
they'll kill us. Now, you fellows keep quiet. I'll do the
talking."

The Indians quickly spotted the lonely flame of the red-
coat and a roar like the roar of all the Inferno's damned
souls on the Day of Judgment burst out of them. It might
have been a shout of welcome or a threat. At the same time
the dance stopped, and the buffalo-headed devils, backed

by thousands of warriors, squaws and children, hemmed in the Dauntless Three beyond all hope of escape.

Dreamy raised his hand in the peace sign, a deathly silence fell on the crowd, and at last Chief Bear's Cap said, in his own tongue:

"How, Shagalasha (Greetings, Red-coat)! What do you want? You must not disturb us now."

Thankful for those lessons in Siouan from Antelope, Red-coat replied, also in that tongue:

"These men say some of your warriors stole two of their horses from them when their backs were turned this morning. You know the White Mother's laws and have promised to obey them. You must give those horses back."

Another roar burst from the crowd. This time it was undoubtedly threatening. Their furious faces and the way in which they pressed in on the whites as if to tear them from the saddle, then limb from limb, said so in language unmistakable even to men who knew not one Siouan word. George and Tom held trembling hands high above their heads but Red-coat kept his quietly on the reins, though he saw that he and his companions were caught in the jaws of death—just like the Light Brigade.

Bear's Cap waved down the shouting, then said:

"Red-coat, you are a boy, with a boy's folly, or you would not come here by yourself among Indians who hate the very sight of white men like those. Take my advice and go away as fast as possible."

"I may be a boy," said Dreamy, "but I am also a red-coat, as you say, and I am not going without those horses."

Another roar. What next? Who would break this deadlock? God alone knew—till suddenly Sitting Bull himself pushed his way through the crowd and the buffalo-headed devils to halt squarely in front of his three visitors.

"What do you want, Shagalasha?" he demanded.

His firm mouth set but his broad face remained calm, his sturdy figure made no threatening move.

Shagalasha repeated his explanations.

For a long minute, Sitting Bull remained silent. He was obviously weighing the pros and cons of the case, considering whether strict obedience to the Queen's laws, the price the Sioux were paying for their Canadian sanctuary, required them to give up the horses of detested white settlers akin to those who had robbed his people of everything.

In that long minute you could almost hear the crack of the coup sticks, the rasp of the scalping knives.

"Find the horses if you can," said Sitting Bull, "then get out of here as quickly as you can. My young men will not be held for ever."

Another roar. But Sitting Bull beat it down, the crowd sullenly gave way, and the evil spell was broken. By the great mercy of God, George and Tom found the sorrel and the black with white points almost at once, then grabbed the head-ropes, still dangling. As the little white group began slowly to ride off, Sitting Bull said to the settlers:

"If you ever come here again, you will probably be killed." Then, taking Dreamy by the hand and shaking it with a grip that almost pulled him off his horse, he added, smiling as if he had overheard Bear's Cap's earlier remark, "Redcoat, you are not a boy but a man."

Tom agreed, "The bravest man I've seen for many a day."

Two sun-dogs foretold a blizzard the next time Dreamy rode out from East End for Sitting Bull's camp. But Sergeant King, that veteran plainsman, was with him, and they expected to reach the camp long before the storm could bother them. Besides, they carried a message of great importance from the Commissioner to the chief, promising that in the hard winter already gripping the Fort Walsh country the Great Mother would not allow the Sioux to starve, though she still denied that they had a right to stay indefinitely in her country. Risks had to be taken to get that message to Sitting Bull before his people took the law into their own hands to save themselves from famine.

But the blizzard struck while the Force men were still two

hours' ride from the Sioux camp but much too far from
East End to turn back, even though, as things were, the
Commissioner would have wished them to do so.

So they rode on, into the white and merciless teeth of the
storm.

It drove the pale, frightened Sun out of the sky, to hurry
home to his lodge in the far west—or so it seemed, as flying,
stinging, paralyzing snow-clouds hid him altogether. It
wiped out the naked, tossing poplars, the lashing jackpine,
the ridges they covered and every single landmark, leaving
the patrol in an utterly formless void. It sheathed riders
and horses in heavy white armour, bit through fur caps and
mittens and even through big buffalo coats and moccasins
with unbelievable cold as if these were made of paper. It
piled enormous drifts in front of them, to stop their
desperately plodding horses. And it roared with a fury far
surpassing any shown by the buffalo-headed devils, "You'll
never reach the camp alive."

"Don't worry, Dreamy!" the Sergeant had said, when its
first breath spattered them with a hissing mist of snow and
played tag with them before settling down to a more deadly
game, "Hang on to me, stick close. I can go the right way
by the lay of the land. In any case, we're only three miles
from Gabe St. Michel's cabin. We can make it long before
things get really bad."

So they still rode on, while the storm got worse and worse,
the riders colder and colder, the horses slower and slower.
All track of time was lost, much, Dreamy thought, as they
lost all track of the trail. And still they did not make St.
Michel's cabin. He could feel the sergeant pressing and
bumping against him, sometimes even see him, like a shadow
beside him, when he could feel or see anything at all. But
of the hunter's little home there was no trace.

He wasn't scared. He had perfect faith in his namesake,
faith too in his idea that before him lay many stirring years
of Force service. All the same, he was almost numb with
cold, almost beaten out of the saddle by the wind and he

would be mighty thankful when he found himself at Gabe's
stove.

Then suddenly he was scared, a little. For, whether he
had somehow fallen into something like the death-sleep
Jerry Potts had warned him to guard against in a fix like
this or whether he had just been careless, he discovered, in
a white flash, that he and his horse were alone in that
howling, merciless void. Sergeant King was simply and
suddenly no longer there.

He thought, as well as he could:

"He's gone into that sleep himself—or had an accident."

And, of course, as Force men stood by each other to the
death, he thought:

"I've got to find him."

He must have spent hours—or maybe it was only twenty
minutes — trying to back-trail along the tracks of the
patrol when there were no tracks, forcing his horse through
enormous drifts, shouting as best he could through that
awful roaring, like a baby wailing against Niagara. It was
utterly and completely useless. And stealthily approaching
dusk told him that soon it would be impossible to see even
the little he could now see through the ice masking his face.

So he had to give up and return to the vital job of finding
Gabe's cabin.

This did not hit him as hard as it might if he had not still
retained that perfect faith in Sergeant King. He felt in the
very bottom of his almost frozen heart that somehow or
other the sergeant would find safety.

But could he find it himself? That was quite another
story. For the first time, now, doubt mounted a pale horse
beside him. He refused to look at it. With his own horse
spurred remorselessly into the wind, he could keep the right
direction. And if he did miss Gabe's cabin, he could not
possibly miss the big Sioux camp.

He came out of what was perilously like another lapse
into that death-sleep to find that he was on hands and knees
among rocks. He must have fallen out of the saddle. Worse,

his horse had vanished, like Sergeant King. Rising, now, to
something like panic, he climbed shakily to his feet—and fell
right over his horse. It lay on its side among those icy rocks,
trying gallantly and pitifully to get up again. He felt through
the white void for its reins, so as to help it, while a great
surge of thankfulness filled and calmed him. His hands,
instead, touched the horse's forelegs. One of them was
broken, thanks to falling on those rocks.

Heavily, clumsily and taking an age to do it, he pulled
out his pistol and shot the animal between its invisible eyes,
to put it out of its misery.

Only then had he time to realize that his own position
was really desperate, so desperate that the grim picture
painted for him by the Commissioner centuries ago in
Montreal—the sketch of fearful risks, particularly of winter
risks, then so lightly tossed aside—came back into his clouding mind, to suggest that perhaps the luck he counted on
had failed him and he was actually going to die.

Die? No chance; "King Bruce and the Spider," try, try
again! So he hunched his shoulders, bore into that awful,
freezing wind and went ahead.

Now, another century later, he found that he had burrowed
his way into a snowdrift, with some idea of writing a
"report" and then boring on again into that wind. He got
his notebook and pencil out, bared his cold right hand to
those merciless teeth so that he could scribble something
and slowly, painfully wrote. . .

Then he felt warm, and strangely peaceful, as if in bed
at home or with the fellows at Fort Walsh and did not really
mind that he could not get out of it.

He was eighteen years and eight months old and had only
six months' service.

Gabe went into the storm to find him as soon as Sergeant
King, with both feet frozen, though fortunately not to a fatal
extent, struggled in and told him that Dreamy was missing.
The search was necessarily short and futile. But when the

storm died enough for the hunter to make another try, he took the Commissioner's letter and the news about Dreamy to Sitting Bull's camp as fast as possible. Sitting Bull turned out every warrior and every horse he could to search and sent a rider at full speed to Fort Walsh, which also sent out all the men and horses available in the same way.

They found him with the notebook open in the drift. His message read:

"Lost. Horse dead. Am trying to push on. Have done my best."

Later the commissioner and all Fort Walsh's garrison turned out to do what was left to be done for him. Watching the scarlet files tramp slowly by, old Scotty said, out loud, "The whole Roond Table, laddie! Ye'd be proud. And ye made a damn' guid saddle!"

But no one heard him, for the tramp of the slow march and the wailing of Sitting Bull's Sioux in their song of departure.

So now Dreamy holds seventh place on the long, long Roll of Honour of Force members "who gave their lives in the performance of their duty."